SPOILS OF WAR

BOOK ONE OF THE IMPERIAL MARINES SAGA

TERRY MIXON

YOWLING
CAT PRESS

Published by Yowling Cat Press ®

Digital edition date: 6/21/2023

Print ISBN: 978-1947376250

Large Print ISBN: 978-1947376649

Cover art - image copyrights as follows:

DepositPhotos | innovari (Luca Oleastri)

DepositPhotos | algolonline (Caroline Rosa Nicolette Atkinson)

Donna Mixon

Cover design and composition by Donna Mixon

Print edition design and layout by Terry Mixon

ALSO BY TERRY MIXON

You can always find the most up to date listing of Terry's titles on his Amazon Author Page.

Note: the links below (ebook only, obviously) redirect you to my website where you can click a button to go to Amazon. This allows me to participate in Amazon's associates program and earn a little more. Sorry for any inconvenience.

Behind Enemy Lines

The Terra Gambit

Hidden Enemies

Race to Terra

Ruined Terra

Victory on Terra

When Luck Runs Out

Gunboat Diplomacy

The Imperial Marines Saga

Spoils of War

Imperial Recruit

Enemy Action

The Humanity Unlimited Saga

Liberty Station

Freedom Express

Tree of Liberty

Blood of Patriots

Single Novels

Scorched Earth

Storm Divers

The Vigilante Series with Glynn Stewart

Heart of Vengeance

Oath of Vengeance

Bound By Law

Bound By Honor

Bound By Blood

Box Sets

The Empire of Bones Saga Volume 1

The Empire of Bones Saga Volume 2

The Empire of Bones Saga Volume 3

The Empire of Bones Saga Volume 4

Humanity Unlimited Publisher's Pack 1

Humanity Unlimited Publisher's Pack 2

Want to get updates from Terry about new books and other general nonsense going on in his life? He promises there will be cats. Go to TerryMixon.com/Mailing-List and sign up.

DEDICATION

This book would not be possible without the love and support of my beautiful wife. Donna, I love you more than life itself.

ACKNOWLEDGMENTS

I want to thank the folks that support me on Patreon. You got to read this book as I was writing it and that kept me working. You have my deepest thanks.

In particular, I want to thank those patrons that supported me at the $10 level:

Bryan Barnes
Bill Colston
Dave Dolan
David Goldstein
Christian A. Michelsen
Dale Thompson
Clark Williams

And my special thanks to John Page for his exceptionally generous donation.

Finally, I want to thank my readers for putting up with me. You guys are great.

1

Lieutenant Grace Tolliver used the optics in her powered armor to scan the icefield that stretched out in front of Third Platoon's makeshift offensive point, looking for any signs of the opposing force. They had to be out there somewhere.

Thankfully, the filters cut the glare down to a manageable level. If she'd been using just her own eyes, the scene would've been lost in the blinding light reflected off the ice of the frozen bay she stood on as she stared out over the ocean that never thawed.

Working in powered armor was a lot better than regular armor, especially out here in the Crag. For one thing, she wasn't shivering her ass off.

Her platoon was spread out over a kilometer and a half between two frozen outcroppings of rock deep inside the Crag, the arctic training ground used by the Imperial Marines on Seward. Like the rest of Delta Company, she was playing defense while waiting for Alpha Company to try and get past them.

The goal of this exercise was to make certain that the opposition force—or OPFOR as the marines called them—didn't surprise the rest of the company. Considering the excellent visibility, she thought the odds of them being able to sneak up on her people were slim, but she wasn't taking anything for granted.

"The hairs on the back of my neck are standing up, Lieutenant," Sergeant Na said over the command channel.

Her top NCO had about twice her experience, and if she felt uneasy, that made Grace feel edgy. Na wasn't given to needless worry.

"Are you seeing something I'm not?" Grace asked, once again scanning the area in front of the platoon. "I'm just seeing sheets of ice and way too much sun."

Na was down at the other end of the line, so Grace couldn't see the other woman. Both of them had enough experience working with their implants and their armor to behave as if they were standing next to one another even when they were so far apart. It made collaboration easy.

"No, ma'am," Na said slowly. "I can't say what's got me feeling this way, but I'm pretty damned confident that somebody is trying to pull something on us. This exercise always seemed just a little bit too easy to me.

"If the opposing force is going to have any chance of success, they can't just walk up to us over the icefield and expect to win. They're going to have to be tricky, and we need to expect something we never saw coming."

That set Grace to thinking about the defensive perimeter again. They had every angle covered. There were even scouts up on the slopes of the rocks to the left and right of the area of operations to make sure that no one made it around them unseen.

How in the world could elements from Alpha Company get past them when they *had* to come into sight at some point?

Going overhead was out. The visibility was excellent, and even if it had been at night, their optics would be more than capable of detecting any vehicles trying to overfly their position. They'd have no difficulty targeting them with the training weapons they used for exercises like this.

But she had to admit that Na was right. The colonel wouldn't set up a field exercise where one side had such a huge advantage. He expected everyone to use their brains. The OPFOR had a path to victory. She just had to figure out the angle they'd use.

Sometimes winning a battle wasn't about the strength of forces one brought to the fight. It was the way one applied that force. If you could finesse your way into attacking an enemy from a blind spot or pinning them against another force, you could win even when you were outnumbered. So, what was she missing?

If the answer wasn't over her head, could it be under her feet?

"Just how thick is this ice?" she asked Na. "Is there any chance they could be going underneath us? Does the ice in this bay go all the way down to the seabed?"

"I'm not certain. Even if it doesn't, exactly how would the opposition force get back up to attack us?"

"Go to infrared and let's see if anything is going on underneath us," Grace ordered. "With all this ice, it's going to shield any action they're taking unless it's close to the surface, but it won't hurt to double-check."

Leaving the observation of the ice field to the marines around her, Grace switched her optics to thermal mode and began looking at the ice both in front of the line and behind it. It all looked the same to her, so she couldn't imagine that anything was going on beneath the surface in her general vicinity.

She turned her attention toward the rocks that rose above the ice to her left. There were a couple of scouts high up on the protrusion, but they wouldn't have a line of sight to the area just below their location. If she wanted to know what was going on there, she was going to have to send a group to check it out.

Or go herself.

She tagged two of the Third Squad marines to accompany her and headed off to examine the area near the rock outcropping herself. If she spotted anything, she'd call for backup.

When she arrived at the base of the rock and started scanning, it only took a couple of seconds to realize that something was wrong. Very wrong.

The temperature of the ice at the base of the cliff was uniformly the same as out in the area she'd been just a few minutes ago, except for an area about twenty meters across that was almost hidden behind a curve of the rock. That area was at least thirty degrees warmer, and she couldn't think of any good reason that would be.

"Breach!" she shouted over the general channel. "We have an OPFOR breach in progress near the base of the left outcropping. I want Second and Third squads on my position ASAP. Sergeant Na, coordinate coverage of our zone with First Squad and sound the alert to Delta Company."

Things were going to get ugly fast. Once the enemy came out from beneath the ice, there would be no cover for her people as they defended against the incursion. All of the barricades they'd constructed would be useless now that the enemy was behind them. She had to come up with a new plan fast.

"Everyone needs to spread out as far as you can while still being close enough to fire on the breach," she ordered. "Get down in the prone position and wait for my signal. They're going to be coming out of a choke point a lot like a hatch on a ship, and we're going to be able to bring a lot of force to bear against them if we can get into place in time."

Grace wasn't certain how long they had before the ice was thin enough for the enemy to come through, but she was sure it would be less time than she'd like.

She found a good position and sprawled out on the ice, bringing her heavy flechette rifle to bear on the target zone. It was loaded with real flechettes, but the rifle was rigged to fire them at a greatly reduced velocity, so none of the marines she'd be shooting at would be in any danger. Their suits would still register the hits and tally them as injured, disabled, or dead.

The two marines with her had barely gotten down when the ice in front of Grace cracked and split. Two marines in powered armor popped out of the fissure and landed with a slight skid on the slick surface, already scanning the area around them.

None of her other marines were in position to take on the intruders, so it fell to Grace to buy them time. Without hesitation, she opened fire.

The two marines in front of her "died" in a hail of flechettes, their armor locking up and freezing them into position. Unfortunately, that told the marines behind them that their plan had gone sour, and they came boiling out of the hole in the ice like disturbed ants.

This was rapidly becoming what Sergeant Na liked to call a "target-rich environment," so Grace had no problem hitting whatever she fired at. Unfortunately, it only took the enemy a couple of seconds to dial in her location, and she had no cover whatsoever.

Within a couple of seconds, her armor went from indicating that she was uninjured to locking up her arms with hits on both and then registering her as dead. Her com system still allowed her to receive transmissions from her platoon, but she could no longer transmit. She was just an angry observer to the debacle that then ensued.

According to her HUD, two entire platoons came out of that hole in the ice. Even if her people had been ready for the attack, they'd probably still have lost, but it still annoyed her that she'd fallen for their trick.

In less than fifteen minutes, Alpha Company had routed her platoon and taken over the bay that they were supposed to be guarding. The breach would cost Delta Company the exercise, and it was her fault.

The final humiliation came when Senior Lieutenant Anatoli Bashir came sauntering up to her frozen armor and squatted down beside her. She only knew it was him because he'd configured his armor to tell her who he was.

The smug bastard.

"Didn't they ever tell you that you're not supposed to lead from the front, Grace?" he asked in a condescending tone. "Once again, you've let me outmaneuver you. I wouldn't want to be you when they start the after-action debrief."

She couldn't respond in a way that he'd hear, but she also couldn't keep herself from growling out an answer. "Screw you, Bashir."

He laughed as if he'd heard her and then walked away to organize his company's incursion into her zone.

She'd be stuck here for the next few hours, so she'd have every opportunity to go over what she'd done wrong. She hadn't considered all the possible avenues of attack. Bashir was an ass, but he was dead right about her screwing up by the numbers.

Grace vowed never to let something like this happen under her watch again. When the ass-chewing came, she'd deserve what she got, but she was going to learn from this. Losing to Bashir was embarrassing. Losing to someone with real weapons would get her marines killed, and that wasn't going to happen.

* * *

"One Twenty-Four!"

One Twenty-Four jerked back to awareness when Keeper's disciplinary rod slapped the desktop in front of her. She'd been daydreaming. Again.

"I'm sorry, Keeper," she lied contritely. "I was considering the implications of your lesson."

The tall woman standing next to her desk obviously didn't believe her. Her face was cut into a thunderous frown that made the swirling tattoos of her social status seemingly stand out from her forehead and cheeks as if they too were angry with her.

Honestly, One Twenty-Four was almost certain that that was an intentional part of its design. The ruling caste of the Singularity needed to be aloof and imposing.

Keeper was all that and more.

Each crèche belonging to the Andrea Line started with two hundred children. One Twenty-Four suspected the more common lines inside the Singularity consisted of significantly more line sibs and hosted their decantings with more regularity. The Singularity needed far more servants than rulers, after all.

One Twenty-Four was identical in every physical respect to her crèche mates, and Keeper was precisely what she'd look like when she grew up, if Keeper permitted that to happen.

If One Twenty-Four could keep her mind focused on her lessons.

She and her crèche mates had wondered—once they were old enough—how Keeper was able to tell them apart. The answer was in the bracelets they each wore. Adults presumably had a different method of identifying one another, but the crèche used bands on the children's left wrists.

Those bands displayed no information that *they* could see, even now that they could read, but were somehow keyed to each of them, and only to them. Switching them only made them stop working, and Keeper had severely punished those who had tried to fool her.

Thankfully, it hadn't been her that time.

Not the ultimate punishment—expulsion from the crèche—but something more than harsh enough to make sure that no one *ever* tried that kind of trick again.

One Twenty-Four thought that since their genetic code was identical, it had to be keyed to their brain waves or some other factor she was unaware of. Perhaps she'd find out what method was used at some point, but such speculation was best reserved for another time.

Right now, Keeper was angry, and it behooved One Twenty-Four to give this situation her undivided attention, because she absolutely didn't want to suffer the consequences of disobedience. She'd been an idiot to let her thoughts stray.

"Your conduct has grown less acceptable with every passing day for the last several months, and it will no longer be tolerated, One Twenty-Four. Do you see your line sibs behaving in such a fashion? I demand conformity, and you will either give it to me, or you will be expelled from the crèche."

Even at only eleven years of age, One Twenty-Four knew that was the ultimate threat: death.

Individual behavior might be tolerated when she was older, but One Twenty-Four knew that the Line demanded compliance during training. She must learn how the Line worked and how she was expected to behave inside it, or she would be purged.

While she might one day be a member of the ruling class of the Singularity, that day was not today. She was only halfway to maturity and, based on what she'd seen, perhaps as few as a third of her current crèche mates would live to see that day. When it came to the ruling caste, the Singularity believed in quality over quantity.

If she wanted to be among the survivors, she needed to focus on the here and now.

One Twenty-Four bowed her head. "I regret my lack of attention, Keeper. It will not happen again."

The stern woman scowled down at her. "I don't believe that, One Twenty-Four. At this point, I'm beginning to despair that you will achieve conformity.

"Such willfulness will not be tolerated in a child of the Andrea Line. Corrective measures will be instituted, but should they prove insufficient, sterner measures will be required. Measures that you will deeply regret, if only briefly."

Keeper turned her head to take in the rest of the crèche. "You will all reach your twelfth year in two days. That's when you'll receive your caste tattoos and become a true part of the Andrea Line. I would be severely disappointed if any of you were to fail before then and be ejected from the crèche.

"I rely upon you to show One Twenty-Four whatever correction you feel appropriate, within the bounds of acceptable crèche behavior. Do not shirk this opportunity to bring your line sib back into compliance."

With her lecture to One Twenty-Four complete, Keeper returned to the front of the classroom as if nothing had happened.

One Twenty-Four felt humiliated, of course. She wanted to sag lower in her seat, but displaying such weakness to her line sibs would encourage them to even greater efforts. She already had a beating to look forward to. Best not to do anything that would make it worse.

Her crèche mates would be certain to leave no marks that could be seen, but One Twenty-Four knew firsthand that the other girls could cause a lot of pain without crossing the boundary beyond which Keeper would be forced to take notice.

After all, she'd done her part with other corrective punishments in the past, even though they had made her feel sick. The Line expected the crèche to regulate itself in ways large and small. Keeper was almost a referee in the ongoing conflict.

With that glum thought, One Twenty-Four forced herself to focus on the electronic board that Keeper was writing on. Today's lesson was in basic calculus, a subject that she still didn't understand the need for.

Others existed to perform calculations, and a leader only guided them to the solution that was optimal for the Singularity. Why would the leader need to do the work that another could do?

Still, her ignorance of Keeper's reasoning was irrelevant. All tasks must be mastered.

She'd rather have been learning about the Singularity and its history. About how it had torn itself away from the Terran Empire, where the heretics now implanted machinery into their bodies to try and compensate for the inadequacy of their genetics.

Why they didn't embrace the glories of genetic engineering was a mystery to her. One she doubted she'd ever truly understand.

What were they like? Why did they do the horrible things they did? How could they possibly put mechanical *things* inside their bodies?

Such questions would likely remain a mystery to her for many years to come. And if One Twenty-Four didn't focus her attention on the task at hand, she'd never have the opportunity to ask them even if she did survive the crèche.

2

Grace had just finished cleaning her armor and weapons, turned them over to the company armorer, and gotten into her duty uniform when her implants pinged with an incoming message. She accessed it grimly, expecting it to be from Delta Company's CO, summoning her to the after-action briefing.

Instead, she found herself reading a summons to the battalion commander's office at her earliest convenience. In marine speak, that meant right damn now.

"That's not good," she muttered to herself. Had she screwed up that badly?

Sergeant Na, who'd been standing beside her and observing the platoon as they cleaned their weapons and armor, turned to face her and raised an eyebrow.

"Problem?"

"Battalion wants to see me."

The Asiatic woman gave her a skeptical look. "This exercise certainly didn't turn out the way we would've hoped, but being called onto the carpet at battalion seems a little extreme. Perhaps this is something else."

"I guess I'll find out soon enough," Grace said with a sigh. "Make sure everybody gets squared away, but have them hang close to the barracks for now."

With the platoon's immediate needs mapped out, Grace set out across the wide parade ground and made her way to the battalion commander's outer office. She was glad they weren't in the arctic circle anymore and just enjoyed the heat. Seward's sun was a shade more to the red than Terra's, so it cast an almost pale orange light.

Once she arrived at the headquarters' building, she marched into the lion's den and smiled at the colonel's adjutant and all-around dogsbody, Senior Lieutenant Pedro van Buren.

As usual, the man's desk reflected his fastidious nature and was as uncluttered as a scoundrel's conscience. Hailing from Terra, the man's complexion and facial features were a mix of South American Latino from his mother and a Nordic profile from his father, just like his name implied.

A handsome man by any standard, Pedro was usually extremely cheerful. Today, his expression was solemn, and that set off additional alarm bells in her mind.

"What's up, Pedro?" she asked in a low tone, planting her hip on the corner of his desk. "Any idea what the Old Man wants me for?"

Considering the efficacy of medical nanites, Lieutenant Colonel Jackson Grimsby looked as if he was in his early forties, though he was undoubtedly twice that age. Still, the name was a tradition as old as the Imperial Marine Corps itself.

Pedro shook his head. "I heard about the exercise, Grace. Ouch. All I can say is good luck."

Perfect.

She nodded, having already known it wouldn't be that easy. "Shall I park it or go on in?"

He gestured toward the door. "He said to send you right in. Good luck."

Having gotten the go-ahead, she rapped twice on the door and waited for permission to enter.

"Come in," the colonel called out in a smooth baritone.

She opened the door and stepped into Lieutenant Colonel Jackson Grimsby's office and braced herself at attention in front of his battered desk. "Lieutenant Grace Tolliver, reporting as ordered, sir."

The man sat behind his battered desk, its surface covered with scattered papers that he seemed to be in the process of examining. That interfered with the built-in computer interface, but the colonel was one of those old-school types that preferred the use of paper.

He gestured for her to close the door. There was a single chair in front of the desk, and he motioned for her to take it, giving her a chance to take in his mood and appearance.

The man's dark skin contrasted well with the pale-grey marine duty uniform he wore. Not the field version like she'd been happy to get out of an hour ago but the noncombat version they all wore on base. His tight curls of black hair were shot through with grey.

Grimsby claimed it was from his marines prematurely aging him, but all in all, he still cut a dashing figure. Not one she'd ever had any interest in because of the chain of command and his exalted rank, but she had eyes, didn't she?

Once she'd settled herself into the less-than-comfortable office chair, he leaned back and regarded her over steepled fingers. "I hear things didn't go so well for Third Platoon at the Crag. Tell me about it."

She mentally sighed but obediently began going through the day's exercise from the very beginning. She didn't try to conceal the blunder that she'd made and had taken responsibility for the lapse.

He didn't say anything for a little bit, only nodding. "I'd imagine that Lieutenant Bashir was pleased that he'd been able to pull this off right under your proverbial and literal noses, wasn't he?"

"He did express some pleasure at having tactically outmaneuvered me, yes, sir." She managed to keep from gritting her teeth at the admission but was pleased to see that her tone had remained professional.

"Want to hear an embarrassing story about Lieutenant Bashir?"

Grace blinked. Of all the things the man could have possibly said, that had never been on her scanners.

"Sir?"

Grimsby gave her a sly smile. "Back when I was a major and

served as the XO in this battalion, Lieutenant Bashir was in pretty much the same position you were today. In fact, somebody else pulled the *exact* same stunt on him, and he fell for it even harder than you did.

"At least you realized right before the end what might be happening. Bashir got caught with his shorts down around his ankles."

"In a few years, when you're a senior lieutenant in charge of a company, you're going to find somebody else that you can pull the same trick on. That's what experience does, Lieutenant. It gives you the tricks of the trade so you can make somebody else's day just as unpleasant as yours is now."

She had no idea why the colonel was telling her this. Nothing like this had ever happened to her before. Gossiping about other officers was not something that the Imperial Marine Corps encouraged.

"Before we get off on the wrong foot, this meeting is not about today's exercise," Colonel Grimsby said briskly. "You did as well as anybody else I've ever seen that's had this trick pulled on them, and better than most. Learn from what happened, and you'll save lives in the future.

"This meeting isn't even about that. I've decided that since Third Platoon is one of the shining lights in the battalion, you and your people deserve an early Christmas present. I'm tagging you to lead an unofficial strike team across the Singularity border."

She'd come expecting an ass-chewing, but this was completely different and totally unexpected.

The Singularity and the Terran Empire weren't *technically* at war, but they'd had border incidents ever since the people that had formed that polity had left the Empire back when the Terran Republic had come crashing down ten thousand years ago.

In point of fact, their departure hadn't exactly been by choice. Their manipulation of the various political groups inside the Terran Republic had led to what amounted to a civil war. When Admiral Andrew Bandar had finally subdued the various factions, he'd recognized who'd been behind everything, and he'd taken decisive action.

After the fighting, he'd brought his fleet back to Terra and overthrown the corrupt government. The rulers for life that had run the damned thing had perverted the election process so severely that it had been impossible to remove them from power via the ballot box, so he'd trashed the Republic itself.

From its wreckage, he'd created the Terran Empire and founded the dynasty that ruled to this day. His first act as the new emperor had been to send his military to find the people behind the machinations.

Those people had believed that cloning was the way for humanity to improve itself and that any kind of equipment implanted inside the body was blasphemous. Their beliefs weren't precisely religious, per se, but that was splitting hairs.

No matter the reason, that was why their members had worked so diligently to pit one portion of the Terran Republic against another. They'd hoped that at the end of the day, they would end up holding the reins of power.

Needless to say, many of them had realized what was coming after their plans had come crashing down, and rather than be arrested, they'd fled in everything from freighters to small warships that had become "lost" during the fighting.

No one could say with any certainty how many people fled beyond the borders of the Empire after the fighting was over, but the number had to have been in the millions. Probably even the tens of millions.

Emperor Andrew the First had eventually sent every member of their sect that his people could catch packing right after them. He hadn't wanted any of that cancer left inside the newly formed Terran Empire.

By the time the Empire's border had once again pushed up against what had become the Singularity, they'd had military forces of their own, and the choice facing the empress who reigned then was whether to wage war to the knife or deal with low-level brushfires along the border every few years.

She'd chosen the latter, so now the Empire engaged in an unofficial rough-and-tumble every few years. And that brought her back to the mission at hand.

"Thank you, sir. We won't let you down."

The older man leaned back in his chair. "I'm sure you won't,

Lieutenant. Or more properly, Grace, since as of this moment, you're officially released from Imperial service."

She blinked at her superior officer. First, she couldn't remember a single time that the man had ever used her given name. In the military —particularly in the marines—it was commonplace to use someone's last name when referencing them, even to their faces.

It was all very regimented, their behavior strictly controlled by precedent that had existed for millennia.

The release from Imperial service shocked her but came as no surprise once she had a moment to think about it. The Empire needed plausible deniability.

Grace had heard stories about previous sorties, of course. Missions like this were *legendary*. The problem was sorting myth from reality.

"Tell me more, Jackson," she said, a bit worried at how the colonel would take that familiarity.

To her relief, her words made him grin. "I'm glad to see that you've picked up on the nature of our discussion. This mission—and even this conversation—is *completely* off the record. You and your people will be operating as private citizens, and what you do next has no connection to the Imperial Marines or the Terran Empire."

The Old Man leaned forward, resting his hands on his desk. "You won't breathe a word of this to anyone except your platoon, and only once you're safely on board the ship waiting for you in orbit.

"This is, in all likelihood, going to be a relatively straightforward raid, much like many of the others that we've carried out over the last century, but as always, complete deniability is paramount.

"If you are captured or killed, the Terran Empire and the Imperial Marines will disavow you and your actions. Any losses that you suffer will not be registered on the Imperial rolls, and no prisoners will be exchanged. You'll likely be executed as pirates if they get their hands on you, just like the Empire does to their raiders."

That matched what she'd heard about other operations against the Singularity. Those had been whispered about over beer, late in the evenings, in dark corners of bars, almost like ghost stories.

Everyone knew the fig leaf that covered the Empire when this type of operation was conducted. The emperor could claim the fighters were renegades turned pirate while knowing that the Singularity didn't believe that for one single second. The Singularity did the same when it sent its troops to attack the Empire.

Both sides knew *exactly* what the other was doing. That still didn't reduce the danger of doing this kind of mission. Or the reward.

Still, it was best to make sure that the rumors and tall tales that she'd heard were correct. Assumptions were bad at the best of times. In the worst, they could get you or your people killed.

"Now that I know the penalties of failure, what are the rewards if we achieve the mission objectives?" she asked.

His smile widened. "Anything that you destroy, a portion of its value will be paid to each of you directly from the black ops side of the Imperial purse. Anything captured by the group as a whole that is of value will be similarly exchanged via a prize court.

"Once you return from your… vacation, you can 'reenlist' and go back to your normal activities, just as if you'd never left, should you wish. You'd get a secret commendation and promotion, as well as your choice of assignments. Pretty much carte blanche.

"The other choice is a quiet retirement, with your service years being bumped up to the minimum required for retirement, still with an associated promotion to a rank matching your extended service date.

"For you, that would likely be major. Or, if you do particularly well, perhaps even my rank. I wouldn't count on me having to salute you, but that's all up to the emperor. One never knows."

That was… sobering.

While she considered that, he continued, leaning forward and whispering almost conspiratorially. "And then there's *tradition*. Anyone who goes on one of these missions is viewed as a pirate. As part of the reward for that—and as part of the cover—emperors since the beginning have decreed that each individual *must* keep one thing seized from the enemy, no matter its legality or value. If it's something big enough to have other things inside it, those are covered, too. The selection of that item is up to the individual, and not even the emperor may gainsay their right to retain this booty."

"Booty?" she asked incredulously. "Isn't that just another word for stolen property?"

The older man chuckled. "Don't get hung up on the peculiarities of language, Grace. By making it so that you get some reward that no one else can control, the emperor is firmly placing you on the side of piracy. Well, privateering, technically.

"Since it's against our enemies, the Empire will turn a blind eye, of course. A Letter of Marque will be entered into your confidential record and the secret mission orders that you and the other senior members of the group will have access to. The Empire will never admit that exists, but it grants you the authority to do everything that I've said and promises the rewards I've specified."

She nodded, though it all sounded so strange. It almost felt as if this were happening to someone else.

"When do we leave?"

"Immediately," he said briskly. "Head back to your barracks and get your people in motion. Change into civilian clothes and only take nonmilitary items. Everything you'll use on this mission will be provided for you. All your other belongings will be secured against your eventual return."

His expression turned grave. "Remember, don't get caught or killed. The Empire is at war with the Singularity, even if no one uses that kind of language. This is your chance to make the bastards pay for what they've done to us in the past. I expect you to make them bleed."

She rose to her feet and stiffened to attention. "You can count on me and my people, sir. We'll extract an Imperial kilo of flesh from the Singularity."

He leaned back in his chair and grinned. "I'd expect nothing less. Good luck, and make sure you find something really sweet to take for yourself, Grace. This is a once-in-a-lifetime opportunity, and I don't want to see you squander it on something that's beneath you. I expect nothing short of an epic piece of booty in your bag when I see you next. Dismissed."

She spun on her heel and walked out of his office. Pedro wasn't at his desk, so she made her way out of the building and headed for her platoon's barracks, her mind swirling with possibilities. There was danger ahead but also a chance for glory against the Empire's enemies.

That was more than enough for her. Money be damned. She'd make sure they remembered her incursion for years to come.

3

The beating that night was just as bad as One Twenty-Four had expected. She'd stayed awake for as long as she could but dozed off despite knowing what was coming.

Her crèche mates had thrown a blanket over her and then used bars of soap inside socks to beat her. The blanket had protected her from serious injury but stopped none of the pain. By design, the beating was impersonal. She had no idea how many of her crèche mates had participated, nor which ones.

Well, with the notable exception of Thirty-One. The girl hated her and made no bones about it.

The beating seemed to last forever, but it eventually ended, and they left her alone on her bunk, covered by the blanket. They'd stayed away from her face, limiting their blows to her body, where they wouldn't be visible once she was dressed.

They knew the rules just as well as she did. This was the crèche's way of making certain that a wayward member knew exactly how badly they'd failed the Line. Frankly, she understood the process quite well, as she participated in these so-called blanket parties herself.

That brought her no pride or shame. It was just the way things were. When someone acted against the best interests of the crèche, they were punished. Emotion played no part.

Well, for anyone other than Thirty-One.

There was a secondary reason that her crèche mates had left her face unmarked. Today was the day that they'd received their Line tattoos. The same pattern that graced Keeper's face would be placed upon them today.

If they'd injured her face, Keeper would have been furious, and that was something to be avoided at all costs.

One Twenty-Four had no idea what the process was going to be like, but she'd been looking forward to this day for as long as she could remember. The bold stylized bird of prey tattooed across Keeper's forehead and cheeks identified her as a member of the Andrea Line, part of the ruling caste of the Singularity.

Even though One Twenty-Four wasn't yet a member of the Line, she'd take that first unalterable step toward becoming one today.

Well, perhaps this was the second step. One Twenty-Four's very creation gave her the genetics of the Andrea Line. Each and every one of them had precisely the same DNA, designed and made into a template millennia ago at the founding of the Singularity. The only difference between her and Keeper was their age.

And One Twenty-Four's poor behavior.

When the dawn chime sounded, she rose stiffly and showered with her crèche mates. Most paid her no mind, as if the bruises covering her torso and legs weren't even there.

The exception was, of course, Thirty-One. Her eyes glittered with smug malice as she washed, brazenly staring at One Twenty-Four.

She had no idea how she'd earned the girl's ire, but the hatred was real and fierce. And One Twenty-Four had to admit that it didn't just go one way. If their positions were reversed, she would feel great satisfaction beating her enemy.

For the rest, the punishment had been delivered, and now the incident was done. It was up to One Twenty-Four to accept the lesson that had been imparted and change her willful ways.

Or fail to do so and die.

Sadly, One Twenty-Four wasn't sure that she could do it. Her view of the world just didn't mesh with that of her crèche mates. She'd tried her very best to be what Keeper demanded, but that was no easy task.

The things that she cared about, the things she wanted to learn, were not the things that Keeper wanted the crèche to be thinking about.

One Twenty-Four was beginning to doubt that she had the focus and fortitude necessary to survive until adulthood under the increasingly strict regime. Perhaps there would be more individuality allowed as things progressed, and that would allow her to find her own path.

She doubted it. The most likely outcome was her expulsion from the crèche.

The thought of that made her stomach twist. In the dark, she and her crèche mates had speculated about what happened to those who'd been expelled. Were they killed and their bodies recycled? Were they ejected from an airlock? Something worse?

The only thing they knew for certain was that if anyone was ejected from the crèche, they were dead within minutes. Keeper had made no bones about that. She wanted the ultimate punishment clearly stated so that there could be no misunderstanding.

One Twenty-Four cleaned herself, dressed in her uniform, and joined the other girls as they made their way to the classroom.

Today, they'd be leaving the crèche and visiting another part of the station for the first time. The equipment that would inscribe the tattoos on their faces was specialized and came on a ship. It would not remain at this station once its work had been completed. It had other crèches to visit and other lines to serve.

No one else was supposed to know that the crèche was aboard the station. The crèche was on an isolated level, and anyone that had to interface with Keeper did so outside its bounds.

One Twenty-Four had no idea how the crèche was marked on whatever maps the station residents used, but she had no doubt that it would seem innocuous.

Since they needed to leave the area around the crèche, Keeper had informed them yesterday that the corridors would be cleared. There would be no witnesses to their passage.

That was disappointing. She'd always wondered what other lines looked like. Or, even better, the base caste that belonged to no line at all.

According to Keeper, twelve lines made up the ruling caste of the Singularity. All were grown from the same template as their line sibs. No deviation was possible. Or perhaps all deviants were culled after decanting. She didn't know.

Below them were the subservient lines that performed tasks as directed by the ruling caste. Only members of these servant classes were allowed to interface with the ruling caste. Members of those lines performed all tasks from guarding the rulers to seeing to their upkeep.

Just like the Andrea Line, they were created from specific templates designed for the tasks they'd perform. The guards were large and fast—or so she'd been told—and the administrators had increased intelligence when compared to some of the other lines.

The ruling caste had that and much more. They were the pinnacle of what was possible in an organic being. Not like the mechanical enhancements that the humans that made up the Empire perverted themselves with.

Outside the servant lines, there were many more lines of lesser importance. And below those were the base caste. These were unaltered humans that did the most menial and degrading tasks.

Those humans came from no template. They were created from random combinations of base DNA and gestated inside the female. Keeper had refused to explain the process of creation or decanting of the base caste in any detail, saying such acts were beneath them and would not even bear contemplation.

The offspring were raised not by a Keeper but by the pair that had spawned them, so long as an examination of the child didn't reveal any apparent physical or mental defects in their yearly inspections. Any that failed were culled for the good of the Singularity.

One Twenty-Four took a deep breath and put the thoughts out of her head. She had more pressing matters to think about.

As they gathered to leave the crèche, she could barely contain her excitement. She'd never seen a spaceship before. She'd been raised in the crèche since the day she'd been created. From her understanding, the nurses that had brought her and her crèche mates to the station had arrived under the same type of concealment as the ship was using now.

No one had seen them arrive, and One Twenty-Four wasn't even certain that they hadn't been created inside the crèche itself. It was possible that a ship like the one they were going to visit now had delivered the necessary equipment and nurses and then taken them away again once they were no longer required.

Her memories of the nurses themselves were vague, but they'd been members of the Andrea Line as well. One Twenty-Four assumed that when she left the crèche—if she did—then she'd serve that particular capacity herself for a subsequent generation of her line sibs.

Once Keeper was ready, the girls moved out in a long line, walking one behind another and keeping quiet as they examined the station corridors with wide eyes. Everything looked similar to what was inside the crèche but seemed a little bit shabbier.

Were the residents less diligent in their cleaning? Keeper allowed no filth inside the crèche. Did no one guide the people out here in the same way?

Well, she supposed it wasn't her place to judge. Yet.

One Twenty-Four thought it was exciting, and now she wanted to see more. She wished she could get out of the crèche and explore the rest of the station. Perhaps even meet some of the people who lived there.

Of course, that was impossible. Children of a line were never seen by anyone outside their line. Only once they were adults would they emerge into the larger society of the Singularity.

One Twenty-Four and her crèche mates traveled through a docking port and into a short tube that led into the ship itself. The vessel wasn't docked inside the station but floated adjacent to it. The interior corridors of the ship were cleaner than those on the station, and once again, there were no people in sight. Obviously, they were not meant to see her and her crèche mates.

Keeper led them through several twists and turns and even into a shaft with a ladder so that they could climb several levels. The torturous path eventually led them to a large room that held ten machines that were of a size that someone like One Twenty-Four could easily fit inside.

After they'd gathered into a group around her, Keeper gave them all a stern look. "This process will not be painless. That is to test your resolve.

"I expect each of you to remain completely and utterly still. If the tattoo is not imprinted perfectly, you will have failed the Line and will be expelled from the crèche."

That news quieted everyone. What little murmuring there'd been between the girls ceased. This was one of those moments where one had to persevere—whatever pain was delivered—or they'd pay with their lives.

One Twenty-Four wondered if she could remain absolutely motionless in the face of intense pain. Even knowing the penalty, she wasn't sure. Though, after the beating that she'd endured this morning—and other mornings—she might actually be more prepared for this test than many of her crèche mates.

She firmed her resolve. She'd do whatever needed to be done, suffer whatever needed to be endured.

Keeper selected the first ten girls at random, with her only criteria being those who were closest to her at the moment she'd decided to pick them. One Twenty-Four was just outside the circle.

Some of the other girls stepped back, likely because they didn't want to be selected for the next batch, but she remained right where she was. Delaying the inevitable wouldn't make this process any easier.

In fact, she envied those that were already climbing into the machines. No matter what happened now, those girls didn't need to worry about what they'd see or hear.

She was working up the temerity to ask Keeper how long the process took when one of the girls inside a pod near her began screaming and thrashing. The top of the pod was semi-translucent, so

One Twenty-Four could see the girl moving about but couldn't tell what was happening.

Keeper slapped a button on the side of the pod, causing it to open.

The girl inside was a bloody mess. It seemed as though a madman had splashed black and red ink all across her face and head. Part of that was a mixture of tattoos gone horribly awry, and the other was blood from whatever injuries her thrashing had caused.

Without saying a word, Keeper pulled the girl—Seventy-Three, her band informed her—out of her pod and dragged her to a door at the side of the room. She opened it and shoved the screaming, sobbing girl through the opening, ignoring her tearful pleas.

Keeper turned back to the group as soon as the door had closed, forever separating the doomed girl from her former crèche mates. If anything, Keeper's expression was even grimmer.

"Seventy-Three is no longer a member of the crèche. I strongly urge you to learn from her failure. No matter the pain you feel or the fear you might experience, you must remain *absolutely* still. Do *not* fail this test."

Now suitably terrified, One Twenty-Four watched as the remaining nine finished their session in the pods.

When they came out, they looked dazed and in pain, but they'd obviously followed the instructions. Their tattoos were perfect, though their faces were red and swollen from the imprinting process. They looked exactly like immature replicas of Keeper.

"You've done well," Keeper told them. "Go into the corridor and wait."

With a sweep of her arms, Keeper selected the next ten. One Twenty-Four was among that group and climbed into the pod that Keeper directed her toward.

Ominously, it was Seventy-Three's pod. Was that an unsubtle hint of Keeper's feelings toward her? Or a grim foreshadowing of what was to come?

No matter.

Using every ounce of will she possessed, One Twenty-Four forced herself to stay completely and utterly still as she willed herself to relax before closing her eyes. The pain would flow through her, leaving her untouched, if she mastered herself.

The lid came down, and there was a moment of utter calm before it felt as if her face was on fire. The pain grew so intense that she wondered if she was going to pass out or lose control of her bladder. It kept growing until she was finally at the limit of what she could stand.

Then, moments away from her losing control of herself, it suddenly stopped.

The lid opened, and Keeper stared down at her. Her expression was somewhat sour as she pulled One Twenty-Four out of the pod and shoved her less than gently toward the corridor without a word.

She'd passed this particular test.

One Twenty-Four stared at her crèche mates in the corridor. That was what she looked like now. She could hardly believe it. She'd survived.

In the end, the crèche lost another six members during the tattooing process. Keeper didn't seem dismayed, so perhaps she'd expected the number to be larger.

One Twenty-Four was happy to get back to the dormitory. Even though it had only been a few hours, it felt as if she'd been running all day and simultaneously beating her head against a wall. Her skin was on fire, even with the salve that Keeper had given them.

Thankfully, nobody else seemed to be in a mood to talk about what had happened. One Twenty-Four lay down on her bunk and let the fire on her face slowly fade until it meshed with the bruises and aches from the beating that she'd endured last night.

She was in a lot of pain, but so be it. That was what it took to survive in the crèche. Pain was proof that you were still alive. She would survive, no matter how much it hurt to do so.

4

Grace made her way back to the barracks and called for everyone to gather in the muster hall. Her platoon was made up of three squads commanded by sergeants, which in turn consisted of three fire teams of four marines, including a corporal to command it. She led the platoon with the assistance of Sergeant Na Fei.

That made for a total of forty-one marines, counting herself. Third Platoon would make an excellent raid group, and she knew that her people would kick some ass.

Sergeant Na assumed her rightful position in front of the neat rows of marines. She brought her right fist to her chest in salute as Grace stepped in front of her and returned it.

"At ease," Grace said automatically, allowing her people to relax in place. "We have a mission. It's an extremely specialized one, and some of the requirements are going to seem very odd.

"First of all, once we're done with this little conversation, I want everybody to change into civilian clothes. In fact, you're going to want to pack *all* of your civilian clothes. When we leave, we'll take nothing issued by the Corps. Second, we'll take a commercial shuttle from inside the port.

"I'm not going to give you any additional information until we're on board the ship assigned to us. I also won't ask if you have any questions, because I have no answers that I can give you at this point. Get to it."

As soon as her people scattered, Na stepped forward and spoke in a low whisper. "What's *really* going on, Lieutenant?"

Grace gave her extremely competent NCO a firm look. "I'm afraid you'll have to find out when we get into orbit. My orders are *exquisitely* clear, so I can't say anything until then. Not one single word."

The other woman nodded slightly, her lips slightly pursed. "You've got my curiosity up, ma'am. I can't wait to find out what we're doing, since this sounds completely ludicrous. What about our weapons? Are we expected to beat somebody with our fists?"

Na was an extremely capable hand-to-hand fighter, so that wasn't entirely out of the question.

"Nope," Grace said cheerfully. "I meant exactly what I said. Pack civilian clothes and associated belongings. Everything else will be provided for us.

"Once everyone thinks they've got what they need, I want you to have them open up their bags and look for contraband. Knives and personal weapons are acceptable. Anything that could be used to link us to the marines or give someone our names is not. It's your job to make sure that none of that makes its way past your inspection."

Na smiled coldly. "You can count on me to make certain that nothing inappropriate gets through. I assume you'll be checking my kit, ma'am. Who's going to check yours?"

"You don't trust me, Fei?" Grace asked with a wicked smile. "Come on. I'm an officer."

"All the more reason to double-check you, ma'am."

Grace smirked. "You'll be checking my bag. Everybody goes through this check so that nobody has to feel like we're any better than they are. Now get busy. I'd like to be on our way to the port in twenty minutes."

That done, Grace headed for her quarters. Even through the thick walls, she could hear everyone carrying out her orders. She had no doubt that at least a few would try to slip something past Na.

Under other circumstances, she'd probably do the same. She was a marine, wasn't she?

Today, she focused on packing every bit of civilian clothes and gear that she had on hand while carefully stripping out any that could identify her personally or associate her with the Corps.

There wasn't much left by the time she'd finished. Even then, some of her clothes would be completely unsuitable for the mission, she suspected, though she'd bring them just in case.

Her little black dress, for example, had no place on a raid. She had no idea what the damn genies wore to fight during their raids— much less off duty—but it probably didn't include sexy dresses.

She wouldn't be forced to assault something in her civilian clothes, she was confident of that. There'd be weapons and armor for them to use. Whatever ship they had would also be capable of sneaking into the Singularity and delivering them onto their target.

It might look like a civilian ship, but whatever it was, she had no doubt that it would have all the capabilities required for the insertion and extraction of her team.

She'd have to pick up additional clothing and gear when they got to the port. She wasn't going to be the only one, she wagered. Their driver could drop them off, and they'd walk to the small craft assigned to them once they finished shopping.

It only took ten minutes for her to get everything packed into the nonregulation bag she used when she went home to visit her mother. Not that she visited her mother all that often, because the woman had never approved of Grace's choice to become a marine in the first place. She'd wanted Grace to settle down, find a nice partner, and raise a family.

Grace didn't see that happening anytime soon. With the longer lifespan marines' nanites gave, she could actively serve for a hundred years. Sadly, the lack of opportunity for promotions meant that it would take her decades before she achieved field-grade rank, much less made it to general.

Unless she kicked some ass on this mission and retired as a major.

If she could bring herself to do that, which she doubted. The Corps was her life.

If she stayed in, the slow pace of retirements meant there were fewer slots available as one climbed the ladder of rank. Her next step was senior lieutenant, which would be covered by the postraid promotion.

There'd be no problem finding a place for her to command a company, though it would take time for a slot to open up. The available slots grew sparser as one looked at the rank of major and above. One had to be genuinely gifted to rise that far.

Especially when one started looking above colonel. As large as the Empire was, there were a lot of marines that hoped to make it into those exalted ranks. Few would have the skill or dedication to make it happen, though.

She liked to think that she had what it took, but the odds were stacked pretty heavily against her. Thankfully, she'd have a long time to work on it. If she did well on this mission, it would open some doors for her, so she'd best make sure they made a strong impression on the Singularity.

At the appointed time, her platoon gathered again, everyone now in civilian clothes. To say that they looked like a motley group of pirates wouldn't have been inappropriate.

She stopped and stared at Corporal Riggio Gomez, leader of Second Squad's Second Fire Team. He was wearing what looked to be an untucked flowered shirt patterned in bright fluorescent colors ranging from yellow to red. The oranges, in particular, hurt her eyes.

Below that, he wore cargo shorts that exposed his *very* hairy legs and shuffled along in ragged sandals. He wore a hat that sat far back on his head and had a bill that extended off to the side. It read "YOLO" across the front in canary-yellow letters.

A corporate logo? If so, she didn't recognize the company.

"Gomez," she murmured as she walked around him, unabashedly looking him up and down. "Be honest. Did you lose a bet?"

The noncom grinned at her. "No, ma'am. On a beach, this kind of getup draws in women like flies. Trust me on that."

She didn't bother to hide the look of disbelief that had to be plastered across her face.

Instead, she gestured for him and the rest to see Sergeant Na. "Open your bags for inspection. If you have anything that someone could trace back to the Corps or learn your name from, you might want to put it back into your foot lockers."

When fully a third of the marines darted away, she suppressed a satisfied look. Yep, marines would always be marines.

After the platoon had passed inspection, Grace handed her bag to Na and took hers to inspect. Neither found anything objectionable, and in a few minutes, they were all ready to depart.

"Let's get out of here before somebody arrests you for wearing that getup, Gomez," Grace said firmly, walking outside the barracks as his mates laughed.

There was a small grav bus waiting for them. It was the kind used to get children to school. It looked as if it had seen better days.

The man driving the bus was morbidly obese and hairy in places that men *shouldn't* have had hair. He was also bald in areas that men *should* have hair. He grinned, revealing a couple of gaps where teeth should be.

"Everybody pile in," he said in a voice far too highly pitched for his size. "I'll get you to the port right quick."

Putting aside her reservations, she went up the steps and sat in front, waiting for her people to file aboard and secure their bags. As soon as they were all seated, the man closed the door, and the grav bus took off, inducing a wave of nausea, because its grav nodes were badly in need of tuning.

If this was meant to make sure that no one associated them with the Imperial Marines, it was a brilliant ploy. If it was a way to save a few credits, she'd love to find the bean counter responsible and conduct some late-night remedial training.

Working up her courage, she leaned toward the man, breathing through her mouth because he smelled like stale onions. "Once we get to the port, we're going to have to stop to get some civilian clothes and gear."

The man nodded. "The guy that hired me already said that. I'll drop you off at a good spot."

Grace leaned back without another word. Being so near the repulsive man made her nauseous.

Twenty-five minutes later, the bus settled to a halt in a large parking area just outside the civilian spaceport. Like most such, it was surrounded by stores that catered to travelers. If someone forgot anything, they'd be happy to provide a replacement at a premium.

Once the bus had left, picking up clothing and gear took about three times longer than Grace had mentally allowed for it. It seemed that her marines were clotheshorses.

Each of them had a specific kind of thing they wanted to pick up, and *none* of it was in the same store. So they ended up trooping from store to store to find the appropriate items.

It would've been quicker to allow her people to spread out and do their shopping on their own, but she had no doubt that unauthorized items would magically make their way into their gear. So she got to be the oversight while Na backed her up.

She honestly couldn't complain about the time spent. She had her own tastes in civilian clothing, and none of the stores that the men had picked were suitable for her. Amusingly, Na had similar tastes.

On the whole, it was actually an enjoyable outing. Her marines horsed around and joked at one another's expense. It was relaxing.

Once they'd secured everything they needed, their next stop was of a more general nature. They had to pick up all the personal supplies they'd need—toiletries mostly—but also entertainment and other things that might not be found on shipboard.

Fleet computers had a vast array of entertainment, but most marines preferred their fun to be of a more physical form. They played cards and other competitive games.

There'd been a resurgence in a game called darts over the last few centuries. Grace had no idea if it actually resembled the original game, because that was from before the Empire. Hell, it was from before the Republic.

Still, the important thing was that her people enjoyed themselves while off duty. Their morale was critical.

As they were wrapping things up, Grace started thinking about what came next. On every mission she'd ever been on, she'd never been read into more than the most fundamental operational planning.

She really had no idea how this trip was going to be arranged. She had no idea what ship they were taking, how large a crew it might have, what capabilities it would be able to provide, and many other things that she had to find out as soon as she got aboard.

Unlike other missions, she was in charge of the entire strike force, and there were aspects of the transport that she needed to become familiar with for them to succeed. Grace had no doubt that the Fleet officers and crew would be top-notch, but they were all operating in new and unusual ways.

In fact, they probably weren't technically Fleet at all anymore. Like her, they'd have been released from service and sent on this mission in a way that was deniable by the Empire. Basically, they were active-duty Fleet officers and crew masquerading as civilians.

At long last, they had everything they needed, all packed away into new bags. They made their way to one of the private shuttle terminals, where a chartered cutter waited to take them up to orbit.

It was significantly more luxurious than the pinnaces she and her marines usually used. Marine pinnaces could hold a platoon and a half in full armor and all their weapons. This shuttle was significantly smaller and could just barely carry them and their luggage.

That said, they traveled in comfort and style. There were plush seats with luxurious padding and attendants to provide in-flight drinks and meals.

Grace considered banning the alcohol but decided not to. She made certain that Na passed the word that everyone was limited to one alcoholic drink and then had to switch to something else.

They weren't going to be attacked in orbit, but she wanted her people sharp, and she didn't want them to make the kind of impression that would linger in someone's mind. Blending in was the most essential part of what they were doing at this moment.

Of course, the fact that each and every one of them had marine-style buzzcuts immediately told everyone who saw them what they did for a living, particularly when they traveled in a group.

That would change in the next week. With the use of modern medical technology, each and every one of them would have what passed for civilian-style hair in an amazingly short amount of time. They could then blend in with the regular populace at need.

On the trip up, several people tried to cajole her into giving them more information about the mission. She politely refused and glared at those who persisted.

She interfaced her implants with the shuttle systems and took a look at the ship that they finally approached. It was a small freighter that had seen better days.

It was still almost as big as a regular marine transport, but the cargo pods took up a lot of that space. The habitation section was going to be tight for the regular crew, much less after adding her people in.

It looked battered and ill maintained, as if it had been repaired in ways that wouldn't pass muster in the core sectors of the Empire. It had to have additional capabilities, but until she spoke with the officers, she wouldn't know the specifics.

The cutter docked smoothly, and her people disembarked. Grace made sure that she was the first person through the hatch so that she could get a look at their new home.

It wasn't much to look at, honestly. The bulkheads hadn't seen a good scrubbing in years, and the air smelled like her gym bag after a few weeks of being forgotten in her locker.

That would be something that she'd have to address. Her marines needed busywork to keep them out of trouble. Getting the ship a bit cleaner would fit the bill.

A glance at Na confirmed the other woman was thinking along those lines already.

Two men waited for them just inside the ship. Based on their hair length, most people wouldn't have guessed that they were Fleet. The thing that gave them away was their stiff, upright postures. These were Fleet officers.

She smiled at them. "Gentlemen, I'm Grace Tolliver. My associate, Na Fei."

The taller of the pair had shoulder-length red hair that framed a ruggedly handsome face with a nose that was just a bit too large. The shorter man's sandy brown hair was drawn back into a ponytail and perfectly complimented his neatly trimmed beard.

"Welcome aboard," the shorter man said, extending his hand. "I'm Jay Anders, and I'm the pilot commander of *Bright Passage*. This is my partner, Alan Kyle."

The taller man inclined his head.

If Grace had to guess, Anders was a lieutenant commander, and Kyle was probably a lieutenant. That would be roughly right for their bearing and apparent age.

Bright Passage was a misnomer for sure. She sensed some irony at work in her name.

"When will we be leaving orbit?" she asked. "I need to see my people settled."

"Right to business, I see," Anders said, his smile widening. "We can leave Seward orbit as soon as you're ready. Alan can see everyone settled if you'd care to accompany me to the bridge. Ah, the control room, I mean."

It looked as if he was still adjusting to the new situation, too.

Grace turned to Na. "Put my bags wherever Mister Kyle says I'm staying and get everyone settled in, Fei."

"Yes... Grace."

Anders's eyes twinkled. "I've got an office next to the control room. This way."

5

The next day's instruction began with one of One Twenty-Four's least favorite classes: physical education. Depending on the day, it involved rigorous exercise or even team sports. Occasionally there were competitions between individuals.

Today, Keeper stood on a raised platform in the center of one of the largest rooms inside the crèche. She stared out over the crowd of girls, who stood straight, their attention focused upon her.

"Now that you've taken your first step toward becoming members of the Andrea Line, it's time for you to learn one of the most important skills that you will have to master. Domination."

One Twenty-Four frowned. Domination? What did that mean in this context?

Keeper waited for the murmurs between the girls to fade. One Twenty-Four remained silent. As one of the outliers in the crèche, she didn't have many friends. Her line sibs associated with those that they believed would help them in the ultimate quest of survival, not those that they thought were marked for eventual elimination.

"I can see that I've confused you," Keeper allowed as she walked to the front of the platform and stared imperiously down at them. "During the second half of your indoctrination—as well as in your lives as rulers of the Singularity—you will often have to project power over your competitors and enemies alike. We call this domination.

"Domination can come in many forms. It can be wrought of subtlety when you outmaneuver your opponent, and they lack any options other than compliance with your will. At the other end of the spectrum, you might have to use force to eliminate competition. And when I say eliminate, that can be anything from making your enemy cease whatever they are doing all the way up to potentially ending their lives."

This wasn't something that One Twenty-Four had ever pondered. Yes, she'd daydreamed about ending Thirty-One's life, but that had only been longing, not belief that such an event was within her power.

The girl was her greatest tormentor. She'd often wondered how much simpler life would become if the other girl was no longer in the crèche. Still, she'd never considered the possibility that creating such an outcome might be an option for her.

Was it allowable to simply slay one's enemies, even within the crèche? Somehow, One Twenty-Four doubted that. If so, the number of girls to reach maturity would be far lower. That couldn't be what the Singularity desired.

She glanced toward where Thirty-One stood with her hangers-on. She and the half dozen girls that belonged to her clique were all staring at One Twenty-Four. Judging by Thirty-One's expression, the other girl's thoughts closely mirrored her own.

That did not bode well for her. Not well at all.

"I can see that some of you are considering the implications of my words," Keeper said. "Let me be clear. You are *not* allowed to kill any of your rivals here. To do so will result in your immediate expulsion from the crèche if I become certain that is what occurred.

"Even as one of the rulers of the Singularity, there are limits imposed upon your behavior. It is unacceptable to use brute force when something more subtle is viable. Outmaneuvering your foes is laudable. Simply slaying them when other options are available is beneath you.

"The Singularity is not ruled by brutes or brawlers. We are led by thinkers and planners who consider potential actions and their implications upon our society before they act. If you cannot do so, then you are not fit to lead."

Keeper paused to allow that to sink in. After a few moments, she continued.

"That does not mean there won't be instances where you must exercise force, so today we will begin learning hand-to-hand combat. If you must fight, it's unseemly for you to have no skill, and I will not have my girls flailing around if they are forced to defend themselves. That would bring dishonor to the Andrea Line and to me personally.

"In this room, and in this class, are the only times that you are allowed to fight one another. I understand that there are times inside the crèche where punishment must be rendered. That is not what I'm speaking about, and you already know your limitations as relates to those actions. Am I clear?"

One Twenty-Four and the rest answered in unison. "Yes, Keeper."

"Good. I will designate partners for each of you, and you must subdue your opponent. I understand that you have no skill at this point. This exercise is meant to exemplify how such training will be helpful to you in the future.

"The basic rules are simple. Each of you will attempt to pin the other to the mat. When one of you cannot rise, you have been defeated.

"It would behoove you to pay very close attention to what your crèche mates are doing. Learn from their mistakes as well as their successes. When the time comes, you will only have the skills you have trained in and those which you can observe and deduce for yourself.

"Use your mind. Outthink your enemy. If you can maneuver them into a position where they have no good options, you'll win. Remember that physical force is the last resort, not the first. Your mind is the key to victory. Use it."

One Twenty-Four stood there as Keeper selected the first two girls, secretly glad that she wasn't chosen. She watched as the two girls struggled against one another, pulling hair and striking one another with their hands. It all seemed so... ineffective. Surely there must be a better way to subdue one's foes.

Why was Keeper forcing them to fight, knowing that they had no skill? What purpose did this exercise *truly* serve?

They couldn't be meant to learn what to do from watching one another. That would simply be idiots mirroring idiots. No, this was meant to show them exactly how helpless they were.

That had to be the purpose of this lesson. The real insight was that One Twenty-Four and her line sibs were dependent on Keeper to make them strong. It was one more way to bind each of them to the Line and cement their obedience to Keeper's will.

Once she understood, she put her concern out of her mind. What Keeper was doing didn't bother her, because that was just the way things were. The thought exercise was still useful, because understanding *why* one did things was often more important than understanding *how* one did them.

The first pair eventually ended their conflict when one of them tripped, and the other jumped upon her back. It was ungainly and uncoordinated but effective, she supposed.

As she watched pair after pair go through combat, One Twenty-Four started to see a pattern. Each of the girls was mimicking what those who'd gone before had done. That meant perpetuating what were obviously ineffective fighting techniques.

What would be more efficient? Fists were better than open hands, that was obvious, but placement seemed to be critical.

And then she saw something that opened her eyes. One of the girls fell, but during her fall, the back of her arm struck the other girl in the stomach. The struck one bent over and gasped for breath, allowing the first to tackle her.

One Twenty-Four knew from personal experience that elbows hurt if you struck them on things, so one would have to be careful about their use, but it seemed that a fast-moving elbow made for a good weapon. It increased the amount of force applied to a specific area. That was just fundamental physics.

The stomach, as she had suspected, seemed vulnerable to this kind of thing. There would undoubtedly be other locations on one's body where such a strike would be effective. She just needed to determine what they were in the time that she still had available.

When the latest girls were sent back into the crowd, Keeper again looked over the group, but before she could speak, someone in the crowd did so.

"Keeper, may we choose our opponents?" Thirty-One asked, a predatory curve to her lips.

Keeper considered the girl for a moment and then nodded. "I will allow it this time. Who do you wish to fight?"

"One Twenty-Four."

One Twenty-Four's blood ran cold. Where she'd been planning on how to simply fight someone, she knew that Thirty-One wanted to injure her. She wanted to cause pain and wouldn't be satisfied by merely winning this fight.

"Both of you step onto the mat," Keeper ordered.

One Twenty-Four stepped onto the mat and watched as Thirty-One took her place across from her. The other girl didn't seem afraid. She was obviously already imagining how she'd cause One Twenty-Four harm.

If Thirty-One won now, her behavior would only grow worse. The only way to stop that—or perhaps only to slow it—was to make the other girl respect her enough to become cautious.

Perhaps that was what Keeper had been speaking about earlier. If you couldn't defeat an enemy outright, you needed to make them weigh the consequences of crossing you.

Now she just needed to figure out how to do it.

When Keeper gave the word, Thirty-One raced forward, her hands already reaching for One Twenty-Four's hair.

Dodging was almost impossible, but she tried to step aside. The move failed, and Thirty-One grabbed her by the hair and struck her on the side of the head.

The blow sparked sudden pain in One Twenty-Four's ear. It felt as if she'd ran into a wall. Her vision spun, and she saw stars.

No, her vision hadn't spun, she'd tried to turn away from the strike and now had her back towards her enemy. That turned out to have been a terrible mistake.

Thirty-One jumped onto her back and wrapped an arm around her neck, squeezing tight until One Twenty-Four couldn't breathe.

She tried to dislodge the other girl, but even though they were precisely the same size, it seemed as if her opponent had a grip of iron. Nothing she did loosened the bar across her throat one millimeter.

If only she could be on top of the other girl. If only she were the one beyond her reach.

And then an idea occurred to her. If she couldn't be behind the other girl, perhaps something else could be.

She threw herself back, and the two of them slammed into the mat. It padded them from falls but wasn't thick enough to truly cushion them from an impact. The force of the landing jarred One Twenty-Four, but it was far worse for Thirty-One. The other girl's breath whooshed out of her body.

With Thirty-One momentarily stunned, One Twenty-Four was able to wriggle free of her grip.

Her first impulse was to run away while she could, but she immediately realized that distance was not her friend. As soon as she recovered, Thirty-One would come after her once more, even angrier than she'd been before.

No, One Twenty-Four had to end this fight quickly and decisively.

She drew her right arm back and struck down with her elbow at the other girl's head as hard as she could. The back of her elbow struck Thirty-One across the face with a dull crack, and blood began flowing from the girl's now flattened nose.

The impact made Thirty-One scream and thrash around, completely uncoordinated now. That allowed One Twenty-Four to spin around, sit on her enemy's stomach, and bring her fists down upon the girl's face.

She struck Thirty-One again and again, her fingers smarting with every blow until she learned to use the bases of her fists as the impact points. After half a dozen strikes, Thirty-One fell limp.

One Twenty-Four paused to consider whether it was appropriate to continue hitting the unconscious girl and decided that it was not. That wasn't the purpose of this lesson.

She stood, stepped away from her unconscious and bloodied enemy, and faced Keeper.

All throughout the fight, the woman had said nothing. Now One Twenty-Four saw that she was smiling.

It wasn't a smile of pleasure. In fact, it bore a marked similarity to Thirty-One's cruel expression earlier. She suddenly realized that Keeper had taken pleasure in watching the violence.

"You have done *surprisingly* well, One Twenty-Four," Keeper said. "Most excellent. You've vanquished your foe decisively, and you've learned to utilize the most potent tool in a physical conflict: your mind.

"Congratulations to you in this moment of insight. Learn from this moment and focus yourself so that you may serve the Singularity with the mind that granted you victory today."

Keeper turned and gestured at several of the girls who'd already fought. "Take Thirty-One to the infirmary, place her on a bed, and wait with her. I'll be along as soon as this class is done."

One Twenty-Four watched the girls carry Thirty-One out of the room. Her enemy's clique was staring at her with dismay and raw hatred now. Far from solving any of her problems, defeating Thirty-One had only made them worse.

Still, she wasn't sure what other choices she'd had. Victory would've emboldened Thirty-One. There had been no reasonable course of action available to her, so she'd picked the one with the most immediate benefits. Now she'd pay for her temerity.

Thirty-One couldn't allow this insult to go unchallenged. Worse, the girl wasn't stupid. She'd learn from her mistakes and make One Twenty-Four pay dearly for humiliating her.

One Twenty-Four sighed and stepped back, rubbing her aching fingers. She'd deal with Thirty-One and whatever came next. That was the way of the Singularity and, she supposed, the ultimate lesson for the day.

6

G race followed Anders through the cramped corridors of the small ship and found herself less impressed with every step she took. *Bright Passage* needed a *thorough* cleaning, and that hinted at trouble for its probable maintenance record as well, unless this was all some big charade.

Fleet might have masked the ship's condition with a false appearance, but until she started poking into corners and asking questions, she wasn't going to assume anything.

The control room—or bridge as Anders had almost referred to it —wasn't set up like an Imperial warship's bridge. In the course of her service, she'd been to a couple of the small ships while she'd been on missions.

On those ships, there'd been a large viewscreen set toward the front of the bridge. A number of control stations and consoles sat in front of it, and the commander's seat was at the rear of the chamber, potentially with a few more chairs and consoles arrayed along the walls behind it.

This ship had a more communal feel. The three consoles were arrayed in front of the command seat, facing inward so the captain could see the operators. There was a wall screen, but it was small and located low on the front of the center console in front of the captain's seat, obviously solely for his use.

Seated at the consoles were two women and a man in civilian clothes. They didn't look like Fleet, but they had to be. Other than glancing at her and Anders, they maintained their focus on their work.

The consoles themselves were different from anything she'd seen on an Imperial warship, too. The controls were made up of *manual* switches. For the life of her, she couldn't imagine why. Who needed to actually flip switches to make things happen? Even merchants used touch screens.

Anders had been standing at the hatch with a somewhat aloof expression as she'd circled the control room. "She's not much to look at, is she?"

"Not really," Grace agreed. "I'm not familiar with civilian vessels, but this seems odd. And I'm not even talking about the ship being run down. The layout is screwy, and the consoles are archaic."

He nodded. "That's because it's not something that we see very often inside the Empire. *Bright Passage* is a merchant ship, but she was built inside the Singularity. It's one of their standard designs and more than two centuries old. Even when she was new, she wasn't at the cutting edge of technology by any stretch of the imagination."

Grace gave the control room another look, taking it in with new eyes. That information changed her calculus. The entire ship was a cover, but not quite in the way that she'd imagined.

"I see. So, this is the way she was when we captured her?"

"She wasn't captured. Assets inside the Singularity purchased her, and she was smuggled out for modifications related to this mission. All of her registration paperwork is intact, and everything is in order. As far as the Singularity is concerned, this is one of their merchantmen."

He turned toward the rear of the control room. "My office is just outside. If you'd come this way, we can finish our introductions there."

She nodded at the officers at the consoles and followed Anders to his office.

Like the control room, it wasn't in the best condition. The smallish compartment held a battered desk, a few cabinets, and a basic computer setup. Everything looked worn and more than a little frayed around the edges.

He made his way behind the blocky desk and sat in a chair that squeaked dangerously under his weight. It had *springs*? Seriously?

He gestured toward one of the other two chairs in the room. "So where do you want to start, Lieutenant? That is your rank, isn't it?"

Grace allowed one corner of her mouth to inch up as she sat. "It used to be. As of this morning, I'm a free citizen. I'll wager that you're in the same position, aren't you, Lieutenant Commander Anders?"

That made him smile slightly. "Touché. My transition came a few months ago, but that's exactly the position I'm in. I think we need to settle a few things up front. The most important thing is to make certain that we've both read our sealed orders. I've had mine a while, but yours came up with the last message packet we received."

Her implants received a connection request, and she accepted. Moments later, an encrypted file arrived, and she studied it. The headers were all correct for the Imperial Marines, and it accepted her authorization codes and began decrypting.

Once the process was complete, she scanned the text quickly. It was as she'd suspected. She was in command of her marines and the raid proper, but she had to work jointly with the Fleet officer to get there. He was charged with operating the vessel and dealing with any issues delivering her platoon to the target and extracting them from the Singularity.

Buried at the bottom of the orders, however, was one bright spot. Anders was obligated to take her opinions and concerns into account and couldn't just overrule her on general principles. There'd have to be some negotiation, but she wasn't entirely at his mercy.

Even so, she supposed it shouldn't bother her. Marines were used to taking orders from Fleet types like Anders. It wasn't unusual for her people to only have control over direct combat operations.

She was pleased to have what influence she did and hoped that Anders wasn't going to prove to be an obstacle to the mission rather than an asset.

When she refocused her attention onto the ex-Fleet officer, he was leaning back in his chair, watching her with much the same expression as Colonel Grimsby had worn earlier in the day.

He was assessing how she was reacting to what she'd read. He probably wondered exactly how much trouble he was going to have managing her.

"You already know that I was a marine lieutenant and that I've brought a platoon of marines," she said. "All of my people have worked together for quite some time, and they're good at what they do. What I don't know is who you are and what capabilities I can count on from you."

Before he could respond, she held up one hand. "I'm sure that you're an excellent officer and that your crew is just as good. Where the sparring is going to come in is how we interpret our orders.

"Neither one of us has complete control over what takes place on this mission, and we both want it to succeed. If we're going to fight, that means that our chances of success go way down.

"I don't want that, and I'm sure that you don't either. What we've got to do is find a way to work together and show the universe a united front."

Anders pursed his lips and nodded. "You're not wrong. I'm not used to sharing command with my senior marine. As you've already guessed, I was a lieutenant commander until I accepted this mission. I commanded a destroyer, and all of the crew on this ship are my people. Kyle was my XO then, too, and he's a damned good man. My people will come through when we need them.

"I expect the same of you and your people. The Empire wants this mission to succeed, and they'd have picked the best people to make that happen. I have zero doubt that we'll find a way to work together and combine our skills to increase our chances of success."

She considered that for a moment and nodded. "I'm in command of the combat operations once we begin the assault. I'm supposed to contribute my thoughts and opinions toward target selection and how we get there. I'll admit that I'm not sure what I have to offer on that front, but I'll be happy to share what insights I can.

"And from what I can see, it's your job to get us there safely and extract us once we carry out the attack. I'm sure the raid is going to provoke some type of military response. Our goal is to get in, take care of business, and then scamper back across the border.

"With all of the cross-border attacks and the suspicion on both sides, I can't imagine they have many systems without military forces between the Singularity and us."

He nodded. "That's why my initial plan calls for us circling around the fringes of the Singularity until we're less likely to arouse suspicion. It's going to take us longer to get into position, but getting across their border is going to be a lot easier.

"From what my briefing said, except where they run up against the Empire, there's not a very hard demarcation between what they consider the Singularity and the fringe systems beyond their borders.

"Sure, they have the usual antipiracy and customs patrols through those areas, but the worlds outside the Singularity in that direction are also populated. Trade takes place, and that's precisely what this freighter has been engaged in for longer than we've been alive.

"Its last owners took it back and forth between fringe worlds, with occasional trips back inside the Singularity. That cover is going to come in very handy for us, because that's exactly what we're going to do. And a check of their records will show that pattern of behavior, so it will reassure the people doing their inspections."

She considered that and slowly nodded. "Aren't they going to expect the original captain to be with us?"

Anders grinned. "Probably. Luckily, he will be. The previous captain was and is an Imperial Intelligence asset. He's commanded this ship for the last decade while passively gathering information about the Singularity for us.

"He won't have any authority now, but he's going to be present and assisting us in getting through any obstacles."

"Is he an Imperial citizen? A patriot in deep cover?"

Anders shook his head. "No. He was born inside the Singularity and does this for money. Everything he's passed along has been reliable so far, but we'll keep a close eye on him. When you have an opportunity to meet him, I look forward to hearing your assessment of the man."

That news was... unsettling. Grace was willing to trust that

Imperial Intelligence had their best interests at heart, but if this person had been born inside the Singularity, he was an unknown factor in the equation.

Could he be a double agent? Would he chicken out and betray them when the full scope of what they intended to do became clear to him?

"Should we really be trusting him even a little bit? If he's a double agent, he could betray us at a moment's notice."

Her words increased the wattage of the man's smile significantly. "I approve of your paranoia, and I share your concerns. We're going to have to watch what he does carefully and manage his interactions with the Singularity. I don't want to take any unnecessary chances.

"He thinks—correctly—that we've installed a lot of classified intelligence-gathering equipment that we didn't want his regular crew to see. That's true enough, so far as it goes.

"*Bright Passage* was scheduled for a major overhaul, and the rest of the crew was paid off. That allowed us to get the work done without worrying about them. The work was done in an out-of-the-way Imperial shipyard, and we've got all kinds of interesting goodies that I know you'll approve of."

"I can't wait to see them," she admitted. "Since you've picked the area of operations, I'll need to familiarize myself with it. Do you have something in mind to recommend as a target for the raid?"

"Not specifically, but the area I'm looking at is a relatively major manufacturing hub in its sector. Based on the merchant trade going through the area, our spy has amassed quite a bit of information about the various systems that should allow us to pick something interesting.

"If we can select the right type of installation to destroy, we might be able to cripple operations in the sector for a lot of industries. A cascade effect like that would be sweet."

Grace didn't know a lot about manufacturing, but at least she'd have time to discuss potential targets with her leadership team. "I can work with that. I'm going to want to have a tour of the entire ship and get an inventory of what equipment we'll have available to us."

"I'll make that happen as soon as you're ready."

"Excellent. It's going to take us months to get to where we need to go, and by that time, we should have already finalized our target selection. I don't know about the rewards you're being offered for success, but the ones my people are getting are pretty good.

"We need to avoid picking a target that's too heavily protected. We can't get greedy. Let's focus on finding something that'll get us what we need while still retaining a good chance of us making it out alive."

He stood and extended a hand across the desk to her. "Deal. Now, if you'd like, I'll take you and your second around to see all the departments on the ship. Fair warning: a ship this size just couldn't hold a full crew *and* a platoon of marines, so you'll be doing double duty. Basically, we've got a core crew of ex-Fleet officers and crewmen, but the noncritical tasks are going to fall to the marines. Are your people up to that?"

She grinned as she shook his hand firmly. "I'm looking forward to finding out. There's nothing like throwing marines into an unfamiliar task to judge how good they really are. If I had to make a bet—and I *am* willing to bet—my people will deliver."

"No bet. I've met plenty of marines, and I know they'll step up. Come on. Let's go get this started while I order the ship out of orbit. If we never get going, we'll never get there.

"And before you brief your people, I want you to meet the ship's former captain. As I said, he's an intelligence source, but he's not aware of the scope of this mission. He thinks this is just a run with classified gear, so no discussions of an attack inside the Singularity. Just keep things general."

Grace nodded. She'd have to meet the man at some point anyway. Might as well come face to face with the enemy in a controlled setting. This would be her first time talking to someone from the Singularity, and it was probably going to be educational.

7

I
t didn't take long for the consequences of One Twenty-Four's upset victory to manifest. Thirty-One came out of the infirmary healed of her injury, but there was something subtly off about her nose. For the first time in the memory of anyone within the crèche, one of the girls looks *different* than the rest.

To say that went over poorly would have been an enormous understatement. Thirty-One stalked into the dormitory and wasted no time confronting One Twenty-Four, with her clique of followers trailing behind her for support.

"You've made a terrible mistake," the girl hissed when she stopped in front of One Twenty-Four. "I will do *everything* within my power to show Keeper what you truly are."

One Twenty-Four set aside the slate that she'd been reading but didn't rise from her bunk. Even though the girls had surrounded her, she didn't feel genuinely threatened. Keeper had made it abundantly clear that there would be no fighting without her direct supervision.

Thirty-One could bluster as much as she wanted, but neither she nor her friends could lay a hand on One Twenty-Four in this setting. To do so would spark the wrath of a woman that none of them wanted to cross.

So One Twenty-Four simply smiled. "Keeper knows exactly who I am. You might be right that I'm eventually going to be expelled from the crèche. I certainly hope not, but there's only so much that I can do to control that."

She focused her attention more closely on the girl's face. "I have to admit that I'm somewhat surprised to see you again, Thirty-One. After we got our tattoos, I was under the impression that Keeper wasn't very accepting of differences in appearance within the crèche. I wonder what she thinks of the fact that you don't look exactly like the template any longer. Do you think that makes her angry, or simply disgusts her?"

Thirty-One's eyes widened, and her already angry expression twisted into rage. With barely a moment's notice, the girl lunged forward, her right hand balling up into a fist and flashing toward One Twenty-Four's face.

One Twenty-Four rolled backward and landed on the other side of her bunk, making the strike miss by centimeters. The action had been unplanned, but it had worked. She'd remember that going forward.

"Temper, temper," she said in a falsely amused tone. "Keeper won't be pleased to hear that you're disobeying her."

It looked as if Thirty-One were going to come over the bunk at her, but her friends pulled her back. She strained against their grip, her mouth almost frothing with fury, her eyes bulging.

"I'm going to see you *bleed*," she hissed coldly. "Keeper's not going to have to expel you from the crèche, because I'm going to kill you with my own hands."

"Do you really think the other girls will allow that to happen?" One Twenty-Four made a show of glancing around. All activity had ceased, and everyone was paying rapt attention to what was happening.

"Do you think that *anyone* here cares about you?" the other girl asked with a sneer. "You aren't fit to live, much less rule. No one will defy me. If they do, they'll have made an enemy that will follow them for the rest of their days, which will be brutally few."

Thirty-One turned and scanned the room. "Mark my words. If

Keeper hears one word of any of this, I *will* find out who's responsible. Anyone that interferes in my revenge will pay a steep price in blood and pain."

With that, Thirty-One spun on her heel and stalked back toward her bunk.

One Twenty-Four picked her slate back up and made a show of resuming her place on her bunk as if nothing had happened, but her pulse was racing. She'd known that things were going to get worse, but she hadn't anticipated just how bad or how quickly.

Could Thirty-One really do as she'd threatened? Could she carry out a murder right under Keeper's nose?

One Twenty-Four didn't think so. Keeper was older and more experienced, wily in the ways of how One Twenty-Four and her crèche mates behaved and thought. She wouldn't be fooled.

There wasn't any guarantee that she'd save One Twenty-Four, though. Keeper didn't like her. She might allow more harm to befall her than any of her crèche mates.

Was Keeper willing to allow Thirty-One to act in contravention to her orders? Would the damage to her authority be severe enough to warrant stopping Thirty-One from killing her?

While she doubted Keeper would allow her to be harmed in defiance to her will, an insidious voice whispered that she shouldn't take this lightly. The outcome of this confrontation wasn't set in plascrete.

Should she tell Keeper? If she did, Keeper *would* act. The only question was, what would her action be? Members of the crèche were expected to solve their own problems. If One Twenty-Four ran to Keeper expecting protection, it would be another strike against her.

No. If One Twenty-Four was going to survive and raise her standing within the crèche, she was going to have to outwit Thirty-One on her own. That meant devising a scheme to defend herself that fell within the rules of allowable behavior.

Now she just had to figure out what that might entail before the other girl killed her.

* * *

GRACE'S TOUR of *Bright Passage* didn't take very long. The interior of the ship was just as grungy and worn down as the captain's office had been, but everything was functional. Anders explained how all of the equipment had been brought up to spec while keeping its original rundown appearance intact.

He'd been right when he'd said that there was very little space inside the crew module. He'd brought along a core group of trained officers and crewmen to manage the ship, but all of the ancillary tasks would have to be performed by her marines. They'd be cargo handlers, engineers' mates, and do any other job that needed doing.

Even so, the crew quarters were stuffed to the gills. Her people— including her—would be hot bunking, because there was no other way that they could get everyone shoehorned into such a small area.

Hot bunking was a process by which each bunk was shared by multiple people. When one was off duty and sleeping, another person assigned to that bunk would be on duty. Extra precautions would need to be taken to be sure that everything was kept clean, but this wasn't her first time in this position.

There were other portions of the ship besides those dedicated to the merchant façade, but they were very cleverly concealed. Cargo inside the Empire and the Singularity was transported in containers that attached to a freighter's spine. Amazingly, cargo pods were the same size and configuration in both polities.

The crew quarters and control center were to the front of the ship while the open spine of the vessel held container after container of cargo that might be destined for many different ports. Engineering brought up the rear, connected to the crew module by a pressurized corridor down the middle of the spine.

As all of the cargo containers were in vacuum, they were assumed by the authorities to be inaccessible to the crew without great effort. They were also sealed by customs agents so that any tampering was supposed to be noticeable.

Each of the containers attached to *Bright Passage* was still sealed, but they were no longer inaccessible. The Fleet engineers had crafted a pressurized tunnel that led through a number of the cargo containers and was accessed from the crew module. Some of them still had their original contents shoved to the side, and others were empty or held equipment.

Three of the containers held marine boarding pods. They were designed to carry a squad of marines to another ship in a ridiculously short period of time and then penetrate the hull to allow boarding.

With those, her people could get to any station and board it the hard way, if that was what it took. She'd rather be sneakier, but sometimes a hammer really was the right tool for the job.

"Everything was either purchased on the open market or came off the black market," Anders said. "Nothing can be traced directly back to the Empire without going through someone else's hands first. The Singularity knows *exactly* who's behind these raids, so that's all for show, of course."

She nodded. "It's a fig leaf, but it'll do. What do we have as far as weapons and armor?"

He nodded as they kept walking. "Everything came from the black market, but it's serviceable."

"What about powered armor? I don't suppose we have any?"

"Afraid not. Powered armor is a little too hefty for pirates. There are limits to what command could afford to do and still maintain the fiction that this wasn't an official operation. I'm afraid that powered armor crossed the line.

"What we do have is some pretty significant unpowered armor. My understanding is that it was acquired from a company that outfits mercenaries on the fringe. It's tough and can even stand up to a goodly number of flechette hits. The weapons come from the same source."

Not ideal, but they'd make do.

"I assume the empty cargo pods are for anything we capture," she said. "I'm still not clear on how much we're supposed to steal versus how much we need to blow up."

"Most of our pods are empty," he said cheerfully. "Whatever you can find, we can steal. We have to make this look like an act of piracy. Like your marines, my people will get a share of everything that's destroyed or captured. We'll get our pick of booty from what you seize."

She grinned. "If I can find something juicy for you, I'll pick it up. I'll task each of my marines to pair up with your crew and get them something sweet during the run, too. Friends look after friends.

"Thanks for thinking of your poor Fleet counterparts."

"I'd best get back to my marines and explain what we're doing," she said. "My original orders were to not give them any details on what we're doing, so they still don't know where we're going."

The two of them started back toward the habitation section of the ship. Deep down, Grace was beginning to feel the same way Anders did. This was a dangerous mission, but they'd make it happen.

8

The following day, One Twenty-Four and her crèche mates were taken to the infirmary. Keeper lined the girls up in the hall and then brought them in one at a time before ordering them to lie down on the table.

When One Twenty-Four had her turn, Keeper placed a device on her head, and she went to sleep. After what only felt like moments, she woke. Based on the time it had taken the other girls, she'd been unconscious for perhaps five minutes.

She quickly assessed her body but could detect no aches or pains. The purpose of the procedure wasn't obvious, and Keeper didn't speak to her. At Keeper's gesture, she returned to the hall and stood in line with the other girls.

There were whispered discussions about what had happened. No one seemed to have any clear theory about what was taking place. It wasn't covered by the crèche syllabus, so One Twenty-Four had no clue.

Perhaps once Keeper finished, she'd explain what had occurred and why. It was also possible that she wouldn't say a word about it. It might end up being one of the mysteries that occasionally swept through the crèche.

When Keeper finally returned to the hallway and gestured for them to proceed to the classroom, almost three hours had passed. Dutifully, each of the girls marched to their seats and stood and waited for Keeper to give them permission to sit.

The large room was made to hold two hundred students. At this point, about forty percent of those seats were empty. That was a grim reminder that as many of two-thirds of their starting number would likely die before they completed their training.

Keeper walked up to her desk and stood beside it, facing them. "You may sit."

Once they'd done so, she continued. "I'm certain that you are all curious about what just occurred. In response to that curiosity, I will ask you a question. What is the main difference between myself and each of you?"

Several hands shot up, and Keeper selected Sixty-Three.

The girl stood. "You're mature, Keeper."

"What exactly makes me mature? Is it just the fact that I'm taller?"

The girl shook her head. "No, Keeper. Your body has developed in ways that ours have not. We're still children, and you're an adult."

"Correct. You may sit."

Keeper walked in front of her desk and crossed her arms over her chest. That move emphasized the fact that she had breasts. One Twenty-Four had always wondered when and how her body would change in that same way.

That was hardly the only difference, either. Keeper's hips were fuller than hers. Where she and her crèche mates were slender, Keeper was tall, muscular, and had a more rounded figure.

The purpose of that had always eluded her. Why not just have adults be like the children, only larger?

"As you can see, as an adult woman, I have breasts, and my body is proportioned differently than yours," Keeper said as her eyes scanned the room. "The reason for that goes back to the dawning of humanity. As you already know, in the base caste, women gestate children inside their own bodies. The changes you see in me are a reminder of how the female body prepares for that task.

"Thankfully, it's a burden that women of the Andrea Line are not forced to bear. It's a dirty, ugly process that you should be grateful that you don't need to know the details of. You're blessed that you were created from our template and raised inside the crèche."

One Twenty-Four raised her hand. She was hesitant in asking a question, but not in the gesture itself. One didn't show indecision inside the crèche. One committed to one's course of action and carried through as if the outcome was inevitable.

When Keeper gestured toward her, she stood. "How does what occurred to us this morning connect with that, Keeper?"

Keeper nodded. "I injected a biodegradable capsule that will release hormones in a controlled fashion over the next few months to initiate these changes inside your body. The somatic stimulator was required because of the location and depth of the injection. This marks the beginning of your transformation from child to woman.

"Your genetics are not the same as the base caste, so the development does not automatically begin for you without this intervention. It was too cumbersome for the designers to make an automatic mechanism for the transition between childhood and adulthood that didn't introduce undesirable randomization into the process.

"This maturation is required for your brains to fully mature. It is our *single* concession to the genetics of those who came before us and a burden that we must bear."

At that point, One Twenty-Four should've sat down, but she wasn't done. She still had questions. She decided to risk asking them.

"What changes are we going to see in our bodies, Keeper? Other than our brains, why do we need things like breasts? I don't understand the purpose for them."

Keeper considered her for several long seconds and then nodded. "I will grant the validity of your follow-up questions. The original purpose of breasts was to produce nutrients for infants. The designers also found the female form—and the male one—to be intrinsically pleasing, and so desired to maintain the appearance of the base caste from which we were refined.

"Another form of maturity that you note in me is that my hips are wider. This originally promoted a safer experience during childbirth. As we've previously discussed, a child of the base caste is gestated inside a woman's body."

One Twenty-Four's stomach churned at the reminder. Nothing had been discussed about the process of how that worked, and for that, she was grateful. It sounded parasitic.

Keeper gestured for One Twenty-Four to sit. "These changes are not going to be comfortable or without distress for you, but they are not without their benefits. In fact, they also serve a recreational purpose.

"While we are incapable of breeding, we still possess all of the necessary sexual organs to copulate with males. Such brings pleasure to both parties, and, when done with the proper person for the appropriate reason, it can also benefit the Line.

"Once you've physically matured, we will have a deeper discussion on the subject of what is involved with copulation so that you may better serve the Line by making good alliances. Men—even within the ruling caste of the Singularity—are susceptible to being influenced by a woman's body."

One Twenty-Four knew intellectually what men were. They must be different than women in some manner, though the details of how weren't exactly clear.

It must have to do with copulation—whatever that was—and the process by which men and women combined genetic material inside a female body. If she understood Keeper correctly, her body was compatible with the physical process, but she was protected from the underlying burden.

What that actually meant would require more questions at some other point and deeper reflection.

Keeper walked behind her desk. "Now, to conclude this lecture so that we may go have lunch, the process of maturing is not an instantaneous one. Over the next several years, your body will continue to change. You will grow taller, your breasts will begin to develop, and your hips will widen.

"Gradually, you'll make the transition between child and woman. Since you all come from the Andrea template, I can tell you that you will finish the majority of your physical maturation by the time you're fifteen. There will still be some growth as you put on mass, but you'll be very much like me at that point.

"The development of your brain will take another decade, but you need not worry about that. The process of education will continue even after you've left the crèche. We will guide you until you are fit to serve the Line."

"The maturation of your body will not require any further adjustments on my part. Your reproductive organs, though nonfunctional in the original sense, will create the necessary hormones now that I have initiated the changes."

One Twenty-Four was unaware of what organs were utilized for reproduction and was still stumped at how the process was supposed to work. How could a male gain access to her organs outside of an infirmary?

Well, she supposed it didn't matter. She wasn't going to meet a man for at least another decade. More likely two.

By the time she did, she'd know what needed to be done. She didn't have time to waste on the formalities of the process. This information—while interesting—wasn't core to her survival.

Keeper had given them the background information, and One Twenty-Four could already tell that there would be no more discussion on the matter for the time being. This was simply a notification on her part so that the coming changes wouldn't dismay them.

One Twenty-Four was looking forward to growing larger. The additional muscle mass would be useful. The breasts were potentially awkward and might negatively impact her balance. She'd have to compensate for that.

Now, she had more important things to worry about. Like whatever Thirty-One had planned.

She suspected that her enemy was working on some plan that would have negative consequences for her, and she wanted to be ready. She'd have to react immediately when Thirty-One executed her plan. Her life depended on it.

* * *

THE NEXT DAY, Anders led Grace back to the engineering section of the ship, where there were a couple of cabins available for use by the engineering team. One of them was under guard by a shaggy-haired crewman, who nodded to the captain as he approached.

"Everything looks good, sir. Other than him taking food, he hasn't requested to be let out or caused any problems."

"Good work, Jester," Anders said. "We've got this covered for a bit. Go grab something to eat and be back in twenty minutes."

The man nodded and hurried off.

"How do you want to play this?" Anders asked as he turned toward her. "He's not stupid. As soon as he sees you, he's going to know that you're not Fleet. How much of the truth do we tell him?"

She considered that. "If we need to drop him off before we get to the Singularity, I'd rather know now. I say we let him in on the full story, and he can decide whether not he wants a cut. He is getting a cut, isn't he?"

"I don't have a personal objection, so long as he pulls his weight. His insider knowledge could be advantageous. If we do as well as we hope, that could mean he can retire. Of course, the same is true for us."

Grace shrugged. "Let's play it by ear. If it looks like he's going to guess most of this anyway, then we'll just fill him in. Give him the option of getting out now with whatever he has saved versus helping us and potentially scoring a much bigger haul."

Rather than responding, Anders rapped his knuckles against the door. There was a muffled response, and he opened the door.

The quarters inside were small but tidy. The man dressed in odd-looking civilian clothes sitting in the chair by the built-in desk was already rising to his feet. He was relatively short, coming in at about chin level for Grace.

He wore his dark hair tied back in a long ponytail and had a meticulously trimmed beard. Grace wasn't sure what the style was called, but it was somewhat pointed and had a vaguely sinister look.

His complexion wasn't as dark as what she'd inherited from her Pakistani mother, but it wasn't light either.

The man's eyes were dark brown—very much like her own—and they were sharp. He was assessing her even as she stepped into the compartment, virtually ignoring Anders.

"And the plot is revealed," he murmured loudly enough for them to hear. "I've been wondering exactly what was going on, and now I understand. You're going to use my ship for one of those cross-border raids, aren't you?"

Anders raised an eyebrow. "What makes you say that?"

The man gestured toward Grace. "Even discounting her hairstyle, this young woman is obviously a warrior. One cannot conceal the grace of a trained fighter.

"I've also been wondering why the rest of my crew had to be dismissed and why I was being kept on board but locked away here in the chief engineer's cabin. Now I understand."

Grace responded before Anders could. "My name is Grace Tolliver. Might I inquire with whom I'm speaking?"

The man put a hand to his chest and bowed deeply. "My apologies. It was rude of me not to introduce myself, since Anders failed at even that simple courtesy in such a spectacular fashion. I am Kayden Harmon of Zarustra, owner of this fine vessel, though I pay my meager earnings to the bank just like everyone else. Am I correct in assuming that you're an Imperial Marine officer?"

His eyes narrowed slightly. "It's difficult to judge ages with beings that use medical nanites, but I'd say that you're probably in the lower spectrum of rank. A lieutenant, perhaps?"

Grace granted him a smile. "You're very perceptive, Kayden. May I call you that? I was a lieutenant once, but now I'm just a civilian. Do you mind if we sit down?"

The man straightened and gestured toward the compact room. "Everything I possess is quite literally yours. If you'd care to use my bunk, then we can all sit. Space is always somewhat limited on a ship."

After they'd settled in, Grace gave the man her full attention.

"Let's say for hypothetical purposes that we are going on a raid. How would you respond to the news?"

"I'd say that someone owes me a ship and future income, first of all. I'll never be able to trade anywhere near the Singularity again. The intelligence service will hunt diligently for me, so it's a good thing that I don't have many close friends or family.

"Am I perturbed that you're going to act against the Singularity? Not at all. Our rulers have never been good to those from the base caste. All I'm concerned about is that I have a future once this is over."

Grace shot Anders a glance and then nodded. "That's something we can work with. It's within our authority to purchase your ship for reasonable market value. As for the future, that really depends on how much help you intend to give.

"Each of us gets a share of anything we capture or destroy. While Anders and I are going to be getting the largest shares, I'm willing to cut you in with a second-tier share if you freely share your knowledge of the Singularity and their weaknesses.

"If you can help us refine our targeting and get us to where we need to get safely, that could earn us all a lot of money. More than enough to live comfortably for the rest of your life somewhere inside the Empire. Maybe you can buy a new ship or two and keep trading."

The man nodded. "I'll cooperate enthusiastically under those stipulations. I know that Imperial Intelligence keeps me on a short leash. They're right to distrust someone from the Singularity.

"But in this case, I have no love for those that rule, and I'm more than willing to guide you to a location that will be harmful to them if it's lost. It's going to make me sad that regular people will suffer, but I have to look out for myself. No one else is going to do so."

Grace turned to face Anders. "What do you think?"

Anders considered the man for a moment and then shrugged. "I think that we should keep him on board. Everything I've read indicates that he's been more than cooperative with Imperial Intelligence. He really doesn't have much love for the Singularity. He's in it for the money, and promising him a share of what we're going to take is a good incentive.

"He has knowledge of how everything works inside the area of the Singularity that we're going to strike. If anyone knows of a good spot to poke them, it's going to be him. And since we don't have to actually capture anything for him to be paid, I suspect he'll be in favor of a swift hit-and-run raid that destroys the target and gets us safely away."

"Then let's cut him in," Grace said. "If you were going to pick a target that had a high value, yet was easily reachable and low on the end of military protection, what exactly would you pick, Kayden?"

The man's eyes narrowed slightly as he considered the question. "I'll need to examine my files in greater detail, but there are several trading hubs that would have a large amount of valuable cargo passing through. Any of them would be quite harmful to the local economies.

"But if you're looking for something to cause long-term damage strategically, you're going to want to find something that affects as many systems as possible. The Singularity isolates each system's economy so that they're all dependent on interstellar trade. No single world is entirely self-sufficient.

"If we can identify a linchpin whose damage will cause great havoc for a large number of worlds, then the repercussions of crippling it would make for a worthwhile target. I assume that the Empire would value such highly."

Grace nodded. "They'll value the damage to the economy. They obviously won't pass us full value for something like that, but it would still be worth a lot."

"Then I'll narrow the target list to linchpins like that. I have an excellent understanding of the economics inside the sector where I traded. I worked mostly on the fringe but came inside the Singularity in that area to trade on several worlds."

He leaned back in his chair a little and pursed his lips contemplatively. "If I'm thorough, it will take me several weeks to refine the data and identify information from my files that will give us what we need.

"If I compare that to systems that don't historically have a large military presence, I should be able to improve our chances of getting in and out again without having to fight. We need to get in, strike the most propitious target, and then get back out again."

Grace smiled. "That's good, but I want you to think a little bit harder. Pick a target like you just suggested but look at any secondary targets along our likely routes of retreat. We don't have to capture something to get paid for it. Yes, seized goods get a higher percentage, but even a destroyed orbital is worth something.

"If you can find two or perhaps even three systems that we're going to pass through that are lightly guarded, it won't take us that much more time to destroy any secondary targets. That's going to make all of our retirements better."

"Would you retire?" Kayden asked. "You're still a young woman. I'm going to assume that you lead a group of marines, so if you succeed in this mission, you might return to your duties. Perhaps with medals or promotions, but I doubt you're going to stop serving your empire. How will the money help you?"

She shrugged. "Everyone retires. Just because I've got a good career now doesn't mean that I'm going to have one in the future. What if I'm injured? They might be able to fix me up, but I'll be cashiered. Having a nest egg means never having to worry that I'm going to be in a position where I have to rely on the charity of others. I'm not mercenary, but I'm not stupid either."

Kayden laughed. "Most excellent, then. I think we can work well together, Grace Tolliver. I'm willing to trust you as far as you trust me. To be more explicit, I'd rather not be locked up in this cabin.

"If I commit myself fully to what's going on, you're going to be able to check every bit of information with the copies of my files that Captain Anders certainly already has in his possession. Let's find if we can work together more closely, because if we can avoid distrusting one another, we can achieve a more satisfactory end result."

Grace nodded, rose to her feet, and extended her hand. "Deal."

Anders stood and shook his hand as well. "It's going to take us about six weeks to get into position to enter the Singularity. I'd like to have our targets picked out at least two weeks in advance of that so that we can tailor our course to get to where we need to go. The more time we have to plan, the better our ultimate chances of success."

"Then I'll get to work," Kayden said. "I have to say that this is a pleasant surprise, and I'm looking forward to working with the pair of you. May our little conspiracy prosper and cause great pain to the ruling caste of the Singularity."

"That's something I can toast to," Grace said. "Let's grab something to eat while we get to know each other better."

Kayden bowed again, this time even more deeply, and he added a flourish with his hands. "I am at your complete disposal, my lady."

9

One Twenty-Four had thought Thirty-One would strike quickly, but the other girl displayed far more patience than she'd expected. Weeks went by with nothing more than glares and snide words. She'd begun to suspect that the other girl feared the consequences of a direct attack.

And, of course, that moment of complacency was the best for an enemy to strike.

Her realization came during their physical education class. Keeper had decided they'd run an obstacle course to improve their strength, speed, and dexterity. This involved going over walls, crawling under things, and climbing ropes that went to the ceiling, as well as other tasks that allowed them to compare themselves to one another.

One Twenty-Four was climbing toward the ceiling on one of the ropes when there was a sharp metallic "crack" from above, and the rope came loose from its mount. In that instant, she'd known that Thirty-One had somehow been responsible.

Not that the knowledge had been all that useful at that moment.

She screamed as she fell but remembered Keeper's lessons and focused on minimizing her damage on landing. She was high enough that she wasn't wholly successful, and there was a loud "pop" when she struck the mat, and her left leg was suddenly torn with agony.

Even so, she managed to roll and absorb some of her momentum. Not enough to avoid flying off the mat and striking her head on the floor hard enough to daze her.

Keeper was at her side in an instant, though One Twenty-Four wasn't able to understand what she was saying. The world spun, and darkness engulfed her.

When she woke, she was laid out on the table in the infirmary. She blinked in surprise and tried to rise.

Keeper put a hand on her shoulder and stopped her. "Remain still. I've finished regenerating the concussion and the torn ligament, but I'm still conducting tests."

"What happened?" One Twenty-Four asked quietly, forcing herself to relax.

"Something interesting," Keeper said. "It could've been a failure of the equipment or something more sinister. That's what interests me.

"There's a lesson to be learned here, One Twenty-Four. I wonder if you have the capacity to grasp it."

Since responding to that by saying that she didn't understand would've been dangerous, One Twenty-Four said nothing.

After a moment, Keeper continued as she ran a hand scanner across One Twenty-Four's leg. "The fitting where the rope you were climbing attached to the ceiling sheared. Perhaps it was manufactured poorly. I'll conduct a more thorough examination of it at some point, but the possibility also exists that it was sabotaged.

"Which do you think is more likely, One Twenty-Four?"

"Sabotage," she said softly.

Keeper paused for a moment and considered her. After studying her for a few seconds, she nodded and resumed her work.

"I think that your paranoia is warranted. Thirty-One doesn't have your best interests at heart, and considering how much at variance you are from the rest of the crèche, I find it hard to blame her.

"On the other hand, the girl has a vicious streak that will have to be tempered if she's to become an effective leader. Figuring out how to balance the two of you into something that can enhance the Andrea Line will provide me with an interesting distraction from my normal duties."

Keeper put the instrument away. "Sit up. While I've used the regeneration equipment to completely repair all of the damage that you've suffered, I think it's time we had a long-overdue talk about your position within the crèche."

One Twenty-Four went cold. That was *not* the kind of conversation one wanted to have with Keeper.

She cautiously sat up, put her hands into her lap, and gave Keeper her complete and undivided attention. "I'm ready, Keeper."

"You're not, and that's part of the problem. There's an acceptable range of behavior inside the crèche. That you know. What you lack is the perspective to understand is that that changes once you become an adult.

"I have to make certain that each and every member of the crèche is capable of doing what needs to be done in a manner that we find acceptable once they leave. You have far too much curiosity, and you're too easily distracted. You lack focus."

That wasn't really telling One Twenty-Four anything that she didn't already know.

Keeper considered her for a moment and then nodded as if making a decision. "If you could focus yourself, that creativity would be of benefit later in your life. There are too many members of the ruling caste that lack subtlety in how they address challenges. Your curiosity could lead you to creative solutions that won't occur to others. Sadly, the crèche is not the place to display that curiosity.

"You think that I don't like you, but you're wrong. When I was your age, I was the one whose behavior put me on the outskirts of my crèche. I ran the same risk of being expelled and executed that you do now."

The revelation astonished One Twenty-Four. Keeper had been like her? How could that even be possible? Keeper was *everything* that she was not.

While she was processing that, the woman continued. "My Keeper pressured me to conform, and I did. It wasn't easy, but it was worth it. Once I became an adult, I found my calling by teaching our young. I don't like some of the things that I'm required to do, but I understand their necessity.

"You undoubtedly think that the crèche is a horrible place filled with the opportunity for death. In that, you're not wrong. Each crèche starts out with two hundred girls, and we're forced to cull them down until only the strongest survive.

"The reason that we must do this is because the Singularity is always at war. The Terran Empire is always pushing at our borders, and they're just waiting for an opportunity to turn us into their slaves and destroy the ruling caste.

"They loathe us because we're genetically constructed. The order and design that went into creating the pinnacle of human evolution offends Imperial Humans because they're jealous and hate us. Only through machines can they elevate themselves, and that humiliates them.

"If they got their hands upon you, you'd be taken to a laboratory and dissected. Then they'd euthanize you as an abomination."

One Twenty-Four wasn't sure that was too much worse than the fate that awaited her if she failed in the crèche, but that wouldn't be prudent to say, so she remained attentively silent.

"The Empire has ruled that all genetically created people are property," Keeper continued. "They see us as things that can be bought, sold, and broken with impunity. Oh, they have laws against the production of genetically engineered people, but I have no doubt that somewhere in their society, there is an illicit trade.

"If you ever fell into their grasp, they could literally do anything they wanted to you with no penalty. Or to me, for that matter. And that's what they want. Absolute and utter domination of those who are not like them."

One Twenty-Four took that in, stunned. Keeper had *never* spoken to her—or any of her crèche mates—like this before. She'd never shown this kind of passion. One Twenty-Four wasn't even sure how she should respond.

In the face of this, she took an awful chance.

"What do I need to do, Keeper?" she asked in a soft voice. "I want to serve the Line, and I want to survive, but it's as if there's a portion of me that I can't control. I'm so curious about everything that it's hard to focus. How do I overcome this?"

"Curiosity is not something that one overcomes, One Twenty-Four," Keeper said, rubbing her eyes tiredly, her energy seemingly gone. "It's something that you have to channel into something acceptable. Daydreaming is a path to inevitable death.

"Perhaps this attack on you is fortuitous. Focus your mind on how to foil Thirty-One's next attempt, lest it be more successful. You can do so while staying within what is acceptable within the crèche.

"There are also many other tasks where your curiosity would be of benefit. What you don't grasp are the boundaries. If you can learn them, you'll not only survive the crèche, but you'll benefit from it in so many ways."

Keeper gestured for One Twenty-Four to stand. "I want you to walk around the infirmary and test that you have no pain or restrictions on your movement. Also, make sure that you have no lingering dizziness."

One Twenty-Four rose gingerly and tested her leg. Once she'd determined that everything felt normal, she walked around the room and even did knee bends. Her session in the infirmary had fixed the damage from the fall.

"How can I use my curiosity to combat Thirty-One?" she asked as she turned back toward Keeper, risking more boldness. "I don't know how she would've done this, but I know that it was her. How can I possibly respond without breaking the rules like she did?"

Keeper smiled. "And here is another valuable lesson for you. She *didn't* break the rules. There's doubt in my mind as to whether or not this was an act of sabotage. If I didn't already know that the two of you have this feud, I'd have believed this to be metal fatigue without a second thought, and that is the brilliance of her action.

"She struck at an enemy in a way that likely wouldn't come back to haunt her. At this point, I'm going to find out exactly what she did, but even once I do, I won't take action against her.

"Thirty-One has also learned a valuable lesson that you must also absorb. Sometimes one's enemies must be disposed of in ways that are untraceable and won't come back to haunt you or the Line.

"That's the kind of situation in which your curiosity can come to your aid. It's more than acceptable within the crèche to utilize your brains to outmaneuver an opponent. That can even include physical action like Thirty-One probably enacted today.

"Act to show Thirty-One the boundaries of your own will. If she fears your response, she will become more cautious. And if you succeed in causing the death of your enemy while making it look like something disconnected from yourself, then you've accomplished something of note and worth.

"If Thirty-One isn't smart enough to overcome this challenge, then she doesn't deserve to survive. The same is true of you. Understand that, and you grasp the Singularity and the ruling caste in one single epiphany."

With that, Keeper opened the door and gestured for One Twenty-Four to exit. As they walked back toward the gym, she considered everything she'd been told.

Keeper was absolutely correct. Thirty-One had to be stopped, and that might mean killing the girl—as much as One Twenty-Four didn't want to do so.

The best outcome would be to find a way to injure Thirty-One badly enough that she became cautious. There was a saying that Keeper had once quoted that came from the time before the Singularity. "Let them hate, so long as they fear."

It didn't matter what Thirty-One thought about One Twenty-Four, so long as she was afraid to strike at her again. To make that happen, she was going to have to take direct action in such a way that it wouldn't lead back to her. That was going to require some thought.

Luckily, now that Thirty-One had struck, she wouldn't dare make another move for some time. She wouldn't want to focus suspicion upon herself.

Perhaps that was an angle to consider. If she made Thirty-One seem as if she'd struck at her a second time, but with such obvious flaws that the action couldn't be ignored, Keeper would eliminate the girl for incompetence.

The problem was that One Twenty-Four wasn't confident she could bring herself to do that. She'd be directly responsible for the death of her line sib.

Still, it was her or Thirty-One, since the other girl *would* keep trying until she succeeded or was dealt with.

That gave her a lot to think about. No matter what needed doing, she'd find a way. Thirty-One would not win. One Twenty-Four's resolve had firmed, and Keeper's encouraging words had given her hope.

If she could control herself, she'd become an asset to both the Andrea Line and the Singularity. Nothing could be allowed to stand in the way of that. Not Thirty-One and not herself.

10

Grace sat at the head of *Bright Passage*'s cramped mess table and looked over her compatriots while sipping a cup of coffee that fell somewhere between mediocre and passable. Maybe they could raid someone's coffee stores before the mission was over.

Joining her for their first major strategy session were Na Fei, Jay Anders, Alan Kyle, and Kayden Harmon. This wasn't their first brainstorming session, but they'd make their final decisions today on what got hit. They were about a week from crossing over into the Singularity, and they needed to know what course to take.

She'd examined the potential targets on her own, trying to determine where she'd strike if it were left up to her. The targets ranged from manufacturing orbitals to massive refineries placed inside asteroid belts.

Any of those would have grave economic consequences for the system in which they were located but wouldn't have much effect outside of that. If they wanted this raid to be more than a pinprick, they needed to up their game.

She looked forward to seeing what Kayden thought the best target was. His in-depth knowledge of this sector had already proven valuable. He'd led them through the fringe worlds in such a manner that they'd raised no eyebrows whatsoever.

In fact, they very rarely saw any armed ships at all. That was by design, Kayden had said. There were some systems where the Singularity performed regular patrols or had forces stationed in case of trouble, but he knew where they were, and that made it easy to slip past them.

Better yet, because he and the ship had a long history in this area, their movement raised no eyebrows. In fact, the one time they'd gotten additional questioning from control in one of the systems, Kayden had personally known the controller.

Their relationship had smoothed the waters. A promise of a couple of bottles of something special the next time Kayden came through was more than enough to ease their passage.

Now that they were almost to the area where they'd chosen to enter the Singularity, it was about to get real, and they needed to firm up their plans.

"I've been looking over the information you gave us, Kayden," Grace said to open things up. "I'll admit that not being a merchant has hampered my ability to understand what I was looking at. I'm a lot more experienced in assessing military targets.

"Did you find anything that will cause widespread damage to the wider economy if we take it out? I didn't see anything."

The man grinned at her. "As a matter of fact, I did. I'll admit that it wouldn't be obvious at a glance, but if one looks at the flow of trade through the sector with a knowledgeable eye, one can find points that are critical to maintaining the distribution of equipment and trade goods.

"For example, let's look at the Aponte system. If you examine the information that I sent you, you'll note that it's four flips from the hard border. Read about it and tell me what you think."

Grace picked up her slate and went through the information that he'd sent to them. She'd uploaded it to her implants, but it felt rude to single him out as different than the rest of them, so she read it the old-fashioned way.

The basic statistics of the system itself weren't all that

impressive. Yes, it had a densely populated world, but it was basically an agricultural breadbasket that fed many of the systems around it. The only way hitting it could hurt anyone else was at the dinner table.

"Are you suggesting that we destroy the supplier of nutrition to half a dozen other worlds?" she asked carefully. "While I have no objection to destroying many Singularity targets, I'm not a fan of forcing billions of people to starve. If that's your idea of a good target, then I think you need to reevaluate your target list."

The man's smile dimmed somewhat, but he shook his head. "You're only looking at the surface information. While I may loathe the rulers of the Singularity, I'm one of the very people that would've starved should something like that have happened when I was younger. I'm not even looking at the main world.

"Rather than leaping to conclusions about how I think, why don't you parse the data in more detail. Once you find what I'm talking about, I think you might understand both our potential target and me a little better."

His reproving tone embarrassed her. She'd made an assumption about him that might have been unwarranted. She really needed to work harder at keeping a more open mind.

If he wasn't looking at the main world in the system, what else was there? There were the almost obligatory manufacturing centers around the planet and refineries in the asteroid belt, but there didn't seem to be anything special about them.

There was some construction not too far from the innermost gas giant in the outer system, but she'd ignored it because no one did anything of importance in the hinterlands of a system. Perhaps that assumption was where her fault lay.

Before she could really dig into what was going on, Na spoke up.

"I think I see what you're talking about," the woman said, her eyes still intently studying her slate. "That's a large installation for such an out-of-the-way place. The information that you've provided doesn't say what it does, but it does tell us how much of that asteroid it takes up.

"It's big enough that it could easily serve a major world as its primary hub of trade. Why put something like that out on the fringes of an occupied system?"

Kayden grinned at the woman. "I think you've grasped the significance of the target, Fei. The reason for your confusion probably lies in your unfamiliarity with how trade works inside the Singularity.

"Main worlds are responsible for their own trade, yes. What they don't oversee is the transshipment of goods from system to system. Unlike inside the Empire, a different network of stations is used for that purpose.

"That is a transshipment center. Cargo making its way through the Singularity passes through orbitals or bases built into asteroids like that. Since they're located closer to the flip points than the main worlds, that cuts travel time by a measurable amount for every cargo container. Those little increments of saved time mean higher earnings, particularly when done in such large numbers.

"The Aponte transshipment center is the central trade hub for this entire sector. Because of this system's fortuitous location and the web of flip points that encircle it, all of the trade coming from the major manufactories across the sector comes through here.

"In addition, the center also has a significant manufacturing capability of its own. It's responsible for taking in the rare elements mined in several different systems and building flip drives.

"In fact, it's the *only* location that manufactures flip drives in this sector. The loss of that capability would cripple shipbuilding in the area for years to come."

That information made Alan Kyle smile widely. "Now we're talking. If we can take out something like that, it's really going to make the Singularity suffer, but not in such a way that it's going to harm the regular people.

"Yeah, taking out all the trade goods stored here for transshipment would hurt a bunch of people, but it's going to be the ones with money. I like it."

"I'm glad you approve," Kayden said with a self-satisfied smile as he leaned back in his chair. "I understand that it's not a major military target, but a ship the size of *Bright Passage* really isn't suitable to attack something like that. We'd prefer to avoid an engagement altogether.

"And that's another reason why this system is such an excellent target. There are several destroyers stationed here, but they spend almost all of their time patrolling elsewhere.

"As Imperial Intelligence is interested in that kind of information, I've made it my business to understand the Singularity military's patrol patterns and where their ships might be found at any given time.

"It's our good luck that I was in Aponte six months ago, and my sources passed along their schedule for the next year. Barring any changes, we can be relatively certain that no military threats are waiting for us there."

Anders grunted and shook his head. "We can't count on that. Circumstances change, sometimes without warning. There's a chance that we're going to find at least one of their ships is still there.

"If we do, we're going to have to abort. We can't strike at something with a hostile destroyer that close. *Bright Passage* isn't fast enough to get away, even with her upgrades. We'd probably get out of the system, but they'd catch us in the next."

"Under those circumstances, we'd abort," Kayden agreed. "I've selected several secondary targets should this one prove too difficult a nut to crack. None of them are as good as this transshipment center, but if circumstances don't permit a strike here, they'll make excellent consolation prizes."

Grace spent the next several minutes reading up on the alternate targets and decided that the man was right. They'd be useful to add to their account but weren't worth as much as the primary target, even when added together.

Eventually, she sighed and nodded. "We're going to have to take the chance. We'll go with the information that we have and strike. The next question I have is about how we achieve maximum disruption. I know *Bright Passage* is armed, but I'm not sure that we can take out an asteroid that big, even if it has surface installations.

"If we intend to destroy the entire thing, we're going to overload their fusion plant. That means boarding and securing that portion of the center for long enough to carry out the mission and prevent them from undoing it once we've left."

"We've got all the gear we need to make that happen, ma'am," Na said with a cold, professional smile. "Rigging the fusion plant isn't all that difficult. If we put secondary and antipersonnel charges in the right places, the locals won't be able to stop it either. We just need to factor in enough time for the locals to get clear of the blast radius."

"And don't forget the rare elements used to build flip drives," Anders said, rapping the table with his knuckles. "If we can identify where they're stored, we can boost them. Either we can load them into some of our empty cargo containers or jettison ours and take theirs if time is on our side. Then we'll have quite the haul when we get out of here."

Considering how costly the rare elements used in making flip drives were, that would be quite the feather in their caps. Actually seizing them would be worth far more than the fee for destroying them. That was just how the tables the Empire used to calculate their rewards worked. A bird in the hand was worth many more in the bush.

"Do we have any idea where the stuff is located?" she asked. "It's not exactly like we're going to have a map of where all the cargo is stored in that asteroid."

Kayden inclined his head. "While I've never been to this particular center, I have some familiarity with the cargo management systems in use inside the Singularity. If your people can get me into the computer systems, I can locate the most valuable containers. If I had the supervisory codes—or a good hacker—I might even be able to have the automatic systems load them onto the ship for us."

"I like that plan," Grace admitted. "We're not going to be able to formulate anything more detailed until we have eyes on the target. Worst case, we don't strike this one at all and move on to one of the secondary locations. Moderate case, we can destroy the center itself but can't take anything. Best case, we take the most valuable containers and blow up everything else.

"No matter what we do, though, we need to allow time for the personnel to escape. I'm not going to be in charge of a massacre. We have to allow enough time for the civilians to get clear."

With that decided, they spent the next half hour settling on the specifics of their ingress and egress. It was going to take *Bright Passage* three weeks to get to Aponte from their current location. If things went well, they'd only be there for several hours before they began their retreat back out of the Singularity.

Even if they struck all of the secondary targets on their way out, they should still be clear of the Singularity in another two weeks.

Of course, that calculus changed if they ran into a warship. If that happened, they'd die.

They were taking a significant risk by going that deep into the Singularity. Most of the other raids had hit border systems and then raced back into free space before any response could be mounted.

If the Singularity had ships in the area they were going to, she and her people might be trapped.

Well, one didn't expect a marine to die in bed. Sometimes you had to take a calculated risk to complete the mission.

The money really wasn't that much of a driving factor for her. She was far more concerned with doing the Empire proud and making the Singularity bleed for everything that they'd done to her beloved Corps over the years.

"I think we're good," Grace said at last. "We'll keep going over the data and refining our plans, but let's make this happen. Next stop: Aponte."

11

———————

One Twenty-Four spent the next few weeks worrying about what Thirty-One planned to do next. She tried to formalize her own plans about how to stop the girl from killing her but found herself reacting to psychological warfare instead.

At seemingly random points throughout every day, she'd find Thirty-One or one of her lackeys staring at her intently. It unnerved her every time. Then at night, there'd be noises and bumps against her bunk as different girls went back and forth to the bathroom. She always woke up terrified that another attack was upon her, but nothing came of the incidents.

All that resulted was her being tired all the time and suffering from increased paranoia. She knew that that had to be the girl's plan. Her enemy was intent on exhausting her and would strike as soon as she felt she could safely do so, counting on all the other disruption to mask her moves.

One Twenty-Four knew that this situation couldn't last. She was exhausted and jumping at shadows. Thirty-One was setting her up for something, and she knew that she was playing into the other girl's hands. She needed to change the parameters of this conflict, or she was going to die.

One Twenty-Four was still seriously considering staging an attack on herself that she could then blame on Thirty-One. She could control all the parameters of the event and make it as dangerous as she needed it to be yet still give herself a method to survive.

She needed to be very careful with that, though. She couldn't afford to seriously injure herself, because any true disfigurement would be cause for expulsion from the crèche, and that meant death.

The slight deformity to Thirty-One's nose didn't cross that line, but if One Twenty-Four lost an arm, she'd doom herself.

In the end, though, she couldn't bring herself to do it. She didn't have it in her to bring about the other girl's death in such a cold-blooded manner.

She knew that Keeper was watching the pair of them closely. How much longer would the woman tolerate their dithering around? If she chose to act, One Twenty-Four was virtually certain that it would not be to intervene on her side.

Her insight into Keeper's background might be useful in turning her situation around. As much as the woman didn't want to show it, she had a history that One Twenty-Four could use to evoke pity.

Sadly, there wasn't much pity in Keeper. Relying on emotion was probably a certain path to death.

What was she going to do? How could she stop Thirty-One?

So her thoughts continued to circle around one another as she sought an answer to her problem. Then one night, one of Thirty-One's lackeys bumped up against her bunk and woke her from a troubled sleep. Even as the girl chuckled and continued on to the bathroom, One Twenty-Four was struggling to remember the fragments of her disrupted dream.

Like most dreams, it was mostly nonsense. Still, there'd been the kernel of an idea buried inside it about how she could flip this situation around. It had provided her with a revelation.

It was time to stop reacting to Thirty-One and make the other girl fear her instead, just like Keeper had advised.

As the bare bones of her scheme became clearer in her mind, she realized the odds against this plan working were high. Still, anything that unsettled Thirty-One was worth the time spent doing it.

If One Twenty-Four could start giving the girl second thoughts about her current approach, that bought her time. What did she have to lose?

She lay there until long after the girl that had disturbed her had returned to her bunk. She had to allow enough time for her to go back to sleep, because she didn't want any witnesses to this confrontation.

Once One Twenty-Four was sure that everyone was asleep again, she made her way to Thirty-One's bunk on quiet, socked feet. She moved carefully, being certain of everything around her so that she didn't make any noise at all. She couldn't afford for the girl to wake up too soon.

She'd brought along her pillow, because it was integral to her plan. She held it tightly against her chest, already anxious about what was going to happen next.

One Twenty-Four had dreamed about using this very pillow to smother her enemy many times, but again, she wasn't sure that she had it in her to murder someone while staring directly into their eyes. That would probably disappoint Keeper. It would certainly get her killed for so blatantly violating the rules.

When she arrived at Thirty-One's bunk, she stared down at the sleeping girl. She didn't look malevolent now, but One Twenty-Four knew that a monster lurked behind the girl's peaceful expression. Thirty-One didn't dream of happy things. She was probably imagining One Twenty-Four's death even now.

Part of her still wanted to call this off. When she made her move, she was committed. If this plan didn't work, she could count on swift retribution.

Of course, that was true even if it worked.

Holding her pillow to her chest, One Twenty-Four grabbed the sleeping girl's hands, clenched them tightly together, and threw herself on top of her.

Thirty-One awoke immediately and began struggling, but she was completely pinned. The girl froze for a moment, fear etched on her face as she stared up into One Twenty-Four's pitiless eyes.

"Are you afraid?" One Twenty-Four whispered. "You shouldn't be.

I wouldn't start screaming if I were you. It'll only make you look weak."

The other girl's shocked and frightened expression immediately morphed into one of rage and arrogance.

"You truly are an idiot," Thirty-One hissed. "You're weak, and Keeper will execute you."

One Twenty-Four smiled. "We'll see. Personally, I think Keeper will kill you instead. You see, I'm going to frame you for ineptly trying to kill me. I'll make you look so incompetent that Keeper will have to expel you."

Her words struck the other girl like a slap. Thirty-One blinked and opened her mouth as if to say something but then closed it again, seemingly utterly confused.

That was perfect. It was exactly what One Twenty-Four wanted.

"Yes, I think you finally begin to understand," One Twenty-Four said quietly. "I don't have to use force to stop you. All I need to do is set up a particular set of circumstances in which you lose your reputation with Keeper. *She'll* kill you for me.

"I've seen how you operate now. All I have to do is make certain that whatever attack I arrange for myself is credible and seems to have your fingerprints all over it. And do you know what the best part is?"

She leaned forward and allowed the tip of her nose to touch Thirty-One's. "If you try to stop me, all you're going to do is strike early and create the exact impression that I want. You'll be playing into my plan."

Without waiting for Thirty-One to say anything, One Twenty-Four rolled off her and headed back toward her bunk without another word.

Her plan was insane, but now that it was in motion, she felt manic. What would Thirty-One do next? Would she attack her right now?

One Twenty-Four's ears were peeled, listening for sounds of the girl coming after her, but there was nothing but silence behind her.

She'd probably shaken Thirty-One to the core. Her enemy was thinking about everything she'd said. That was good. The more she could get inside Thirty-One's head, the better.

Whatever plans the other girl had had in motion, One Twenty-

Four had probably just upset them. Thirty-One was on defense now, second-guessing everything and trying to figure out how she could adjust for One Twenty-Four's insane plan.

A plan that wasn't even real. One evoked to cause the other girl to panic and doom herself with her own actions.

One Twenty-Four returned to her bunk and lay in the darkness, a smile spread across her lips for the first time in weeks. Her heart was pounding, but she felt alive. This might be crazy, but she'd never felt happier in her entire life.

Whatever came next was going to be complicated. Thirty-One was going to be even more vicious than she usually was. One Twenty-Four had frightened her, and the other girl couldn't allow that to stand.

Thirty-One was probably going to strike soon, and One Twenty-Four had to be ready. Within a month, this situation was going to be settled one way or another.

Or perhaps Keeper would tire of their antics and kill them both.

Either way, One Twenty-Four was satisfied that she'd at least acted decisively. In the crèche, sometimes that was all one could do. She was done living in fear. Never again. Better death than that.

12

———————

G race had expected crossing the Singularity border to be a nerve-wracking situation, but it proved anticlimactic. In fact, their ship wasn't even inspected by customs after it made the transition—another benefit of having an owner with a sterling reputation.

That wasn't to say that the border wasn't protected. Far from it.

The Singularity version of Fleet had a significant force in the system they'd chosen for their ingress. According to the files that Kayden had provided, the system sported a dozen destroyers, about the same number of light cruisers, and a core of three heavy cruisers. The Singularity kept the force in this system to ward off invasion.

In addition to the flip-capable warships, some non–flip-capable system defense boats were watching over the orbitals. They also patrolled the areas around the flip points and ran along the major transit corridors.

These boats were tasked with keeping the peace in the system and providing an early warning should problems occur. That was when the heavier units would make their appearance.

The system defense boats were responsible for herding the merchantmen to various inspection points if that was what the customs officers decided. They seemingly picked ships at random, but Kayden told them that it was a more complicated process than that.

Each ship that came through the system had a reputation. Ships that kept their noses clean and whose crews never caused any problems were rarely searched. Those with issues were examined more often. Captains whose reputations were poor got the most attention.

Thankfully, *Bright Passage* made it through the border system without anything more than basic contact with Control. They made their way from one flip point directly to another and headed deeper into the Singularity.

Kayden said that this was normal. Depending on the speculative goods one picked up, a particular world might not be the best location to perform their trades. If there were better opportunities for profit in systems farther down the line, a ship would continue on.

Each flip after that brought them closer to the target system and also raised the tension level aboard the ship to a fever pitch by the time they made that final flip.

While they weren't technically restricted to passive scanners, they'd decided that using active scanners had a greater potential to draw unwelcome attention. That meant hours of poring over data to find out what was waiting for them in the Aponte system.

With the upgrades that Imperial Intelligence had made to the ship's passive scanners, they pulled in a lot of information. The concealed equipment had an incredible amount of processing power built in to massage the data and draw useful tidbits of insight from the soup they were picking up.

The first thing that they needed to be worried about was warships in the system. If there were flip-capable destroyers, then they'd have to move along rather than strike. That would be annoying, but sometimes that was just the way the coin toss went.

According to Kayden, the Singularity based its warships out of an asteroid that they'd be passing close to on the way to the gas giant. That was where their passive scanners would come in handy.

She wondered why the Singularity kept their larger ships stationed further away from the habitable world but decided that it didn't really matter. Perhaps they wanted a location that would be more responsive to issues in other systems. Or maybe they just wanted to make sure that there was no possibility of ambush.

The reason didn't matter so long as the outcome served their ends. It was just interesting trivia for someone in her line of work.

Anders and the bridge crew were bent over their consoles, examining every piece of information that they could pull out of the passive scanners as they closed range with the Singularity base. Judging from the tenseness of their shoulders, she knew they hadn't gotten the answers that they'd hoped for yet.

Kyle eventually straightened from his console and grinned at the rest of them. "I'm not seeing any destroyers. There's a couple of system defense boats there, but that's it. I suspect they're pretty quick, but so long as we can make it to the flip point before they catch us, it's not going to make much of a difference.

"Also, the few that I can see aren't going to have enough weaponry to take us down. We might look like a freighter, but we can deal with a couple of these boats pretty handily. About a third of the cargo containers are really missile launchers. We don't have any reloads, but we can deal with a bit of trouble."

"So, we're go to proceed?" Grace asked, hardly daring to believe it.

"You're go," Anders confirmed. "You should head back and finalize everything with your people. I'll keep you informed about our progress and let you know when we're ready to make our move.

"We'll be able to adjust our speed of approach somewhat, but I'd appreciate a heads-up about any glitches that you experience. Good luck to you and yours, Grace. Go kick some ass and bring us back some juicy cargo that we can trade in for a lot of money when we get back to the Empire."

She grinned at the man. "You've got it."

"Remember," he cautioned her. "Our timetable is going to be tight. I want to be done before the system defense boats get here. We *can* win that fight, but it'll be a lot better for us if we never exchange missiles with them at all. Take care of business as quickly as you can."

Grace nodded to him and exited the bridge.

The trip down to the cargo containers they were using to launch their assault only took a couple of minutes.

From the outside, those containers looked like every other container the freighter carried, but inside, they were completely different. The one they were using to launch the assault had a large airlock that could be used to get them out onto the hull a squad at a time.

It was a hive of activity by the time she arrived. All of her marines were in armor and finalizing their loadout. While they didn't have powered armor available for the assault, they were still pretty well protected in the mercenary gear that Imperial Intelligence had picked up for them. It would have to do.

Thankfully, being a mercenary out here meant that one might have to do work in a vacuum or under bad atmospheric conditions. Each suit of unpowered armor came with a life-support system that was more than capable of getting them across to where they needed to be and a thruster pack that could get them there quickly.

The attack plan called for them to detach from the freighter and make their approach with just the velocity imparted by the ship herself. When they were close to the transshipment center, they'd use their thruster packs to decelerate and make their way to potential entry points.

Their preference would be completely bypassing some relatively unused airlocks and getting inside without notifying the residents that they were there. Na would lead the way to the engineering section and begin setting up everything they needed for overloading the fusion plant.

Grace's mission was more complicated. It was up to her to make sure that Kayden got to the cargo management area so that he could help them seize whatever valuable containers they could get their hands on. That was a riskier proposition, and there were a lot of things that could go wrong.

She raised an eyebrow at Na and took her nod as an acknowledgment that everything was on track. That left her free to focus on her own group and the man they were going to have to protect during the mission.

He was also the man they'd have to keep a close eye on just in case he decided to betray them. She really hoped that didn't turn out to be the case, but if he was going to turn coat, this was the worst time for him to do it.

All it would take was him slipping away from them or using one of the consoles to sound the alarm, and they were cooked.

Even as she thought that, the man himself stepped into the container, spotted her, and headed over. "What do you need me to do, Grace?"

She gestured for him to go over to the open packing containers that held their armor and weapons. "We'll get you armored up and verify that your vacuum gear is functional. Do you have experience operating outside of a ship in zero-G?"

"Some," he said with a nod. "I started out as an engineer, so I've worked in vacuum before and operated without gravity. I'm probably not as adroit as your people, but I can get the job done and not embarrass myself too badly.

"What about once we get to the orbital itself? We're going to have to force our way into an occupied section of the transshipment center, and there's always the possibility that they're going to open fire on us. They have security to ward off pirates.

"Even with a naval base inside the system, piracy is still a concern. If someone thinks that they can just walk in and take a lot of valuable things and get away without retribution, they'll be tempted, so the people on this asteroid are going to have the ability to defend themselves."

"We'll do what we can to avoid any direct confrontations," Grace said as she started fitting his armor to him. "I'm surprised to hear that you have a problem with piracy, though. I thought the Singularity was a lot more orderly than that."

He chuckled as he held his arms out. "The more authoritarian the regime, the more the people under their heels that want to express themselves. Sometimes that comes out via dissidents disseminating information and at other times as criminal elements that want to make money while sticking it to the ruling caste.

"Such endeavors never prosper for long, but you can't completely stop them. As soon as you stomp one group, another one springs up to take its place. Don't you have a similar problem inside the Empire?"

She shook her head. "Not so much. We have piracy and smuggling, but they aren't widespread. Smuggling is far more prevalent, since Fleet actively goes after pirates but leaves smuggling to each system's customs service."

When she had Kayden armored up, she considered adding a weapon to the mix. While she still had concerns about him, he might need to defend himself.

After a moment's thought, she grabbed a holstered stunner and held it out to him. "I assume you know how to use this."

"I do," he said as he took it. "I give you my personal bond that I will do everything within my power to make certain that your mission succeeds. If you give an order, I'll carry it out. If I have misgivings, I'll keep them to myself until such time as we're away. Unless, of course, they endanger the mission while we're there, in which case I'll speak up. I'll be a good partner, Grace. I promise."

"See that you do."

She really hoped that he was as good as his word, because she'd grown to enjoy his dry sense of humor and would hate to have him turn against her. If he did, she'd handle it, but the betrayal would make her sad.

Getting Kayden into his armor and attaching the thruster pack only took a couple of minutes. By the time she was finished, all of her marines were ready to go.

Grace went to the communication panel set in the wall and opened a connection to the bridge. Since the ship's crew wasn't supposed to have implants, they didn't dare install any receivers that would allow them to use their implant coms. There was too much chance that a random customs search would find something incriminating.

Kyle answered the call. "Talk to me, Grace."

"We're ready to go. How close to the transshipment center are we, and what kind of time frame are we expecting before we're ready to detach from the ship?"

"We're still on approach. Control hasn't contacted us yet, but there's a fair number of ships loading and unloading cargo. I expect that we'll get instructions to change course in the next couple of minutes for the final approach.

"As soon as we get the word, we'll let you know. It's probably best if you go ahead and move out to the exterior of the ship and get ready to detach.

"I want to second everything that Jay said. Be careful and come back to us. Don't put yourself or your people in any undue danger. I'd much rather have all of your marines come home than have a fat bank account."

His words made her feel good. She'd dealt with Fleet officers that didn't value the lives of the marines under their command. It was nice to have these guys looking out for her and her people.

"That works for us," she agreed. "We'll do the best we can. Give us a call when you're ready for us to deploy, and we'll be able to detach in just a couple of seconds. I figure that you can rotate the ship so that our own momentum will carry us away as you change course. Does that work?"

"Absolutely. Good luck, Grace."

She killed the channel and started her people out onto the exterior of the ship. They'd use their magnetic boots to lock on around the airlock until all of them were outside and ready to deploy.

It wasn't going to be long now. In just a couple of minutes, they'd disengage from *Bright Passage* and be on their way.

She grinned as she watched her marines moving out. It was their job to make damned sure that the Singularity remembered their visit for a very long time. Anders would get them clear once it was all done, but the lion's share of the work was going to be on her and her people.

Five minutes later, she stood outside next to Kayden and watched the growing speck of light in front of them that was the asteroid housing the transshipment center. She could see dimmer dots moving around that must be ships maneuvering, but she really couldn't get a scale of the place.

Not that she needed one. The raw data that Kayden had supplied had told her that the place was huge. She didn't know how much cargo was moving through here or how many people were inside the massive structure, but she was looking forward to seeing it completely and utterly destroyed.

Grace hoped that the people working there could evacuate in an hour. That was the amount of time they'd decided would be appropriate. The place should have enough escape pods to get every single person clear, and an hour was a lot of time to make that happen.

"Grace, this is Anders," the Fleet officer said over the short-range com in her suit. "Control just gave us an approach vector, and we're rotating the ship. Stand by."

"Copy that. Go for rotation."

Moments later, the ship rotated and then stopped again once the stars had realigned.

"You are clear to detach," Anders said. "Be bold and be careful."

"Will do. Keep a light on for us. Tolliver out."

She switched to the general marine channel on the short-ranged suit com. "Heads up, people. We detach in ten seconds."

Without prodding from her, Na took over the countdown duties, and Grace cut the magnetic latching system in her boots right on zero. She was pleased to see that Kayden did the same.

They drifted slowly above the hull of the freighter for a few seconds, and then the ship changed course and began pulling away from them and accelerating slightly. Moments later, they were floating alone in space, still headed toward the transshipment center.

They were utterly committed now. All that lay before them now was victory or death.

13

One Twenty-Four was pleased to see that turning the tables on Thirty-One had unnerved her over the next several weeks. Whatever the girl's plans had been, she seemed to be reassessing them. Every time One Twenty-Four stared boldly at the girl, Thirty-One looked away.

Of course, this would only be a temporary setback for her enemy. One Twenty-Four had no doubt the girl would strike soon enough. With that in mind, she made it her business to watch everything that was going on around her.

If someone was working with a piece of equipment, she paid close attention to that. If any of Thirty-One's lackeys seemed to be manipulating how people were doing things, she took note of it.

And her attentiveness eventually paid off.

About three weeks after she'd confronted Thirty-One in the dorm, she found another bit of sabotage. In this case, it was something in their advanced chemistry class. Some of the chemicals in her mobile cabinet had been tampered with.

How did she want to play this? She could tell Keeper that something was going on. Keeper would have no trouble determining that the chemicals had been altered.

Some had been relabeled and were different colors than they should've been. If anyone was paying even the slightest bit of attention—or bothered studying chemistry—she'd notice the substitution.

As assassination attempts went, it was clumsy. That made her smile.

One Twenty-Four took the time to look at all the chemicals and then began assessing her equipment. Some of it had also been modified. The burner, for example. When turned above a particular setting, it would create a flame that was *significantly* hotter than anticipated, and it would do so with little warning.

After she conducted an experiment that proved that, One Twenty-Four realized that she'd made a mistake. Thirty-One could easily have rigged the equipment to simply explode. If flaming wreckage had landed all over her, she'd have been badly burned. Perhaps enough so that she'd be expelled from the crèche. She needed to be more careful.

In the end, she came up with a straightforward solution to her problem. It would take too long to sort through everything in the cabinet. So she wouldn't.

The cabinets were heavy but had wheels allowing them to be relocated. The chemical containers inside the cabinets were well secured, so unless she accidentally dumped the entire thing over, she should be able to move it without difficulty.

Needless to say, when she began rolling her cabinet to one of the unused stations, that garnered a lot of attention from her line sibs. Particularly Thirty-One and her cronies.

Keeper also observed her move the cabinet but didn't say anything. She simply watched passively, her expression neutral. Once One Twenty-Four had finished moving the cabinet, she took Seventy-Three's cabinet and rolled it back to her lab station. Her dead line sib wouldn't be using it, so it hardly mattered if she took it.

Thirty-One looked as if she wanted to leap to her feet and accuse One Twenty-Four of wrongdoing.

But she didn't. After all, what exactly could she say?

Keeper! One Twenty-Four is getting rid of all the equipment that I sabotaged! Make her put it back so that she can die!

No, that wouldn't have looked good for the girl at all.

Once One Twenty-Four had her new cabinet of chemicals and equipment back to her work area, she now had to overcome the challenge of the cabinet's lock. Thirty-One or her lackeys had managed to bypass her original cabinet's lock, but they'd had time and secrecy to aid them.

She quickly decided that boldness was her best option.

Once she had the cabinet of chemicals and equipment locked down so that it couldn't move, she walked up to Keeper's desk and stood impassively, waiting to be acknowledged.

"Yes, One Twenty-Four?" Keeper said, one eyebrow raised. "Is there something that you desire?"

"Keeper, I'm unfamiliar with the combination of my new cabinet and don't wish to damage Line equipment. Would you open it for me?"

Keeper stared at her for several seconds before rising to her feet and walking over to One Twenty-Four's work area. There, she entered a code into the lock, and the cabinet opened.

"You'll need to reset the code," Keeper said before returning to her desk and settling back into her seat, acting as if this sort of thing happened every day.

One Twenty-Four changed the code and took a few minutes to go through all of the equipment and chemicals stored in her new cabinet before starting the experiments that she'd been assigned for the day.

She stared at Thirty-One often, reveling in the other's impotent fury by smiling sweetly at her. Discovering this plot wasn't going to stop Thirty-One from trying to kill her, but it showed Keeper that One Twenty-Four wasn't a patsy. That she wasn't going to just roll over and take whatever her enemy dealt out.

She had no doubt that Keeper would go through her old cabinet. If Thirty-One had been too sloppy, that might still be the end of her. After all, wasn't that really the best outcome? To let Thirty-One sabotage herself to the point she was censured?

Hopefully, this would cause her enemy to become even sloppier when she made her next attempt. An attempt that One Twenty-Four would be watching for with every bit of her intellect.

* * *

GRACE FELT calm as they approached the asteroid, and that kind of surprised her. She'd expected her heart rate to be up, anticipating the fight that was to come. Yet she was calm, cool, and collected. All of her training was paying off on the biggest mission of her career.

Based on the intelligence they'd gotten from Kayden, she had a reasonably decent idea of where the engineering section of the center would be and had dispatched Na in that direction. She had First and Third squads to help her.

He'd been a little less clear about where the cargo control area would be, but it had to be somewhere close to where the loading and unloading took place. They just had to find an airlock that would be close enough to get them to where they needed to go.

Her preference would be to find a disused airlock. The longer they avoided being seen by any of the locals, the more they could accomplish. Their mercenary combat armor was going to stand out like a priest in a strip club, so the moment they revealed themselves, the alarm would be out.

It turned out that gaining access to the transshipment center wasn't nearly as difficult as she'd feared. Her squad didn't have to use an out-of-the-way airlock because there was an open cargo bay that wasn't currently in use. Someone must've decided that it made more sense to leave it open to space than to spend the time repressurizing it.

That might mean that a ship was going to be docking to the attached umbilical and transferring cargo soon. She made note of its location, because it might become useful when it came time to leave, particularly if they had to move in a hurry.

While *Bright Passage* was going to be in position to load cargo shortly, she wouldn't know which bay their ride was going to use until Anders sent them a message. When that came, it was going to be an encrypted burst that their gear was designed to pick up. To the locals, it would be a random bit of static.

Once they had that information, they'd have to find a map to get them to where they needed to exit the transshipment center. Her preference was to directly board the ship rather than having to use the thruster packs again. Faster would be better, and she had no qualms about abandoning unneeded equipment.

Her people stashed their thruster packs in a disused locker as soon as they were inside the bay. The last thing that they needed was for an overly observant cargo handler to wonder where the new stuff had come from.

Once they'd done that, everyone loaded themselves into the personnel airlock, which took them inside the transshipment center. The corridor outside the bay was made for moving cargo containers and had an overhead rail system that was more than capable of moving the massive boxes without human intervention.

That was actually a lucky break. So long as they could move around the station without garnering any attention, that would ultimately improve their chances of success.

While it might seem backward, she was leading the secondary team. Na and her people would see to the destruction of the asteroid via overloading the fusion plant. That task—though critical—was also *significantly* more straightforward.

That was why Grace had Second Squad. Her group only numbered fifteen people, including herself and Kayden Harmon. So stumbling into an automated system like this was a godsend.

A noise from farther up the corridor attracted their attention, and they crouched, weapons ready. Ahead of them, an automated rail car hoisting a container came around the gentle curve. It almost filled the corridor.

"Everyone to the sides," she ordered. "It looks like there's enough room for it to pass by without touching us, but let's not get anything snagged."

The extra space made sense. Maintenance work couldn't interfere with the job of loading and unloading cargo, after all.

Her group split in two, and Grace was pleased to see that the container cleared her with maybe a third of a meter to spare. It passed by and continued on its unknowable journey.

"Is this the kind of automated system you were talking about?" Grace asked Kayden as they resumed their advance.

He half turned toward her and nodded clumsily in the armor.

"Everything that can be done without human intervention is. If we can find the system controlling the rails, we can order it to take whatever we like and put it on board *Bright Passage* once we have the docking bay number that she's going to use.

"Sadly, none of the computer interfaces in these corridors is likely going to be of use to us. They don't have the command-and-control software on them. All they're responsible for is interpreting the orders sent from elsewhere or perhaps local control of a specific container.

"Still, if we can find a terminal, we can locate the nearest command-and-control interface. We'll probably be able to get a map of the rail system, too. That'll make our lives a little easier."

"Excellent. Do you think the terminal is going to be protected from intrusion?"

"Undoubtedly. Leaders inside the Singularity worry about sabotage all the time. A disgruntled worker could use automated systems to cause a lot of havoc. I suspect that management here is more worried about that sort of thing. Theft seems less likely than sabotage in the grand scheme of things."

They continued on, passing branching corridors that were just as large as the one they were in, obviously meant to take cargo containers to and from different areas.

She was beginning to fear that they weren't going to find any terminals when they came across a recess that had one in it.

"Overwatch positions," she ordered.

The squad deployed with half aiming their weapons the way they'd come while the rest took up positions watching the forward part of the corridor.

The terminal looked unremarkable, but she knew that wasn't the case. Singularity computer systems differed in many ways from the ones used in the Empire. When these people had left the Empire behind, their technology had diverged significantly when it came to computers.

That wasn't to say that her people couldn't manage. Ships with Singularity computer systems were captured on a fairly regular basis. Some systems had even been purchased by Imperial Intelligence for study. Through cutouts, of course.

Needless to say, the necessary people inside the Imperial Marines were trained on how to utilize Singularity systems. In this case, her specialist was Riggio Gomez, and he was damn good at what he did.

After a few minutes of work, Gomez turned his head toward her and grinned. "I'm in, Lieutenant."

"No ranks," she gently admonished him. "Kayden, can you find the nearest command-and-control terminal?"

The man stepped up to the terminal and typed in a command.

Grace read past his shoulder. She was both curious about what he was doing and making sure that he didn't give them away. Since Gomez didn't seem concerned about what he was seeing, she relaxed a little.

"I've got a listing of the authorized terminals, and I even have a rough idea of how we can get to one without exposing ourselves," Kayden said after the terminal display changed to show a list in text.

She and her people had training in the Singularity's language—called the tongue—both written and spoken. Her accent was atrocious—as Kayden had gleefully pointed out—so she was glad that the man was fluent in Standard.

"Great," she said. "How far is it? Can we tell if we're going to cross any areas with personnel traffic?"

"Six levels up. I've got access to a map of the rail system as well as the cargo management control area. Nothing else, though. If you pass me your slate, I'll transfer it."

Grace handed him her slate, which had all the modifications needed to link up with Singularity systems and also to read the files from them. "How long is it going to take us to get there?"

"Not long. We can go a little farther up this tunnel, and there'll be a ladder built into the wall. It'll lead us up to a maintenance corridor directly adjacent to the control area. There's always the possibility that we'll run into somebody doing maintenance, but I think your people can handle anything like that."

"You're damned right they can," she said with a nod. "Get me that map, and let's be about our business. We've got a cargo to steal, and then we can get the hell out of here."

14

One Twenty-Four's inevitable confrontation with Thirty-One came that evening. The girl and her clique of followers barely waited until all the girls had filed into the dorm before they confronted her. With Thirty-One in the lead, the group surrounded her, leaving no avenue of escape.

Even though she knew that Thirty-One probably wasn't stupid enough to attack her so blatantly, One Twenty-Four was still afraid. There was something wrong with the girl. Her rage made her do things that weren't wise.

"You've embarrassed me for the last time," Thirty-One hissed as she stepped into One Twenty-Four's personal space, jabbing her in the chest with a finger and forcing her back a step.

One Twenty-Four chose to smile in spite of her fear. "Your attack on me was uninspired. Even an idiot would recognize that some of the chemicals had been altered.

"Was that really the best you could do? Based on your attack in the gym, I thought you at least had some cunning. Is there nothing but brutishness hiding behind that bent nose of yours?"

Her insult had the desired effect and more. Thirty-One actually *growled* as she grabbed One Twenty-Four by the blouse and yanked her close.

"You think you're so smart. Let me tell you the hard truth. Keeper hates you, and so does everyone else in the crèche. You don't belong here. You deserve expulsion and death, because you aren't worthy of the Line."

"And you're an idiot for touching me," One Twenty-Four responded just before she drove her fist into the other girl's stomach.

Thirty-One staggered back, taken completely off guard by the physical strike. The girl gasped for air even as her supporters gathered around her.

Things were about to get ugly. While One Twenty-Four felt justified in responding with violence since the girl had touched her, that wouldn't protect her from their retaliation.

Even as Thirty-One and her supporters advanced on her with bloodlust in their eyes, the atmosphere in the dorm changed. Where before, the rest of her line sibs had been watching curiously, they were now closing in on the confrontation from all sides.

One Twenty-Four was suddenly and deeply afraid. Was this the end? Had the crèche decided that she should be eliminated? She could posture against Thirty-One and her cronies, but she couldn't fight the crèche.

Instead of attacking her, the other girls placed themselves around One Twenty-Four in support. That stopped Thirty-One and her friends from advancing, their expressions now changed to shock.

"What is the meaning of this?" Thirty-One demanded. "Stand aside."

"Your behavior is unacceptable," Twelve said firmly. "Your attack on One Twenty-Four in the dorm is too blatant. It stops now."

Thirty-One put her hands on her hips and glared at Twelve. "How *dare* you? I will see you exterminated along with this trash."

Twelve raised an eyebrow. "Will you? You have the support of half a dozen girls. I have the support of the crèche. We outnumber you twenty to one. Are we the enemies that you wish to make today?

"I understand that in the future, we may be required to maneuver against our enemies. That time has not yet come. Here in the crèche, we are expected to learn, and you have failed to comprehend the offered lesson."

Twelve turned toward One Twenty-Four. "That isn't to say that One Twenty-Four won't find herself expelled from the crèche. In fact, I believe the odds of her surviving to adulthood are slim, and that saddens me.

"The Singularity needs each and every one of us. The Empire will have no mercy, and we cannot waste time exterminating ourselves. Both of you are behaving in a manner that is not befitting of the Andrea Line."

"And what shall we do?" One Twenty-Four asked. "How shall Thirty-One and I resolve our differences?"

Twelve turned back toward Thirty-One. "You are the aggressor. I speak on behalf of the crèche when I demand that you cease such direct action inside the dorm. If you don't, I will speak with Keeper, and she will learn of *all* the things you've done. If that happens, Keeper will *not* be pleased."

"I don't bow to the likes of *you*," Thirty-One sneered. "Do not insert yourself into this conflict, or you will find yourself next on my list of enemies. Do I make myself clear?"

"Once again, you fail to understand," Twelve said with a sad shake of her head. "I don't speak for myself. I speak for the crèche."

All of the girls that were not part of Thirty-One's coven of friends stepped forward and surrounded the smaller group. They didn't behave aggressively, but they didn't act like they were afraid either.

"You are at a turning point, Thirty-One," Twelve said into the sudden silence. "If you act in such a direct manner again, we *will* deal with you. If you attack me, someone else will step forward and see that the crèche's will is done. Defy us at your peril."

One Twenty-Four could barely see Thirty-One through the other girls, but she could see that her enemy *was* intimidated. She tried to put on a good face, but who wouldn't be daunted at this kind of confrontation?

Without any response whatsoever, Thirty-One turned on her heel and headed back toward her bunk with her supporters streaming behind her. As soon as they'd backed down, everyone else dispersed.

Everyone except Twelve.

"Do not think that this absolves you of your failures," Twelve said softly. "I was being honest when I said that I don't think you're going to survive. Your behavior is too far outside the norms expected in the crèche.

"Perhaps you can reform yourself, but this is less about protecting you and more about making certain that Thirty-One does not believe that she rules here. If you strike her in the dorm again, rest assured that you'll receive all the negative attention that I promised her.

"This conflict between the two of you needs to be subtle. This kind of overt confrontation will not be tolerated. Is that clear, One Twenty-Four?"

"I struck her because she touched me. If she does so again, I will hit her again. The crèche doesn't forbid self-defense."

Twelve considered that for a moment and nodded. "So long as you don't initiate a physical confrontation, you can defend yourself. See that you don't make the mistake of abusing that allowance.

"I'd warn Thirty-One about that as well, but she won't listen to me. She has a cruel streak inside her that the rest of us do not. She won't wait long before she finds a way to strike at you, so be wary. The gymnasium and the chemistry lab were just the beginning.

"For whatever reason, she's decided that she must *personally* end you. Never take your eyes off of her or her lackeys."

Without waiting for a response, Twelve turned and walked back to her bunk, resuming her life as if nothing had happened.

The girl was right, One Twenty-Four decided. Thirty-One wasn't going to be deterred. In fact, after being told that she couldn't do this, she suspected that Thirty-One would act sooner than she otherwise would have, and perhaps even more violently.

The war between them wasn't going to last long. If One Twenty-Four were to guess, one of them would be dead within the next month. Perhaps they'd both be dead.

She needed to watch everything around her. When the viper struck, she would only have moments to react. Inattention could and would get her killed.

One Twenty-Four felt her resolve harden. Whatever it took for her to survive, she'd do it. No matter the consequences.

* * *

ONCE THEY'D SECURED the terminal again, Grace and her team made their way farther down the corridor. Several more cargo containers passed them as they advanced into the transshipment center, but they saw no one else.

After about ten minutes of walking, they came to the ladder that Kayden had found on the map. Seeing how far they'd walked, Grace had to reassess the scale of the asteroid.

On the map, the distance hadn't seemed significant, emphasizing just how large the transshipment center truly was. Its loss would be a tremendous blow to the economy in this sector of the Singularity.

Ascending the ladder was straightforward until they reached the level they wished to exit on. It was blocked by a locked hatch. Management obviously wanted to make certain that no one accessed the cargo delivery corridors without the proper authorizations.

Thankfully, just like the computer system, they had a way of bypassing such locks. In this case, the lock itself was electronic, and Gomez had it overridden in less than a minute. She suspected that overriding it from the other side would've been more difficult. After all, saboteurs wanted into the tunnels, not out.

The hatch opened into a deserted maintenance corridor. She gestured for Gomez to disable the lock. They might be coming back this way in a hurry.

When that was done, Kayden consulted the map and started them to the left. They traveled as a group, tightly packed and in the same formation that they'd used in the corridor below.

Sadly, there just wasn't enough space to spread out properly. Hopefully, they wouldn't run into anyone with grenades.

Their good luck ran out when they chanced across a pair of technicians in light-blue coveralls working on something behind a wall panel. The men gaped at them in shock just before her lead elements took them down with stunners.

Grace cursed under her breath. She'd hoped to avoid running into anyone before they reached their target.

She assigned a pair of marines to carry the two. When they reached the cargo control area, they'd make sure that they weren't overlooked. She'd stunned them, so she was responsible for their ultimate safety.

It took them almost fifteen minutes to reach the control area that they'd decided to breach. That was far more time than she'd initially allocated, but they hadn't gotten word that Na and her people had reached the engineering section yet, so they were still good.

When Na arrived in engineering, Grace would get a burst transmission, indicating that that part of the operation was ready to execute on her command.

On the positive side, she hadn't received word that her subordinates had run into resistance, either. So far as she knew, they were still undetected. Or, if they had been spotted, they'd managed to stun whoever had chanced across them, just like her squad had.

When they reached the hatch they'd decided to use, she put half of the squad into a defensive perimeter and stacked the rest to go through as soon as they got word from Na and Anders.

"Remember the plan," she said softly. "Stun everybody you can and try to keep this quiet. The longer we can keep them from knowing that we're here, the better. Clear?"

Acknowledgments flowed back from everyone.

She tugged Kayden over to stand next to her. "Unless you absolutely have to, leave that stunner in its holster. Let the professionals do this. That's what we're trained for. You're only to use that stunner if things go completely to hell, understood?"

"Understood, Lieutenant," he said with a grin. "And yes, I know I'm not supposed to use your rank. I just couldn't resist doing it this once. It makes you sound so… official."

She smiled in spite of herself. The man was incorrigible.

Bypassing the lock on the access hatch took about the same amount of time it'd taken to crack the last one. That accomplished, they waited for the rest of the platoon to get into position. Until and unless Na was ready to go and their ride was in place to receive them, it made no sense to kick things off early.

What she did do was send a burst transmission about their readiness. That way, the rest would know that they were okay and prepared to proceed.

Less than five minutes later, her implants pinged with an incoming transmission. It was from *Bright Passage*. The ship was docked and awaiting cargo.

Amusingly, the freighter had docked at the same cargo bay they'd used to enter the facility. Sometimes Lady Luck really did smile down on them.

Now all they had to do was wait for Na to get into position. Once that portion of the project was underway, they'd have one hour to steal everything they could, get back to *Bright Passage*, and get away from the transshipment center.

Things could still go wrong, but she was pleased that they'd gone smoothly thus far. That could all change in a moment, though, so she wasn't going to get too cocky.

Ten agonizing minutes later, a second burst transmission came in, this time from Na. The rest of the platoon had made its way to the engineering section and was ready to begin its assault.

Na's report indicated that they'd stunned a couple of people already and would be bringing them into the engineering section with them. Unlike the cargo control area, they could be relatively confident that engineering held a lot of people.

They weren't going to be able to stun everyone there, so they'd have to make sure that whoever they did take down was accessible to rescue parties once the word was given that there was a timer on the evacuation.

With any luck, there'd be escape pods present in the engineering section that they could eject before they began withdrawing.

Grace composed a response. "You are go to proceed with the attack on engineering. I repeat, you are go to proceed on your own discretion. Give us a time hack when you start the overload countdown."

Once done, she compressed and sent the message.

That was it. In just a few seconds, the Singularity forces on this station would become aware of their presence in the most unpleasant manner. Time to get her part of the operation underway.

"Breach the cargo control center," she ordered.

Her people flowed through the access hatch one after the other, each sweeping different areas of the control area with their stunners. Unlike in the vids, she came in close to the back, ready to add her fire to theirs but safe from any initial resistance.

Somewhat anticlimactically, this particular room was empty of people. Even as her people spread out to cover the other hatches in the compartment, she turned quizzically toward Kayden.

"Shouldn't there be people here?"

He shrugged. "The control center is probably a fairly large affair. This might be an overflow room of some kind. I'd imagine that they have times where they're busy and times when they're not. Perhaps they only use this room when there's a lot of traffic or if there is maintenance required on the consoles in the main area."

"Well, let's not look a gift horse in the mouth. You and Gomez break into the system and get control of the portions that we want. *Bright Passage* is at the same bay we arrived in, and they're ready to take on cargo. You have the list of empty containers, so just have the system swap them out."

The two men got to work. Ninety seconds later, Gomez gave her a thumbs-up.

"We're in. I'm going through the cargo manifests now, locating where the cargoes we're looking for are located and determining what the possibilities are for extra goodies."

"Prioritize the rare elements used for flip drive construction, because that will have a lot of value, but if you find anything else that's in the same range, don't hesitate to snag it. Maybe completed flip drives. Whatever you do, be efficient. I want to be on our way as soon as we can."

"I found the cargo you were looking for," Kayden said. "And I've bumped *Bright Passage* up in priority, so she'll get serviced first. We should be able to get quite a bit of cargo loaded in the next half hour.

"I'll have the empties that we had aboard the ship just left in the cargo bay. It's not going to make any difference now and will speed the process."

"What are the chances that someone is going to notice what we're doing?" Grace asked, eyeing the hatches around them that might open at any second.

"With everything else that's going to be going on shortly, probably very little. Even if they do, what are they going to do about it? They're under attack in engineering, and that's going to command a lot of their attention.

"And as soon as they get word that they have an hour to get off this orbital, they're going to have far more pressing matters than somebody stealing their cargo."

Gomez nodded. "I've put a security lock on the cargo transfers. Even if someone sees them, they'll have to override what we're doing. Certainly doable, but I think it's unlikely, given the timeframe."

It had taken them over half an hour to get here. If they wanted to get back to the ship before everything went to hell, they were going to have to find a place where they could put their prisoners and get moving soon.

Standing orders aside, they weren't going to have time to search for booty. That was actually something of a relief. The idea of personally stealing something of value struck her as wrong. Yes, she and her people would profit from this mission—if they survived—but that wasn't the same thing.

Perhaps they'd find some stuff in the cargo containers for everyone. That should count. It would have to.

"Lock the console down," she ordered. "Stack up on one of those hatches and be ready to go. Once we find the crew, we need to make sure that they take these people with them."

"You're underthinking this," Kayden said, popping his helmet off. "Going in and mowing down everyone in sight is not the simplest answer. That's just going to cause more chaos. May I suggest an alternative?"

Grace raised an eyebrow, choosing to ignore the implied insult. "I'm listening."

"Take your people back into the maintenance corridor and leave the hatch unlocked. I'll go find someone and tell them that I found a couple of unconscious maintenance people in here. That's going to cause a stir, but it's not going to be as messy as an active-shooter alarm.

"And if they get suspicions, I'll stun them and run for my life. You have my promise on that."

Part of her wondered if this was a way for him to get away from them, but she rejected the idea. While it was possible that he'd betray them, it hardly mattered at this point. Her people were already assaulting engineering, and if the people in control didn't know that already, they would in extremely short order.

The marines taught their officers not to dither when making decisions. That was almost always worse than making a less optimal choice. That made her decision easy.

"Do it," she said as she gestured for her people to retreat into the maintenance corridor.

Once there, they set up a defensive perimeter and waited. Less than a minute later, the hatch slid open just enough to admit Kayden, who slipped through and eased it closed again. He manipulated the lock and sealed it from their side before turning to face her.

"It's done. As soon as they started looking at the unconscious men, I slipped away. They never even thought to ask who I was or why I was wearing this armor. In other words, they thought that I was one of them.

"That's one of the benefits of having a good accent in Singularity space. You really should let me give you elocution lessons."

He added an arch smile to his assertation.

"You're hilarious," she said in a deadpan voice. "Now, let's get the hell out of here. We've got to get back to *Bright Passage* before everything goes to crap."

They began withdrawing along the same path that they'd come. They hadn't gone ten steps when a low alarm began thrumming through the corridor. The attack in engineering had been detected, and the clock was sure as hell ticking now.

15

The afternoon class on leadership theory had only barely begun when a low, throbbing tone sounded throughout the classroom. One Twenty-Four frowned. She'd never heard anything like it before. What did it mean?

Keeper immediately walked to the wall behind her desk and uncovered a screen behind a wall panel that slid up when she touched it—a wall panel that One Twenty-Four hadn't even suspected existed.

She pressed her hand to the screen and said something softly. From where One Twenty-Four was sitting, she could see lines of text begin scrolling down the screen. Whatever it said displeased Keeper.

The woman turned toward them and gestured toward the doorway. "We are vacating the crèche. Form up in a single line, and I will lead you to our designated evacuation point."

Evacuation? This wasn't a situation that they'd trained for. What could be going on that was so serious that they needed to leave the crèche?

Curious to know more, One Twenty-Four violated protocol and placed herself at the very front of the line. Three, who typically occupied the lead position, looked scandalized but didn't have an opportunity to complain about the violation before Keeper started walking briskly toward the exit.

Keeper led them into the corridor outside the crèche, just like she'd done when they'd gone to the ship for their tattoos. This time, however, it hadn't been cleared. For the very first time in her life, One Twenty-Four saw people that didn't belong to her line.

The corridor was half filled with people rushing to and fro on tasks that she had no way of knowing. Some of their faces held caste tattoos, but many did not. Most looked markedly different from one another and from Keeper.

It took all of One Twenty-Four's willpower not to stare at the strangers around them. Then she decided it was stupid to waste the opportunity, and she did stare. That was when she noticed that not all of the people around her were female.

Shocked, she realized that she was seeing men for the first time in her life. Knowing that this opportunity would be fleeting, she stared at each of them as Keeper led them through the throng, trying to commit what she saw to memory.

Interestingly, the people seemed just as astonished to see her and her line sibs. She supposed that made sense. Children of the Andrea Line were never so openly on display. It made her feel a little self-conscious.

That didn't stop her from gawking. This was just the kind of experience that she'd always longed for, and her curiosity was being sated at an incredible rate. She couldn't have been more excited.

Sadly, her examination of the people around them was cut short when Keeper took a turn down a side corridor that opened into a larger room. There were more people here, but they were different.

Each wore some type of clothing that seemed to be made up of hard shells. Their heads were covered by helmets with dark visors that hid their features. They held what One Twenty-Four suspected were weapons.

These must be the protectors of the crèche. Since the inhabitants of the crèche didn't come out, she'd never had the opportunity to see one of them face to face, though they'd all known the crèche was guarded.

Keeper marched up to another screen set into the far wall, and, unsure of what to do, One Twenty-Four followed closely behind her. The woman reached the wall and placed her hand against the screen.

One Twenty-Four stepped to the left to get a better view of what was going on, and Keeper didn't see her when she turned to the right and gestured for everyone to line up against the wall.

She knew that she should back away, but she hesitated. She really wanted to know what was happening.

Keeper spoke softly. "Override authorization Andrea Seven Seventy-Six."

"Authorization provisionally accepted," a monotone voice said. "Passphrase?"

"Oblivion sunrise."

"DNA sequencing in progress. Identity accepted, Andrea Seven Seventy-Six. What are your instructions?"

"Initiate self-destruct sequence. Set timer for forty-five minutes. Engage on my authority with no audible countdown."

"Command accepted. Self-destruct sequence engaged."

One Twenty-Four stepped away from Keeper and headed back toward the wall where the rest were waiting, but she wasn't fast enough. Keeper must've seen her moving out of the corner of her eye, because she turned and glared at her.

"One Twenty-Four, this is not the time for your nonsense. Go to the back of the line and stay there. I'll deal with you when we're safely away from the station."

She turned toward the other girls as One Twenty-Four made her way to the rear of the line, her face aflame.

"Let me be bluntly clear," Keeper said coldly. "Keep up, or you'll be eliminated. I don't have time to coddle you and cannot allow even a single member of this crèche to fall into the hands of whoever has attacked this facility. If you become separated from the group, I will dispatch guards to find and execute you. Do you understand?"

"Yes, Keeper," they all intoned.

"We'll see. Guards, lead the way. Detach a small detachment to bring up the rear. Do not allow any of the girls to become separated from the rest. If any are, you are to utilize their wristbands to track and eliminate them before they can be captured."

As one, the guards silently slapped the butts of their weapons.

One Twenty-Four was frightened. Nothing like this had ever occurred, and she was worried. Had the Empire come? Were they trying to capture the crèche so that they could dissect them?

This worry so filled her thoughts that she barely paid attention to the course they were navigating through the station. The wide corridors had shrunk down by the time she finally began paying attention again, and she saw that they were now traveling through what was obviously not a public thoroughfare.

She turned her head to look at the guards behind her and saw that their attention was primarily focused in the direction that they'd come from. In fact, they were walking backward, their weapons pointed toward the rear.

One twenty-Four was so absorbed by what was taking place around her that she almost missed that they were passing by a partially open hatch. What was in there? Did it lead to some other portion of the station? Could enemies be lying in wait there?

Even as those thoughts ran through her mind, someone grabbed her. She tried to scream, but they'd clamped a hand over her mouth. Those rough hands wrenched her head around, and she found herself staring into Thirty-One's hard eyes.

"You heard Keeper," the other girl whispered. "If you get separated, they're going to kill you. I win."

One of the girl's lackeys pushed the hatch open while Thirty-One shoved her through. One Twenty-Four drew in a breath to shout but found herself plummeting into the darkness.

She did scream then, but it was far, far too late to do her any good.

* * *

GRACE and her team were nearing the bottom of the ladder when she heard a shrill scream above them. As she was toward the back of the group, she was able to see the two marines above her on the ladder and something falling toward them from the darkness.

She barely had time to register the falling form before the person slammed into the uppermost marine and knocked her off the ladder. She, in turn, struck the marine below her, who landed on Grace.

Thankfully, Grace was only half a meter above the deck, so the fall didn't injure her. She stood and pulled her stunner, covering the person that had fallen down the maintenance shaft. That was when she realized it was a child.

A girl of perhaps eleven or twelve years lay sprawled on top of her marines, who were struggling to get to their feet. She had strange, predatory tattoos swirling along her forehead and cheeks and was dressed in what looked like some kind of school uniform.

Before Grace could decide what to do, there were shouts from above and the sound of booted feet on the ladder. Someone was coming after the girl, so she'd be rescued.

"Leave her," she ordered.

That was when the people above began firing flechettes down the shaft. Since they couldn't see who was at the bottom of the ladder, that made it pretty damned clear that they were after the girl and had hostile intent.

Grace had no idea why the girl was running from them, but she wasn't going to leave a child to be slaughtered. She grabbed the semiconscious girl and clutched her to her chest as she turned to run.

The girl cried out in pain. She was undoubtedly injured, but they didn't have time to address that now. Running would potentially magnify her injuries, but that beat getting shot dead any day of the week.

"Extraction plan bravo," she ordered into the com on the squad frequency.

They reoriented themselves so that two-thirds of their number were toward the rear of the party as they raced up the corridor. When whoever was coming down that ladder arrived at the bottom, they were going to get a *very* warm welcome.

"Kayden, to me," she said.

The man from the Singularity was at her side in a moment, staring at the girl as if she was an armed plasma grenade. "What are you doing? We can't take her with us. Leave her."

The look Grace shot the man could've frozen helium. "Imperial Marines do not leave children behind to die."

"That's not a child," he argued, his voice almost a hiss. "That's a viper."

"I don't have time to argue with you. Why are they after her?"

"Look at her tattoos. She's a member of the Andrea Line. That's one of the twelve ruling lines of the Singularity. Children in those lines are hidden away until they're adults.

"No one really knows what goes on with any of our rulers, but it's safe to say that they don't want their members to fall into the hands of their enemies. In this case, quite literally. If they're shooting, that means they've decided that she has to be eliminated. They won't stop coming."

"Then it's doubly important that we get away with her," Grace said firmly. "I'm going to be asking a lot more questions when we get to *Bright Passage*, but I want you to put aside the ill will you have toward the ruling caste of the Singularity. Until I say differently, this child is going to be treated as a prisoner."

"Even the laws of your empire say that she's not a prisoner," he argued as they ran. "She's a genie, as you call them. A being designed and grown from a genetic template. According to Imperial law, she's not a person, she's property."

"What? That's *bullshit*."

"It's true," he insisted. "I'm sure it's a legal fiction designed to outrage the Singularity, but those laws are real."

The idea of someone being owned sickened her. Still, that law gave her a way to bring the girl with them and to protect her, even from her own people.

"If she's property, then I claim her as my booty."

"Your what?" Kayden asked incredulously. "What's booty?"

"I don't have time to argue about this," she said as she ran past where the lead elements were guarding a connecting corridor. "Shut up and do what I'm telling you to do."

At that moment, the marines behind the fleeing group opened fire. She didn't have access to the standard marine tactical net, but the mercenary armor did let her see what was going on through small windows on her HUD.

The ambush that she'd set up had been quite effective. The group behind them wouldn't be bothering anyone else. That didn't mean that they were out of danger, though.

One of the marines in the front shouted a warning over the tactical net about an ambush ahead of them. The warning was immediately followed up by the attackers opening fire on them from a cross corridor.

The lead marine—Anne Marie Scott—stood her ground, firing to buy time for the rest of the squad to take what cover they could. The woman started backing up even as flechettes ricocheted off her armor in bright flashes, but she was far too close to the enemy.

"Advance," Grace ordered, and spun to protect the girl with her body.

Flechettes slammed into her, and her armor began to degrade as she struggled to get the child's limbs out of the line of fire. Alerts flared to life on her HUD, and she felt a stabbing pain in her upper back.

Her implants reported that the injury wasn't deep, so it had to be a shard of her armor. She rotated as much as she could to get the compromised area out of the line of fire but kept shielding the girl.

Even with her back turned, she could see her people moving up to support the now-wounded Scott through her HUD. That meant she also saw someone on the enemy side throw a grenade around the corner and toward her people.

Scott snatched the grenade out of the air as it tried to sail past her, clutching it to her chest and hunching over to protect her squamates just a single moment before she vanished in a ball of superheated plasma.

The woman's body disintegrated but lasted just long enough to channel the destructive energy away from the squad. It was still enough to send them all staggering, but no one else was killed.

Anne Marie's final act of bravery had saved them all.

The squad didn't hesitate to capitalize on their second chance and rushed the side corridor. Someone on their side threw a grenade of their own, and that ended the ambush once and for all.

The blast that had vaporized Scott had left a hole in the plascrete that revealed the rock of the asteroid itself, but Grace managed to get around it. It tore at her heart that there was nothing left of her dead marine to bring home. All they'd be able to take with them were memories of her life and of her sacrifice.

There was no time to grieve. She had to save the rest of her people first. There would be time for tears, toasts, and memories later.

"How did they know we were here?" she demanded.

Kayden blinked at her and then stared at the girl. He pulled a band off her wrist and hurled it to the deck before crushing it under his boot.

"That had to have had a tracker in it," he said. "Now they won't be able to find us again, but they obviously know that we're down here. Please, Grace, leave the girl behind. They'll never stop hunting her."

"We've killed everyone in both groups. When the asteroid blows up, they won't know what happened. Maybe they'll think that their people killed her."

"And maybe pigs will fly."

Ignoring his cynicism, Grace signaled Gomez as they ran. "How long until the cargo is loaded?"

"Fifteen minutes, LT. It's going to take us at least ten to get there if we maintain a good lookout for other ambushes."

"Be ready to cut the cargo feed as soon as I give you the word. Whatever we've got, that's what we've got."

She opened a channel to Na. She didn't use a burst transmission this time since she needed real-time feedback. The encryption was going to have to be good enough.

"Na, this is Tolliver. We've come under attack. What's your status?"

"We've got the fusion plant booby-trapped, but somebody on the outside sent an override and started a self-destruction timer of their own before we'd fully isolated the damned thing. It's going to blow in just over half an hour.

"We tried to get into the communications system and warn people to evacuate, but they're locked down. We're withdrawing, and I suggest you expedite."

"Crap," Grace said. "You're going to have to get out of the orbital the same way you came in. We'll pick you up."

"Copy that."

Grace killed the channel and called Anders.

"We're coming in hot. We've run into enemy security and have casualties. Team Two will be exfiltrating the way they entered. Be ready to undock as soon as we get there. The countdown to Code Omega is thirty minutes."

"Isn't that a little sooner than planned? What about the civilians?"

"Something is going on, and they've decided to blow the station on their own. We're locked out of the com system. So far as we know, there's no warning to evacuate."

"Crap. Hurry up, and we'll have medics standing by."

Grace killed the com without responding. This was going to be *very* tight.

"Gomez, are you still in the cargo control system?"

"I can be."

"See if you can worm into the general com system. If so, have Kayden broadcast an evacuation order with the correct time to detonation."

"On it."

A minute later, concealed speakers overhead came to life, and she heard Kayden's voice ordering people to evacuate in the tongue. Warning them that the fusion plant was going to blow. Then an automated countdown began.

Perhaps that had something to do with why they made it to the cargo bay without running into anyone else. Gomez was a little off, as it had taken them almost twelve minutes to get there.

It only took Grace a few seconds to retrieve a rescue ball from one of the lockers outside the cargo bay. She stuffed the now unconscious girl into it and strapped her to the outside of her armor as her people crammed into the airlock. Sixty seconds later, they were in the cargo bay.

They ignored their thruster packs and headed directly to the open hatch, where they could see *Bright Passage* on the spar just outside, cargo containers still being loaded as they ran.

She reached the edge, judged the distance, and jumped with a bit more energy than she'd intended. Once she was in motion, she was committed, but her jump was good. She was able to spin in place using the microthrusters built into the armor itself and landed on her feet, her knees buckling to mostly absorb the impact. Her magnetic boots locked on before she could bounce off, and she was quickly making her way toward the now-open airlock on their ship.

They were going to have to get out of there fast, because no one wanted to be close by when a fusion plant exploded. She'd already lost one person, and she didn't want to lose any more.

"What's our time, Gomez?" she demanded as the squad crammed into the airlock.

"Sixteen minutes and thirteen seconds."

"Where are we on cargo?" she asked as the airlock on the false container cycled.

"The final two containers are already being loaded, so we can't save any time there. Sixty seconds until we can undock."

The Fleet medics had a team waiting inside the airlock. Grace handed the rescue ball to them.

"The girl fell onto us from a height of at least several levels. Keep her secure and treat her as an injured prisoner."

"Yes, ma'am," one of the medics said as they started extracting the girl from the rescue ball and assessing her condition.

Grace raced to the com panel and called the bridge. Anders answered.

"What's our status?" she demanded.

"Loaded and moving. There are a lot of ships leaving the transshipment center, so we have good cover. Na and her people are in space, and we'll pick them up in five minutes. Then we'll boost as they get into the ship."

"I'll come up and brief you now."

"Looking forward to it. I'm sorry about your marine."

"Me, too. Tolliver out."

That done, she headed for the bridge. There wouldn't be time to tell them about the complications with the child, but she could at least oversee getting the last of her people picked up.

16

One Twenty-Four awoke in pain, unsure of where she was. The last thing she remembered was falling into darkness. Her head, left arm, and ribs hurt so badly that she could barely think.

She was in an unfamiliar place, lying on a table with a man and woman she didn't recognize looming large over her. She shrank back from them, uncertain of who they were or their intentions.

The man said something, but the words had no meaning. She couldn't even comprehend what his intent might be because she'd never heard anything like it before. It was gibberish.

One Twenty-Four had no idea how this could be possible. Were there other languages inside the Singularity that Keeper hadn't taught them? She'd only heard a conversation between Keeper and people outside the crèche one time, and that had been to the guards that worked for the crèche. She'd understood that.

Perhaps what they'd been speaking all along was a secret language used inside the crèche or within the Andrea Line.

When it became apparent that she couldn't understand what he was saying, the man went to a panel on the wall and spoke into it. After a few minutes, a woman entered the room.

One Twenty-Four studied her as carefully as she could through the blinding haze of pain inside her skull. She was tall, taller than Keeper. She was also muscular, her skin was a dark brown, and her hair was a deep black.

She wasn't certain, but she thought the woman looked tired. Worn out as though she'd been exercising or studying some extremely difficult math problems.

The woman stepped over the table and looked down at One Twenty-Four, her expression guardedly friendly. "My name is Grace Tolliver. You're safe here."

One Twenty-Four wasn't sure what surprised her more: the fact that the woman could speak the language of the crèche—if that was what she'd really been speaking—or the fact that she spoke it so *poorly*.

It took all of One Twenty-Four's limited ability to concentrate to make certain that she could actually understand what the woman was saying.

"Where am I?" One Twenty-Four asked slowly. "Who are you? Do you work for the crèche?"

The woman shook her head. "I don't work for the crèche. In fact, I have no idea what a crèche is. Before I explain who I am, I need to know who was trying to kill you."

The memories of what had happened came flooding back. How Thirty-One had thrown her into the darkness beyond the hatch. How she'd fallen for a seeming eternity and crashed into something at the bottom.

Suddenly panicked, she reached for her injured arm, ignoring the stab of pain in it. She had to get rid of the wristband, or they'd track her.

But the wristband was gone.

"I had a wristband," she said hurriedly. "The guards can track it."

"It's gone," the woman said gently. "They can't get to you here. You're safe. Now, tell me what happened and why they wanted to kill you."

"One of my line sibs betrayed me. She pushed me into the darkness, and I fell. She wanted to kill me, and I suppose she's succeeded."

The woman scowled. "Why would she do that, and why would anyone shoot a child?"

"Because the Line cannot allow us to be captured by our enemies. If the Empire were to get their hands on us, they would do terrible things to us. Unthinkable things."

"Like what?"

One Twenty-Four felt her eyes narrow. "Surely, you know. They see the uplifted lines as things to be studied and eradicated. They would dissect me, study every portion of my insides until they understood how I worked, and then dispose of my remains. We're not people to them."

The woman shook her head and sighed. "I think both sides of this fight have some misunderstandings that they'll have to overcome if they're ever to have peace.

"My name is Grace Tolliver. My people and I have just conducted a raid on the transshipment center where we found you. Because your associates were trying to kill you, we took you with us when we left. You're on our ship, and we're headed back to the Empire."

For a moment, One Twenty-Four was sure that she'd misheard the woman. Then she gasped as horror flooded her. She had to get out of here.

She tried to rise from the table, but the woman put a hand on her shoulder to stop her. One Twenty-Four pulled the woman's hand away, causing pain to flash across her face.

Before she could rise, the other two people were on her, holding her down as she thrashed wildly. Even if she'd known how to fight, she'd have been at a severe disadvantage with her injuries. They pinned her to the table as she wailed in terror.

The woman leaned over her. "You don't have to fight us. You're under my protection, and I won't allow anyone to harm you. You have my word. These people are doctors. You were injured in the fall, and they're trying to care for you. Stop fighting us."

"How can this be?" One Twenty-Four whispered as she stilled. "This isn't possible."

"It is. We don't want to hurt you, but they'll have to strap you down to keep you from further injuring yourself. You don't know me, but I'm asking you to trust me. Let the doctors help you."

What should she do? Was it her duty to fight? Did she still have an obligation as an outcast?

One Twenty-Four just didn't know enough about the situation, and she couldn't fight effectively. Perhaps she should wait for a better time to escape if she decided that she should. As it was, her own people would kill her on sight. Death awaited her no matter what she did, so why was she fighting so hard?

She tried not to shake in terror. "My name is One Twenty-Four, and I'm a child of the Andrea Line. Or I was. Now that I'm gone, they'll kill me as soon as they find me. If, of course, they find me before you have the opportunity to do so."

The woman looked down at her for a few moments and then stepped back, rubbing her wrist where One Twenty-Four had grabbed it. "The only way to change your mind is to give you time to understand who we really are. I have to go talk to the rest of our leaders, but I'll be back. Please, these people only want to heal you. Don't attack them."

What was it the woman had said? "You have my word."

Whatever word that might be. Did she have her own word? What might it be?

The woman narrowed her eyes in a way that reminded One Twenty-Four of Keeper. "That's a promise among my people. If you break it, others will doubt your word in the future. Stay true to it. I'll be back shortly. I'll also send someone to keep an eye on you."

With that, the woman turned and exited the room.

One Twenty-Four supposed it made no difference if she allowed the doctors to do as they would. If they were going to cut her apart, there was nothing she could do to stop them. She'd just hope that the end wouldn't be too painful.

* * *

GRACE MADE her way back to the container where the marines had stored their gear. Now that they'd successfully picked up the rest of the platoon, she was finally beginning to unwind.

The timing had been tight. There'd been less than eight minutes left by the time they'd retrieved Na and the rest. Far too close for her taste.

They'd raced away from the transshipment center as quickly as they could, and she'd watched in horror from the bridge as the place exploded, destroying a lot of ships that still hadn't gotten clear of the blast radius.

She didn't know how many people had died, but it had to have been a lot. The only solace she had was that it hadn't been her or her people that had done this. The Singularity had. Once again, they'd shown their true colors.

That last thought made her feel guilty. Someone had shown their true colors, true, but she couldn't paint the entire Singularity with too broad a brush. The perpetrators had to be the same people that had sent armed guards to murder a child. What kind of monsters did that?

The rage that thought shot through her made her pause and take a deep breath. Whoever they were, she'd likely never get her hands on them. If she did, she wasn't sure that the rules of war would save them from her retribution.

Yet her side bore some responsibility for the bad blood. She thought back to all the talk she'd been part of, the disdain and disgust she'd used when talking about the people of the Singularity. Her view of them had to be slanted, but she'd let her feelings pass by without much conscious scrutiny.

The fact that the girl had thought that nothing but death awaited her made Grace want to retch. She'd *never* be part of something like that, but she probably wouldn't have to look too far to find someone who relished the idea.

She had some hard thinking ahead.

She resumed walking and cornered Na as soon as she was in the container. "How's the platoon?"

"We've got a few injuries, but nothing life threatening," her second said. "Other than Scott, we all made it out."

Grace heard the sorrow in the other woman's voice, but Na's expression never wavered. She was an Imperial Marine. Grief didn't stop them from doing their duty.

"She died as a marine, saving her comrades," Grace agreed. "Sometimes, a death that means something is the only reward we get in our line of work. What kind of injuries do we have?"

"Mostly flechette hits that chewed up that mercenary armor. Basically, shrapnel wounds. A few got actual flechette penetration, but nothing fatal. The medics checked everyone out and said they'd live. Turn around."

Grace frowned. "What?"

"I saw your armor. Someone shot the hell out of your back. Let me make sure you're not bleeding out. That would look bad on my next efficiency report."

"I probably caught some shrapnel, but I'm not bleeding out."

Na raised a single eyebrow and made a circling motion with her finger.

Giving in to the inevitable, Grace turned her back to the NCO and started to unseal the skinsuit. As a marine, she'd long ago lost any hint of body modesty. When it came time to don armor, there was no time to be sensitive. There was nothing sexual about duty-related nudity.

The other woman didn't bother trying to get her skinsuit off. Being much more direct, she pulled her marine knife and used its almost monomolecular edge to cut the back of the skinsuit away.

Then she hissed. "You're all chewed up. No serious bleeding, but you've got armor fragments in there. Maybe even a flechette that lost most of its velocity, since you're still alive. How did they manage to shoot you in the back? Running from danger isn't your style."

"I'll get it looked at as soon as I take care of the postcombat briefing. I got shot in the back because I had a little girl in my arms. Better me than her."

Na grunted her agreement. "I heard something about that. It takes a lot of guts to take hits like that to shield an enemy civilian. So, how did it happen?"

"She literally fell on us as we were making our escape. She's maybe eleven or twelve, and a member of their ruling caste. She has full-face tattoos and said her name was One Twenty-Four of the Andrea Line. I'm not sure why she had a number rather than a name.

"Kayden told me that I should've left her behind. He told me that I couldn't keep her as a prisoner because the Empire doesn't see genetically modified people like her as human by law.

"Speaking of Kayden, where is he?"

Na shrugged as she grabbed a medical kit. "He's in his quarters back in the engineering section. I gather being shot at wasn't on his bucket list. I secured his stunner.

"He's probably cleaning up and decompressing. He might also be supremely pissed that you didn't listen to him about the girl."

"Perfect."

Grace grimaced as she stripped out of the ruined skinsuit and allowed Na to clean off the worst of the blood.

"That law is a legal fiction to stick a finger in the eye of the Singularity, but he's right," Grace admitted. "Legally, that girl is nothing but a thing. So, to make sure that she stays alive, I've declared her as my booty."

Na stopped cleaning and leaned around Grace's torso to look at her face, her expression one of incredulity. "Seriously? You're going to own a person?"

"No," Grace said, shaking her head firmly. "That's as much a legal fiction as the law itself. I'm doing this to protect her from having somebody in Imperial Intelligence decide that maybe dissecting her is a great idea after all.

"Which, by the way, is what she thinks is going to happen to her. She's certain that the Empire is going to butcher her at the earliest opportunity so that they can figure out how she works. I heard it from her own very lips when I saw her in the medical center."

"That's complete and utter bullshit, ma'am," Na said as she got back to work. "She's not an enemy combatant."

"Still, she's bound to have critical intelligence that we'll need to extract from her. How are you going to balance what duty requires while keeping somebody like her safe? Hell, it's not like she's a pair of boots. Even if you won that fight, where would you keep her?

"It's not exactly like you can have a child wandering around in a duty area. We're Imperial Marines. What we do isn't safe for regular civilians, much less a child."

Grace nodded. "I'm wondering all that and more. The first thing that I'm going to have to deal with is the fact that some people on this ship aren't going to be happy about what I've done. I don't know who they are yet, but I'm confident that there's going to be someone who's convinced that I've lost my mind.

"I want to ask you directly. Do *you* have a problem with what I'm doing? No judgment from me if you have reservations, but I need to know that you have my back."

"I'll back your play, ma'am," Na said immediately, not pausing as she cleaned Grace's wounds. "The fact that you have to do this makes me sick."

Na finished her work and grabbed a new skinsuit for Grace, handing it to her and starting to clean up the supplies she'd used in treating Grace.

"It might even be someone inside the platoon," the NCO admitted. "I'll talk with them and find out if anyone has a problem. If they do, I'll address it."

The finality of her tone made it clear that she'd address it firmly, too. Good. Grace loved her people and didn't like putting them in this kind of bind, but she wasn't going to compromise when it came to the girl.

"Thanks," Grace said as she slid her legs into the new skinsuit. "I'll talk to Anders and Kyle about her. It's going to be their responsibility to deal with any problems on the crew side. I want you to post two marines outside the medical center. I don't want them intimidating the girl, so make sure that they're unarmored and only have sidearms. Women only to start with.

"They'll be there to make sure the girl doesn't get into trouble because she's from the Singularity, so make *sure* that they don't have any axes to grind. We can hate the Singularity, and we can hate what it's done to the Corps, but we can't let that bleed over onto a civilian child. Nits do not make lice, Sergeant. Is that absolutely clear?"

Na braced. "Clear, Lieutenant. I'll make damn sure that none of our marines is going to give this girl any problems. I'll talk to her as well. The best way we can prove that we aren't monsters is to be decent with her."

Grace nodded, satisfied. She grimaced in pain as she slid her arms into the sleeves of her new skinsuit and made a promise to herself to see the medics as soon as she'd finished a longer briefing for Anders and Kyle.

"I'll leave you to it, then," Grace said. "We're going to have a ceremony for Scott tonight. We can't lay her to rest, and we have no uniforms, but we'll do her full honors."

"We'll be ready, ma'am," Na assured her. "Go make sure those Fleet slackers don't screw this up."

Grace laughed and headed toward the passageway. Neither officer was going to be happy about what she'd done, but she was sure they wouldn't take it out on a child. The crew might have other ideas, though, and that was what she needed to make sure they were watching for.

And, of course, they'd want to take full advantage of the briefing to chew her ass off for putting them in a difficult spot.

Time to face the music.

17

One Twenty-Four eventually decided that the people seeing to her injuries weren't going to harm her. It wasn't anything they said, since they couldn't speak a language that she understood, but they only seemed to be trying to mend her hurts.

She'd never been injured so badly before and so took some interest in what they were doing to her. The various medical processes that she'd gone through in the crèche were very different than what was happening now.

They had portable devices that they ran over her body that made her feel somewhat better, and then one of them spoke with her briefly and prepared to put a somatic stimulator on her head. She drew back a little at that, and the person spoke in a reassuring tone. She finally allowed it.

When she woke, she didn't feel any pain. Whatever had been wrong with her had been fully healed.

Her situation had also changed. The two people that had healed her were gone. In their place was a short woman with black hair and a dark-skinned face. Her eyes looked strange. There was something odd about how her tear ducts were shaped.

After a moment, she decided that the woman was pretty. She wasn't certain what criteria she'd used to come to that conclusion, but it felt right.

The woman was seated in a chair near the portable bed on which One Twenty-Four lay. She wore some type of dark gray coverall. On her hip, One Twenty-Four saw that there was a weapon of some kind.

The woman said nothing while One Twenty-Four examined her. And even when she'd finished, the woman just sat there with a slight smile on her face. She seemed content to wait and see what One Twenty-Four did.

With the woman's seeming invitation, One Twenty-Four sat up and examined her curiously for a little while. Once she felt as if she'd learned what she could by sight, she spoke.

"Who are you? My name is One Twenty-Four."

The woman's smiled grew slightly. "My name is Na Fei. My given name is Fei, and I don't mind if you use it. In my culture, the family name comes first. So, where Grace Tolliver's given name comes first, mine comes at the end.

"If that's confusing, I won't be offended if you make a mistake. A lot of people do, and one gets used to it. I work with Grace as her second-in-command. She asked me to keep an eye on you and to make certain that you felt safe. Do you mind if I ask you a few questions?"

Fei didn't make her feel as threatened as the others had. One Twenty-Four decided that her desire to know more outweighed her concerns about cooperating with these people. After all, she was their prisoner.

They wouldn't stop asking her questions. If she could learn things herself, perhaps that was the best that could be hoped for.

Also, the woman's command of her language was much better than the first woman's. She still pronounced things oddly, but her meaning was clear enough.

"Am I allowed to ask questions as well?"

The woman nodded. "Certainly. Why don't we trade? I'll even allow you to ask first. Ask whatever you like, and I'll answer if I can. If it's on a subject that I'm not allowed to speak of, I'll tell you so and allow you to ask another question. The same applies to you. Is that acceptable?"

One Twenty-Four thought about it and nodded. "I can't think of anything that I know that I won't answer a question about. I grew up in the crèche. It's not like I know very much about the Singularity or their secrets."

She studied the woman. "You said that you're the other woman's second-in-command. What does that mean? Were you here to attack the crèche?"

The woman's smile widened slightly. "That's actually two questions, but since they're related, I'll allow it. Grace and I were once Imperial Marines. My rank was sergeant, and I was a noncommissioned officer. Grace was the commanding officer of my platoon and a lieutenant. The Imperial Marines use that kind of rank structure so that people with varying levels of authority know where they fall inside the hierarchy.

"As a sergeant, I had a number of others that I commanded, but I took my orders from the lieutenant. She, in turn, took orders from those in higher-ranking positions. And at the very top, our senior officers took orders from the civilian government of the Empire. If one goes up far enough, one finds the emperor.

"As for what we were doing here, are you aware that the Singularity and the Empire are in a state of not-quite-war where they send raiding parties back and forth across each other's borders?"

One Twenty-Four shook her head. "I know that the Empire is our enemy, and I know the consequences of falling into your hands, but I don't know anything about the fighting itself."

She felt her eyes narrow slightly. "You speak of your membership in the Imperial Marines, yet you're here working together. If you brought others you once worked with on this raid, then I begin to doubt part of your story. It seems too coincidental."

The woman shook her head. "You're entirely too clever. Yes, our departure from the Imperial Marines is a fiction. I'll explain that in a moment.

"Now, I understand that you're worried about your future. Grace has ordered that no harm befall you, and that's why I'm here. In addition to myself, I have two marines stationed outside this compartment to make sure that there are no disturbances.

"No one is going to offer you harm on this ship, and Grace is taking every step that she can to make certain that nothing untoward comes to pass. Personally, I don't believe that anything terrible would happen to you in any case.

"I'm sorry, but you're a victim of propaganda. Will there be people inside the Empire that hate you just for being from the Singularity? Sadly, yes. There are people like that everywhere. I suspect the same is true inside the Singularity.

"Having captured you puts Grace into an unusual position. I think she's come up with a creative way to deal with most objections to what she's done, and I believe that she can protect you. I and the rest of the marines will endeavor to assist her in doing so.

"As far as the raids that brought us here, we were instructed to leave our positions as Imperial Marines so that we could act on our own and strike at the Singularity. The Singularity does much the same to the Empire.

"Both governments know that's a legal fiction, but it allows us to have a level of conflict that doesn't rise to full-scale war. Our mission was to find an economic or military target inside the Singularity and destroy it. We happened to choose the cargo transshipment center where we found you.

"To say that the mission went somewhat awry from there would be an understatement. We planned to overload the fusion plant and destroy the transshipment center after allowing everyone to leave, but someone overrode what we were attempting to do and set a shorter destruction time.

"They also didn't want anyone to know that the end was coming and blocked us from making a public warning until far too late. So, while we escaped, many others did not. That saddens me, because such a loss of life was not in our plans."

One Twenty-Four felt a wave of cold wash through her.

"I know what happened," she said in a whisper. "Keeper gave the order. She instructed everything to self-destruct and gave a time limit of forty-five minutes. Then we were supposed to escape.

"I suppose the rest of them did. Keeper wouldn't have set a timer that was too short. I wonder if they think that I'm dead now."

The other woman watched her for a few moments and nodded. "Perhaps. That may be a question that you never get an answer to. Who is this Keeper?"

"Keeper is… Keeper. She is an adult of the Andrea Line. It was her duty to teach us the ways of the Line and to make certain that only those who met expectations survived the crèche."

The woman's expression froze. "What do you mean by 'survived the crèche'?"

"Each of the twelve lines in the ruling caste decants children every six years. Each line is responsible for educating and training their own children. Those that are unsuitable or fail to meet expectations are culled."

Fei's eyes narrowed dangerously. "Are you telling me that they killed children?"

"Isn't it my turn to ask a question?"

"If you'll humor me, I'll let you ask two for each one I take out of turn. I need to understand what you're telling me before I can move on."

One Twenty-Four shrugged. "Yes. Of the two hundred children that started in the crèche in my cycle, we were down to one hundred and twenty-one when this happened. Keeper told us that perhaps only seventy would live to see the end of our training. Those that are culled are immediately killed, though we never had to watch."

The woman's calm expression remained frozen, but One Twenty-Four could see rage burning in her eyes. Fei remained still for a few moments and then stood, turning her back to One Twenty-Four and staring at the wall. Her shoulders seemed tight, and her hand rested on her weapon.

"Are you going to kill me now?" One Twenty-Four asked, her voice a little unsteady despite her resolve to accept whatever came with a brave face.

The woman turned slowly back toward her, taking her hand off her weapon. She crouched down in front of One Twenty-Four and took her trembling hands into her own.

"No, Little One," she said softly. "I will *never* allow anyone to hurt you. You have my word on that."

"I don't know what that means, but Grace said that I shouldn't give my word—whatever word that is—unless I mean to do what I say. That it was important."

"She's right. It's a promise, not a specific word, and one should always keep their promises. No one on this ship will hurt you. If they were to try, I'd hurt them first, and I'm *very* good at hurting people that deserve it.

"I'm sorry that you grew up in a place where such horror was acceptable. The Empire isn't like that, and hearing that you had to suffer under that kind of dystopian nightmare makes me want to find this Keeper and introduce her to my fist. Many, many times."

The idea of someone striking Keeper was so strange that One Twenty-Four couldn't wrap her mind around it. "She's very strong, and she knows how to fight. She started teaching us how to fight one another. That's how I broke Thirty-One's nose and turned our rivalry into something more. That's why Thirty-One threw me into the darkness and why Keeper sent the guards to kill me."

Fei took a deep breath and resumed her seat, her hands in her lap. "Are all the children in the crèche physically the same? Is that why you use numbers?"

"We're all grown from the same template, so we're exactly the same. The only way we could tell one of us from another was via our wristbands. Except for Thirty-One. Her nose was different after I hit her. I'm not sure why, but that made me happy. Keeper is what we will grow into."

The woman shook her head. "I can assure you that you won't grow into a monster like that. Grace will make sure of that, and we marines will help her. You can't see that what was done to you is wrong because you don't have the proper frame of reference yet, but you will one day. Then you'll be as pissed off as I am."

"Pissed off? You use such strange words. By the way, you speak the language of the crèche much better than Grace. She's… hard to understand."

Fei chuckled. "That's the language used in the Singularity. It's simply called 'the tongue.' We all know it, to a degree, and she just needs to practice. Perhaps you can help her, and we can teach you to speak Standard, the language used in the Empire."

One Twenty-Four felt herself smile. "I didn't know it had a name. Thank you for telling me. I like learning new things. A lot of the lessons in the crèche were about subjects that I didn't like. That's why Keeper warned me that I had to stop daydreaming, or I'd be culled. What happens if I don't like something now?"

"Then we'll talk about it. Not everything one must do is fun, but if you know *why* you need to learn it, that makes it easier. You're young, so you don't have to worry about that for a while yet.

"I know I owe you some questions, but I want to ask a few more. Were you born with those marks on your face? And what do they mean?"

"That's two questions, but since they're related, I'll allow it," One Twenty-Four said with a smile, using the woman's words against her. She didn't know why, but she liked Fei and felt safe around her.

"I only got my caste tattoos a few months ago. They hurt so bad, but we couldn't move, or they'd go on wrong. We lost six of my line sibs that day. It was just before Keeper gave us the shots to activate our sexual organs, though I'm still not sure which ones they are. We needed them to grow breasts and mature."

Fei smiled slightly. "I have some knowledge of sexual organs, so I can probably give you a basic rundown. Why did you need shots?"

"Because members of the ruling caste are designed to be sterile. I don't know why we needed something to start producing the hormones needed to make us develop, but we did. Our brains, mostly, but Keeper said that we would also one day be able to use our bodies to make men in the other lines more amenable to doing what we wanted. That came later, and she was going to train us on how to do it."

Once again, anger flashed in the woman's eyes. "That sounds a little too… hands-on for my taste. We also have sexual education, but it's more of an intellectual exercise. We leave our kids to explore the specifics with people of their choice when they're ready."

Just then, One Twenty-Four's stomach rumbled.

"Are you hungry?" Fei asked. "I can have something brought in, and we can eat while we talk."

One Twenty-Four nodded. "It's been a long time since I ate. I'd like that."

"Then that's what we'll do," Fei declared as she rose to her feet and walked over to the hatch. She opened it, revealing a woman on the other side in the same kind of coveralls.

"Jane, could you head down to the mess and grab something for the two of us?"

The woman looked at One Twenty-Four, her expression blank. "Sure. Anything in particular?"

"Whatever they have handy. Thanks."

One Twenty-Four knew instinctively that the second woman didn't like her. Perhaps she even hated her. Her sense of safety evaporated.

Fei closed the hatch and started back toward One Twenty-Four but came to an abrupt halt. "What's wrong?"

"That woman. She hates me. I can see it in how she looked at me."

Fei considered her for a moment and then pulled her chair over beside One Twenty-Four. "It's complicated. She doesn't hate you, specifically, but she lost a friend when we rescued you. Anne Marie Scott was her name, and she died when those guards came after you."

"How?"

"The details aren't important," Fei said. "What matters is that she gave her life to save her friends and you."

"Me?" One Twenty-Four blinked in surprise. "Why would she die for a stranger? An enemy."

"Because she was an Imperial Marine, and we don't let people kill children. Grace had you in her arms and allowed someone to shoot her in the back to keep you from harm. It's who we are and what we do.

"Jane understands that, but she lost a close friend. It's going to take her a while to get over that. She doesn't hate you, but she wants to hurt the ones that killed her friend. She wants that *very* badly, and so do I. Those people are not you, so you don't need to fear us."

"Grace… what? I still don't understand."

"Maybe one day, you will. All you need to know right now is that we're going to keep you safe. Grace is going to talk with you in more detail soon. Right now, she's making sure that we get out of the Singularity alive."

One Twenty-Four had never been more confused in her life. Why would enemies do that for her?

After a few moments, she simply shrugged. It would either become clear in time, or it wouldn't. For right now, she'd just accept what Fei said. Grace was doing what she could for her, for her own reasons, and she'd explain why when she was ready.

For now, One Twenty-Four would eat with Fei and find out more about her captors. She really wanted to know more about the Imperial Marines and why they did what they did. She owed them a debt, it seemed. Only time would tell if she could ever repay it.

18

"Have you lost your ever-loving mind?" Kyle demanded from across the wardroom table. Anders, seated beside him, didn't look much happier.

Grace had just told them everything that had happened during the mission, the final straw being her claiming the girl as her booty.

She'd expected the executive officer's explosion. In fact, he'd only be the first of many. And, conceivably, one of the milder cases.

What she didn't know how to predict was Anders's response. As their captain, he was going to set the tone for the rest of the Fleet personnel. If she had to fight with anyone about this, it was going to be him.

And that was a fight she *had* to win if she wanted to secure the girl's place as a person in Imperial society. Not as something that could be destroyed at someone else's whim.

That seemed counterintuitive, since she was claiming that One Twenty-Four was property, but she had to make sure the spooks didn't disappear the girl first. Then she could set up for the fight ahead of her.

Grace didn't directly answer Kyle's outburst, instead focusing her attention on Anders. She raised one eyebrow, prompting him for a response.

The man grimaced slightly. "I understand why you're doing this, but I have to question if you've considered all the implications. Imperial Intelligence is going to want that girl in their custody. They're going to want to drain her dry of every bit of information they can get.

"She's a member of the ruling caste of the Singularity. Even as a child, she has to know some juicy secrets. And then there are the negative repercussions to having her. It took everything I had to keep Kayden out of this meeting. The man is frothing at the mouth about how dangerous the girl is.

"And you know what? He's right. If the Singularity knew that we had her in our possession, they'd send everything they have after us. Even the border of the Empire probably wouldn't protect us."

Grace shrugged. "If they knew where we were right now, they'd send everything they had after us anyway. We just blew up one of their transshipment centers, or at least we were going to before they blew it up themselves. By the way, does that still count? Inquiring minds want to know."

Anders sighed and rubbed his eyes. "Our actions prompted them to blow it up, and we'd already booby-trapped their fusion plant, so I'd say yes. Our mission was a complete and utter win, beyond our wildest dreams of success, since we pulled this girl out of there.

"But I have to agree with Kyle. Making her your booty is going to open up a world of hurt for you personally. You're going to come under immense pressure to backtrack. Hell, they'll probably just take the girl anyway. I can't stress how much this could harm your career."

"They'll get her over my dead body," Grace said flatly. "From what I can see, she was raised in some kind of dystopian hellhole. Na sent me a brief update via one of the guards, using her implants so that the girl couldn't overhear.

"Fei is the most even-tempered, levelheaded NCO that I've ever served with, and she's so pissed off right now that she wants to break things and kill people. I've never heard her drop an F-bomb until today. She's frothing.

"And to be clear, I want to get information from the girl, too. I just want to be a damned human being while I do it. She's terrified that the Empire will dissect her. That we're going to butcher her to find out how she was made. Do you really think that someone in Imperial Intelligence won't be tempted?"

Neither Anders or Kyle said a word, confirming her guess about their opinion of the spooks. Imperial Intelligence was good at what they did, but no one could call their methods clean.

"The way that this was explained to me, not even the emperor can gainsay what I've chosen to seize," Grace said when they offered nothing more. "Imperial law states that a genetically engineered being is property. I've verified that. The doctor is running some tests, but Kayden has already confirmed that the ruling caste is made up of twelve lines of what amounts to designed beings. Genies.

"Even though that law is undoubtedly meant to be a poke in the eye for the Singularity, it means that—technically—she's property. And, as any good lawyer will tell you, technicalities are the very soul of the law.

"So, who's going to tell the emperor that his edict doesn't carry any weight? Is it going to be you, Kyle? Are you going to tell the emperor that you can flout his word?"

The man looked like he wanted to bang his head on the table. He settled for pulling at his long red hair.

"I want to," the man finally admitted. "Do you realize what you're doing? That girl *isn't* a human being. They cooked her up in a lab somewhere. That means that there are other people *exactly like her* running around. How can you see a copy as a person?"

"How can you not?" Grace put her hands on her hips and, even though she was sitting, she hoped it carried her defiance across to the man. "Are you really going to get into nature versus nurture with me? Just because someone designed her genes doesn't preclude her from being human. For God's sake, she's a twelve-year-old child.

"The people that left the Empire to form the Singularity were just as human as you and I. From what Kayden says, their base caste still is. I'll bet you any amount of money that that girl is fully human once you get down to the genetic level.

"I have no idea what all they've tweaked, other than perhaps clean out recessive genes and modify certain attributes, but they didn't change very much, because she's still *human*. It doesn't take a genius to figure that out. We have eyes, don't we?"

She said the words, but some doubt crept into her mind as she unconsciously rubbed her wrist. The girl had been *strong*. Maybe even stronger than Grace. That had to be intentional. What other tweaks were they going to find before this was all over?

"I honestly don't know what to think," Anders said with a shake of his head. "I'm going to have to think long and hard about this before I decide how I feel. What I do know is that it's not a decision I have any control over.

"Imperial law says the girl is property. The emperor said you can seize whatever property you want. Right or wrong, you're the girl's owner, and you're responsible for her. I can't change that.

"But is that really who you are? Are you the kind of person that owns another human being, even for altruistic reasons? Can you live with that?"

It was Grace's turn to sigh and shrug. "She needs someone to watch out for her. I'm not her owner, I'm her guardian, and that's how I'm going to look at this. I thought I was going to go back into the Imperial Marines when we got home, but now I'm really wondering. I didn't plan for this, so I don't know how things will play out.

"What I am sure of is that there are going to be plenty of people that feel just like Kyle does. Or worse. Maybe even on this ship."

She stared at the executive officer. "Tell me honestly, do you hate the girl? Do you blame her for what the Singularity has done?"

The other man opened his mouth to say something but then stopped and closed it again. After taking a deep breath, he shrugged.

"I sort of do, but even I get how stupid that sounds. Does that mean I want to hurt her? Hell, no, but I'm still not a fan of your decision. She needs to go to Imperial Intelligence for debriefing, and then they can decide what needs to be done about her.

"With you keeping her, what kind of life does that mean for her? Your career is over. Even if there were no reprisals against you personally—which I certainly wouldn't count on—do you dare take your eyes off her? If you go on a mission, what happens without you around to protect her?"

Grace deflated a little. "I don't know. My mother could help, but I have no idea how she's going to feel about this either. I don't want to stop being a marine, but I probably don't have much choice. I hope we had a good haul, because I might be living in an armed compound somewhere in the woods on some backwater world."

Anders snorted. "No worries there. I haven't had time to more than skim what Kayden grabbed, but there's a lot of rare elements used in flip drive construction. He also got some finished drives, which are even more valuable. Your share is going to keep you sitting pretty for as long as you like."

He drummed his fingers against the tabletop. "You're right about some people hating that girl with all their hearts and souls. Some of them might even be on board *Bright Passage* right now. It's probably a good thing that you've got your marines guarding her.

"But how sure are you that your own people aren't going to take out the loss of your marine on that girl? The people chasing her were the ones that killed Scott. They're hurting and mad. In their place, I'd be considering some payback."

Grace shook her head. "Na is watching the girl, and I trust her judgment. She won't put people on that duty that would be a threat to the girl. At this point, she's as much an advocate for the girl as I am. That'll work for now.

"We've got a few weeks until we get out of the Singularity. All this could be moot, since we might be dead before we get back to the Empire, so let's not borrow trouble. I'm sure that we're going to have plenty enough of it when we get back home."

Anders chuckled darkly. "You are, anyway. So, if you don't go back into Imperial service, what will you do?"

Grace shrugged. "I honestly have no idea. This was never on my scanners. I had my future all mapped out, and now this girl has changed everything. You might end up being right. Imperial Intelligence might take her away, no matter what the emperor says. Or the emperor might change his mind.

"I'll have to play this day by day and see what happens. And while

I do, we're going to have to deal with the fact that we have someone on this ship that needs both protecting and assessing.

"I don't want to be the only one talking to her. We should all have our turns discussing things with her and trying to figure out what we can about where she came from and who she is. We may never get a better chance to understand the inner workings of the Singularity."

"Maybe later," Anders said. "We don't want to overwhelm her. For the moment, I think you and Sergeant Na are the best people to interface with her.

"But once we do have a chance to start talking to her, maybe she'll change your mind about her, Alan. Kids are kids, after all. They have a way of getting inside your heads."

"I hope she does," the man admitted. "I already feel like a jackass about how I feel. I'll talk to the crew and start finding out if we have any brewing problems. The last thing we want is a confrontation between the crew and the marines."

Anders nodded. "Good. Pass along that I'll come down like the wrath of God on anyone that offers this child so much as a harsh word. If they can't do that, then they need to tell us so that we can make accommodations before the fact."

He rubbed his face and looked at Grace. "I don't envy the position you've put yourself in, Grace, but I'm going to back your play. It's the right one to make, and I'll do my part to shield that girl from the worst elements in the Empire. Better get a big compound. I might need a place to crash."

She laughed. "You'll be able to afford your own compound. Maybe we could be neighbors. Are you in, Kyle?"

The redheaded man sighed and nodded. "God save me, I suppose I am. So, now that we've all screwed up our careers, I think we should focus on the next target. It's one flip from the next system and should be straightforward. We have more than enough concealed missiles to take it out.

"But once we do, our anonymity is gone. Hell, I'm surprised we got out of Aponte without being ID'd as the bad guys. Outright shooting up an orbital is going to blow our cover for sure."

"We'll just have to hope that Kayden is right about there being no organized defensive force close by," Anders said. "If there is, we'll pass it by."

He turned to Grace. "Will there be a ceremony for Scott? If so, do you mind if we attend?"

"We'd be happy to have you both," she said. "It's going to be a sad time, and more friends will only lighten the load. If there's nothing else, I need to have a long conversation with One Twenty-Four. And I need to have my back looked at."

Anders frowned. "Do we have to keep calling her by a number? That's too damned impersonal for my taste. And what's wrong with your back? I didn't see anything about an injury in the report. Dammit, you should've gone there first."

"Duty before pain," she said as she rose from her seat. "Na cleaned it up enough for me to get by. Thank you for your support, gentlemen. I deeply appreciate it."

As she left the wardroom and headed for the medical center, she felt relieved. That had gone better than she'd had any right to hope. She might just pull this off—if she could convince the girl that she really was on her side.

19

One Twenty-Four spoke with Fei for at least an hour before the hatch opened and admitted Grace. She was accompanied by the man who'd treated One Twenty-Four's injuries when they'd captured her.

Fei rose smoothly to her feet. "It was a pleasure meeting you, Little One. I look forward to getting to know you better. I'll see you again soon."

One Twenty-Four felt a little lost now that the woman was leaving. She really was the only one of her captors that she knew.

Yes, she'd met Grace, but she barely knew the woman. They'd only spoken for a couple of minutes.

She certainly didn't know the man. One Twenty-Four still wasn't certain exactly what he was. She had much learning to do.

To her surprise, Grace went over to another one of the tables and hopped up to sit on it so that the man could begin helping her to undo the top of her coveralls. The woman winced a little as the man helped her to get her arms free.

That left her, surprisingly, without clothes on her torso.

She'd never seen Keeper in anything other than her uniform, so she had only an approximate understanding of what breasts were supposed to look like. Grace's were larger than she suspected Keeper's were, so that meant that they'd be larger than hers, once she matured.

The woman's breasts were more aesthetically pleasing than she'd imagined. They weren't simple mounds of flesh like she'd imagined. They had curves and a visible firmness that she hadn't expected.

"You can come over," Grace said. "I don't bite."

The sound of the woman's voice, and her terrible accent, startled One Twenty-Four out of her reverie. Then the meaning of what she'd said came through, and she frowned.

"Do people in the Empire bite others? Why?"

Grace chuckled. "It's just an old saying. I'm not quite certain where it came from. It means that I'm not going to cause you any harm. Just come over, and we'll talk while Gerard works on me."

One Twenty-Four hopped off the bed she'd been sitting on and picked up the chair that Fei had been using earlier. She carried it over close to the other table and was about to sit when she wondered what the man was doing.

Then she remembered that Fei had said Grace had been injured while defending her. Rather than sitting, she walked around to the back of the bed and gasped when she saw the bloody mess that was Grace's upper back.

Something had cut it up and punctured it in numerous places. There was dried blood and red, angry flesh everywhere. She'd never seen an injury so grievous before.

"Someone shot you," she said. "Fei said that happened while you carried me from where I fell. I should thank you for your kindness, though I'm still uncertain whether this is kindness at all. Why did you risk your life for me?"

"You think so poorly of us," Grace said as the man began using a set of tweezers to pick bits of debris out of the injury. "I protected you because I'd rather die than allow someone to hurt a child. I'm not alone in feeling that way. You don't really know us yet, so I hope that, in time, you'll come to accept that some of us don't mean you harm."

"Meaning that others do," One Twenty-Four countered, her gaze still captivated by what the man was doing.

"That remains yet to be seen. Will some people dislike your

presence? Yes. Will some dislike you simply because of where you came from? Absolutely. Will they hate you personally? I hope not."

"What happens to me now?" One Twenty-Four asked quietly. "Will Gerard hurt me?"

"No. Other than the fact that he's a gentle soul, he's a doctor. They take an oath as healers to cause no harm, and he embodies it. You're perfectly safe with him."

She watched the man pull bits of debris from Grace's back and marveled that the woman's expression remained serene. It had to hurt, but the woman allowed no hint that pain to reach her expression.

One Twenty-Four stepped closer and looked at the debris that the man—Gerard—was placing into a small pan. Most of it seemed to be small chunks of some material that she wasn't familiar with, but one of the objects was different.

She reached down and picked up a small metal dart whose tip was severely deformed. It was made of an unknown material and seemed to be designed to fly through the air. It looked dangerous.

"What is this?" she asked, frowning up at Grace.

"It's called a flechette," the woman said. "The weapons we carry and the ones carried by the guards who came after you fire those at very high velocity. That one struck the armor on my back, penetrated a weak spot, and went to me. Hopefully, there aren't too many more of those in there."

One Twenty-Four set the flechette down. The idea of intentionally killing someone was strange. Yes, she'd fantasized about ending Thirty-One, but this felt different. Where her anger with Thirty-One came from something between the two of them, weapons that killed with these small pieces of metal seemed much more… impersonal.

"And this is because you're an Imperial Marine? Fei tried to tell me you were no longer marines, but I can see that that is a fiction. So, you fight others because your emperor says you must? I suppose the Singularity has troops that do so as well, but I've only met the crèche guards. I don't really understand how any of that works."

The man—Gerard—finished pulling the bits of debris out of Grace's back and then used a liquid to clean it. Once that was done, he picked up the same handheld device that he'd waved over One Twenty-Four to make her pain go away, and she watched, fascinated, as the flesh of Grace's back began to heal before her very eyes. In just a couple of minutes, it was as if it had never been damaged at all.

Once that was done, Grace slid her arms back into the sleeves of her coveralls and shrugged them back over her shoulders before sealing it. She turned her head toward the man and said something in their language. Standard, Fei had called it.

He said something in return, nodded toward One Twenty-Four, and left the room.

When the two of them were alone, One Twenty-Four wondered what the woman was going to do next. This moment felt charged with energy, as if something were going to happen, but she didn't know what.

"Fei said that you've already eaten," Grace said. "If you're still hungry, we can get more."

One Twenty-Four frowned. "When did she say that? Or did Jane tell you?"

"It was Fei. She sent a message to me through our implants. Jane did pass it along, since this ship doesn't have the right kind of repeaters to do so."

"Implants?" One Twenty-Four asked. "What are those?"

The woman considered her for a moment before speaking. "The Singularity has prohibitions against putting machines inside the body, so you won't like the answer. In the Empire, we have small, purpose-built computers inside our heads. They allow us to remotely control equipment and process information. Also, they allow nonverbal communication."

One Twenty-Four's frown deepened. "*That* is forbidden, and we've been taught that it was a poor attempt to compensate for your random genetics, attempting to approximate the pinnacle of human development as embodied by the ruling caste in the Singularity. It sounds… disgusting."

"Opinions vary," the woman said. "In point of fact, implants were in use before the founders of the Singularity were thrown out of the Empire. Since the ruling caste didn't exist then, I could argue that the

Singularity was trying to match the performance we'd already achieved through genetic manipulation.

"But I don't want to argue about it. You asked a question, and I answered it. I'm only informing, not persuading."

"My education isn't complete," One Twenty-Four admitted, "but Keeper was quite clear that the ruling caste came first."

"Then she was either mistaken or basing her conclusion on bad information. Propaganda can be used on people inside a society, too. Or she might have known better and said that anyway."

"Perhaps it was you who was misled."

Grace smiled slightly. "I don't think so, but I'll allow for the possibility. We can argue philosophy later. Are you still hungry?"

"What is philosophy?"

"That's the field of study revolving around questions about existence, values, reason, and knowledge. If I remember correctly, it came about in ancient Greece, long before humans ventured away from Terra.

"I'm no philosopher myself, but it involves posing questions that have to be resolved via critical discussion and rational arguments. A systematic presentation of the argument is also important."

One Twenty-Four blinked at the woman. She'd never heard of anything even remotely like that.

"In the crèche, we are told how the universe works, and we learn to test things like chemistry, but nothing like philosophy. Keeper wouldn't like any of us disagreeing with her."

"Then that's another difference between her and me. I don't mind a reasoned discussion when I have time. Still, you'll probably want to do some research before you argue your point. Food?"

One Twenty-Four shook her head. "I'm not hungry. I'm worried about what will happen to me next. Everything has changed, and I don't like it."

"No one likes change, particularly when they don't have any control over it. Stability is important. Would you like to go see where you'll be staying?"

The idea of new living accommodations hadn't occurred to One Twenty-Four. Obviously, she wouldn't be sleeping in the crèche anymore. The crèche didn't even exist. Though, she supposed, the crèche was the people rather than the place.

That was when it hit her. She wasn't going to be sleeping with her line sibs anymore. She'd never see any them again. She was alone.

This was the first time in her life that she had even *been* alone. She knew no one here. No one was like her. Suddenly, she was terrified.

Her throat felt constricted, and she swallowed, trying to clear it. "What happens to me now?"

"Nothing bad," the woman said as she stood and held out her hand. "I'll take you someplace where you can sleep if you're tired. If not, we can talk. We've got a lot to discuss.

"I know almost nothing about you, but I'm responsible for you in ways that neither of us understands yet. The two of us are going to have to get to know one another a lot better.

"I'm glad you feel comfortable calling Fei by her given name. She's showing you how much she likes you by allowing it. I'd like you to call me Grace for the same reason."

"Very well. Do you have a sequence number? I didn't ask Fei. I suppose not. Is that what the family name is for?"

"Right," the woman said with a nod of her head. "Also, while this may seem strange, I don't feel like calling you One Twenty-Four. It makes you sound like you're interchangeable with the others.

"You're not. You're a person in your own right. Andrea is a pretty name, though. May I call you that?"

"I suppose that would be like my family name in the Singularity. It will feel odd, but if that's what you wish to call me, I cannot stop you."

"The Imperial Marines have a long tradition of calling people by their family names, so it's more natural than you'd guess. Come on."

Grace led her into the corridor, and One Twenty-Four saw two female marines there. One was Jane, and the other was unknown to her.

The second woman was short and thick, with brown hair cut close to the scalp. It amazed her how everyone looked so different from one another.

Each wore the same coveralls that Grace and Fei had worn. Were they uniforms? She wasn't sure.

The two women fell in behind them, and, together, they walked down the corridor and passed several others who were dressed in other kinds of clothes. All of them stared at One Twenty-Four as if they'd never seen anything like her.

Maybe they hadn't.

They went up a ladder and onto another level. Then they stopped by a hatch seemingly at random.

"This compartment is next door to mine," Grace said, gesturing to the next hatch. She pressed the control, and the hatch in front of them slid open.

The room inside was small. Barely two meters by two. It had two bunks that folded out from the wall, one above the other. It also had a desk and chair, as well as a hatch set further into the room.

"The head—the bathroom—is on the other side of that hatch. We'll share it, as it opens into my room, as well. You can come to see me that way if you'd like. That way, the guards can just keep an eye on the corridor without disturbing you."

The room dismayed her, though she'd known she wouldn't have others around her. She'd never felt so isolated.

"Does it become easier once one has lived alone for a while?" she asked.

"Did you live with other girls like yourself?"

"Yes. We shared a dorm. We were never alone. Only Keeper spent time apart from us."

"Good, then you know that it can be normal. I know this will feel scary, but you'll get used to it. If you feel lonely, you can come to me at any time—day or night—and we'll talk."

Grace stepped inside the small room and took a seat in the chair. "Come on in. This will be your home for at least the next few weeks, so you'll want to get used to it.

"There's a built-in computer that you can use to watch entertainment or read a book. We have slates that work for that as well. I'll make sure that you get one.

"Meanwhile, I need to explain the situation in which we find ourselves. It's unusual and will pose problems for us both."

One Twenty-Four walked into the room, hardly noticing when the hatch slid shut behind her. She sat down on the lower bunk and rested her hands in her lap.

"I'm ready."

"I very much doubt that," Grace said, "but we'll make do. I'll bet you're tougher than you imagine. We'll find a way through this together."

One Twenty-Four wanted to cry, but showing weakness wasn't the way of the crèche. She might not belong there anymore, but it would always be a part of her.

"I'm ready," she repeated. "As ready as I can be."

And she was. She had to be.

20

Grace stayed with Andrea longer than she'd planned, but she needed to get used to spending time with the girl. She was going to be at her side a lot over the next decade, at least. It still hadn't really sunk in yet just how big a commitment she'd made.

Children had never been on her scanners. She was an Imperial Marine, and that meant no time for even a steady partner, much less offspring. This was more daunting than anything she'd ever faced before, including death.

It was easy to like Andrea because she was so earnest. And she was so *curious*. Every time they'd start discussing something about the Empire or Singularity, questions would come up, and the conversation would go down a rabbit hole.

Grace didn't mind that. It was all part of the journey of becoming comfortable with one another. It also illuminated the seemingly intentional holes in the girl's education.

Just like she'd never been exposed to the concept of philosophy, Andrea's understanding of history as it pertained to the Empire, or even the Singularity, was skewed. The girl had never questioned how it came to be that so many people served the ruling caste or how there was no mobility between the various strata in her society.

It was simply just how things were done. Just as expulsion from the crèche and death were the price of failure for her and her line sibs.

Concealing her anger at that had been impossible, so she hadn't tried. Andrea already knew how furious the crèche and Keeper had made Na, and that was good enough for Grace, too. She'd explain why killing little girls was evil after they had a bit more of a connection and had built some trust.

What had happened—and was no doubt still happening to other children in the various crèches inside the Singularity—appalled and infuriated her, but Andrea didn't even know how to process a world where her upbringing didn't reflect reality.

The girl had asked Na if she was going to kill her because she'd thought she'd asked the wrong question. It made Grace want to drop a few F-bombs herself. And to kill the people responsible, though she'd likely never have the chance.

Na would almost certainly stay in the Corps, but Anders was right about Grace's career being over, one way or the other. She'd never have a chance to strike at the people who'd done this.

It made her see red every time the girl explained how the crèche system worked. She'd read her share of dystopian novels over the years, and if anything, the crèche was worse.

Talk about being under pressure. Andrea had to perform every single day, because failure meant expulsion and execution. The girl had seen dozens of her line sibs—girls exactly like her—taken away never to return.

She was terrified of making a mistake, and that engendered a level of caution in everything she did. It was going to take time and patience to change how Andrea saw the world.

Bold action wasn't the girl's strong point and might never be.

It was also going to take them time to adjust to just how different their worldviews really were. Grace had understood that everybody viewed the universe around them through the prism of their own experiences. That was brought home now by just how differently Andrea saw *everything*.

People, in particular, were a wonder to the girl. She'd only ever met those who were genetically identical to her. Grace couldn't imagine living around hundreds of other girls, all exactly the same age, that looked precisely like she did.

Grace had grown up wishing for a sister but not a dorm full of identical twins. That was just plain creepy.

The idea of all of those little girls being forced to behave exactly like one another sickened her. Individuality in the crèche wasn't just frowned upon, it was crushed. The Andrea Line believed in hardline conformity, at least during the formative years.

Oddly, Grace had a lot of familiarity with that type of training, because it was how the Imperial Marines trained their recruits. They brought them in from whatever world they came from, whatever society in which they'd been raised, and then broke their individuality.

They remade each and every recruit into the same mold. Each got the same training, ate the same foods, and behaved in the same manner. Any hint of resistance was met with overwhelming verbal force.

There was nothing quite like having a group of drill instructors swarm you, screaming at you because you'd done something wrong. That type of example certainly made an impression on the recruits. No one wanted to draw that kind of attention to themselves, so they complied and were molded.

It was only once the recruits had finished their basic training that they were allowed to begin displaying individuality again. The Corps had built a new foundation upon which the marine would then grow.

It never failed to amaze her how much the world had changed after she'd gone through basic training. In actuality, the world hadn't changed: she had. Even now, many years later, she still saw the world as a marine and could hardly remember who she'd been before she'd joined the Corps.

It was as if Andrea had been born into a sadistic form of basic training, a brutal existence where not only were you yelled at, you might have your throat slit.

Of course, Grace had no idea how wayward children in the crèche were euthanized, and—thankfully—neither did Andrea. Probably something coldly clinical, since that seemed to fit the personality for this Keeper.

The very idea that human beings were discarded because they couldn't conform or excel enraged Grace. She understood exactly why Fei was so angry, because she was too.

Sadly, there was absolutely nothing that either one of them could do about it. The Singularity might be smaller than the Empire, but a war between the two would result in uncounted deaths on both sides.

No, all she could do was make a difference for one person: Andrea.

When she finally excused herself, Grace worried that the girl wasn't going to be able to adjust to what amounted to solitary confinement and instructed the marines on guard to check in with her every once in a while, just to make sure that she was doing okay. She'd do the same before she went to bed.

Grace went back to her quarters and spent the time required to get herself into the mental headspace she'd need for the ceremony to come. Saying goodbye to fallen friends never came easily, and it shouldn't. Every loss should be a tragedy. If it ever became routine or casual, she'd have lost her humanity.

This wasn't the first time that she'd had to preside over a service like this and far from the only time she'd participated in one. She knew what to do. Tonight had to be a celebration of Anne Marie's life.

Since they were on this particular mission, none of them had uniforms, so they'd wear their skinsuits. Now that the raid had taken place, unless they came across a situation where they had to pretend to be regular crew, they'd go ahead and wear them. That would make getting into armor quicker.

When she arrived at the container with the airlock, she found all her people gathered and ready. Joining them were Jay Anders and Alan Kyle. Also present was Kayden Harmon. She wasn't sure why the man was there, but she didn't find it objectionable.

An empty equipment crate would be jettisoned to represent Anne Marie's casket. That would help them all find closure.

She walked up to a small lectern that somebody had put together in front of the makeshift casket and faced her people. She could see sorrow and anger on their faces. She knew that her face would mirror those same emotions if she allowed it to.

That was what grief was: rage at the universe for taking someone that you cared about. She wouldn't feed their anger today. There wouldn't be any patriotic speeches calling for bloody retribution. Today, they would remember their departed friend.

"When I first met Anne Marie, it was a little bit uncomfortable," Grace said without preamble. "I'd just been appointed to command the platoon and was taking an unofficial tour of the barracks.

"She and I actually bumped into one another at the entrance to the head, and she almost spilled a bucket of soapy water all over me. She was taking extra care to make sure that our area was prepared for inspection, even though I had no intention of doing one.

"Anne Marie just wanted to go the extra kilometer to make sure that everything was perfect. That's the kind of person she was. She'd literally give someone the shirt off of her back if they needed it. She was selfless, brave, and I will miss her."

Grace paused to let that sink in. "I don't want us to be thinking about how the Singularity took her from us, though. Today isn't about them, it's about her. What I'd like each of you to do is to share a memory of our friend so that we can all grieve for what we've lost."

She walked to the back of the room to stand beside Anders and Kyle as each of her marines came forward and told a story. Some of them were funny, some of them were gut-wrenchingly sad. All of them were personal and reflected their profound loss.

Grace shed her tears unabashedly. This wasn't the time to suppress her emotions. Marines didn't hide their grief for the loss of a friend.

The last marine to speak was Na. She told a story about how she'd set up a birthday surprise for a friend, but the gift had failed to arrive on time. Anne Marie had somehow, miraculously, found a replacement gift, and the party went off without a hitch.

It was only later that Na had discovered the gift had actually been one of Anne Marie's prized possessions. She'd given it away so that someone else could get pleasure from it.

Na didn't cry when she told her story. Her face was instead flat with controlled anger. Everyone could see that she still wanted to see someone bleed for this.

She was far from alone in that.

Grace was about to go back to the lectern and close the ceremony when Kayden stepped forward to replace Na. The move shocked her. Hell, every single one of the reasons there could be for him to do this was wrong for this crowd.

She started forward to cut him off, but Anders blocked her with his arm. "Let him speak. You need to hear what he has to say. You all do."

Uncertain that she agreed, she backed down and waited. Na was right there. She wouldn't allow things to get out of hand. Hopefully.

Kayden placed his hands on the lectern and looked out over the marines. "I know that many of you don't want to hear what I have to say because I'm from the Singularity, but you need to. I hate the rulers of the Singularity even more than you do, so please open your hearts to my words.

"I ask you not to lay blame for this on the regular people inside the Singularity. They're slaves in everything but name. Reserve your rage for the ruling caste and their willing lackeys. I know that goes against the rules Lieutenant Tolliver laid out, but it had to be said.

"With that out of the way, I need to acknowledge that Anne Marie Scott gave her life for me. I didn't know her. I'd never even *spoken* to her, but she selflessly sacrificed her life so that I might live.

"Oh, I'm sure she didn't do it for me. She gave her life for you, her friends and comrades, and that's as it should be. One shouldn't squander one's life for a stranger, yet to my utter incomprehension, that's what she did.

"Even more confounding to me, she traded her life for that of a member of the ruling caste of the Singularity."

His hands tightened on the lectern, and his expression hardened. "You can't begin to understand how much I loathe each and every one of those people. The things that they've done to our society, to our people, are unimaginable. I've been inside the Empire, so I know just how bad we have it, even though many of our people don't understand what they're missing.

"But Anne Marie Scott's sacrifice has made me reconsider some core truths that I've held for all my life. If she could sacrifice herself for someone that she didn't know, for someone that might one day have grown up to be one of the cold bastards that rule over untold trillions of people, then perhaps I'm being too hard.

"I told Lieutenant Tolliver during the retreat to the ship that she should leave the child behind to be killed. That the girl was going to grow up to be a monster.

"When she didn't, I became angry, but now that I've had time to reflect on Anne Marie Scott's sacrifice, I realized that I was just as locked into the caste of my birth as the girl was in hers before we found her.

"If people are the sum of their experiences, then it's never really too late to change. Or perhaps it might be better said that one's life can be changed for the better if those around them are willing to give them a chance so long as they're willing to try.

"Anne Marie Scott's sacrifice demands something equivalent from me. A life for a life. Isn't that how it used to be on old Terra? If someone saved your life, you owed them one in return.

"Sadly, since I can't save Anne Marie's life, I must pay it forward, as the saying goes. I'll speak with Lieutenant Tolliver when we're done here and offer my services with the girl. Perhaps I can help shape her into someone that might one day redeem Anne Marie's sacrifice.

"I ask you to look inside yourselves and find the courage and strength to help me. Together, perhaps we can make a difference for this one child. Will you help me? For Anne Marie?"

Na stepped forward without hesitation. "Changing this girl's future will be a powerful blow against the Singularity. I pledge myself to this task, and you have my full support, heart and soul."

Almost as one, the rest of the marines stepped forward and pledged their support as well, their expressions hardening with resolve.

Grace wept.

She'd expected grudging cooperation from her people but now knew that they'd watch over the girl as if she were their personal charge. In effect, they'd be her godparents, uncles, and aunts.

It took Grace a moment to realize that Kayden had stepped away from the lectern before she got herself moving to take his place. She took a deep breath and wiped the tears from her face.

"I also pledge myself," she said quietly. "You've probably heard that I've claimed the girl as my booty to keep her from falling into the hands of Imperial Intelligence and anyone else that just wants to use her. I wanted to salvage a life for her, but I wasn't sure how to do it.

"With your help, I believe that we can do it together. Let's make the redemption of this child Anne Marie's legacy. Let's make her a person that Anne Marie would be proud of.

"Not for the child's sake—even though it will be—but for Anne Marie's, so that her death means more than saving any single one of us. Perhaps Andrea can do something in the future that will save many more marines than we could ever dream possible.

"Thank you for your support and for coming to listen to your comrades' memories of Anne Marie. We're all going to miss her, but now we know how to honor her. Now, let us inter her into the deep where she can rest in peace, her work and pain finally done."

Six of the marines stepped forward and grabbed the crate by the rails, hoisting it and marching step by step into the airlock. They set it down and retreated to the ranks.

"Attention on deck!" Na shouted. "Present... arms!"

They all saluted, their right fists to their chest as the interior hatch slid closed. The airlock was already programmed to open without bleeding off the atmosphere. Moments later, the outer hatch opened at maximum speed, and the crate went flying into the eternal darkness of space.

They all held their salutes until the outer hatch once more slid closed.

Grace dropped her salute and turned to face her marines. "Double alcohol rations are authorized, but don't forget that we're still in enemy space. Dismissed."

The marines filed out of the compartment in small groups, talking amongst themselves. Anders and Kyle nodded toward her and followed them out. That left her alone with Kayden Harmon.

"I had no idea that you were going to say that, much less that you'd feel that way," she said as she walked up to him. "I'm not certain what to say."

"I didn't do it for you or the child," he said quietly. "I really didn't even do it for Anne Marie Scott. I did it for myself.

"Hate is something that festers inside you, that eats at who you are to the point where you lose yourself. Hope is the opposite of hate. By dedicating myself to helping this child, I regain a little bit of my soul.

"That doesn't mean that this will be easy. I might understand the girl better than you, but I'm going to come into this with preconceptions developed over a lifetime in the Singularity. I know what kind of person she'd have become if we hadn't intervened, but I don't really understand who she might be now that we've broken the cycle."

"None of us do," Grace said. "We can't imagine who someone else is going to become based on what we've experienced in our own lives. We can provide her with examples of the kind of person she could aspire to be, and we just have to hope that she can exceed our expectations.

"I'll accept your help, but we're all going to have to be careful that our preconceptions don't get in the way of helping her. We're also going to have to fight against Andrea's own preconceptions."

"If the leaders of the Andrea Line knew that we were calling her that, they'd be outraged," he said with a chuckle. "I heartily approve. I'll need to speak to her."

Grace nodded. "You do, but she's had a very rough day. Rougher than ours. She needs sleep and a little time to adjust. We can meet for breakfast.

"I'd also ask you to be patient with her. She's a curious child, but she's got some landmines that her education and indoctrination have laid for her. I don't think you understand how rough she's had it."

The man nodded slowly. "Perhaps not. The two of us should have dinner so that you can explain the challenges we're going to face. I need to be prepared so that I can provide support for both you and the girl."

She smiled at him even as her eyes narrowed. "I think you just want to have dinner with me."

"Of course I do," he said with a grin. "What kind of ladies' man would I be if I didn't use our exigent circumstances to get such a beautiful woman all to myself?"

She laughed and shook her head. "You really are horrible. Come on. Let's go have that dinner, but remember to keep your hands to yourself."

"I'll be the perfect gentleman," he said with a slight bow. "Tonight, in any case. In the future, who knows?"

"We'll see. Since you're buying, I demand the good stuff."

He laughed. "Have you met our cook? Raymond is a delightful man, but one mustn't set their expectations too high. To make up for the inevitable disappointment, I'll bring a bottle of something I've been saving for a special occasion."

"Lead on, Macduff."

The corner of his mouth twitched. "I believe that Macbeth said, 'Lay on, Macduff.' It's an invitation to start fighting, or so I understand, so that's in effect the opposite of what I had in mind."

"Only if you do it wrong."

He laughed, and the two of them headed for the galley.

Grace found herself looking forward to the meal. Since he wasn't getting his bottle of drink now, she suspected he'd invite her back to his compartment for a nightcap.

She was inclined to accept his offer. The death of her friend made her want to reaffirm that she was alive, and she liked Kayden. It might add some complication to their lives, but what was life without a dash of spice?

21

_____

With the marine guards and Grace checking on her at various points during the evening, One Twenty-Four found it difficult to go to sleep. Her mind continued to race across unsure ground.

Even if she had been inclined to sleep, it was too quiet. There were none of the sounds that one would expect when living in the crèche.

She felt so alone.

And then there were the unfamiliar sounds. The various mechanical noises seemed constant, but sometimes there were other sounds that she couldn't decipher. Were they normal? What made them? Those thoughts kept her staring up at the bunk above her for long hours.

She didn't recall falling asleep but woke to a loud knock at the hatch leading to the bathroom—or the head, as Grace had called it.

The name seemed nonsensical. Why not the tail? That would at least account for most of what took place in the room.

Whatever it was called, it had amazed One Twenty-Four. Everything was so small, seemingly designed for a single person.

Nothing in the crèche was designed for one person except the bunks. All showering and other activities took place in a group setting. That made the head feel even more alien than her quarters.

Just one more thing to adjust to.

When the knock repeated, One Twenty-Four sat up and rubbed her eyes. She was exhausted and ached all over. A lingering effect of her fall?

She took a deep breath and rose, making her way to the hatch. It was lockable from her side, but she'd decided that wasn't prudent. She was a prisoner, and a prisoner shouldn't act as if she were doing something that mandated closer scrutiny. Just as in the crèche, one had to behave as if one were being watched at all times.

In fact, she couldn't dismiss that possibility. There could be vid cameras hidden in her quarters, monitoring everything she did. For that matter, she wouldn't have been surprised if there had been some inside the crèche doing exactly the same thing.

Keeper always wanted to know what they were doing. Why should Grace be any different?

She opened the hatch and found her captor on the other side.

"I'm prepared," she said evenly.

"You don't look like you slept very well, which isn't surprising, I suppose," the woman ventured. "I hope that improves as you get used to us.

"Before we get breakfast, I think we need to see about getting you some new clothes. Those look like you slept in them, and they're also inappropriate for you now.

"I'm sorry, but that life is behind you, Andrea. We'll come up with something more suitable, though it will have to wait for a while. In the meantime, I'll bet we can get something rigged up for you to use on the ship."

One Twenty-Four blinked in surprise. She'd seen others wearing different kinds of clothing yesterday. She wasn't certain that any of the styles she'd seen actually appealed to her, but what did she know?

Not that her preferences mattered one way or another. If they said that the uniform of the crèche was inappropriate—and she supposed it was—she'd have to adjust to whatever they selected for her.

She nodded, accepting the inevitable. "I didn't sleep well. I kept thinking about… everything. Then I fell asleep before I could prepare for bed.

"I know that doesn't make much sense, as I should have prepared for bed first, but I couldn't seem to get my mind to work. Too much has changed in the last day, and I don't know how to compensate for it. I just don't have enough information."

The woman smiled at her. "We'll address some of that today. Come on."

Grace closed the hatch leading to the head and led her out of her compartment.

Two different marines stood outside the hatch to her quarters, both still women. The two examined her without bothering to hide the fact that they were doing so but fell in behind them as Grace led her to another part of the ship.

Since they were openly examining her, One Twenty-Four turned and walked backward to consider them in turn. Like the other marines she'd seen, these two seemed athletic and capable. Their eyes told a tale of experience.

In a way, their eyes were similar to Keeper's. They hinted at knowledge that she didn't have.

She was grateful that their gaze didn't seem hostile, but they were taking her in with a lot more interest than the first two marines had. It was if they were weighing her to determine if she was worthy of living. It was… unsettling.

Walking backward, she almost missed the turn that Grace made to take them into a side corridor but was able to adjust with only a single hiccup in her step as she resumed walking forward.

That pleased her. She'd always been agile and enjoyed the physical education class.

She wondered if there would be more training like that now that she was outside the crèche. What form would it take? She would have to ask if the time ever seemed appropriate to do so.

Grace led them to a small room whose hatch was open. Inside it, there was what appeared to be a concealed door that was wedged open. Interesting. Why hide this particular hatch?

The strange opening led into a long tube that fed deeper into the ship. Several side hatches came and went at uneven intervals. Most of them were closed, but several were not, and she saw men and women dressed in the same coveralls that Grace wore.

Their tasks seemed obscure, but they must serve a purpose. In one room in particular, she saw them working on weapons and armor. She knew that was what they were because they were similar to what the crèche guards had carried.

They finally arrived at a compartment where a familiar face awaited them. Fei stood with her arms crossed, leaning back against a table.

One Twenty-Four resisted the urge to go to the woman. Of all the people she'd met thus far, Fei made her feel the safest. That was undoubtedly an illusion, but it still made her feel better.

As if sensing her emotions, Fei squatted down and held out her arms. "Come here, Little One."

Unsure of why the woman was holding her arms out, One Twenty-Four walked over. She was shocked when the woman wrapped her arms around her and held her close to her body. She wasn't sure how to respond.

"What is this?" she asked, stiffening.

Fei turned her head so the two of them could see one another. "It's called a hug. When people like one another, they hug. This is my way of showing you that I'm happy to see you."

"Should I... hug you back?"

She'd never hugged anybody in her life. She had no idea what was going on, and her heart was racing.

"I'd like it if you did, but if you don't, I'll understand. It's undoubtedly going to take some time before you trust people enough to give just anyone a hug."

"I trust you," she declared. "At least as much as I trust anybody."

She slid her arms around the woman and squeezed her slightly. She didn't want to use too much of her strength, because Fei wasn't doing so. She tried to match the level of engagement that the other woman was using.

Her reaction appeared to be the correct one, because the other woman grinned and then stood. "Grace brought you here so that we can get you into something a little more suitable for use aboard a ship. Being marines, our options are fairly limited.

"We're going to fit you with a skinsuit similar to the ones we're wearing. It's a very versatile piece of clothing that will serve you well as general shipboard wear. They're also quite comfortable."

One Twenty-Four found herself frowning. "So, you mean the coveralls? We had to wear something similar when we were doing particular kinds of work that would get us dirty."

The woman nodded. "They're similar to coveralls, but not exactly the same. A skinsuit is something that can fit inside armor or a vacuum suit. In a pinch, you can go into space with one and be protected, though obviously your head would be exposed, and you couldn't breathe. It also acts as a basic set of armor, protecting as much as it can against damage.

"For example, say that you got into a knife fight while wearing a skinsuit. It's strong enough to blunt stabs and protect you from slices, at least for long enough to defend yourself."

One Twenty-Four blinked at that description. It seemed that fighting and the effects of combat were more prevalent in the lives of marines than she'd considered. There was nothing wrong with that. Everyone needed to serve a purpose.

She had absolutely no idea what her purpose would be now. Growing up, she'd known she'd either be one of the rulers of the Singularity, with everyone else following her directives, or she'd be dead. There had been no middle ground.

With her a prisoner of the Empire, she didn't know under what circumstances she'd be permitted to live or what tasks might be required of her. Now she might be in the servant class, or even lower in the hierarchy.

If, of course, the Empire had such hierarchies to begin with.

She'd discovered that her education in that respect had been lacking. She'd listened to what Grace had said about the Empire and decided that Keeper had given them flawed data about the other polity or had at least failed to mention certain details.

Keeper's understanding might even be completely incorrect in certain areas. More study was needed to be sure, and some direct observation.

She had only a child's education and was beginning to understand that her outlook on the world could be manipulated by the information she was given, as well as that which was withheld.

Interestingly, once she'd begun to use the available translation software to examine some of the books written in Imperial Standard that Grace had provided, she'd started getting information that was at odds with what she'd been taught. The data in the tongue matched what Keeper had said.

One or the other was definitely incorrect. Perhaps both. A deeper study would require her to develop actual skill at reading and speaking Standard. The process wouldn't be quick or easy, but it seemed mandatory to uncover the truth.

The woman had described hers as a much freer society than the Singularity, and based on the information that One Twenty-Four had read in the Imperial books, that seemed to be true.

In any case, she didn't have a choice about changing clothing. Grace had said that the crèche uniform was inappropriate, so she should feel honored that the marines were giving her something of theirs to wear.

"I'm sure that I'll get used to it," she said, inclining her head slightly toward Fei. "I don't pretend to know anything about fighting. Keeper had only just begun teaching us about hand-to-hand combat, and I wasn't very good at it.

"None of us were. It was never expected that we would come to blows with anyone else because we had guards to protect us, but she insisted that we fight one another to learn how incapable we were at it."

Fei's eyes narrowed. "She just pointed you towards one another and said fight? No training at all? You'll forgive me if I find that pathetic.

"If you're interested in learning more about fighting, I have some knowledge of the process and would be happy to educate you on the basics of how one goes into combat with another."

For the first time since she'd found herself in these unexpected circumstances, One Twenty-Four smiled. "If Grace allows me to do so, I would like to know more. I've felt helpless for so long."

The fact that it would allow her to bond with her captors also held merit. Keeper wouldn't approve, but that only made the moment feel sweeter. Keeper didn't rule her world anymore, and she'd do whatever was required to assure her survival.

Making new friends was the first step and one she was beginning to enjoy. Her world might come crashing down at some point shortly, but she was done letting uncertainty freeze her with fear.

22

———————

Smiling, Grace shook her head as she watched Andrea and Na interact. The sergeant had never struck her as potentially being anyone's aunt, but she certainly looked up to the role. She just had a certain way about herself that seemed to make Andrea trust her.

Grace didn't have any objection to the girl learning how to fight. It would also give her something to focus on other than her current circumstances.

"You wouldn't know it from the way she underplays her skills, but Fei is an extremely competent hand-to-hand fighter," Grace offered. "If you choose to take her up on her offer, pay very close attention, because you're not going to find many people more skilled at close-range fighting on this ship, or off it, for that matter. Teaching others to fight is one of her primary responsibilities."

Andrea nodded at that and turned back to face Na. "I would be honored. I don't know anything about what my future will hold, but having something that I can focus my attention on might help me better adjust to my new circumstances. Thank you, Fei."

The Asian woman smiled. "It will be my pleasure, but I'm not certain that you should thank me just yet. The training will not be easy. In fact, there are times when it's going to be painful and discouraging."

Andrea shrugged slightly. "The crèche taught me that there are painful things that either must be accepted or overcome."

Grace stepped over to stand beside Na. "That's not always true, but when it comes to hand-to-hand combat, you're right. Now, we're going to have to take off your uniform, and Fei will measure you. Once she has all the appropriate dimensions, she can tailor one of our skinsuits to fit you.

"It's going to be a little bit more involved than just wearing coveralls though. You're going to have to be shown how to fit the waste removal system. Basically, you're going to have to wear a catheter.

"Solid waste is more problematic, but the suit can handle isolating that if you really need to go. You'd be much better served if you use the bathroom before you put it on, though. That's a lot simpler. The systems are meant to handle issues like those when it's inconvenient to take a restroom break. Like in the middle of combat."

The girl frowned. "Is it absolutely necessary that I wear this… catheter?"

Grace shook her head. "No. In fact, I would suggest that you don't insert it unless you anticipate really needing it. Still, if you don't know how to fit it, you're going to be in a bind if you need to. While I could walk you through it, it might be best if Fei showed you what to do."

"I think you would be a better choice for this," Na disagreed. "As her guardian, it should be you who performs this instruction."

Grace was surprised at the other woman's quick rejection but nodded. "I suppose I can do it. The process isn't very complicated. I apologize now for any embarrassment or discomfort it causes you."

Both Grace and Na had instructed any number of marines—male and female—in the use of catheters. She'd never performed this task for someone so young and anticipated that it was going to be an embarrassing matter for the girl.

Her concern that Andrea would be self-conscious was unfounded. The girl stripped off her clothes without the least indication that she was bothered by public nudity. That was probably one of the side effects of growing up in a communal setting like she had.

Once Fei had tailored a skinsuit for her, Andrea began putting it on, and Grace instructed her on how to fit the catheter at the appropriate point in the process. It took a couple of tries before Andrea grasped the basics, but with a little bit of practice, Grace thought that she wouldn't have any difficulty with it.

Then she showed the girl how to change out the catheter tip. In an emergency, they could be sterilized, but it was best to simply dispose of used ones to avoid the chance of infection.

With that done, they helped Andrea finish donning the skinsuit.

Grace walked around her and eyed the fit critically before nodding in satisfaction. "Excellent. Fei, if you'd make another couple of suits, I think she'll be able to use these for the rest of the trip."

"I'll take care of it," Na said. "While I do that, you should probably explain to her what a guardian is and what her responsibility to you will be as your ward."

Grace still wasn't certain that she was ready to have that conversation, but Na was right. It needed to be done. In fact, the girl needed to understand exactly what her status was going to be inside the Empire. If, of course, this worked out anything like what she'd planned.

She took a deep breath and faced Andrea squarely. "It's important that you realize that some of what you've been told about the Empire is correct, even though it's been taken out of context. Imperial law states that a designed being like yourself is property.

"That was never meant to be something used against an actual individual, I think. It was enacted to enrage the ruling caste of the Singularity. In other words, it's more of a political ploy than a punishment intended for real people."

The girl frowned slightly. "I'm assuming that a law is something like the rules we lived under in the crèche. Intent doesn't mean anything, only compliance with the rule."

"Let me be absolutely clear about something," Grace said seriously. "No one is going to harm you. Everything you were told about somebody cutting you apart and experimenting on you, that is *never* going to happen. You have my word on that. If anybody means you mischief, it'll only happen over my dead body, and I'm *damned* hard to kill.

"When I agreed to come on this mission, I was told that I was required to seize a piece of property inside the Singularity to cement the ruse that I was a pirate. I'm going to use the technicalities of the law against those who would like to take you away and declare you as my booty."

Andrea's frown deepened. "What is… booty?"

Fei put a hand on the girl's shoulder. "Back in the old days on Terra, there were pirates. When one of them seized someone else's property, they called it booty. So, while the precise origin of the word is lost in the sands of time, we were issued what they call a Letter of Marque and Reprisal.

"Rather than being pirates, the Empire considers us privateers. It's a fine distinction that the Singularity wouldn't recognize, but it legally protects us from the consequences of the instructions we were given in the Empire once we get home.

"It's my understanding that the Singularity does something similar. That gives both sides a level of plausible deniability so that outright war doesn't break out.

"One of the end results of this is that the emperor has instructed that these pieces of property that we seize as our own personal booty belong to us and may not be disputed by anyone, not even the emperor himself.

"And that's how Grace is going to protect you. By declaring you as her property, she shields you from anyone else that might want to take custody of you. Under the law, they cannot."

Grace nodded. "Even though the Empire labels me as your owner, I see myself as your guardian. You are not my property. All of this is a legal fiction meant to protect you."

"How can I know that's true?" Andrea asked. "I don't know you. You could be telling me this to keep me calm until you hand me over to whatever butchers are going to cut me apart."

"Actions speak louder than words. I think the easiest way to show you how you're going to be treated is to let you make up your own mind about the situation that you're in. All I'm doing is telling you so that you'll know what I'm thinking.

"When I agreed to this mission, I became a private citizen and was promised that I could return to the Imperial Marines as soon as it was done. If, of course, I survived.

"With you as my booty, the career that I've worked so hard to build is gone. They're never going to allow me back into the Corps. I'm going to have to find a new way forward, and you're going to be a big part of it."

"First, why do you refer to the Imperial Marines as a dead body?"

The question startled Grace, and she almost laughed. "Sorry. The words sound similar in Standard but mean different things, and I mispronounced it in the tongue. In this case, 'Corps' refers to the marines as a military organization."

"Okay... So, why would the Imperial Marines not let you back in? That doesn't make any sense to me."

"There are several reasons. First, they're going to be upset that I've done this. They're going to apply a lot of pressure on me to change my mind. It's not going to work, and that'll make them even angrier.

"Second, as an Imperial Marine, there would be no place in my life for a child. It's a dangerous job, and any of us could die at any moment, just like Anne Marie Scott. I don't know if you remember her death, but we lost her while escaping from the station. You might've already been unconscious by then.

"So, the level of danger means that a marine really can't risk having a permanent relationship with anyone. Casual lovers are fine, but spouses are not. Neither are children. The risk of leaving them orphaned or widowed is just too high. It would be cruel of us to do that, and I won't be a party to it."

The girl stood silent for a few seconds. "I don't remember very much after I fell into the darkness. I'm sorry that someone became too close to you. The crèche taught me that it's unwise to allow others to be too close to you. It hurts when they are taken."

"I think you've learned the wrong lesson," Grace said as she squatted down beside the girl. "Life is fleeting. Treasure it while you can. Marines know that death might await us around any corner when we're on a mission. Things can go wrong, and you might have to make a choice that trades your life for someone else's.

"Anne Marie Scott offered up her life so that her friends and comrades could live. She didn't know you, but she traded her life for yours as well. That's part of what makes being a marine special.

"With a child as my responsibility, I don't have that luxury anymore. I've got to take care of you, and that's going to be my focus. That means that I can't be a marine anymore since I can't make those hard choices. In effect, I'm giving my life for yours right now, only I'm not dying.

"That stings a bit, but we'll be building a new life together. The two of us will figure out what we need to do.

"I'm not saying that it's going to be easy. I'm sure that there are going to be times when you hate me. I'm sure that there are going to be times when I want to pull my hair out. We'll get past them together."

Andrea nodded slowly. "I think I understand, and I'm willing to give you a chance to prove that you're telling the truth. I think I'd like to know more about this person who died for me.

"I've known line sibs who've died, though I was never there when it happened. They were always taken away and simply never returned. None of us would have considered exchanging our lives for any of them. It just wasn't done.

"I need to know more about the person who did that for me. I need to understand why she did it. Perhaps in doing so, I will understand the Empire and the Imperial Marines better."

"I'll explain it to you," Fei said. "I have helmet video of her death, though it's not pretty to watch. If you'd like to see it—and Grace approves—I'll show it to you."

"If Andrea wants to see it, then show it to her," Grace said. "She can handle it, I think. Now, we need to get something to eat. We're also going to meet someone special today. Someone from your society who's been working with us."

"You found someone inside the Singularity that was willing to work with you?" Andrea asked, sounding surprised. "I would've thought that the hatred between the Empire and the Singularity was too great for something like that."

Grace chuckled. "Remind me to explain to you how money can open doors. In a society like the Singularity—or the Empire for that matter—money talks. Not literally, but you'll find people willing to do just about anything if you have enough of it."

"Money? I don't understand what that is."

That turned Grace's chuckle into an outright laugh. "I think I'll leave explaining that to Kayden. He's the man who used to own this ship before the Empire bought it. He was a merchant inside the Singularity and worked with Imperial Intelligence to help us spy on your former people.

"He's a complicated man who has no love for the ruling caste, but he's made it clear that he wants to help you adjust to life outside of the Singularity. I'm not saying that it's going to be easy for either of you, but I ask that you give him a chance.

"He's going to explain how the ruling caste treats regular citizens of the Singularity. He comes from what you'd call the base caste. He doesn't have any tattoos like yours, and he knows the Singularity from the bottom up. He's traveled inside the Empire and knows what life there is like, too.

"If you can listen to what he's saying with an open mind, then I think there's a lot he has to teach you. He can show you how things are from both points of view. He can interpret for you, if you allow it."

"I'll try," Andrea declared. "I'd never met anyone from outside the crèche until yesterday, and I'm not sure why he would hate the ruling caste, but I want to understand. I'm beginning to get the feeling that I've been told lies my entire life, and I want to know the truth."

"Then let's go start down this new path together. It'll be much easier for everyone that way. Besides, I'm starving."

23

O nce her new skinsuit was fully fitted, One Twenty-Four followed Grace to the ship's mess. That was another use of a word that she just didn't understand. The room was both spotless and neatly organized, so it was the opposite of messy.

Why did these Imperials have such strange names for things? It was incomprehensible.

While the room was large enough to hold at least a dozen people and had plenty of tables for them to eat at, it was almost empty when they arrived, though she could hear the sound of someone moving around in a connected room.

The single occupant was a man dressed in oddly bright clothing with his feet propped up on a chair, seated at a table that sat against one of the walls. He smiled and motioned for them to join him as he rose.

Grace stopped short of the table and gestured toward the man. "Andrea, this is Kayden Harmon. He's the former owner of this ship and worked as a merchant throughout this part of the Singularity and the fringes around it for the last several decades. Kayden, Andrea."

Though the man smiled at her, One Twenty-Four could see that the emotion he was feeling was not happiness. She wasn't quite certain what he felt, but based on what Grace had told her, it wasn't likely to be a pleasant emotion.

Nevertheless, he extended a hand toward her. "I can't say that I'm exactly happy to meet you, at least not yet. Perhaps that will come in time. Please, have a seat. We got a lot to talk about."

Though his enunciation was somewhat different than what they'd used in the crèche, he was significantly more fluent with the tongue than Fei. That meant that he was *far* better than Grace.

Feeling more than a little intimidated, One Twenty-Four said nothing as she sat where the man's feet had been propped up. Grace took the seat next to her just as someone stepped in from the other room with a tray holding what One Twenty-Four assumed was food.

It seemed that eating on the ship was different than how it had worked in the crèche. All food preparation there had been automated, with each portion size determined in advance. Food was nothing more than fuel for their bodies, so it didn't warrant very much attention.

One Twenty-Four examined the contents of the platters as the man laid out eating utensils and began pouring an orange-colored liquid into tall glasses. Everything smelled interesting.

Once he'd finished that task, he poured black liquid into smaller cups. She noted that she hadn't gotten any of the black liquid and wondered why.

In the crèche, breakfast had consisted of oatmeal mixed with fruit and nuts. Based simply on the smell of these new foods, this meal would be a very different experience than she was used to.

The largest platter held flat, circular pieces of bread that seemed to have been poured into place while being cooked. Another platter held clumps of yellowish material that she couldn't identify. The final platter held long strips of what seemed to be blackened meat of some kind.

"What are these?" she asked Grace while gesturing toward the bread.

"You've never had pancakes?" the woman asked. "Basically, you take the ingredients and mix them into a thick liquid, which you then pour onto a hot griddle. Yeast causes them to rise as they're heated.

The containers beside the platter hold butter and syrup that you can use to flavor them."

She pointed toward the clumps of yellowish material. "These are scrambled eggs. Have you ever had eggs?"

One Twenty-Four shook her head. "No. Our breakfasts consisted of oatmeal with fruit mixed in. Lunch and dinner were different every day, but there was never anything like eggs. Or anything else on this table, for that matter."

Grace's lips curled slightly up. "Then I think you're going to be pleasantly surprised. The final platter holds bacon, or as I prefer to call it, the king of meats. They're thin strips of pork that have been fried. They're quite savory.

"You can try whatever you like. If nothing suits you, I'll have Ray whip up something more to your taste."

"Would you show me how these are best eaten?"

"Of course." Grace grabbed One Twenty-Four's plate and used several serving utensils to retrieve a couple of pancakes, a scoop of scrambled eggs, and a couple of strips of bacon. She set the plate in front of One Twenty-Four.

"I suggest that you take a bite of the pancakes before you add butter or syrup to see if you like the flavor. As far as the eggs, we have both salt and pepper to season them with, but do a little testing to find out if you like the flavor before you add too much.

"Your tall glass is filled with orange juice. Oranges are a fruit that originated on Terra and are very common in both the Empire and the Singularity. You haven't had that either?"

Grace shook her head. "No. What's the black liquid?"

"The nectar of the gods," Grace said solemnly. "That's coffee. It's where we get caffeine from, and that helps keep marines going. Caffeine is a stimulant. The reason Ray didn't pour you any is that children typically don't like the taste, and caffeine isn't good for them, as they're still developing."

One Twenty-Four considered that and frowned. "Can I try it?"

Kayden, who'd been watching the interplay with interest, slid his cup of coffee over in front of her. "You can have mine, and I'll get another. Coffee is quite bitter without sweetener, so you might want to add a little bit of sugar and creamer. If those aren't to your taste, there are artificial sweeteners as well.

"The sweeteners take a bit of the bite out of the coffee, and the creamer blunts the edge of the bitterness. When you find the right mixture for your coffee, it's often a drink that you don't want to pass up in the morning.

"Some people—like me—prefer it without additions. I believe that black coffee is the perfect wake-up call. I find it bolsters one quite well to field the day."

The man looked over at Grace. "I've read that the intake of caffeine isn't a big deal with modern medical care. I don't think that it's anything to really worry about."

With so many things to try, One Twenty-Four wasn't certain where to begin. She decided to start with the tall glass of orange juice. The cold liquid ended up being sweet and somewhat acidic. On reflection, she decided that she liked the taste.

Coffee, on the other hand, was *very* bitter. Still, because she saw Grace drinking hers with a form of reverence, One Twenty-Four didn't reject the drink out of hand.

She added some sugar and creamer, and it became somewhat more palatable. She'd reserve judgment and give it a more extended trial before making any lasting decisions about it. Perhaps it would grow on her.

The pancakes were light and fluffy, but somewhat dry. The addition of butter removed some of the dryness, and she approved. The butter itself was creamy, and she liked it.

It was the addition of syrup, however, that made her close her eyes in pleasure. She knew without a doubt that she was going to be a big fan of pancakes and syrup.

The eggs were interesting but bland. The addition of salt and pepper improved their taste considerably. They were certainly better than oatmeal, but she didn't think that they were even half as good as pancakes and syrup.

The bacon was unlike anything she'd ever eaten. Meats used in the crèche were just elements of whatever stew or dish was being served. Everything was prepared automatically, so she'd never seen individually cooked pieces of meat before.

These strips were both crisp and yet slightly chewy. Their flavor was intense, and it made her mouth explode with pleasure. They were *far* better than the pancakes. The two strips that she'd been given were quickly consumed, and she grabbed a couple more, adding syrup on top of them, which made them even more delicious.

She considered taking more bacon but decided that would draw too much attention. This was still a time where she couldn't afford to stand out. Perhaps there would be more tomorrow morning.

None of them spoke as they ate, but she could see that Kayden was watching her closely. As Grace had said, his lack of facial tattoos indicated he was part of the base caste. If she'd graduated from the crèche, she'd never have met someone from his stratum of society.

Every time Keeper had mentioned them, it had been in a disparaging tone. If he held a similar opinion of the ruling caste, it would be perfectly understandable if he disliked her. Perhaps even hated her.

She turned her attention to Grace as they sat drinking another cup of coffee. The woman wasn't looking at her, though she certainly tried to make it appear that she was. Her gaze rested on Kayden, though she seemed to be trying to conceal that fact.

Interesting. One Twenty-Four wondered why. Whatever the reason, it was just one more mystery to try to figure out on her own, as it wasn't her place to inquire.

Kayden set his coffee cup down and focused his attention entirely on her. "Do you mind if I call you Andrea? I'm quite certain that the ruling caste wouldn't approve of you using that name, which means that I like it quite a lot."

One Twenty-Four shrugged. "It's my new name, so I'm not certain what else you'd call me. I can no longer use One Twenty-Four."

He laughed. "They referred to you by a numeric designation? How very practical, while still being cold and uncaring.

"Well then, Andrea, I know that Grace has told you about some of the differences between the Singularity and the Empire. While I don't know the specifics of what she's said, I intend to expand upon your knowledge. It will be my duty to guide you through the process of transitioning to the world outside the crèche over the next few weeks or months.

"While I have no knowledge of what went on inside the crèche, I do have a fair bit of insight into how the ruling caste behaves in the society at large. You've undoubtedly led a sheltered life, and I'm afraid this news is going to be shocking to you.

"Then again, you appear to have had a tough existence inside the crèche, so perhaps this information won't be as big a shock as I believe."

He leaned forward and clasped his hands in front of him, resting them on the table. "What I need you to understand first is my goal. I believe that you can live a better life than what was planned for you.

"Quite frankly, the ruling caste is filled with monsters. Coldhearted people that enhance their lives to the detriment of everyone below. Then, when those people are no longer useful, our rulers dispose of them.

"The vast majority of people inside the Singularity are slaves in everything but name. Do you understand what that term means?"

She'd never heard the word before, so she shook her head.

"I thought not. A slave is someone who's entirely under the control of another. They don't have the freedom to do as they choose, and their lives are spent solely for the benefit of those who control them.

"The entirety of the base caste are slaves by that definition. The rulers of the Singularity can come in whenever they like and take whatever they want. In an instant, those people can lose everything they've spent a lifetime achieving.

"Their children can be killed if they deviate from what the ruling caste deems genetically acceptable, their spouses can be sent to other areas in the Singularity without appeal, they can be told what work they'll perform—whether they like it or not—and they can be executed without any consequence simply for existing."

"I hear your words, but I don't understand their meaning," she said slowly. "Inside the crèche, all of those things were true for me as well. Perhaps Keeper had a better life, but I don't know how she behaved outside the crèche."

Kayden nodded. "I suppose that's a fair point. Like I said, I don't have any information about what your life was like there. I'm sorry that you had to go through what you did.

"I suspect that you'd have gotten more training in ruling as you became older. You'd have learned how the ruling caste are groomed to become the strategic leaders of the Singularity. How they allocate resources in a manner that benefits themselves and use people as if they're simply supplies to be expended.

"To your credit, you're not as cold as they are. You're not withdrawn and superior. I believe that there's still a chance to save you, and I've dedicated myself to the task of helping Grace and the marines to make sure that you don't become the kind of person you'd have become without our intervention.

"I'm going to be honest with you. I hate the ruling caste with all of my being, and seeing those tattoos on your face makes me so angry that I can barely speak. I'm doing the best that I can to give you the benefit of the doubt, but I've got a lifetime of experience that tells me who you were meant to be."

He held up a hand when she made to speak. "Allow me to finish, please. I'm going to grant you a clean slate, as much as I can. It's going to be challenging for me, but I'm going to do everything that I possibly can to not hold any of my feelings against you personally. I beg your forgiveness if I slip. If so, I ask that you remind me that you're not a member of the ruling caste."

She considered his words and slowly nodded. "I'll do that. I could see that kind of coldness in Keeper. She was of the Andrea Line, just like I was, but older. It wouldn't surprise me at all if she behaved in the manner you've indicated and would've trained the rest of us to do the same when we'd grown older.

"I don't yet understand what it means to be different, but I'll pledge myself to try and understand what you're teaching me. I have no idea what it means to forge a new life, but I'm no longer a member of the ruling caste or resident of the crèche.

"The moment that Thirty-One separated me from my line sibs,

my fate was sealed. If I'm ever captured, I'll be executed immediately. I can't think of anything that would make a separation from my old life more immediate and permanent than that.

"Honestly, I don't think I'd have made it out of the crèche alive in any case. My curiosity was just too great. I'd get sidetracked from the assignments because something else interested me, and Keeper had to chastise me again and again. That kind of behavior simply isn't tolerated inside the crèche. My time was likely short."

She took a deep breath and turned her focus to Grace. "You've said that you're my guardian and that you're to guide me when we make it to the Empire, where they'll see me as property. Am I to be some type of curiosity for the amusement of others? Is that all I can look forward to in my new life? I have to be honest: that doesn't sound very appealing."

"I'm going to fight to give you as full a life as I can," Grace said seriously. "If I get everything that I want, you'll be treated just like any other citizen of the Empire. I want you to have the same options and choices that any free human being should have.

"As I said, I'm pretty sure that that law was written to be a poke in the eye of the Singularity's ruling caste. Few Imperials will genuinely believe that you're property. Even those that do will have to readjust their expectations and beliefs when confronted by a real person rather than an abstract concept.

"I'm not saying that it's going to be easy, but with hard work and a lot of pain on both of our parts, it should be possible to forge a new life for you that pleases you. Once I've secured your immediate safety, the next step is going to be finding some accommodation under the law that allows you to live your life as a normal person.

"Sadly, that's not going to happen quickly. The law will have to be changed, and that will take years. Hopefully, by the time you're an adult, we'll have made the changes that you need to live your life as a free person."

They sat in silence for a few minutes as One Twenty-Four digested everything she'd learned.

"What about your government?" she finally asked. "Are you sure that they aren't going to want to perform experiments on me?"

"I'm sure that no one would actually want to cut you apart. There's no need. What would they find? Even though your DNA has been edited, you're still a human being. There's no purpose to be served by that kind of butchery.

"Even if someone had a mind to do so, the law inside the Empire gives me complete and utter say over what happens to you. Perhaps, if I was an evil person, I'd allow something monstrous like that to happen, but I won't. You're going to be safe."

"They could just kill you," One Twenty-Four countered. "If someone in your society behaved like Thirty-One, they'd arrange to eliminate you. They could then take possession of me and do what they wanted."

Grace opened her mouth to say something but closed it again without speaking. She took a deep breath and then started again.

"As I said, I'm a lot harder to kill than I look. For the time being, I'll make sure that all of my property is inherited by Fei. Frankly, she's even harder to kill than I am. I'll set up a legal framework that makes absolutely certain that only people who have your best interest at heart will represent you."

Before One Twenty-Four could respond, a hidden speaker overhead came to life. "Grace, we need you on the bridge. We've got a situation."

Grace stood. "I'd best go see what's happening. Kayden, if you'd be so kind as to escort Andrea back to the marine area when you're done, I believe that Sergeant Na has some hand-to-hand training that she'd like to begin."

With that, Grace strode out of the room without another word.

One Twenty-Four was more than a bit concerned about what was happening. Had the Singularity caught up with them? Might her new life be over before it had really begun?

That would be a tragedy, and she hoped with all of her heart that Grace could handle what was coming next. Whatever it was.

24

Grace made her way up to *Bright Passage*'s bridge and found Anders examining a readout on one of the consoles facing the command chair. She stepped around to stand beside him and was able to tell that it was a navigational plot but not much else, since she wasn't trained to read that kind of display.

He turned toward her, his expression concerned. "We're about halfway to the next flip point, and a pair of destroyers just flipped into the system. They're headed directly toward us."

"Do you think they're on to us?"

The ex-Fleet officer shrugged. "It's hard to say. They could be heading for the Aponte system, since its flip point is directly behind us. Freighters of every size and shape scattered before the transshipment center blew up, and you can be sure that news of attack is spreading like a shockwave. There's been enough time for the next system over to have gotten word about what happened. Barely."

Grace considered that possibility while she rubbed her nose. "We have to plan for the worst-case scenario and assume that they've gotten word of the attack. The question now is whether or not they intend to stop us or are going directly to the source.

"Dozens of the ships running from Aponte are in this system and are even now in the process of scattering toward various destinations. There's no way that those destroyers are going to stop every single one of them, so why should we assume that they're coming for us?

"As far as we know, there's nothing to connect us with the attack. *Bright Passage* didn't do anything to directly draw attention to itself, so it's unlikely that anyone pointed us out as the source of the marines when we invaded.

"Hell, that Keeper woman blew up the place with almost no warning. They might not even suspect the Empire was involved yet."

Anders slowly resumed his chair. "True, but we can't count on that being the case. If either of those ships decides to board us, we're screwed. With two destroyers, they could stand off and blow us up without any difficulty at all.

"Just the marines on those ships are more than capable of overwhelming your platoon. No matter how this plays out, if they've singled us out for attention, we're done for."

Everything the man said was true, but Grace wasn't going to give up hope just yet. Since they were on a direct path toward the flip point that the destroyers had come from, they couldn't jump to the conclusion that they'd been targeted.

"Nothing in the information that Kayden gave us indicated there were destroyers deployed in the system ahead of us," she said. "We didn't come through it on our way in, so we don't know for sure, but that system is mostly supposed to be used for transit."

"It isn't supposed to be guarded," he agreed. "That said, we can't count on our intelligence being perfect. As a marine, you already know that. Just because none of the destroyers stationed at Aponte was supposed to be in the next system over doesn't mean that they weren't.

"For that matter, these ships might've just been passing through on their way to another posting when they got word of the attack. If that's the case, they could've diverted on their commander's orders. All that really matters is that they're going to pass right by us."

That was true. The back story didn't change the results. All that mattered was whether they were challenged or fired upon.

Well, if they were going to have trouble, she might as well get the marines ready to dance. Grace walked over to the wall communicator and signaled Na. As soon as the noncom came on, she ordered her to get the marines into their battle rattle.

If it looked like they were going to go down fighting, she'd head back and join them. It was far better to die with a weapon in one's hand then stand around bleating about their bad luck.

With that done, she returned to Anders's chair. "How long is it going to be before we know for sure what their intentions are?"

"We'll be in weapons range in about an hour and a half. If I were in command over there, I'd wait until my ships were inside weapons range before opening communications. They're not going to want to telegraph their intentions.

"There are five other freighters from Aponte traveling in a rough cluster around us, and we're all headed for the flip point that they just came through. It's possible that they'll just command us all to heave to.

"If that happens, we can play dumb and then open fire with our concealed weapons if they come close enough. We've got enough firepower to cripple one or both of those ships but probably not destroy them. If it comes down to shooting, they're going to blow us into little bitty pieces, and then they're going to board what's left."

Grace considered heading back to join the marines but decided against it. They'd be much better prepared if she knew exactly what was happening. To know that, she needed to stay here and see how things played out.

The next hour went by so damn slowly. She gave in to temptation and paced the rear of the small bridge to bleed off some of her tension. Eventually, she gave up on that and went to pester the navigator on some instruction about how to read his display.

Anders ordered the man to put something up onto the small screen on the front of the console that the captain faced. It showed a blue dot that represented *Bright Passage* in the center of the screen. Some of the other freighters fleeing Aponte were scattered loosely around them and represented with amber dots. Ahead of them, two red dots crawled toward them.

Even though those red dots weren't moving very quickly on the scale of the display, Grace knew that they were coming as fast as they possibly could. The navigator had informed her that the destroyers were moving at flank speed.

In Fleet parlance, that meant that they were going even faster than what was normally considered their top speed. They were pushing their engines as hard as they could to eke out every single bit of velocity.

Grace thought that was a good sign. If their only intent was to intercept the freighters, they didn't have to rush. The civilian ships weren't going to get away. *Bright Passage* couldn't outrun a destroyer even with its upgraded engines.

Her expectation at this point was that the destroyers were going to fly past the freighters without giving them a second look.

To her immense relief, that was exactly what happened.

The destroyers sprinted past the cluster of freighters and continued on toward the Aponte flip point, no doubt racing to help secure the system against whatever attack they thought was taking place.

She finally let out a sigh of relief once the destroyers were outside weapons range again. Anders looked as relieved as she felt. Nobody wanted to die on this mission, even though they all knew that was still a real possibility.

They'd escaped immediate confrontation, and now they could continue on to the next system in line and make the flip on to engage the first of their secondary targets in the system beyond that.

Personally, Grace doubted they were going to be able to hit all three secondary targets. That was just begging for trouble. If they managed to just hit one, she'd be pleased. If they got two, she'd be ecstatic.

She stayed on the bridge until *Bright Passage* finally flipped to the next system. Once they did, she waited anxiously as the officer manning the scanners began gathering passive information from deeper into the system.

Grace didn't expect there to be much. This system wasn't a major hub for the Singularity. It served as a transit point between more populous systems, containing no habitable worlds of its own and holding no military bases.

There was some mining going on in one of its asteroid belts, and one of the gas giants had a commercial orbital used in harvesting hydrogen for industrial processes elsewhere, but that was it. Unless there were other warships in the system, *Bright Passage* should have a smooth transit to the next system.

When they got there, Grace expected that news of the attack at Aponte would've already arrived. Gossip traveled at almost the speed of light, after all. Bad news spread even faster than good.

The man monitoring the scanners looked up with a quizzical expression. "Sir, I'm picking up active scanners at the gas giant. I'm still gathering the details, but I think they're military grade."

Anders rubbed one hand across his face and sighed. "Why am I not surprised? What can you tell me about the gas giant and the scanner signature?"

"The gas giant has only one commercial orbital used for siphoning off hydrogen, according to the information listed by Imperial Intelligence. It's not supposed to have any military presence whatsoever.

"I'll get better data on the scanner source as we get closer. Our current flight path will take us near the gas giant as we make our way to the next flip point. It's only a single scanner signature, and now that I'm getting a longer exposure to it, it looks odd."

"In what way?" Anders asked sharply. "Are they scanning for us?"

The man shook his head. "No, sir. It looks like a general scan of the area around the gas giant, but it's the modulation that's strange. It's not utilizing the frequencies that I'd expect from a Singularity warship. Frankly, it's a lot closer to Fleet modulation."

"Are you saying that's a Fleet warship?" Grace asked incredulously.

The man shrugged. "It's not an exact match for Fleet frequencies, but it's not far off either. That's what makes it strange."

Anders leaned back in his seat, crossed his arms over his chest, and shook his head. "This doesn't make any sense. First of all, there shouldn't be any Fleet vessels inside the Singularity at all. Second, if there were any, why the hell would they be advertising their presence?

"And yes, I understand that it's not precisely using normal Fleet frequencies, but if it's not a Singularity vessel, then we have to start asking questions about who it really is and what they're doing."

"You said that we're going to be passing fairly close by the gas giant," Grace said. "If so, why don't we deviate a little and see how close we can get to whatever is generating that signal? It's not going to see anything other than a freighter on its way to the next flip point. If we can get close enough to get some real data, that might be valuable to Imperial Intelligence."

Anders considered her suggestion for a few seconds and then nodded. "Helm, adjust our course as much as you can without being obvious about it. I don't want to seem like we're taking too great an interest in the gas giant, but any additional reduction in distance that we can achieve is going to help our passive scanners pull in more information about it.

"Without raising anybody's suspicions too much, let's go find out what the hell's going on."

"I think I'd better head back and join the rest of the marines," Grace said. "I should've already told them to stand down. If it turns out that we're going to need to fight in the next several hours, we need to take a break before that happens."

"Good idea," Anders agreed. "I should've thought of that myself. My apologies. Go get your people in order, and let's find out what the hell we're dealing with."

25

One Twenty-Four remained in the mess, talking with Kayden Harmon, for almost an hour. Despite his stated dislike of her, the man was chatty, and their talk veered off onto a number of tangents. He seemed just as curious about her as she was about him.

Honestly, their conversation was less about her new circumstances and more about getting to know one another. As they spoke, she could see him relaxing and becoming more comfortable in her presence. In turn, she became more used to him as well.

Considering that he was only the third person she'd spoken with at any length outside the crèche, she thought things went very well.

Even as they spoke, she continued to worry about the issue that had drawn Grace away. In the end, she was forced to put the entire situation out of her mind and focus on her interactions with Kayden. Building that relationship was of great long-term importance and deserved her complete attention.

When their rambling talk finally drew to a close, the man rose and gestured for her to accompany him. "I think we've gotten to know one another as well as we can for the moment. I should take you to

Sergeant Na so that she can get on with giving you that lesson you've been looking forward to."

She cocked her head slightly as she stood. "How do you know that I've been looking forward to it?"

He chuckled. "You've been fidgeting. I think that subconsciously you've been looking forward to getting back to someone that you know better than me. I fully understand that, and I'm not offended.

"We've made progress, and you should be proud of what we've accomplished. Over the next several weeks, we'll have plenty of time to discuss the Singularity, the ruling caste, and the Empire. Trust me when I say they have their own set of flaws and weaknesses, and that their nobles can be just as arrogant, though they have limits on how much raw power that they wield."

She didn't argue. She'd have the rest of her life to learn about those things.

Even after speaking with him, she still didn't know Kayden very well and wasn't certain about his ultimate intentions. That continued to make things awkward between them, but she expected her feelings toward him would improve with time and exposure.

The one person she did trust—so far as she trusted anyone—was Fei. She wasn't sure why, but the woman engendered a sense of safety in her. It was probably illusory, but she wasn't going to reject that relationship out of hand simply because she thought it was all in her head.

The two of them walked out of the mess, and he led her to the part of the ship that the marines were using. When they arrived, they found all of them dressed in armor and performing tasks that centered around weapons.

That certainly wasn't a good sign.

It only took a few seconds for Fei to spot them. "Thank you, Kayden. I'll take care of her now. You should probably go to the bridge. There are a couple of destroyers coming toward us. We don't know that they're going to interact with us, but if they do, we should have a fluent speaker of the tongue ready to answer."

He shook his head slightly. "They won't need me, since they have fluent speakers of their own. If someone demands to speak to the captain, and they know who I am, I'll go up and perform my function.

"My place right now is in engineering, making sure that I keep an ear on what's happening and that the ship continues to function as designed."

Fei raised an eyebrow. "I thought you were a merchant, not an engineer."

The man grinned, showing a lot of white teeth. "I'm a man of many talents. I began my career as an engineer, and I still think that I'm a damned good one. Being able to trade and haggle over cargo has made me a lot of money, but it's not as enjoyable as fixing something that's not working the way it should.

"In any case, I'll leave you to your business. Good luck, Sergeant. Andrea."

Fei watched Kayden walk out of the compartment before turning to One Twenty-Four. "So, what am I going to do with you, Little One? We might be in for a fight before very much longer. Perhaps I should complete your transformation and fit you with armor.

"Not that I intend to let you fight unless things go very badly, but it might be best to make sure that you're fully protected. You're already wearing a skinsuit, and I have your complete measurements, so it's not going to take very long to get you outfitted."

One Twenty-Four felt her heart skip a beat. Even though she wasn't looking forward to further conflict, the idea of being able to defend herself sounded good. And she had to admit that she was curious about the process of being fitted for armor and how the weapons were used.

As Fei led her over to some formed containers at the side of the room, she ventured a question. "How likely is a fight?"

The woman shrugged. "I don't know, but it's better to be prepared than to be surprised, so let's assume that we will."

"Then it will be good that I'm ready to fight," One Twenty-Four said, deciding on boldness. "If the Singularity boards this ship, my life is just as forfeit as yours. I will try to stop as many of them as I can."

That made the woman smile. "Excellent. Marines run toward a fight, not away from it. It's best we die in action and not like sheep."

"What's a sheep?" One Twenty-Four asked with a frown. "Never mind. It's just one more thing that I'll need to look up later."

Fei laughed and started pulling pieces of armor out of one of the containers. It didn't take long to get her ready. Having One Twenty-Four's measurements must've made the process easier.

When they were done, One Twenty-Four stood there with a helmet tucked under her arm and outfitted with armor just like Fei.

The marine nodded approvingly. "Now, let's look at weapons. It won't do you much good to give you a stunner, because any boarders are going to be armored as well. That means I need to outfit you with flechette weapons. I think you'll need both a pistol and a rifle.

"You're not to use either one of them unless I explicitly order you to do so or someone is shooting at you. Is that understood?"

One Twenty-Four nodded. "Only use the weapons you give me if I have no choice. Understood."

Fei walked her over to another container and pulled out a pistol. "This weapon is deceptively simple to use. This small lever on the side is the safety. Whenever it's in the upward position, the weapon cannot fire. When you flick it down, it can.

"Once we put it into your holster, you are not to remove it unless you intend to shoot someone or I tell you to. Don't even put your finger on the trigger unless you intend to fire the weapon. Clear?"

One Twenty-Four nodded. "Yes."

Fei gripped the weapon and rubbed her thumb on a button where it sat on the grip. "This release is how you drop an empty magazine. The flechettes inside are not infinite. When you squeeze the trigger, you will fire one flechette. When the weapon sounds a tone, you'll know that it's empty, and you must eject the magazine and replace it with a full one."

She pressed the button, and a part of the weapon at the base of the grip fell away. Fei extended the magazine toward One Twenty-Four. The interior of it was filled with flechettes similar to the one that she'd seen pulled from Grace's back. Only these were sharp and lethal looking but embedded in some kind of clear gel.

"What is this stuff the flechettes are in?" One Twenty-Four asked. "What purpose does it serve?"

"That's called a discarding sabot. It stabilizes the flechette as it is fired but comes off before it strikes its target.

"Just leave any empty magazines where they fall. As one would expect, the sharp part of the flechettes goes toward the front of the weapon. The magazine won't fit if you try to put it in backward, but that will waste time when you'll probably have none to spare.

"Slide it in and push it up until you hear a click. That's how you know that the magazine is completely seated. The weapon will know that it can fire again as soon as you've completed that action, and you can once more begin shooting at the enemy.

"Do you have any questions about the pistol?"

When One Twenty-Four shook her head, Fei gave her the weapon and made her eject the magazine several times and reinsert it so that she could become used to the process.

The pistol felt strangely heavy and more than a bit awkward in her hands. It was made for someone larger than she was, and it was difficult to grip. She needed two hands to be certain that she didn't drop it.

It felt a bit frightening to hold something that she could use to end someone else's life. If she'd had a pistol like this when Thirty-One had attacked her, she could've ended the girl with almost a thought. That was a lot of power to hold over others. It was sobering.

Once Fei was satisfied that One Twenty-Four understood how the pistol worked, she took it from her and slid it into the holster on One Twenty-Four's upper leg.

"I want you to slowly pull the pistol out of the holster and extend it toward that bulkhead over there. Keep your finger off the trigger and move both slowly and carefully. I want you to get used to the idea of extending the weapon before you're ready to fire. Watch me."

Fei dropped her hand to her own pistol and slowly drew it. She brought her other hand up to wrap around the one she had gripping the weapon, raised the weapon to her chest with the barrel pointing toward the bulkhead she'd indicated, and then extended both of her arms.

"Pay close attention to how I have my feet positioned. Your stance is important for your stability even though the weapon has almost no recoil. You're the aiming platform, after all.

"Now, see how I never let the barrel point at anything that I'm not willing to shoot? You need to do the same. Accidents happen, even in training, and if you make certain that your weapon is never pointed at another person, you can't accidentally shoot them."

Under Fei's close direction, One Twenty-Four drew her pistol and extended it just like she'd been shown. The woman had her do it several times and corrected how she was holding it, the position of her hands, and how she was standing.

When the woman was satisfied, she grinned. "If we make it through this, we'll set up a firing range and have you get in some practice with a live weapon. That's the only way to really get comfortable with one."

That done, Fei had One Twenty-Four holster her pistol while she retrieved a rifle like the one that hung from around her own neck and laid it on the table. She explained all the features of the weapon as if she'd done it many times before.

The rifle was similar in function to the pistol. Other than its size, the major difference was that it had a setting to fire multiple flechettes with one pull of the trigger. Thankfully, its magazine was also significantly larger to support that kind of output.

Fei demonstrated how the weapon was held with the stock pressed against her shoulder and the end of the barrel aimed at where the enemy would be. Like the pistol, there was a sighting mechanism that had a red dot. So long as one looked down the barrel, it was visible. If the weapon was turned slightly, the dot vanished.

"Think of your weapon like the ultimate point-and-click interface," Fei said. "The sight is smart enough to be able to determine the range and adjust for the flight characteristics of the ammunition, so all you have to do is put the dot where you want to hit and squeeze the trigger. These weapons don't have any recoil to speak of, so don't yank it, or you're going to jerk your weapon off the target."

Just as Fei was hanging the weapon around One Twenty-Four's

neck, Grace walked into the compartment. She took one look at them and grinned. "Don't you look like a proper little marine?"

"I thought it best for her to be ready to fight if that's what it came down to," Fei said.

"You'll get no argument from me. Luckily, it looks like we're not going to need to right now. The destroyers passed us by, and we're safely into the next system. We're not quite free and clear just yet, but we've got some breathing room. Stand everyone down."

Fei nodded and began giving orders to the marines, who started stripping off their weapons and armor.

Grace took One Twenty-Four by the elbow and guided her back toward where Fei had gotten the weapons. She gave One Twenty-Four virtually the same set of instructions on how to treat the weapons as she took them away, separated the ammunition from the weapons themselves, and stored everything away.

One Twenty-Four thought that was amusing, but it never hurt to hear safety instructions more than once. Getting another chance to do things correctly the first time was worthwhile.

Once the weapons were put away, Grace helped her strip out of her armor until she stood in her skinsuit. By that time, Fei had finished giving instructions to the marines, shucked her own armor, and rejoined them.

"What would you have done if it had come to fighting?" Grace asked One Twenty-Four seriously.

"My life is forfeit in the Singularity, so I would've done whatever was required to survive. It benefits me to make certain that the marines survive as well, since they're protecting me."

"That's very well thought out," Grace said approvingly. "Now that we've got a little bit of time, I think we should show you the helmet footage of Anne Marie's death. It will be difficult to watch, but it's important that you know what it means to be an Imperial Marine."

One Twenty-Four nodded and followed the two of them as they left the room. She wasn't sure that she wanted to see someone dying, but everyone attached such importance to the act that the woman had performed that she felt as if she had no choice.

Both Grace and Fei were prominent in her new life, and they were Imperial Marines. If she wanted to understand them and perhaps even begin to think about the universe in the same way that they did, she needed to see this recording, no matter how ugly it was.

26

G race's plan fell apart five seconds after they exited the compartment where the marines had just finished divesting themselves of weapons and armor. She'd just made it into the corridor when the overhead speakers came to life again.

"Grace and Kayden, I need you both in the wardroom," Anders said. "Grace, there's no need to stand your marines back up. I think we know what we're dealing with, and I want to get everyone briefed."

It annoyed her that, once again, duty had pulled her away from Andrea when she'd tried to connect with her. If things kept on at this rate, maybe Fei would make a better guardian than her.

No, that was just her frustration talking. This had been a busy couple of days, and she just needed to remember that they had the rest of their lives to figure this out. Once they got out of the Singularity, things would calm down. For a little while, anyway.

"I'd best go see what this is all about," she said with a growl. "Fei, take Andrea somewhere quiet and show her the vid. If you'd explain what it means to us, I'd appreciate it."

She squatted so that her eyes were closer to Andrea's. "I wanted to be there for you, and I'm sorry that I can't be."

"I understand that these circumstances aren't of your making," the girl said earnestly. "It's your job to keep everyone safe. We can talk about the vid later."

Grace found herself smiling slightly at the girl's word choices. They made her sound older than she was.

While Grace could understand the tongue well enough, she knew that her pronunciation made her sound like an imbecile. Sadly, she was going to have to spend years getting better at speaking the girl's native language to better bond with her. It was going to be far easier teaching Andrea how to speak Standard, she suspected.

"I'm still sorry," Grace said seriously. "You deserve my full attention. Hopefully, whatever this is isn't too serious, and I'll be back down shortly. If not, I'll find you when I can."

Grace rose and headed toward the wardroom without waiting for a response.

She ran into Kayden right outside the wardroom hatch, but before she could say anything to him, the hatch opened, and Anders gestured for them both to come in.

The cramped table already held Kyle and the man who'd been operating the scanners on the bridge earlier. Once Anders had resumed his seat at the head of the table, Grace sat down beside Kayden and focused her attention on the captain.

"Evan here believes he knows what we're dealing with," Anders said, gesturing at the young officer.

The earnest young man looked odd with blond hair falling down to his shoulders. She thought he'd look a lot better with a standard Fleet haircut. Despite his civilian appearance, his voice was professional.

"To bring Mister Harmon up to speed, we've detected an active military-grade scanner signature around the innermost gas giant in the Lyteara system. The source is trailing just behind the commercial hydrogen collection orbital.

"We've only been able to use passive scanners, so the data is more nebulous than I'd prefer, but it's not a Singularity warship. Also, the frequencies used don't precisely match Fleet either, though they're close."

The man tapped his slate, and the small screen set into the wall came to life. It displayed an image of a ship. Grace wasn't familiar with many of the vessels used by Fleet, so she didn't immediately grasp what she was looking at.

"I believe our subject is a Zombie-class destroyer," Evan continued. "They're pretty common inside the Empire and have been for almost a hundred years. They're light, fast, and relatively well armed for their size. They don't have beam weapons or battle screens because they don't have the power-generation capability to support them.

"I suspect the difference in frequencies that I've detected are explained by battle damage that's been repaired using Singularity parts. I'm making an educated guess on the ship's class based on our passive data gathering and the scanner signature itself. The ship is mostly occluded by the orbital, so I won't have any confirmation for another half an hour or so.

"My best guess at this point is that the ship was captured in battle years ago. If we can figure out who she was, we can report her status to Imperial Intelligence when we get back home."

"Or we could take a more proactive approach," Kyle disagreed with a grin. "If this ship really is an Imperial destroyer that the Singularity captured, I'm proposing that we take her back."

Grace found herself blinking in shock. She pressed her palms against the table and leaned forward.

"Excuse me? We're on a freighter that doesn't have anything but concealed weaponry, I only have a platoon of marines, and you want us to board and capture an enemy destroyer? Have you lost your mind?"

"While I'm not supporting Alan's plan just yet, let's take the time to hear him out," Anders said, his tone placating. "If we decide that it isn't feasible, we can reject it. I know this sounds crazy, but we do have certain advantages if we can figure out a way to get around the obvious downsides.

"There haven't been any battles where we've lost a destroyer in repairable condition in at least a decade. The computer systems on that ship have undoubtedly been replaced with the Singularity versions, but that doesn't mean that all of the original equipment has been removed. In fact, it almost certainly hasn't, and that works in our favor.

"You see, there are programs buried in Fleet secondary systems that someone with the appropriate authentication codes can use to bring them online. As a former destroyer captain, I have those codes.

"So long as that ship wasn't lost more than sixty years ago, I should be able to subvert the antiboarding weapons and use them to disable the crew. The big downside of that is that I'd have to be on board the ship to make that happen."

Grace started to say something but stopped herself before taking a deep breath and letting it out slowly. When she felt that she had a good grasp on her frayed temper, she allowed herself to speak.

"First, why would Fleet put something like that on their ships? Second, how do you keep it from being used against you? That seems like a crazy thing to have, since anyone in the know can just use them to turn a ship against her own crew."

Anders shot her a small grin. "The program has to be activated by the ship's assigned senior officers. That's only done if they feel that the ship is about to fall into enemy hands. It's part of the protocol that wipes all the data on the computers. Only after that's done can someone like me waltz in with the right codes to use the system."

Grace didn't see the point of having that capability, but it hardly mattered. If he said the capability was there, that was all that really mattered. Still, it didn't make Kyle's plan any more palatable.

"Even so, you're making a lot of assumptions there," she argued. "You can't be sure that the Singularity hasn't stripped out the program you intend to use. Even if they haven't, how do we get you aboard that ship? Let's say that we actually manage to take her back. How do we get her out of the Singularity?

"Leaving those questions aside, why would we possibly do any of this? We've accomplished our primary mission, and we've got a freighter full of valuable cargo that will set us up for the rest of our lives. Why in the universe would we take an insane risk like this?"

"Honor," Anders said simply. "Every objection that you've raised is valid, and so is every question that you've asked. The thing is, that ship was once one of ours, and we have to at least consider if it's possible to get her home.

"I don't think this will be quite as insane as you think. In fact, it might not even be that difficult to get on board her."

He turned his gaze to Kayden. "If we were to do so, it would require some duplicity from you, but we wouldn't even have to lie about what we were doing. After all, we've just come from the system where a transshipment center blew up.

"For whatever reason, this destroyer stayed here rather than going with the other two. The captain is going to want to know what happened.

"If we make a stop to perform a small repair in orbit and transmit a courtesy itinerary to control and the ship, it's an almost certainty that they're going to want more information. I'm certain that a clever fellow like yourself could wrangle a dinner invitation for himself and his senior officers to tell that story in person."

Kayden shook his head. "I find myself in agreement with Lieutenant Tolliver. We'd be putting everything we've already accomplished at risk, and I'm not willing to endorse something like that without a very good reason. One that I'm afraid Commander Kyle and you have not made a case for."

"Have you considered how large a share recovering a functional Imperial warship would be?" Kyle asked with a big grin. "That isn't some ancient relic. That class of ship is currently in use by the Empire today and will be for the rest of my life, most likely. It's a modern warship.

"Bringing him back into service would mean getting shares based on almost his full value. The cargo we have is worth a lot, but that ship has to be worth nearly as much. Maybe even more.

"At the very least, we need to consider our options carefully. If we decide not to go after him, we can always continue on our course, but we have to at least talk about it while we have a chance."

"What use is money you never live to spend?" Kayden countered. "They could reward you with a noble title and a promotion, but how much would you enjoy them posthumously?

"And you've now referred to that ship with both female and male pronouns. Please explain."

"It's a Fleet thing," Grace said before Anders could respond. "Our ships are she or her. Hostile ships are he or him. Since this was once a Fleet ship, it's she in the historical sense but he when considering her current owners."

"That seems needlessly complicated," the merchant complained with a sniff. "Couldn't you just use the same term for everyone?"

"It's tradition," Anders said. "When you've done something a certain way for thousands of years, it takes on a life of its own."

There were a few seconds of silence as Grace thought about the plan they'd laid out. In the end, she just shook her head.

"It's a mirage. A pool of water seen in the desert when it's not really there. Don't allow the illusion to lure you to your death."

"Once again, the Lieutenant has the right of it," Kayden said seriously. "Let's say we were unreasonably lucky and captured that ship. Marvelous! What would we do next? We already have to use her marines to perform basic tasks aboard *Bright Passage*. Are you telling me that we're going to be able to do that and also man a destroyer?

"I understand that you once commanded a ship like that, Captain Anders. I want you to put aside your emotions and think very carefully. With one platoon of marines and the small crew from this freighter, can we even minimally man that ship while still bringing this freighter home?

"I also doubt very seriously that the cargo containers we have aboard would fit onto a destroyer, at least not many of them."

Anders grimaced and tapped his fingers against the table. "We wouldn't be able to operate the missile batteries, except perhaps one or two in a pinch. We'd also be running back-to-back shifts with minimal personnel, but it's still possible."

Before anyone else could say a word, Anders sighed and shook his head. "Still, I get your point. A man's reach should always exceed his grasp, but perhaps not by that far. Sadly, I'm afraid that I have to agree with you, even though I really don't want to. We'll continue on and just settle for getting the best information that we can to pass on to Imperial Intelligence."

Grace leaned back in her chair, more relieved than she was willing to admit. Marines were crazy but not *that* crazy. Trying something like that would've been suicide.

A chime sounded from Anders's tablet. He frowned, picked it up, and tapped the screen. "Yes?"

"We've received a transmission, Captain," someone said, her voice loud enough for Grace to hear. "It's from the warship in orbit around the gas giant. They're instructing us to change course and assume orbit near them."

The unexpected news made Grace sit bolt upright. Had something tipped them off? Why the hell did a Singularity warship want them to heave to? Was it just them looking for news or something more sinister?

"Did they tag us specifically or all the freighters?" Kyle asked, leaning forward so that the slate could pick up his voice.

"Just us, Commander. It might be because we fell a little bit behind the other freighters while we were gathering information. The rest of the pack is a bit farther along in their trajectory leading to the next flip point.

"It might also be that we're the smallest of the freighters, and they don't want to inconvenience any of their big commercial carriers. Honestly, I don't know."

"It doesn't matter," Anders said with finality. "We can't outrun that ship, so we're going to do what they say. If possible, we'll keep our options open, but we might have to consider Alan's plan after all."

That was absolutely not what Grace wanted to do, but she understood that their circumstances had changed, and not for the better. If they had to execute Kyle's insane plan, she really hoped it worked, because they were out of good options.

"I have one other piece of information, Captain," the voice over the com said heavily. "They've identified themselves as the heavy cruiser *Ever-Loyal Warrior*."

Anders squeezed the bridge of his nose between two fingers. "Evan, remind me to make note of this epic blunder in your next efficiency report, on the off chance that we survive. Confusing a heavy cruiser for a destroyer isn't a good look for a tactical officer of your caliber.

"Dark humor aside, this just turned a difficult task into an almost impossible one. We're all going to have to be on our A-game, or this is going to end us.

"Grace, you might need to be visible on the vid pickup, so get into something other than your skinsuit. They'd know that's military. And hurry. We might not have much time."

—————

27

One Twenty-Four followed Fei into a compartment filled with crates of varying sizes that almost reached the ceiling in places. She had no idea what they contained, but if they were for the marines, they probably held something useful in combat.

The woman pulled down a couple of smaller crates and set them up as makeshift benches. She helped One Twenty-Four up onto one and then took the other for herself.

"This isn't going to be easy to watch, and if you don't feel comfortable doing so, I won't judge you," Fei said, her expression somber. "If you'd like, I can simply tell you what happened."

One Twenty-Four shook her head. "This woman died protecting me, so I think that she deserves my complete attention. I was unconscious when she died, but I was there. As difficult as it may be, I need to see what happened for myself."

Fei nodded and handed her a slate. "If at any point you change your mind, there's no shame in that. Watching something like this is difficult, even for a marine."

There was a vid already queued up to play, so One Twenty-Four tapped the button. The scene showed a large corridor through which a number of marines were moving with their weapons up and apparently searching for anyone that was a threat to them. She'd never seen anything like it before.

The crèche guards had certainly never behaved in such a manner. Their movements had been clumsy in comparison, and it was obvious that the marines had far more experience at this sort of thing.

When the ambush came, the marines found places to squat and minimize their aspects before returning fire. Well, almost all of them.

One had been caught in the open by the ambushers and was furiously returning fire, seemingly to give her teammates time to respond. One Twenty-Four knew instinctively that this must be Anne Marie Scott.

She almost missed the device that the ambushers threw at the marines but witnessed the figure standing in the corridor snatch it out of the air, clutch it to her chest, and bend over to shield the marines behind her from whatever it was.

A tremendous blast of light and energy blanked the video. When the display cleared, Anne Marie Scott was gone.

There was nothing left of her. It was as if she'd never been.

One Twenty-Four watched the remainder of the fight. She saw the marines overrun the crèche guards and kill them. It was bloody and ugly, but part of her felt a vindication that she couldn't explain. A satisfaction that was undeniable.

They'd been after her, and if they'd caught her, she'd have died. One Twenty-Four regretted Anne Marie Scott's death, but she still didn't understand why the woman had done what she'd done.

When the vid ended, One Twenty-Four handed the slate back to Fei. "I don't understand. She could've allowed the weapon to fly past her and perhaps survived. Why would she do something that made her own death inevitable? Her act was obviously intentional, and she knew exactly what would happen. Why did she do it?"

Fei took One Twenty-Four's hand into hers. "Many people think that marines exist simply to kill others. While that's certainly part of our duties, I'd argue that it isn't our primary purpose at all.

"Each of us dedicated our lives to the protection of others. In our training, we learn to be the guardians of our fellow marines. The battlefield isn't a safe environment, and so we often face death or injury. If we can save a fellow marine, we don't hesitate to act.

"Anne Marie did have a choice. She could've allowed that plasma grenade to land in the middle of the squad. She might have survived the explosion, but it would've certainly resulted in the deaths of almost everyone else, including you.

"In that split second, she made the choice to exchange her life for her friends and for you. She was a genuinely selfless person and made an incredibly brave sacrifice that I'm not certain many marines could or would match.

"As human beings, our survival instincts are strong. Marine training focuses us so that we're fighting the enemy rather than running to preserve our own lives, but no one wants to commit suicide.

"She chose to give the squad a chance to survive and paid for it in blood. She chose to give a child a chance at life at the cost of her own. Though the rest of us probably wouldn't have done something so dramatic, if it came down to a choice between allowing a child to die, of allowing our friends to die, we'd plant ourselves in that position to buy them time. We each know the cost of what we do, and we do it because we're Imperial Marines."

One Twenty-Four had never heard of anyone possessing that level of dedication to others. Inside the crèche, such behavior was unheard of.

She cast her mind back over what she'd seen of the marines during her time on board the ship. She didn't know them well enough to know if Fei was accurate in her assessment, but she had to assume that she was. The woman knew these people far better than she did, after all.

What was blindingly obvious was that the strangers were willing to risk their lives for her sake. That certainly didn't fit with the information that Keeper had presented about the Empire.

One Twenty-Four came to them as their enemy—or at least she bore the markings of their enemies—yet they'd made a conscious decision to risk themselves for her. To die for her. That spoke of a completely different type of morality than existed inside the crèche.

Grace had been gravely injured in the fighting. One Twenty-Four remembered the doctor pulling a flechette out of the woman's back. It had gone through the armor that she'd been wearing, which One Twenty-Four knew to be thick because she'd now worn it herself.

She'd intentionally turned her back to the enemy to shield One Twenty-Four with her own body. The possibility of death from that act had to have been high. A few more seconds and the flechettes would certainly have penetrated the damaged armor and killed her, yet she chose to risk her life for One Twenty-Four.

All of this was so very different than the crèche. Her line sibs might stand up to someone like Thirty-One if their behavior became destabilizing, but every individual was expendable.

If Keeper had decided to eliminate One Twenty-Four, it wouldn't have bothered anyone in the crèche other than One Twenty-Four herself. No one would've raised an objection.

Some would've been pleased.

She hadn't raised any objections when Seventy-Three and the others had been killed after their failures during the tattooing process. The concept of resisting had never even occurred to her.

What would Keeper have done if she'd objected? That act would've almost certainly shocked the woman, but it wouldn't have stopped her.

In all likelihood, One Twenty-Four would've joined them in death because of her defiance. Keeper didn't tolerate insubordination. Each of them had learned that lesson at a very young age.

But now the crèche was behind her. If Grace was victorious, One Twenty-Four would have a new life inside the Empire. Whatever form it took, she now realized that she had to have a greater purpose to give it meaning.

The marines had a purpose. They served their Empire and emperor, but more importantly, they served one another. Would she have the strength and commitment to do something like that?

She didn't know. How could she?

One Twenty-Four realized that she'd been sitting there for quite a while, just thinking. Fei had been quietly allowing her to process what she'd seen. She looked up at the woman's face and cocked her head to the side.

"The Imperial Marines saved me. Anne Marie Scott died, at least in part, because she was protecting me, an enemy of your people. Why did you take me with you, knowing that it would draw those that would kill to get at me?"

Fei smiled slightly. "Because we could no more stand by and leave a child to die than we could stomach any other atrocity. We know right from wrong, and we're willing to use force to stop monsters like that. We're willing to die to stop them if need be.

"I wish I could explain it better, Little One, but I can't. It's who we are.

"When you get older, you're going to be the sum of all your experiences and training. Part of that is going to be what you've learned in the crèche, for good or ill, and part of it will be what you experience in the years after. Remember this: the past is immutable and cannot be changed, but the future is an open road.

"If you want a different life than you currently have, you can always turn aside from your current path and choose a different course. Don't be fooled into thinking that your future is decided by others.

"Envision a life that appeals to you and work to make it a reality. If there's an obstacle in your way or someone that wants to deny you an opportunity, use grit and determination to overcome their resistance.

"I'm not saying that needs to be with violence like the Imperial Marines often use, but if you're committed to making a change in your life, only you can make it happen.

"And always remember that sometimes we're not able to effect the changes that we want. Failure is just as much a part of life as success. In fact, failure is often a better teacher than success.

"Whatever obstacles life throws in front of you, the creativity and determination that you use to overcome them defines you. The harder the journey, the stronger the person that makes it. Never give up, Little One, no matter the pressure that you face. Scream your defiance, keep fighting, and die on your feet like Anne Marie if that's what's called for."

One Twenty-Four realized that she had a lot to think about. She admired Fei, Grace, and the marines. They were so strong and determined. They'd sacrificed so much for her.

Could she dare to dream of becoming an Imperial Marine? Was that even the kind of life that she'd choose for herself?

She didn't know, but perhaps it was a good place to start. As Fei said, she could always change her mind later.

"If I wanted to become an Imperial Marine, how would I go about doing so?"

Fei's smile widened. "You don't think small, do you, Little One? I suspect that would be a difficult journey indeed. Frankly, I can't imagine how you'd overcome the resistance that you'd face in doing so, but at least it's a life that I know something about. If you truly want to learn what it means to be a marine, I'll help you.

"Perhaps it's even a good intermediate goal. You can always decide that you'd rather do something else with your life, right up until the moment you officially swear the oath. Over the next several weeks, I think we can teach you the basics of what it means to be a marine and start some kind of training for you.

"If that's your heart's desire, I'll stand beside you, and so will Grace. We'll fight for your freedom to make that choice. You have my word on that."

One Twenty-Four hopped to her feet and nodded decisively. "When can we start?"

* * *

WHILE THE REST of them went to the bridge, Grace raced to her quarters and quickly changed into a light-green blouse and tan pants before racing after them, taking up a position at the back and watching the main display as they approached the heavy cruiser. Kayden Harmon stood beside her, also casually leaning against the bulkhead.

Even though he feigned casualness, she could tell he was tense.

She felt the same. They both knew that this situation could spin out of control at any moment and end them.

"Any idea what's going to happen?" she asked quietly.

"I've been stopped a number of times, but this one's a little unusual. Normally, the military doesn't take an interest in small freighters like *Bright Passage* unless we're doing something demonstrably wrong.

"This has to be related to the destruction of the transshipment center. I'm hoping that Captain Anders is right, and this is simply to gather information from someone who actually witnessed the events in question.

"If so, we're not really in that much danger, but we'll have to be on our guard. If we make a mistake and arouse their suspicions, that will doom us."

He turned slightly toward her and smiled. "You won't be taking any part in discussions with them, I'm afraid. You don't exactly have the verbal skills to pass as a native speaker like the bridge crew does.

"I've been thinking about that, and it surprises me. I'd have figured that everyone on this mission would have had adequate language skills, at a minimum."

She gave him a toothy grin. "My skills lie in other areas."

"Indeed, they do," he murmured.

Grace found herself blushing. "That's *not* what I meant, but thank you anyway."

The woman sitting at the communications console raised her head and signaled to Anders. "We've got another request for a connection, Captain. They sound annoyed at the delay."

Anders stood and gestured for Kayden to take his seat. "Remember the plan. Play it nice and easy."

"What about me?" Grace asked. "Should I get out of sight?"

Anders shook his head. "No. Come over and stand next to me. We'll be bringing you on board with us if we go, so you need to be a familiar sight."

Kayden shook his head. "I think portraying her as a crewmember is a mistake. She's not going to have any of the skills, and she can't speak the tongue very well. I have a different cover story if need be, but it's somewhat… demeaning."

Grace felt her eyebrows rise. "What does *that* mean?"

He grinned at her. "I'm going to have to play this by ear, but just accept that what I'm saying isn't unusual inside the Singularity, and I'm not choosing it to be crass. In fact, I believe it might provide you with a great deal of latitude in your behavior.

"Now, we've delayed long enough. We had to look like casual merchants, but if we keep ignoring their attempts at communication, they're going to become suspicious. Everyone, clear your expressions, please."

Kayden made a gesture, and the woman who'd spoken earlier tapped her console. The main screen cleared, and Grace could see the ship's commanding officer sitting at his console. There were a couple of others whose backs were turned as they worked at consoles set against the rear bulkhead. Based on other Fleet bridges she'd seen, there were also consoles arrayed in front of the commanding officer.

He wore a severe, dark-gray naval uniform and sported facial tattoos, but they were different than Andrea's. His forehead and cheekbones were covered with what looked like an intricate geometric pattern of small blocks.

If their delay in answering his hails had overly bothered the man, it didn't show. His expression somehow managed to be both bored and casually arrogant. He gave off the air of a man that was very comfortable with his authority.

"*Bright Passage*, this is Legate Lucius Seven Fifty-Three of *Ever-Loyal Warrior*. Shut down your drives and prepare to receive my cutter."

Kayden smiled as if he wasn't worried in the slightest. "Understood, Legate. Might this one inquire as to the nature of this matter? My schedule has a little bit of play concerning the delivery of my cargo, but I need to know what you require in order to better serve you."

The man smiled slightly, not really showing any humor at all. "I require you and your ship to perform a service for the Singularity, so your cargo is going to be delayed.

"I also require information. It's my understanding that you just came from the Aponte system. Is that correct? You were at the transshipment center before whatever occurred there took place?"

Kayden nodded. "That's correct, Legate. What service might my ship and I provide for the Singularity?"

The man's humorless smile widened slightly. "You'll discover that in due time. My cutter will bring you and your senior staff to answer a few questions in person first."

"It shall be as you order, Legate," a seemingly subservient Kayden said with his head bowed. "May I bring a non-crew guest?"

The man showed interest for the first time, raising one eyebrow slightly. "Non-crew guest? Explain."

Kayden casually reached out and placed a hand on Grace's arm. "My mistress. She's from the fringe worlds, and I rather enjoy having her around to liven up my day. If there are no objections, I'd like to bring her with me."

That earned Kayden what looked like a genuine smile, though a small one. "I have no objections. Be ready for my transport. My marines will search you before embarkation, so bring no weapons."

The screen went dark, and Grace turned to glare at Kayden. "Your mistress? Seriously?"

"Hear me out before you punch me," he said with a smirk. "I realize that it's sexist, but this type of arrangement is common inside the Singularity and will explain why you can't speak the tongue very well.

"If you make any social faux pas, they'll just assume that you're there to be pretty and aren't terribly bright. You can use their preconceptions to their detriment."

"Well, I suppose it could be worse," she grumbled. "What do we do when we get there?"

Anders gestured toward the bridge hatch. "Let's go back to the wardroom and discuss our options before the cutter arrives. They've undoubtedly ripped out the transceivers, so we're going to have to see if we can stash something on Alan that he can use to allow an implant connection to the ship. If he can slip it past them, I should be able to overpower everyone on board."

"And if they don't have the necessary program?" she asked. "What if the ship is too old to have it?"

"That's a Gauntlet-class heavy cruiser, so she has it. Still, unless we have to, we won't act. We'd be safer behaving like ordinary merchants and going along with whatever mission they have for us. I understand that we need to get out of the Singularity as fast as we can, but we don't have a choice in this matter."

"I certainly hope that's the way it works out, Captain," Kayden said. "We're in grave danger that grows worse with every moment that we spend inside the Singularity. Also, anything that we say or fail to say aboard that ship could trigger a negative response.

"Grace, I'm going to give you a brief rundown of everything that I can on a fringe world that I'm familiar with. I'll upload the data to your slate so that you can transfer it to your implants and be able to answer at least basic questions about it. Not that I'd expect any of them to be familiar with it, or to even question you on the subject, but one can't be too careful."

She approved of his thoroughness. "What about our implants? If they're going to scan us for weapons, are they going to be able to detect our implants?"

Kayden shook his head. "The wands they use for weapon detection aren't meant to look inside bodies. They won't be looking for Imperials on every ship they stop. That's not their function."

"Let's hope you're right," Grace muttered. "Come on, let's get ourselves set up."

28

One Twenty-Four hadn't actually expected her training to start right then, so she was surprised when Fei took her back to the other marines and put her into armor and armed her with the weapons that she'd had earlier.

With the chances of a battle being very high, she tried to settle her mind into a place of determination but had to keep fighting the fear that tried to worm its way into her mind.

How did the marines keep fear from freezing them in place? She'd have to ask Fei when time permitted.

Fei started by teaching her how to use the HUD—the heads-up display—inside her helmet to both communicate and get information about the marines. It was even possible to bring in visual and audible feeds from the exterior cameras on their armor.

To make it work, Fei had to add One Twenty-Four to the platoon as a member. Once she'd done so, One Twenty-Four could see all of the marines on her display as small dots. By focusing on them more closely and using her chin controller to manipulate the data, she was able to see information specific to each and every one.

She focused on herself and saw that Fei had reused Anne Marie

Scott's ID rather than creating a new one for her. She supposed that made sense since they were pressed for time.

It was fitting that she was taking the place of the woman who'd saved her. It was also potentially an omen—which might also be fitting, if still a reason for concern.

The basic principles were simple enough for her to master, though when combat began, she'd undoubtedly find herself unable to figure out how to do something, almost certainly when she needed to be doing it very badly.

Once she'd run through everything with her helmet, One Twenty-Four went to stand next to Fei. "What happens next?"

"We wait," Fei said. "Right now, we're at the mercy of that ship. It's a heavy cruiser, so he's more than capable of handling anything we can throw at him. Even if we used all of our concealed weapons to open fire on him with no warning at all, he'd be able to shrug aside the damage and burn us down."

"So, we're helpless?"

"I wouldn't say we're totally helpless," the woman said as she squatted down next to One Twenty-Four. "If we need to, we can get to their ship in a hurry. Some of the containers have boarding pods, and we're close enough that they'd be effective.

"The problem is that they have far more marines than we do. On a ship that size, I'd expect to find a full company, so roughly three times our number.

"And that's just in numbers. Unlike us, they'll have access to powered armor. With our unpowered armor and lighter weaponry, the fight would be severely uneven.

"If push comes to shove, we might as well fight, because we'll all be dead anyway, but our best hope at this point is to remain hidden from view. As long as they never suspect that we're here, they won't come looking for us.

"And those of us that they do see, so long as they believe that they know who they are, can remain disguised. The enemy's preconceptions will influence their understanding of what they see."

One Twenty-Four frowned slightly and tilted her head just a little to the side. "I don't think I understand that. Are you talking about some kind of technology that projects an illusion over a person?"

Fei laughed as she stood. "Not precisely, though I understand that the advanced armor available to the Marine Raiders can do that. As an example, if you ever need to get into someplace that you're not supposed to be, wearing a bland uniform—preferably with a hat—and carrying a slate makes you look official.

"People are conditioned to ignore folks like that. You can pass unnoticed if you act as if you belong somewhere and don't draw attention to yourself. The exception is if you're in an area where they know you're not supposed to be or doing something unusual. Even then, a good bluff can sometimes get you through.

"So, the basic lesson is that if you behave as if you belong and dress nondescriptly, the odds are excellent that no one will even consciously notice that you're there. They won't be inclined to stop you or ask questions, because they'll believe they already know who you are and what you're doing."

One Twenty-Four thought about how such an act might work. It was an interesting concept that she'd never considered before, but it had implications beyond the current situation. She'd have to ponder it at length when she had time.

Pulling herself back to the situation at hand, she decided to ask about something else that bothered her. "What do we do if they send marines to *Bright Passage?*"

Fei shrugged. "We have places that we can use as defensive redoubts, but they're only going to be of limited utility. We'll hold the enemy off as long as we can, but at that point, it will be an exercise in futility. They're going to win, but maybe we can take a few of them with us."

"Your plan does not inspire confidence."

Her dour comment made the woman laugh. "Hopefully we won't have to do anything like that. Grace is going over with Captain Anders, Commander Kyle, and Kayden. The people on that ship have no reason to suspect that we're anything other than what we look like, so our people should be able to fool them and perhaps even capture the ship through trickery."

One Twenty-Four found herself blinking. How could such a thing be possible?

"Why would they do that?" she queried. "If you captured the ship, how would you keep such a great number of people under control?"

"That's trading up when it comes to problems," Fei said with a shrug. "If we have to figure out what to do with a ship full of prisoners, that means we've won. If that happens, I'm not going to look a gift horse in the mouth."

That offhand comment derailed One Twenty-Four's retort, making her scowl. "What's a horse, why would anyone look in its mouth, and what does that have to do with our situation?"

"We're getting a little off topic," Fei admitted, putting a hand on One Twenty-Four's shoulder. "You'll have time to look up sayings and terrestrial animals once we're out of this mess. Right now, since you're dressed as a marine, you should probably be focusing on marine things.

"Grace is going to be over in a little while, and if things go well, we'll get the signal to assist them. If things go poorly, we might be fired upon. If it's somewhere in between, we'll just have to see how things play out.

"While we're doing that, I want to take you to one of the empty containers and give you a chance to fire flechettes into something. I've had a couple of marines put up an armored barrier to protect the container from flechettes overpenetrating the targets and blowing out our atmosphere, and now I want to give you a chance to fire your weapons so you won't be surprised by how they behave if you have the need to use them.

"If it comes to that, you're only going to get one chance to get it right, and I want to be sure that you do."

Fei took One Twenty-Four to another container where the far end had been packed with crates and then covered with slabs of what looked like gelled material. Tacked to the gel were silhouettes in the form of human torsos.

That was more than a little disturbing.

"Take your pistol from its holster and aim it at a target," Fei commanded. "I want you to fire a single shot when you're ready.

Aim for the center of the chest right where the breastbone would be."

Taking a deep, settling breath, One Twenty-Four drew her pistol the way she'd been taught, brought it up her body with the barrel pointing toward the target, and then extended it until her elbows were almost locked. She focused through the sight and picked the appropriate place to aim the weapon before slipping her finger into the trigger guard and gently squeezing the trigger.

She tensed, afraid of what the weapon was going to feel like when it went off, only nothing happened.

Frowning, she remembered the safety, flicked it down with her thumb, and felt the click that indicated the weapon was now ready to fire. She then sighted on the target again and squeezed the trigger.

The flechette slammed into the target with more force than One Twenty-Four had anticipated, splattering some of the gel off of the barrier itself. The weapon bucked slightly in her hand, and the movement startled her enough that she inadvertently squeezed the trigger again and fired a second flechette.

Shocked, she took her finger off the trigger and almost turned to face Fei before she realized that that would bring her weapon away from the target and froze.

"I'm sorry," she said carefully. "The movement of the weapon surprised me, and I accidentally fired it again."

Fei grinned at her. "That's actually more common than you might think. My compliments on keeping your weapon on the target. I'd have been really upset if you'd swept the barrel across me. You did well. Safe the pistol and holster it for now. It's time to try your rifle."

With her failure fresh in her mind, One Twenty-Four followed Fei's instructions and then brought the rifle up to her shoulder and focused on the target before using her thumb to move the selector switch to single fire.

When Fei gave the order, she slid her finger inside the trigger guard and squeezed the trigger, exerting all care to ensure that she didn't fire again when it discharged.

The impact of this flechette was *significantly* more potent than the one from the pistol, blowing a large hole in the center of the target.

The weapon also jerked more strongly than the pistol, but because of its size, it was easier to control. The fact that the stock was wedged into her shoulder meant that she never lost sight of the target through the sight.

"Excellent," Fei said with a nod of approval. "Now flip the selector switch to burst. There's a trick to using burst that I want you to practice. If you simply squeeze the trigger and release it, the rifle will fire three flechettes at the target.

"If you squeeze the trigger and hold it, the rifle will fire until you let off or the magazine runs out of flechettes. I want you to start with a single burst and pay attention to the behavior of your rifle."

One Twenty-Four focused her attention on the target, flipped the selector to burst, and squeezed the trigger. As advertised, the rifle fired three flechettes in rapid succession. The muzzle of the weapon tried to rise, but she had no difficulty controlling it.

"Very good," Fei congratulated her. "Now, hold the trigger down and try to keep your weapon on target while you empty the magazine."

With growing confidence, One Twenty-Four did as instructed. The muzzle of the weapon rose more aggressively, but she mastered it, emptying the magazine into the target's chest, shredding it.

Once the last flechette had fired, the rifle emitted a brief tone that she knew indicated the magazine was empty. Without being told to, she ejected the spent magazine and replaced it with a full one from her harness.

"Excellent, Little One!" Fei said with a grin. "I'm shocked that you managed to keep your weapon controlled while on fully automatic. That's one of the most challenging weapons-related tasks a new recruit trains on during the early stages of training.

"Automatic fire is mainly used to keep the enemy's heads down so that your teammates can advance or retreat without being under fire. Most people stick with bursts because they're more controllable. How did you manage to keep your weapon focused on the target? Honestly, you shouldn't have been strong enough to do that."

One Twenty-Four shrugged as she moved the selector switch back to safe and allowed the rifle to hang from her harness. "It wasn't *that* difficult. Why can't most people keep it on target?"

"The muzzle rises when you fire it. Even though you're not feeling much of the recoil, the weapon does have a reaction to the high-speed flechettes coming out of the barrel. You didn't have any trouble controlling the muzzle rise?"

"No," One Twenty-Four said with a shake of her head. "It didn't even require that much strength. Are you sure it's supposed to be that difficult?"

"Make certain that your weapon is safed and put it back on your shoulder," Fei commanded.

As soon as she'd done so, Fei reached out and put her hand under the barrel.

"I'm going to lift the weapon as if it were firing. I want you to keep it on target."

One Twenty-Four nodded and prepared herself to deal with the rising muzzle. When she felt Fei applying pressure, she used her left arm to pull the barrel back down and kept the rifle aimed at the target.

When the muzzle didn't go up, Fei frowned and increased her upward pressure to far more than the weapon had actually generated. It was still barely manageable, but One Twenty-Four kept the weapon on target.

After a few seconds, Fei released the weapon and stepped back. "You're stronger than you look, Little One. Just based on my impression of your arms, I wouldn't have believed that you could resist that much pressure. Exactly how strong are you?"

One Twenty-Four shrugged. "As strong as my line sibs. I've never had an opportunity to test my strength against anyone outside the crèche."

"Have you ever heard of arm wrestling?"

"No. I know what arms are, but I don't know what wrestling is."

Fei laughed and gestured for One Twenty-Four to come over to where a few crates sat in the corner of the container. She took up a position on one side and rested her elbow on top of the box before gesturing for One Twenty-Four to do the same.

As soon as she'd done so, Fei gripped One Twenty-Four's hand firmly. "When I tell you to, I want you to apply pressure and force my hand down to the top of the crate. Don't take your elbow off the top, just use it as a lever."

One Twenty-Four didn't understand the purpose behind this ritual, but she was more than willing to give it a try. There was no way that she'd be able to move Fei's hand very much, of that she was certain. The woman was much larger than she was and also a trained warrior.

Once she had a good grip on Fei's hand, she waited for the signal to begin. As soon as Fei nodded, One Twenty-Four began applying pressure.

To her surprise, the woman's hand began moving. Fei frowned and increased her efforts, seemingly trying to get her hand back into the upright position. One Twenty-Four brought the full pressure of her strength to bear, and Fei's hand continued down until the woman's leverage failed, and One Twenty-Four slammed the woman's arm onto the crate.

They stared at one another for long seconds. One Twenty-Four wasn't sure which of them was more shocked.

"You're *much* stronger than you look, Little One," Fei said as she rubbed her forearm. "I think your genetic modifications may have increased your base strength beyond that of a normal human. If we'd been of equal strength, I'd have been able to use my superior arm length to win this contest, so you must be somewhat stronger than me, even at your age.

"Honestly, I think you might be stronger than any of the men in the platoon, too. A fact that I'm tempted to use to my advantage in the near future, just to see their reactions."

One Twenty-Four opened her mouth to say something but couldn't figure out what she wanted to say. She didn't know what to think. What Fei was suggesting was ludicrous.

"Are you telling me that normal humans aren't as strong as members of the Andrea Line?" she finally ventured. "What purpose would such a modification serve? I wasn't meant to be a laborer or warrior, so why would *I* require enhanced strength?"

Fei shrugged. "If you don't know the answer now, the odds are good that you'll never know for sure. You'll just have to accept that that's the way it is.

"With modified genes, the differences between you and unmodified humans may be legion. Your intelligence could be significantly increased, your speed and dexterity—or any other trait that the original designers chose to augment—could be higher.

"Hell, since you're a member of their elite lines, they might have decided to enhance *everything*. Until we get to a place where we can do more noninvasive testing, we won't know for sure.

"And I use the word noninvasive *very* specifically. We can measure many of the things about you and figure out how they fall into the range of human norms without looking at your insides. Or, if the thought of that makes you uncomfortable, then we won't."

One Twenty-Four considered what Fei had said and shrugged. "I need to know what differences there are so that I can compensate for them. If unmodified humans view me as a threat, that could make my life more difficult. I think it best if I blend in, so I need to know what to expect. I still want to know why, though."

"I think you're wise to be cautious, Little One. As far as why, I think chasing that answer is a fool's errand. It's much more useful to focus on the what rather than the why. All that matters under these circumstances is that you are who you are.

"If you ever get into a fight with an unmodified human, that kind of advantage could very well make a difference in your favor should they underestimate you—which is an almost certainty."

As if the matter were settled, Fei handed the magazine back to One Twenty-Four. "Let's fire some more with both the rifle and pistol. I want you to become comfortable with moving and shooting at the same time. Standing still while someone shoots at you is an excellent way to die.

"We'll also discuss how to take cover and the basic signals that marines use and what they mean."

Before they could start, there was a thump, and it felt as if the ship moved slightly.

One Twenty-Four frowned and looked over to Fei. "What was that?"

"The cutter just docked," Fei said seriously. "It looks like the great game has begun. Now, let's focus on what we can before we're required to act. We'll go over what I need to teach you quickly, and then we'll head back to join the marines and start getting them into the boarding pods.

"You're not going to be going with us if we attack the other ship, but I want you to be at least marginally familiar with the process.

"And that's another lesson for you, Little One. The learning never stops. As soon as you think you know everything, you'll find something else that you need to master."

One Twenty-Four nodded as the two of them got to work. If she needed to defend herself or the marines, she needed to be ready.

29

To Grace's relief, the Singularity marines' search for weapons was perfunctory. In fact, the two didn't even bother using scanner wands. Instead, they patted each of them down by hand, and that was it.

The process was professional enough that they'd have found any weapons but not so thorough that she felt groped. While these troops weren't top of the line, they seemed competent, so she was glad whatever Kyle had stashed to try and get into the ship's systems passed undetected.

The marines grouped the four visitors together inside the cutter and then sat around them in good overwatch positions to make sure that they didn't cause trouble. Once again, professional behavior. She really hoped they didn't end up fighting marines of this caliber, because it would be an ugly fight.

The cutter was an Imperial model, though not of the most current generation, so it must've been captured with the ship. Its age meant very little since Fleet was so extensive. Even the generation of cutter previous to this one was still in service in some places. If it worked, there was little call to replace it.

The pilots undocked smoothly, but their maneuvering seemed

clumsy. She found that peculiar. She'd have figured that even though the equipment wasn't Singularity gear, they'd have accrued enough experience to use it without issues.

Grace considered attempting to connect her implants to the cutter to see if it still had the systems to receive such communications but decided that that was just begging for trouble. It was far better not to take chances like that.

Trying to look casual yet still somewhat nervous about what was to come wasn't that difficult, so she didn't feel like she was straining her almost nonexistent acting skills too much. If things went badly, not only would she die, but so would everyone else back on the freighter. There was a lot at stake.

The flight from *Bright Passage* to *Ever Faithful Warrior* was brief. The marines escorted them into the ship and directly to a lift once they'd docked.

Unlike Imperial protocol, none of the ship's officers was there to greet them. Maybe it was because of their supposedly low caste. She'd bet an officer would be there to welcome anyone of real status.

As they made their way through the ship's corridors, she began noticing that not everything was as it should be. There were occasional scuffs and scratches on the bulkheads and deck that looked as if they'd been caused by flechettes.

She was pondering why the crew wouldn't have cleaned things up after capturing the ship when they rounded a corner, and she found something far more anomalous.

The side corridor they'd turned into was partially melted from a plasma discharge. Based on the amount of damage, it looked as if someone had fired a plasma rifle and ruined one of the bulkheads and several hatches on that side.

The group edged over so that they were only traveling through the undamaged portion, but it begged the question of why the battle damage hadn't been repaired. The only thing that she could think of was that the ship had only recently been captured.

That changed their calculus, but she was concerned that they hadn't heard of any battles larger than the usual border skirmish. Something this significant would've caused waves.

While she was still thinking about that, her implants pinged with an incoming communication, shocking her. It was Anders. She couldn't believe that he was taking this kind of risk but accepted the call. It wasn't as if doing so was more dangerous than what he'd already done.

This looks recent, right? he asked.

It does, she confirmed. *What's going on?*

This has to be a new capture. Did you notice how the pilot didn't seem to be familiar with the cutter? Add that together with the fact that they haven't repaired this damage, and I don't think they've had this ship for very long. It wouldn't take much to replace the plates here to make this part of the ship whole again. Obviously, they're still working on the critical systems.

Grace, I'd stake every bit of money that I'm going to earn on this raid that they haven't had this ship for more than two months. In fact, it has to be more like one, or they'd have fixed the corridor here.

I haven't heard of any large-scale battles, though I suppose with only a couple of months since we started on this raid, we might not have gotten the word before we left, she said. *How did the Singularity get their hands on this ship, and what are they doing with it?*

They're taking her deeper into the Singularity, probably so that she can be fully converted for their use, he said, looking curiously at the damage as they passed. *We've captured Singularity ships in the past, so it doesn't shock me that they've gotten some of ours as well. I can't imagine how they got their hands on a ship this large without one hell of a fight, though.*

At a guess, I think they must've caught her somewhere relatively isolated and overwhelmed her quickly. That's the only way I can see that they could've forced her captain to surrender intact.

Does this change our plans? she asked.

I've already tried connecting to her with my implants, but the transceivers are down. No shock there. Why keep them online if you don't have any people that can use them?

Or they've got prisoners on the ship, she said.

Anders almost stopped in his tracks before covering the motion with a fake stumble. The Singularity marines gave him funny looks but didn't say anything.

I suppose that we have to consider the possibility, he finally said. *If so, they're going to be locked up tight and under heavy guard.*

That changes things. We're going to have to take her. I'm not going to potentially leave our people in these bastards' hands. They'd just pretend that everyone died in the fighting and then disappear the survivors.

We'll have to play this by ear, she said. *Is there any way that we can clue Kayden in on the change? This might alter how he behaves when the talking starts.*

I suggest you whisper it in his ear. Isn't that what mistresses do? Give him a very brief rundown of what we're thinking and planning.

She and Kayden *had* had sex, but this was still going to be awkward. Still, if she wanted them all to make it out of this alive, she was going to have to sell it.

Grace stepped up to Kayden and allowed her eyes to widen dramatically. "Honey, did you see what happened back there? It looks like someone shot the place up. What's happening? Are we in danger?"

Even though she'd been speaking softly, she'd made certain to pitch her voice so that the Singularity marines would hear. She had to play this straight and make them feel sure that they knew what her reasons were for getting so close to Kayden.

If the merchant was surprised by her actions, his expression didn't betray it. He simply grinned impishly back at her and put an arm around her waist.

"Just think of this as a display of our military power, dear. There's nothing to worry about."

Grace squeezed him more tightly and put her face next to his, stopping them both in the corridor. "Are you sure? I'm scared."

"You're perfectly safe. I promise."

She put her lips next to his ear and whispered softly. "Anders thinks that they still have the original crew aboard. That changes the equation, and we're taking the ship. You need to plan for that when you talk to the leaders."

Kayden said nothing, merely kissing her on the forehead and gently pushing her back.

One of the marines shook his head at her display of supposed weakness. She could imagine what he was thinking and was pleased to see that her ruse had worked.

If they had to throw down on these marines—which was looking more likely by the second—the fact that they thought she was helpless and weak would work in her favor.

"Where is she from?" one marine asked Kayden. "Her accent is the worst I've *ever* heard. How can you stand it?"

"It grows on you," Kayden said with a grin. "Besides, she can pronounce my name perfectly, and at volume, at the appropriate moments and with the right... stimulation."

The marines laughed, and Grace had to school her face to keep from glaring at Kayden. He was going to pay for that later.

She didn't know the layout of a heavy cruiser, but it didn't seem like they were headed toward the bridge. Grace would've thought the captain would meet them in a briefing room somewhere close at hand in case he needed to get back to the control area quickly.

Instead, their goal seemed to be near the senior officers' quarters based on the signs that were still attached to various locations to guide the original crew. That was another sign that the ship hadn't been in Singularity hands for very long.

The marines led them to a hatch that was different than any she'd ever seen before. Someone had gone to the trouble of sheathing it in what looked like real wood.

Grace was no expert when it came to that sort of thing, but it was pretty and was probably expensive. What the hell was something like that doing aboard a Fleet warship?

The hatch opened moments after the marines signaled their presence, and the visitors were ushered into a briefing room. Like the hatch, it was far different than what Grace would've expected on a Fleet vessel.

Rather than being an ordinary briefing room, this was a VIP affair. The table in the center of the room was a long, thick, heavily polished tabletop that seemed to have been constructed from a single piece of lustrous wood. That would've made the tree that it was taken from massive and likely made it even more valuable than her initial guess.

The displays along the bulkheads encircling the compartment were also made of expensive-looking wood but closed in with what seemed like glass doors. They wouldn't be glass, but something sterner. Glass could shatter and injure people in combat.

Inside the display cases sat a wide variety of knickknacks. She didn't have time to examine them closely, but her guess was that they were some kind of archeological artifacts. They looked old.

The room had an almost diplomatic feel to it. Or maybe a corporate board room. Neither of which made sense. Diplomats wouldn't have used a warship, and this couldn't be something rigged up for a flag officer, because they'd have used a battlecruiser or superdreadnought as their flagship.

Whatever the answer was, it was going to have to wait until later. It was show time.

Legate Lucius Seven Fifty-Three sat at the head of the table with two Singularity officers flanking him. Though there was plenty of room at the table, there were only four other chairs in the room, and all were grouped at the far end of the table from the Singularity officers.

As Grace and her friends sat, the two Singularity marines took up positions along the bulkhead behind them. She surreptitiously eyed the distance between her and them. If she positioned herself well, she'd be able to reach them before they could get their weapons out.

Thankfully, the marines were unarmored and only had pistols at their waists. Based on the heft of the weapons, she thought they were flechette pistols rather than stunners. She'd have rather had the option of stunning people with the captured weapons, but beggars couldn't be choosers.

Attacking the two would be dangerous, but she couldn't allow them to get the drop on her and her friends. When push came to shove, she'd take these two out fast and hard.

Kayden took the center chair at their end of the table, with Anders and Kyle sitting on his right. That left her to take the seat on the left, and she positioned her feet and body in such a way that she'd be able to come out of the chair and straight at the marines on a moment's notice.

Then she turned her attention to the Singularity officers. All three sported the same geometric pattern on their faces, though they weren't of the same genetic heritage. She'd thought that the tattoos marked them as coming from certain genetic lines, but apparently, her understanding of that aspect of their society was incomplete.

Whatever the case, their appearance didn't bother Kayden at all. He simply inclined his head toward them and waited for the Legate to speak.

The man in question let them stew for about ten seconds before he started talking. "*Ever-Loyal Warrior* was recently captured in battle. We're taking her to a shipyard for refit, but we've suffered an engineering casualty. One of her two fusion plants became unstable, and we were forced to shut it down. That leaves us with only one, and its behavior has now become suspect.

"Our escorts left us here to go investigate the attack in the Aponte system and will return in a day or so, but I've come to the conclusion that it would be prudent to send your ship back to Aponte to bring back trained technicians skilled in the maintenance of fusion plants to perform what repairs they can. I don't want to see my new command suffer a complete power failure before I've even had her six weeks."

The officer leaned back slightly in his chair and considered them. "Now, tell me what you can tell me about the attack in Aponte. Were you at the transshipment center or merely somewhere else in the system when it occurred?"

"We'd docked at the transshipment center and were transferring cargo, Legate," Kayden said deferentially. "I'm not sure what exactly happened, but there was an alert sent to all the ships as we were finishing up, indicating that a destruct sequence had been initiated and the timer was very short. We had less than half an hour to disengage our ship and gain as much distance from the transshipment center as we could.

"I have no idea what prompted such action, because no one from Control contacted us directly. No general transmissions were sent about why the transshipment center felt the need to destroy itself either. Frankly, I was unaware that facilities like that were even equipped to self-destruct.

"In any case, there were still many ships, either docked or too close to the transshipment center when it exploded, and they were destroyed. That's really all I know."

The Singularity officer frowned. "This is going to require more investigation, so I may have to divert to Aponte myself once I'm confident that my remaining fusion plant is stable.

"I'll want my people to go over everything that you recorded during the incident and question any of your crew that might have seen or heard something of note. You will make them and your systems available as soon as you return to your ship."

Grace blanched inside. If the Singularity put people aboard *Bright Passage*, the chances of discovery went through the roof.

We're going to have to execute Kyle's plan, she sent to Anders through her implants. *If they board us and start digging into everything, they're going to find the marines or something else sketchy. This would be far more invasive than a customs search. What kind of position does Kyle need to be in to get into their system?*

He's working on it, Anders said. *There are access ports underneath the table, and he's taking his apart so that he can connect the implant reader right now. If he can do it, we might be able to end this fight in the next minute.*

Keeping a vacuous smile on her face, Grace glanced over at Kyle and saw him attentively paying attention to the Singularity captain. There was no indication from his posture or expression that his hands were busy trying to get their equipment connected by touch alone.

She was impressed. That took a lot of skill. As a marine, she could disassemble and reassemble her weapons in the dark and under fire, but she'd never thought of Fleet officers as being able to do the same sort of thing. Kudos to the redheaded man.

The Legate stood, and his men stood with him. "I think I've given you enough information to carry out my instructions. My officers here will accompany a squad of marines back to your ship and began going through your files and interviewing your crew immediately."

Kayden stood smoothly, and Anders and Grace followed suit. Kyle didn't. In fact, he dropped out of sight under the table, drawing everyone's attention.

"What is your man doing?" one of the secondary officers asked, obviously confused.

Moments later, an implant port appeared in Grace's virtual perception of the room. Kyle had gotten them in. His idiotic plan might just work after all.

Without saying a word, Anders threw himself at the three Singularity officers, with Kayden following a beat behind. Kyle rose and followed them.

Taking that as her cue, Grace launched herself at the marines who were still gawking behind them. Neither of the men had even begun reaching for their pistols by the time she reached them.

No matter how capable they were, the men were starting this fight from the unenviable position of having been taken completely by surprise and having vastly underestimated her capabilities. She had no intention of allowing them time to recover.

Grace planted one foot squarely between the first marine's legs with all her strength and instantly disabled him. One down.

The second man had only just begun to realize how much trouble he was in when she grabbed his arm, twisted herself around, and used the leverage to flip him over her shoulder. He slammed face-down into the deck with bone-jarring force.

While he was momentarily stunned, she pulled his pistol out of its holster and took a couple of steps to the side, glancing at the weapon quickly to make sure that it was similar in function to the ones she was familiar with. It was, and it only took a moment to flip the safety off and have the weapon ready to fire.

As the man she'd kicked in the crotch was still curled in a ball and unable to defend himself, she leaned in and retrieved his pistol as well, stepping clear of them both and making the second weapon ready to fire.

Grace half turned to assess how the fight was going, making sure to keep her prisoners inside her cone of vision, as well as watching the hatch to be certain that no one came in and surprised them.

One of the secondary officers was down with Kyle on top of him. The Fleet officer was pounding him in the face with his fists and seemed to have the upper hand.

Anders and the Legate were trading blows in the far corner of the compartment, while Kayden and the remaining officer were battling on the other side of the table.

The merchant was getting the worse end of the deal. The officer was far better trained in hand-to-hand combat and was in the process of whipping his ass.

To even things up, Grace fired a flechette into the officer's leg. The injury would be bad but probably not lethal. Still, the man's survival wasn't her problem. Mission success was.

The man staggered and gasped, allowing Kayden to punch him in the gut before throwing him to the deck and stepping clear of her field of fire.

The distraction of her shooting the man gave Anders the opportunity he'd been looking for to lay a truly impressive right cross into the Legate's jaw. The Singularity officer's head snapped around, and he struck the bulkhead with a thunk as he reeled back before sliding bonelessly to the deck.

Anders turned toward her. "I've activated every antiboarding weapon on the ship and received responses from most of the system. Not all of it, unfortunately. There were some sections of the ship that might not have fired. We need to get your marines over here as quickly as possible to secure the ship. Make the magic happen, Grace."

With implant access to the secondary systems available, she was able to link up with the com system and send a signal to *Bright Passage*. She encoded it with Imperial Marine headers that would immediately forward the message directly to Na.

We've ambushed the ship, Fei. Execute Operation Pincushion immediately.

With the order given and no response expected, Grace turned her attention toward the hatch. If there was a counterattack, she'd need to hold this room against all comers until help arrived. She only hoped that her platoon arrived in time to save the day.

30

———————

One Twenty-Four had just finished going through Fei's familiarization training with the boarding pods when a chime came over the speakers set into the top of the container. The woman hurried over to the panel beside the door and accessed it quickly.

After a few moments scanning whatever was shown, she tapped the screen again and spoke, her voice ringing out over the overhead speakers. "All marines to the boarding pods! We launch in sixty seconds!"

Even as the marines in the container were rushing into the pod behind her, One Twenty-Four took a step toward Fei. "What about me?"

"I need you to go back to your quarters, Little One," the woman said briskly. "It's still possible that the enemy will send boarders to *Bright Passage*, so keep your weapons with you and wait for us to come back. If the crew gives you any orders, obey them."

Without waiting for a response, the marine rushed out of the container.

One Twenty-Four only considered her options for a moment before turning around and following the marines into the boarding pod behind her. If they were going to be fighting for their lives—and for hers—she was going to be fighting with them.

The boarding pod was large enough to hold an entire squad. Since she was dressed in the same style armor as everyone else, there was an excellent chance that they wouldn't realize that she wasn't supposed to be there.

She was grateful that the marines were focused on their own tasks, since that prevented them from noting her short stature. None of them even gave her a glance. As Fei had said, if one acted as if one belonged, those around them only saw what they expected to see.

Her mentor had mentioned that this particular pod was the one that Anne Marie Scott had been assigned to, so she wasn't running any risk of them running out of seats.

None of the marines paid her the slightest bit of attention, all of them focused on their own tasks, so she strapped herself in.

The squad leader, Sergeant Andy Tanaka, came in last. He threw himself into his couch and quickly strapped himself in just as the hatch closed.

Without warning, a crushing weight slammed onto One Twenty-Four's chest, jamming her into the acceleration couch and taking her breath away. She'd never felt anything like the pressure.

Lacking implants, she wasn't able to mesh herself with the rest of the marines but heard the squad leader counting down the time until impact. Even that small number of seconds felt like an eternity.

In spite of the acceleration, his voice was impossibly calm and level, seemingly unaffected by what was happening to them.

As his count hit zero, their pod slammed into the heavy cruiser and came to an abrupt and immediate halt. She was thrown forward against her straps and was deeply grateful that she'd tightened them as instructed.

She expected the marines to exit through the same hatch they'd used to board, but the sides of the pod blew off and provided them with broad access to the wrecked compartment that their pod had come to rest in.

One Twenty-Four had no idea what the room had been used for, but now it was filled with debris. Her HUD indicated they were in a vacuum, but her armor protected her.

Without waiting for orders, the marines around her began piling out. Not wanting to be left behind, One Twenty-Four clumsily released her restraints and followed.

She was the last one out of the pod, but she wasn't far behind everyone else. Her cover seemed intact. Everyone was focused on the marines setting up a portable airlock around the hatch leading into the ship.

"Form up around me," Tanaka ordered over the squad channel once that was done. "Our target is the bridge. If you see anyone moving, stun them. If you see anyone with a weapon, you are authorized to use lethal force. Move out."

Without another word, the marines arrayed themselves and began flowing through the airlock and into the corridor beyond. The airlock could only hold three marines at a time, so that took several nerve-wracking minutes.

Uncertain of exactly where she was supposed to be inside the squad, One Twenty-Four decided it was probably safer for her to remain near the back of the group so that the squad leader didn't see her. Every opportunity he had to observe her meant one more chance that she'd be discovered.

Sadly, he was waiting for her as soon as she came through the airlock.

"Dammit, kid," he growled over a private channel as he grabbed her arm when she came through. "I saw Anne Marie's beacon, but I didn't think a single thing about it. What the hell were you thinking?"

Tanaka held up his hand before she could answer. "Never mind. I don't want to know. Keep your skinny ass next to me. Do you understand?"

He followed that up with a word that she didn't understand. Based on her conversations with Fei, she suspected it was a curse word, probably Imperial in origin. She really needed to learn Standard so that she could understand how to correctly interact with the marines.

"Yes, Sergeant," she said as she moved up beside him.

She didn't try to explain herself. The man was bright enough to figure out why she was there, and none of her answers would matter in any case. The situation was what it was. He'd make do, just as she would.

The corridors on the ship seemed both taller and broader than the ones aboard the freighter and were filled with the unconscious forms of the crew. None of the marines paid them the slightest mind.

The squad ignored the lifts as well, taking to the stairs and moving upward in an organized pattern where one group would take up positions covering their advance while the next group passed by them and then took up similar positions in turn.

It was almost like a game. One with potentially lethal consequences if anyone made a wrong move.

They exited the stairwell several levels later and began heading down a corridor just like the one they'd been traveling in before. Unfortunately for them, they quickly discovered that not everyone on this deck was unconscious.

Ahead of them, a dozen men and women dressed in armor somewhat similar to their own raced around the corner and immediately began firing at them. The marines hunkered down and returned fire.

Sergeant Tanaka pushed One Twenty-Four behind him and also returned fire.

Ignoring his unspoken admonition, she brought her rifle up and stepped to the side to free herself up to shoot as well. Of course the first squeeze of her trigger failed to do anything because the safety was still engaged.

Muttering the word that she'd heard Sergeant Tanaka use, she flipped the selector switch to burst mode, put the red dot on one of the enemies, and squeezed the trigger. The rifle fired, and her flechettes struck the man, but she wasn't sure if her actions caused his death or merely contributed to the carnage of all the other marines that were shooting him.

She suspected that she should be horrified or frightened but didn't have time to feel any emotion at all as she mechanically followed the directions that Fei had given her. She'd process what was happening when there was more time.

One Twenty-Four kept her weapon on burst mode as Fei had taught her and kept switching from target to target as more men and women poured around the corner behind the enemy. How many were there?

Flechettes flew up and down the corridor. Some of them even struck her torso, the impacts more powerful than she'd anticipated. None of the hits penetrated her armor, and she was able to continue firing.

When her weapon sounded, she dropped the spent magazine and replaced it with a fresh one, continuing to fire as Fei had trained her to do. In her uneducated opinion, it looked like the marines were winning the fight.

Then another figure stepped around the corner—one dressed in armor that looked significantly thicker. There wasn't even a face visible inside the helmet, only flat metal. The weapon this figure carried was also much larger than those everyone else was using.

A sharp warning from Sergeant Tanaka caused the marines to shift their aim, but their flechettes didn't seem to be able to penetrate the heavier armor. If this was the fabled powered armor that Fei had told One Twenty-Four about, her weapon wasn't going to be able to damage it either.

Several of the marines around her were already throwing grenades, but all she could do was continue firing her rifle. She shifted her aim from the armored form to the weapon it carried. Perhaps that would be vulnerable to attack.

She held her finger down on the trigger and zeroed in on the bell of the weapon with every flechette she could fire even as it began glowing.

One Twenty-Four had a moment to wonder if she was about to die before a massive explosion hurled her back and slammed her into the deck, sending her skittering along its surface and into the bulkhead behind them with bone-crushing force.

She lay there for a moment, stunned. The only thing she could see was her HUD, but she couldn't make any sense of it.

Realizing the danger of just lying there, she scrambled to her feet, raised her rifle, and took stock of the situation.

The corridor in which the armored figure had stood was a blazing wreck, torn apart by the explosion of the grenades. One Twenty-Four had no idea whether she'd disrupted the weapon or not, but that was a question that would have to wait for later.

Sergeant Tanaka made a quick assessment of all the marines and gestured for them to get moving again.

He stepped over beside her and gave her a once over. "You don't look like you're breached, but you need to stay behind me. This is dangerous. Now replace your empty magazine in case you have to use your rifle again."

One Twenty-Four was shocked. The rifle was sounding the tone that indicated an empty weapon, but even though she'd heard it, it hadn't meant anything to her. She felt like an idiot.

Without responding, she quickly dropped the magazine and replaced it with another, feeling humiliated. Her lapse could've cost someone their life. Perhaps even her own.

With those thoughts still in her mind, she ran beside Tanaka as they made their way past their dead enemies and arrived at the massive hatch leading into the bridge just a minute later.

It was wide open, and One Twenty-Four could see that everyone inside was either sprawled in their seats or lay across the consoles. The bridge was much larger than she'd imagined it would be.

Tanaka gestured toward the hatch, and several marines went around, moving the bodies to the side of the room. They searched them for weapons but otherwise left them jumbled together on the deck.

"Seal the hatch," the squad leader said. "Gomez, get into the system and see what's going on. If there's organized resistance on this ship, I want to know where they are and how many people we're talking about."

One Twenty-Four was about to follow the marine and see what he did, but Tanaka held out a hand and stopped her.

"What you did was exceptionally stupid," he said over a private channel. "You not only put your own life at risk, you endangered every single member of this squad because you're not trained to be here. Give me your weapons."

"No," One Twenty-Four said flatly. "I've used them to defend myself and the marines. I might not be one of you, but I'll do what you tell me to. Other than disarming myself."

The two of them stood there, staring at one another for several seconds, before the squad leader used that word again and turned away.

One Twenty-Four was more confident than ever that it was a curse word. The idea thrilled her a little bit. She wanted to learn more. To learn them all, no matter the language.

"Sergeant, we've got a problem," Gomez said, half turned away from the console that he was now sitting at. "It looks like they've replaced the computer system with something made in the Singularity. Somebody was able to lock the controls, and I can't access anything."

31

To Grace's relief, Na and her marines were the next people through the hatch. She'd been on pins and needles waiting for the Singularity forces to counterattack, but none had come. Whether that actually meant there were none still active aboard the ship or not, she didn't know.

"You can't believe how glad I am to see you," she told Na once the woman had signaled through her implants that the marines had arrived and Grace had opened the hatch. "That guy over there against the bulkhead is the captain. The ones near him are his senior officers. Secure everyone. I don't suppose you brought my armor and weapons, did you?"

Na gestured for one of the marines to lay a large bag on the conference table. "What kind of adjutant would I be if I just let my commanding officer wander around the battlefield naked?"

The woman turned and looked at the two marines glowering at Grace from where they sat in the other corner. "Though it seems you didn't do too badly. Medic, work on the man with the leg wound. Stabilize him, and we'll post a guard to keep watch over them."

"We don't have time to deal with them right now," Anders said. "Sew the one guy up and then stun them all."

The marines quickly did as instructed, stunning all the prisoners except for the one being worked on by the medic. As soon as he was taken care of, he joined the rest in enforced slumber.

"What's the status on the assault?" Grace asked as she finished stripping down, changing into her skinsuit, and donning her armor.

"Second squad has already seized the bridge," Na said. "Tanaka said that the computer system is locked down tight. Gomez believes that the Imperial computer has been replaced by a Singularity model. He's unable to access the system."

The noncommissioned officer gestured toward the aft section of the ship. "Third squad is in engineering now. Some of the crew there are still awake, and there are marines in unpowered armor holding part of the compartment. It's going to be a tough fight, but I think we've got the edge, particularly if we reinforce them quickly."

Grace shook her head. "If we have conscious marines, our first stop has to be the ship's armory. If there's powered armor in there, we've got to keep them from getting their hands on it. If it's in good shape, perhaps we can even use it ourselves."

Na nodded. "Second squad ran into someone in powered armor wielding a plasma rifle. They took them out with grenades before they fired, so that turned out well enough, but it could've been ugly."

The other woman made a face. "I know you don't need this kind of complication right now, but Andrea ignored my instructions to return to her quarters. Sergeant Tanaka didn't realize that she was on board his pod before he launched. She's on the bridge with him now."

Grace pinched the bridge of her nose and took three deep breaths only to let them out slowly. Yelling wasn't going to help. She'd deal with that complication later.

"Is she okay?"

Na nodded. "Tanaka said that she was involved in the combat despite his orders to stay behind him. She was knocked around a bit, but her armor held. Until I review the vid feeds from the squads' helmets, I won't be certain exactly what happened, but he says that she's in good shape.

"He also says that she's stubborn. He ordered her to hand over her weapons, and she refused. Speaking for myself, I think that kind of backbone from a girl with her background is promising."

"Isn't that the way of the world?" Anders asked. "You want your kids to have a spine right up until the moment they defy you. Now, if we're finished discussing parenting challenges, I need to get to the bridge.

"You can take Kyle with you to engineering. That way, we'll have an officer in each place, and we can try to get this ship under our control. If they end up calling for help, we might have incoming forces from the orbital."

Kayden shook his head. "It's a commercial operation. They won't have heavy security, and the orbital isn't equipped to fire on ships.

"At most, they might've noticed your boarding pods and begun calling ships passing through the system for help, though even that's not likely. Control doesn't closely monitor ships that are already parked. I learned that as part of my smuggling operations."

Grace shook her head, amused. "Sergeant Na, dispatch a fire team with Captain Anders and get him to the bridge. See that Second Squad sends a fire team to meet you.

"Kayden, you're with me. Stick toward the back and let us go around corners first. Everyone move out."

Moments later, they were all on their way. Grace fell into her usual position inside the squad.

There were a lot of unconscious people scattered throughout the corridor. The antiboarding weapons had done a good job. Too bad they hadn't been entirely effective.

They reached the armory inside marine country several minutes later and surprised a squad-sized group of Singularity marines trying to get some powered armor online.

Sadly for them, their armorer had locked everything down nice and tight. After all, you wouldn't want just anyone wandering around the ship in something like that without supervision or orders, right?

The exchange of fire was short and brutal. None of these marines were armored, so they'd missed a bet trying to get into the powered gear rather than armoring up when they could—a fatal mistake that they didn't live long enough to regret.

Grace took a moment to look around the armory and noted that it was an eclectic mix of Imperial and Singularity equipment. The new owners hadn't gotten rid of any of the Imperial weapons and armor, but they'd brought Singularity weapons and armor to stock it with. That meant that the gear was piled high in places.

There was one rack for powered armor that was empty. That must've belonged to whoever had been fighting Second Squad. She noted that the rack was grouped with the Singularity armor.

She wondered if she'd be able to unlock the Imperial armor. If she could, that would end this fight quickly. It was worth a try.

Grace set half the marines to guarding the corridor outside the armory while she attempted to bring one of the Imperial sets of powered armor online. Whoever had stored it—almost certainly the original armorer—had engaged the lockouts, which would've prevented the Singularity forces from being able to use any of the systems, but she had the codes. One of the perks of being a platoon leader.

It only took a few seconds for the armor to come to life at her order. Whoever had been maintaining it had done an excellent job. All systems were green. She wasted no time stripping off the mercenary armor and tossing it into the corner of the armory. This was no time to be neat.

As soon as she slid inside the powered armor and closed it up, the HUD came to life. She'd chosen a suit that looked to be about her size, and even though it wasn't fitted for her, it would do.

It would do damned well.

Grace detached herself from the rack, grabbed one of the large flechette rifles, and began loading herself up with ammunition and grenades. As soon as she was ready, she took up a position in the corridor and ordered the rest of the squad to armor up.

She used her codes to remotely activate each set of armor they chose and was pleased to note that all were operational. If the armorer was still alive, she'd be buying him beer for the rest of his life.

Grace used her armor's com system to connect with First Squad to get a status. They had the Singularity engineers and marines pinned down in one corner of the large compartment. On the plus side, the enemy wasn't close to the fusion plants. On the negative side, they were far too near to the flip drive for her comfort.

Her people were well trained, and everyone was ready to go in less than five minutes. She detached one fire team to hold the armory under Na's supervision and led the remaining fire team to engineering.

She met up with Sergeant Emily Kurtz just outside the main hatch. Her people were inside and keeping the enemy pinned down.

"What's your status?" Grace asked over a private channel.

"They've got roughly two squads' worth of marines," the squad leader said. "They outnumber us, but we've got them jammed back into the area around the flip drive. That's a real concern, because the engineers might be working to sabotage it. If we want to take this ship in operational condition, we can't let them fry the flip drive."

"We're going to have to hit them hard and fast," Grace decided. "As soon as they realize that we've got powered armor, they'll know the jig is up. If they've got the engineers working on sabotaging the flip drive, they'll either hurry them up or use their weapons to damage the equipment themselves. We need to make sure they don't have time to make that happen.

"I want you to get your people ready to follow us in. My team and I will take out any active threats, but you're going to have to be ready with stunners to take out anyone working on the equipment."

A situation like this was where all the training her platoon had put in paid off in spades. It only took a few seconds to select an appropriate battle plan and send her marines in to engage the enemy. The hatch leading into engineering was big enough to move equipment, so it was more than large enough to handle powered armor.

Her people went through, immediately racing toward the corner of the room where the defenders were holed up. The enemy was quicker on the uptake than she'd hoped and immediately engaged her people, but they only had flechette rifles. Thankfully, no plasma grenades came arcing out at them.

The heavy flechettes fired from the large rifles her people carried tore the Singularity marines apart and damaged the equipment behind them. Her people were pros though, so they managed to avoid shooting the flip drive.

First Squad was right behind them, using stunners to shoot every single engineer they laid eyes on. In less than two minutes, the fight was over, and the enemy was either dead or unconscious.

With that done, her marines spread out to search engineering for any holdouts. No one would rest easy until they declared the compartment secure.

Several of the marines in unpowered armor had injuries, but nothing the Singularity marines had possessed was powerful enough to damage her powered armor. The outcome had been inevitable.

To her untrained eye, the flip drive looked intact. It didn't seem as if they'd even been messing with it. That was good news.

Unfortunately, all of the engineering consoles were locked down. Someone—probably down here, since this was where most of the conscious people they'd encountered were—had managed to run the program to deny access to intruders. Without access to the computer, they wouldn't be able to use any of the ship's major systems.

She supposed it was a good thing that Anders had suborned the antiboarding weapons, or this would've been a very short attack.

"Kayden, check the flip drive," she ordered over her external speakers. The merchant rushed off with a pair of marines to provide him with cover.

"We need to get into these computers," Kyle said after several attempts to bypass the lockout failed. "We don't know how much time we have left, but we're going to have to make a decision about whether we can take this ship with us or if we have to destroy her fairly soon."

"That's not all," Grace said. "We've got to go through this ship deck by deck and make sure that we don't have any holdouts. I'll leave a fire team in powered armor to guard the entrance to engineering. That should be more than enough to make sure that you're undisturbed.

"The rest of my people are going to have to spread throughout the ship in groups to check everything out. Heavy cruisers are pretty large, so that's going to take hours. Even then, we might miss some clever people, so be careful. Hopefully, we'll find the original crew somewhere along the way."

She didn't know how they were going to get into the computer systems. Frankly, that was Anders's problem. Hers was to make sure that the ship was as secure as she could make it.

Maybe during that process, she'd figure out what was so unusual about this ship. There was something weird going on, and she was determined to find out what that was.

32

One Twenty-Four waited on the bridge, standing to the side as the crew tried everything to dig into the consoles and gain control of the ship. Based on the language they were using, they weren't having much luck.

While that was unfortunate, it did allow her to pick up a wider variety of likely curse words to use going forward.

Captain Anders arrived shortly after they'd seized the bridge and assumed the central seat, snapping out orders to the crew so that the vessel could be secured. He motioned to her to come over as soon as he finished doing that.

"Take your helmet off," he ordered.

She did so and waited passively for him to lecture her on her most recent failures.

He studied her face for long, silent seconds. "You're something of a cipher to me, Andrea. Or do you still think of yourself as One Twenty-Four?"

His grasp of the tongue was quite good, she decided. Much, much better than Grace's.

She shrugged slightly. "I still think of myself as One Twenty-Four, but I suppose that will change over time. It really doesn't matter what my designation is. As Fei says, you can call me whatever you want, so long as you don't call me late for dinner."

The joke caused the corners of his lips to curl upward slightly. "I think I like your sense of humor. You realize that you've made Grace and Fei very upset by sneaking onto this ship, don't you?"

One Twenty-Four nodded. "I did what I needed to do. I refuse to stand by while others defend me when I can defend myself and help them do the things that they need to do."

The man nodded. "Completely understandable, and I sympathize, but Grace is going to tear a strip off of you when she finally finishes securing this vessel. I'd also expect a very stern lecture from Sergeant Na.

"Even when you do the right things in life, there are always consequences when you disobey orders. I'm told that you want to be an Imperial Marine someday. I believe I speak for all Fleet officers in saying that I'm pretty sure that marine command has a *very* dim view of disobeying orders."

"That day—if it ever comes—is in the distant future. Today, I'm still property," she said with a shrug. "I personally doubt that the Empire will allow me any freedom whatsoever, much less the opportunity to become an Imperial Marine."

"I hope you're wrong. Of course, if we can't get out of the Singularity, then it won't matter. We've got to undo whatever they've done to this ship and then get the hell out of here before those destroyers come back. Our time is short, and we may have to head back to *Bright Passage* and destroy this ship."

"If I might ask, how can you get around this computer lockout?"

"We either have to bypass the computer itself or somehow hack one of the command codes. I doubt very seriously that we're going to get any of the senior officers to unlock the computer for us.

"And, since we've stunned all of them, we're not going to be able to get them to do anything for us in the short term, even if we wanted to. It's all up to Corporal Gomez at this point. He's a very competent computer guy, but this isn't a civilian system that we're worming our way into. It's military, and it's designed to keep unauthorized persons out. Only someone important enough to have an appropriate override is going to be able to do anything."

One Twenty-Four frowned slightly. "Perhaps I can help. Genetically, I'm a member of one of the ruling lines of the Singularity. That must carry some form of authority."

The man started to say something but stopped and rubbed his chin thoughtfully. "Maybe. And you'd be willing to help us to do that? Such an action would brand you a traitor in their eyes. Right now, all you are is a prisoner being taken away from the Singularity."

"I don't think you understand how they'll treat me if they ever catch me, Captain Anders. My life is already forfeit. My choice to join the Empire was made for me. I'm willing to do what I can to help you in the hope that it will perhaps allow me a more meaningful life inside the Empire."

"We have a saying for that too," he said. "If you scratch my back, I'll scratch yours. If you can do something to help us, my officers and I will do what we can to help you in turn. Go see if Corporal Gomez can put you to use."

One Twenty-Four nodded and stepped over to where Gomez was working on a console. He had it partially disassembled and was muttering something that didn't sound very complimentary.

He looked up at her in surprise when she cleared her throat. "I'm a little busy, kid."

"Captain Anders said that I might be able to assist you. I have no skills with computers, but I'm genetically a member of one of the ruling lines of the Singularity. Is it possible that you can use that to help override this lockout?"

His face took on a thoughtful expression, and he was silent for several seconds. "I did see a DNA reader on the captain's chair. Nothing ventured, nothing gained, right?"

The man rose and walked over to Anders. "Sir, can we borrow your chair?"

With a somewhat nonplussed expression, Anders stood and gestured toward the chair. "It's all yours."

Gomez gestured for her to sit and take off her right gauntlet.

When that proved somewhat troublesome, he assisted her in disconnecting it and sliding off her hand.

"You'll get used to those things with practice," he said in a conspiratorial tone. "Put your hand on this reader plate, and let's see what happens."

She rested her hand on the plate that looked like it had been recently added to the chair.

"Override authorization Andrea Seven Seventy-Six," she said, deepening her voice to mimic Keeper's. She and her line sibs had gotten a lot of practice at imitating the woman over the years, and they'd become very good at getting the right tone and cadence to her speech.

For a moment, One Twenty-Four was afraid that the computer would reject her, but then it spoke.

"Authorization provisionally accepted," the voice said. "Passphrase?"

"Oblivion sunrise."

"DNA sequencing in progress. Identity accepted, Andrea Seven Seventy-Six. What are your instructions?"

She looked at Captain Anders for guidance.

"Tell it to remove the computer lockout," the man said, his expression both stunned and hopeful.

"Remove the computer lockout," she said firmly.

"Processing. Computer lockout overridden."

Gomez raced back to one of the consoles and touched it. It sprang to life with a display that she didn't recognize. He spun in place and grinned at them.

"We're in!"

Anders started tapping the controls on one of his chair's arms. "This looks like a Singularity system to me, but the Imperial computer may still be on board. Gomez, I want you to go through this thing with a fine-toothed comb and make sure that we change every single control code that we need to. No one gets to pull this trick on us."

"There's no need to, sir. She's unlocked all the systems that we were locked out of. If you have her press her hand on the panel again and tell her to disable all user accounts except for her own, I believe that'll keep anyone else from screwing with the system. She could probably even add you as a user, and then you can add the rest of us as authorized personnel."

Without waiting for instruction, One Twenty-Four pressed her hand to the reader and spoke. "Computer, disable all user accounts other than my own."

"Processing. All standard user accounts disabled. Only the ruling line overrides are still enabled. You lack the authorization to lock those accounts."

Interesting. So, someone—or perhaps a group of someones—could lock even Keeper out.

"That's probably fine," Anders said. "I doubt very seriously that there are any other members of the ruling lines aboard the ship. Add me at the highest level of authorization that you can."

"Computer, I want to add a user to your system. I want him to have the highest level of authorization that I can give."

"Processing. Identify user?"

"Jay Anders," he said.

"Jay Anders," she repeated.

"User Jay Anders, please state your passphrase. Choose something that no one can overhear and be advised that your DNA will be required."

Anders gestured for her to stand and step away from the chair. He placed his hand on the plate and said something in a low enough tone that she couldn't make it out clearly.

That was smart of him. She'd just demonstrated how one could potentially steal another's identity.

"Account created, Jay Anders," the computer said. "You have been granted complete access to all systems and files on this computer. Will you be replacing Legate Lucius Seven Fifty-Three in command of this vessel?"

That was a smarter question than One Twenty-Four had expected the computer to ask.

"Yes," Anders said evenly. "I'm the new commander of this vessel."

"Command authority granted. As no other accounts are currently active, you may designate your officers and delegate the authority that they require so that they may create user accounts for their subordinates."

Anders grinned at her. "You did it, Andrea! I wish to hell I could give you a share in this raid, because you've more than earned it. I can't, but there is something that I *can* do to return the favor. Something I'll probably get in trouble for, but it'll be worth it."

She was about to respond when Fei stepped through the hatch. She was dressed in a variation of powered armor that was similar to —but not identical with—the one that One Twenty-Four had fought earlier. This must be the Imperial variant.

With her helmet off, One Twenty-Four could easily see that the woman's expression did not promise a joyful reunion.

"Ah," Anders said with a smile. "I see that consequences have arrived for you. Sergeant Na, I'd like you to escort this young lady to the medical center and make sure that she's fully checked out. Doctor Dubois should be on board by now and will be treating any of the injured that have made their way to him. See that she gets looked at."

"Yes, sir," Fei said. "Come with me, Little One. We need to talk."

Unpromising indeed. Those four words never heralded anything positive.

Then the woman's eyes widened and shot toward Anders. They must be communicating through their implants. Whatever Anders had said shocked Fei.

"Are you sure, sir?" she asked out loud.

"I am," he said firmly. "Consider it an order. I accept full responsibility for any blowback. And, to save Grace from some of those consequences, let's just not tell her. Those are my orders."

"She'll be angry with both of us, but I concur. In your case, this might be what they call a career-limiting decision."

"I doubt it, but if so, so be it. I can afford to retire."

"I'll see to it. Andrea?"

One Twenty-Four followed Fei out of the bridge, and they headed down the corridor. A pair of marines in powered armor fell in behind them as they made their way to one of the stairwells.

"What you did was exceptionally dangerous," Fei said flatly. "I gave you that order because I intended to keep you safe. By disregarding it, you've offended me. There will be consequences for that."

"And I will accept those consequences without complaint," One Twenty-Four said. "I did what I needed to do."

Fei chuckled. "You're going to give Grace gray hair. Are you injured?"

One Twenty-Four shook her head. "My armor is damaged, but I took no injury."

"Were you forced to shoot anyone?"

"Yes. I'm not precisely certain how I feel about that, but they were not giving us a choice."

Fei nodded without saying anything as they started down the stairs. When they'd gone down four decks, they exited into another corridor and continued on.

"I think that your background is going to complicate your emotional reactions to combat, but you've seen the elephant now. There's no going back.

"And before you ask, that's another Terran saying. An elephant is a creature that is so different from what one would generally expect to see that once you've seen it, your life can never be the same.

"You realize that by going into combat, you could've been maimed or killed. You don't have medical nanites like the marines do. I have no idea how well you heal from injuries, but something that one of us could shrug off might end you."

"It was a risk that I had to take," One Twenty-Four said simply. "Debts must be paid, and sometimes that payment is in blood. I read that.

"Perhaps I made up for it somewhat by helping Captain Anders gain control of this ship. I was able to use my DNA and a passphrase that I overheard Keeper use to convince the computer that I was her."

"I see. That explains his instructions to me. You did him a great service, and he's offering to do one for you as well if you're willing to take that step. I know that your people have an almost religious rejection to implanting machines inside their bodies. Yet you also want to be an Imperial Marine. Those two things are mutually exclusive. Have you considered that?"

One Twenty-Four nodded. "I'm no longer of the Singularity. I refuse to be limited by their restrictions. If implanted machines are good enough for you and Grace, they're good enough for me."

"Captain Anders has authorized Doctor DuBois to use the equipment in the medical center to give you a set of Fleet implants, which is what the Imperial Marines use as well.

"That's a small transgression in the greater picture, but he's also authorized the doctor to implant a marine-grade medical nanogenerator into your system. They're significantly more capable than the medical nanites that Fleet uses, and *someone* is going to have a cow as soon as they find out what he's done."

One Twenty-Four almost asked what a cow was, but she stopped herself. One more thing to look up.

"I really should get Grace's approval since she's your guardian, but if she doesn't know, she can't be blamed for not stopping us. Which, if you're overly clever, you'll think you can use to get away yourself. Don't try that, or I'll make you deeply regret it. Do as I say, not as I do."

Fei waited until One Twenty-Four nodded before continuing.

They stopped outside an open hatch where injured marines were being walked through. This must be the medical center.

"The choice is yours, and I'll support you in it, but it's not something you can take back," Fei said. "Once the implants are in your brain and the nanites are in your body, they won't be coming out. If you truly want to be an Imperial Marine, Captain Anders is risking his career to give you a huge leg up. Do you want to do this?"

One Twenty-Four didn't even hesitate. "Yes."

"Then let's get you fixed up before Grace comes howling in like the wrath of God to stop us."

33

―――――――

Searching the heavy cruiser for holdouts took hours. Thankfully, they'd found none. The process was complicated by the fact that she and her people still had to secure all of the stunned Singularity crewmen, and there were a lot of them. For that, they'd had to bring over every single crewman they could spare from *Bright Passage.*

By the time the task was complete, four hours had passed, and she was exhausted. So was everyone else, but it felt as if the weight of the universe had been lifted from her shoulders.

During the search, she'd also located the heavy cruiser's original crew. Some of them, at least. It was hard to tell based simply on numbers, but she thought that perhaps only half of the required people were stashed away in what had originally been cargo areas toward the rear of the ship.

She suspected that that was why there were so many marines in engineering. They'd been guarding the prisoners. Apparently, the engineering crew had been in the process of removing the antiboarding weapons and had started with engineering and the surrounding area.

That hadn't saved the prisoners, because they hadn't gotten to that section yet, or they'd decided to leave those in place, but it had allowed the guards in the aft of the ship to remain conscious.

The simplest way to store all of the Singularity prisoners was to relocate them into the makeshift prison that the original crew had previously occupied. Once again, that required carrying a lot of limp bodies. The only suitable area for the original crew was the ship's mess.

By the time they'd finished, she'd had a choice to make. She could either report to Anders or wait for the prisoners to start waking up.

She'd decided that Anders could wait. He had a decent idea of what was going on, and she needed to figure out a few of the mysteries aboard this ship.

One of those mysteries had been the captain's quarters. Someone had gone to the trouble of ripping out the bulkheads around it and making an almost palatial suite of compartments. Like in the conference room, they looked costly and were stuffed with luxuries. Definitely not something one found in Fleet.

All of the prisoners were dressed in orange ship suits, undoubtedly to make sure that if any of them got loose, they'd be instantly recognizable. Doctor DuBois had made a pass through the unconscious prisoners and said that without a more detailed examination, he couldn't be sure, but they looked healthy enough.

Her decision made, Grace took up a spot against one of the walls, ate a ration bar, and drank some water. She watched with interest as the prisoners began groaning and twitching.

Having been stunned herself, she knew they were going to have ugly headaches for hours after the event. Still, she'd bet they'd be happy enough at having been freed.

The new surroundings confused the befuddled crew. Or at least most of them. One in particular was very quick on the uptake.

She watched the middle-aged man with shoulder-length brown hair and striking gray eyes staring around the room after he'd sat up. He seemingly only blinked twice before he stood and took a narrower scan that settled on her.

He staggered when he started walking but managed to make it to her without falling over.

"Who are you?" he demanded. "What happened?"

His voice was raspy and dry, but he had the tone of someone who was used to giving orders and being obeyed. Perhaps he was the ship's captain or one of her senior officers.

Or, based on some of the other oddities, something completely different.

"I'm Grace Tolliver," she said. "We've seized this ship and freed you. Whoever you are."

The man frowned as he sank into a handy chair, already rubbing his temples. "A cross-border raid, then. That would mean that your people are operating under a Letter of Marque and Reprisal. So, you're basically active-duty Fleet and marine personnel operating under cover of having been released from service. Is that correct?"

She smiled slightly. "If you're familiar with the process, then you know that I'm not supposed to confirm that. Let me repeat my question: who are you? In fact, what is this ship, and how did you get captured?"

"That's something of a tale. Shouldn't we be focusing on our safety first? Not that our captors were giving us much information, but we have to be inside the Singularity by now. I can't imagine how you captured this ship, but they won't have been traveling alone. What are we going to do next?"

Grace put a little bit of iron into her tone. "*We* aren't going to do anything unless *you* tell me who you are."

He chuckled darkly. "You'd hardly know it by looking at me, but I'm Lord Reginald Fowler, Duke DeSantis."

The Imperial nobility wasn't commonplace—which was kind of the point—but there were enough of them, and they were spread out to the point where Grace certainly didn't know very many of them at all by name, much less sight.

A duke might have heavy responsibilities or none at all. It wasn't as if a noble title necessarily meant one was qualified to do important work. Though, she had to admit that if the man had a heavy cruiser outfitted for his use, he was probably somebody of note.

"I'm afraid that I'm not familiar with you, Your Grace," she said.

"Perhaps you could add a few details. How did the Singularity capture you?"

"I'm fairly sure that I was betrayed," he said as he scanned the compartment and his waking people. "I command the Parasis Sector militia. I was moving between worlds when we were ambushed by half a dozen Singularity warships that were concealed inside an asteroid belt.

"We were a couple of flips away from the border, so we weren't really expecting to contact enemy ships, particularly in force. Someone that knew my schedule had to have leaked it for them to be able to find us so readily."

"And you chose to surrender?" she tried to keep any judgment out of her voice, because there were circumstances in which surrender was the right choice.

"We didn't have an option," he said bitterly. "Someone sabotaged both of our fusion plants. We lost power, and they were able to board us before we could stop them. The captain did the best he could, but they were shielded against the antiboarding weapons, and we just couldn't stop them.

"Our marines died trying to anyway, but they boarded us so quickly that my people didn't even have time to get into powered armor."

Grace had never heard of any kind of cross-border raid with this kind of sophistication. If true, the Singularity had set out to capture one of the high nobles of the Empire. That by itself would be enough to start a war. A real war.

"I should get you and your senior officers to brief Captain Anders. Formerly Lieutenant Commander Anders. He'll be able to sort out what's going on while we're formulating a plan to get this ship out of the Singularity."

Fowler shook his head. "The bastards executed every single officer on the ship and all the surviving marines. All that's left are the enlisted crew. A lot of them are formally Fleet, but not all. *Gargoyle* used to be a Fleet heavy cruiser until she was seconded to me. Having former Fleet personnel serve on her made a lot of sense."

At least Grace now had a name for the ship and an idea of why some of the things about her were so unusual.

"According to the Singularity officer in command when we seized the ship, one of the fusion plants had failed completely," she said. "The other one was questionable, and they were waiting for repairs. They sent their escorts off to investigate what we blew up during our raid.

"Our time is short, and we've got to get this ship in motion if we intend to keep her. Otherwise, we're going to have to scuttle her and stuff all of you into the freighter that we're traveling on. If we can get you all."

The man rose to his feet, clutching at the side of his head. "I think we'd best go to see your commander. If my people can help, you'll have them. If *I* can help, you have me. Time is exceptionally short, Lieutenant. You are a marine lieutenant, correct?"

Grace nodded as she stood. "I used to be. Do you have any staff that you need?"

He shook his head grimly. "No. They shared the fate of the officers. The bastards spaced them."

Hearing that enraged Grace, but she didn't have time to deal with it now. They had the bastards prisoner, and they'd pay. She'd see to that.

While they still had a chance of getting out of the Singularity with this ship, every minute that passed made the challenge more difficult. Those two destroyers were going to come back at some point, and when they did, there was going to be a fight. A fight they'd almost certainly lose.

* * *

ONE TWENTY-FOUR WOKE ABRUPTLY, blinking as she saw Fei removing the somatic stimulator from her forehead. She sat up and saw that Gerard Dubois, the doctor that had performed the procedure, was already working on other patients, leaving her alone with her mentor.

"Everything went as planned," Fei said. "Since Gerard doesn't speak the tongue, he thought it best if I take you through your testing to be sure that everything is working properly. Besides, I have a lot more experience working with this kind of hardware than he does.

"We're actually very lucky that the Singularity didn't destroy the equipment. I'd imagine that would've happened in due course, but they hadn't gotten around to wrecking the implantation hardware or dumping the implants and nanogenerators themselves."

"Why didn't they?" One Twenty-Four asked. "From the way that Keeper spoke about that kind of thing, I'd have expected it."

Fei shrugged. "I suppose we'll find out when we start questioning the Singularity crew. They should be waking up about now. No need to worry. All of them are safely locked away under heavy guard. How are you feeling?"

One Twenty-Four considered the question. How did she feel?

Honestly, no differently than she had before. For someone that had just had a machine implanted in her head, she felt amazingly... normal.

"I feel fine. How does it work?"

Fei helped One Twenty-Four swing her legs over the side of the bed and sat next to her.

She was still wearing her skinsuit, so the surgery on her torso must've been conducted with it open, and then the doctor had resealed it. Or perhaps Fei had done so.

Fei put a hand on One Twenty-Four's leg. "There's a lot to learning how to use implants. Each person's experience is different. Think of it like an artificial person listening for your instructions, which then attempts to carry out your orders and present you with information. It's going to learn from you while you're learning from it.

"It may seem intrusive, but the implants are always listening for you to issue them an order. I'll walk you through accessing it for the first time, and after that, it's going to be a matter of you experimenting to see what works best for you. Are you ready?"

One Twenty-Four felt as if she should be terrified, but she wasn't. This felt like the right step for her. She was almost like an Imperial Marine, and no one could take that from her now.

"I'm ready," she said after taking a deep breath.

"I want you to think this as concisely as you can," Fei said. "Focus hard and act as if you're speaking inside your mind. 'Implant initiation status check.'"

One Twenty-Four spoke those words in her mind, and information suddenly blossomed onto her awareness. It was almost as if she were reading a screen of data, but it wasn't visual. It wasn't like something was speaking to her, either.

Everything seemed to be working as designed, though she wasn't sure how she knew that. Her cranial implants were represented in the list, and so was the nanogenerator. Her medical nanites were inactive, though they had been customized to her DNA.

Based on what Fei had told her, active medical nanites would influence her developing body, and the results of that weren't always predictable. None of that was guaranteed to be bad, but the Empire was cautious in how they treated their young.

Perhaps overly so.

One Twenty-Four knew from personal experience that the Singularity didn't share that viewpoint.

When she'd wondered to herself about what the medical nanites could do to a developing child, it was as if she'd read several articles on the subject, and the information was impressed on her mind. It all happened in an instant and made her smile. It was like having the knowledge at her fingertips even though she hadn't known that she needed it.

According to the information her implants provided, the medical nanites had a genetic image of what her body should be. The fact that her body was still developing meant that their perception of her was that of an adult. Prematurely activating them had the potential for the nanites to attempt to "heal" her from "injuries" that were, in fact, part of her being a child.

She wondered if she could instruct the medical nanites to only look for trauma. The answer came back immediately that she could not, but that the doctor might be able to do so.

It was as if an operating manual for her medical nanites was present in her mind. It felt as if she had been reading it for minutes, but her implants informed her that only a couple of seconds had passed.

It seemed that her cranial implants could provide her with the time as well. That might be useful.

"I have questions," she said slowly. "The medical nanites indicate that the problem with a child having active medical nanites is that they can inappropriately alter a body that's still developing.

"Is it possible to have the medical nanites perform an assessment of my body on a daily basis and use that as a template for its repairs? I can't imagine that my body would develop too much in such a short period of time.

"If I was actually injured, then they could perform their designated function without harming me or my development. If I was hurt, they could be instructed not to use the damaged areas as part of the template for future updates until I'd healed."

Fei seemed to think about that for a moment and then slowly nodded. "I've just checked my own implants and asked some questions from the data that I took the time to store there about medical nanites. Data that I made sure was uploaded to your implants as well.

"It should be possible, but I'm not an expert. We should ask Doctor DuBois."

The marine waved a hand at the doctor, and he came over. They spoke in Imperial Standard, so One Twenty-Four wasn't able to understand what they were saying.

Or was she?

She instructed her implants to translate what they were saying into the tongue and was immediately presented with a translation of the words being spoken. It sounded a little rough but was more comprehensible than Grace's accent.

"Gerard," Fei said. "Andrea has a question that I'm not comfortable answering, and we'd like to hear your medical opinion. She thinks that it should be possible to have her nanogenerator update its template of her body on a daily basis rather than keeping them inactive.

"That would allow them to protect her while not putting her body in danger as it's developing. What's your opinion?"

The man shrugged slightly. "I can update them to do that. Since her implants are active, it's going to take her approval for the change, but it will only take a minute. Even young adults that get medical nanites have to go through this process, because their bodies don't actually stop developing until their mid-twenties.

"Even longer, really, because of the regenerative properties of the nanites themselves. If I do, her development will slow down and she'll look like she's in her mid-teens when she becomes a legal adult.

"The final programming doesn't usually go into place until the recipients are in their mid-thirties. We're starting this way earlier than I'd prefer, but with proper monitoring, it shouldn't be dangerous, though she might not be fully developed until she's in her forties. Considering how much risk we're at, it's probably a prudent decision."

Fei considered that and slowly nodded. "I'll explain this to her, and we'll do it now."

"I… understand you and… concur," One Twenty-Four said haltingly in Standard.

Her mentor's eyebrows shot up. "You're *very* quick on the uptake, Little One. Most people don't figure out that they can have their implants translate for them for quite some time."

Fei turned back toward the doctor. "Let's get this done so that I can get her out of here and leave you to your work."

While the doctor brought out his equipment, One Twenty-Four looked at Fei and switched back to the tongue. "What are we going to do next?"

"Grace said that she found the people previously in charge of the ship. They're going to be briefing Captain Anders very shortly. I think it would be best if you're in the room."

One Twenty-Four frowned. "Why?"

"Apparently, the owner is someone very powerful inside the Empire. Grace feels that if you're presented appropriately, he might make a powerful advocate to speak on your behalf.

"The best way to do that is for you to be present when they explain how your actions and your background helped turn the tide of battle.

"Then, when he questions you, you can explain how you've left that life behind and what you want in your own words. If you can convince him of your sincerity, he could be a powerful protector."

The idea of having to convince someone to protect her was unsettling, but One Twenty-Four steeled her nerve. If she needed to convince someone of her value, then she'd do so.

What Fei hadn't mentioned was that if she failed to win this man's support, he could just as easily condemn her. No pressure.

34

After consulting with Anders about the meeting location, Grace led Duke Fowler to the briefing room just off the bridge. Unlike the one that now was obviously the Imperial noble's territory, this one was spare and military in appearance.

Anders sat at the head of the table with the officers that Grace recognized as being in charge of the major departments aboard *Bright Passage*. The only one that was missing was Alan Kyle. That probably meant that he was on the bridge, keeping watch in case trouble came calling.

As soon as she and Fowler entered the briefing room, Anders stood, and the rest of his officers stood with him. It was a show of respect for someone socially superior to themselves even though the man was still dressed in prison orange.

Anders started to give up his seat, but Fowler waved a hand in negation and sat farther down the table. "Let's not stand on ceremony. I understand that we're in a very bad position, and I don't want to waste any time bowing and scraping. You've seized *Gargoyle* from the Singularity, and that puts you in command. We can sort everything else out when we have time."

Without bothering to argue, Anders resumed his seat, and his officers followed half a beat later.

Grace leaned against the wall just as Na came in with Andrea in tow. The girl had her helmet on, so her tattoos weren't visible. That was probably a good thing right now, because that was a needless distraction when they were on the clock.

Andrea wouldn't stand out, because there were a couple of marines in the mercenary armor stationed at the back of the briefing room with their helmets on.

Well, Andrea wouldn't stand out because of the armor anyway. The fact that she was so much shorter and slimmer than the marines would probably register at some point, but for the moment, Fowler hadn't noticed.

When he did, there was going to have to be an explanation, and then she'd see how he responded. As a powerful Imperial noble, his support could open a lot of doors. His resistance could also hamper Andrea's ultimate chances of success. It was a gamble but one that was worth taking.

"Let's start by laying out the situation as we find it for Duke Fowler," Anders said. "*Gargoyle* is currently in orbit around a gas giant about three flips away from the Singularity border. My people and I have seized control of the ship, and we have the previous crew locked up where we found him and his people.

"With the able assistance of an ally, we've managed to bypass the lockout on the computer. The original hardware was disassembled. It's in the hold, and a Singularity system was installed in its place. There won't be time to swap them out, so we'll have to make do.

"With only the crew from *Bright Passage*, we can potentially maneuver this ship, but it would be helpful if some of the original crew could bolster our forces. We're stretched incredibly thin."

Fowler nodded. "You'll have every assistance that my people and I can provide. We don't have any officers because the Singularity executed them, but the enlisted people are competent and skilled. I figure that we lost maybe half the crew during the fight, so we'll still be stretching it, but you should be able to run the ship if the power situation can be sorted out."

Anders gestured for Kayden to stand.

The Singularity merchant rose and bowed slightly toward Duke Fowler. "My name is Kayden Harmon, and I'm a former merchant working for Imperial Intelligence inside the Singularity. Captain Anders will vouch for my loyalty, as I think I've proven it multiple times on this mission.

"I started my life in space as an engineer, and while it's been some time since I've filled that role, I know enough to check the systems. This ship is down to one fusion plant, and while it's operational, its output is fluctuating in a manner that makes me suspect that if we push it too hard, it will destabilize.

"If we can slip out of the Singularity without pushing it, I believe that we can continue to use it, but there's going to be some risk. If it fails, the ship will be without power until I can bring it back online."

Fowler grimaced. "I can't say that I'm surprised. Both fusion plants were sabotaged as part of the ambush. I have my suspicions about who was responsible based on some of the engineers being absent from the prison, so I'd definitely like to review who you're holding prisoner.

"We managed to lock the computer down, so I'm not surprised that they had to replace it. What does shock me is the fact that you were able to gain access to the Singularity system when they undoubtedly did the same. You must have some very skilled hackers."

Anders grinned. "While we do, I have to say that credit for gaining access goes to an asset that we picked up on the raid. Someone with a... unique background that gives them authority over computer systems like that."

Fowler's eyebrows shot upward. "You've intrigued me, Captain. If we have time, I'd like to meet this asset and hear their story. But for now, we really need to get underway, don't we?"

"We do, but we've got to make a decision first. Do we destroy *Bright Passage* or try to take her with us? She's got a lot of valuable cargo that we've seized, and I'm loath to just abandon it. The ship itself now belongs to the Empire, but the loss of the cargo will hurt the shares of every man and woman under my command."

"Abandon her," Fowler said firmly. "The Empire will pay the full amount as if you'd delivered it, and if they don't, I'll make up the difference myself. My chancellor of the exchequer will scream like a gelded bull, but I can afford it."

"That does make the decision easier, Your Grace, but it's still a lot of money. We packed that thing full of rare elements used in the construction of flip drives and even flip drives themselves. The value of the seized cargo is… substantial."

"I believe that the Emperor will honor my promise to you," Fowler said firmly. "And with the recovery of this ship, he's going to be paying a lot more if we get out of here. The original sum is only going to be a fraction of what you're owed.

"Of course, many of the containers could be transferred to *Gargoyle*. Supplies for a ship of this size come in the same containers that are used for standard cargo transport. You'd have to make the decision about what to keep and what to abandon."

Kayden nodded. "With the assistance of someone on *Gargoyle*, we should be able to transfer a goodly number of cargo containers if we have time. You should be aware, however, that two Singularity destroyers are expected to return in roughly a day. I think it would benefit us if we could leave as soon as possible and arrange what transfers we can while we're moving toward the next flip point."

"I'll give the order for us to pull out as soon as you go over the remaining fusion plant," Anders said. "We left a skeleton crew aboard *Bright Passage*, and they'll be able to keep pace with us while we transfer what cargo we can. The flip point we'll be headed toward is on the other side of the sun, so we'll drop the freighter into it as we pass.

"If we can get out of this system before the destroyers catch up with us, our chances of success improve dramatically. I don't want to push our engines, but those smaller ships are faster than we are. Once they figure out what's going on, they're going to come after us with everything they have.

"With your crew to boost us, we should be able to operate the weapons, but we run a risk with every hit of losing all power. If we can manage to get out of this system and lose those destroyers by going in a direction that they don't expect, we'll be much better positioned to eventually escape the Singularity."

"If you're looking for my blessing, Captain, you have it," Fowler said. "You're in command of this ship. Hell, by interstellar law, you own the damned thing, and the Empire is going to have to buy her back from you.

"Do whatever you have to do to get us out of here safely, and I promise you that I'll have a reward of my own for each and every one of your people. A performance bonus, if you will."

"Then that's what we'll do," Anders said as he rose to his feet. "We've got a lot of work to do and very little time to do it, so if you'll excuse me, I've got to get busy.

"If you can locate your senior noncommissioned officers and have them available for my people to coordinate with, we'll get them spread throughout the ship and start bringing the weapon systems online and getting the ship ready to fight."

Grace watched as the Fleet officers made their way out of the briefing room and headed for their departments. She knew that Anders had once commanded a destroyer, so being in charge of the heavy cruiser was going to be a stretch for him, but she thought he'd manage.

Once everyone else had departed, Fowler stepped over to her and nodded at the marines. He then frowned at Andrea.

"Aren't you a little… short to be an Imperial Marine?" he asked curiously.

Before Andrea could say anything, Grace inserted herself into the conversation. "She's not a marine. The armor is simply for her protection. This is the asset that Captain Anders spoke of that got us into the Singularity computer system."

Without waiting for a response, Grace gestured for Andrea to remove her helmet. She watched the Imperial noble closely as the girl did so and saw his eyes widen in recognition and shock.

"That's… not what I expected to see," the man muttered. "I can't say that I'm familiar with all of the facial markings inside the Singularity, but I *think* that's a line high in status.

"I've never even heard of a child from a line like that ever being captured or even *seen* by anyone outside the Singularity."

"If you've got time, I'd like to sit down with you both and have her tell you her story," Grace said. "Then I'll tell you what I'm doing that's going to get me into a lot of trouble and ask for your help."

His gaze swiveled to her face, and he scrutinized her for several seconds. "You intrigue me, Lieutenant Tolliver. I sense a *fascinating* story to come, and it just so happens that I have some time to listen to it.

"If you'd send one of your marines to the mess and tell Chief Burns to get all the senior enlisted to coordinate with Captain Anders and his people, I can hear your story right now."

The next few minutes were going to set the tone for how Andrea would live inside the Empire, she knew. This was her chance to make an impression on someone very powerful.

Andrea would be arguing for her very life, and Grace thought that the girl could make her case well, but the proof was in the pudding. It was time to see how Andrea made friends and influenced people.

35

At the man's gesture, One Twenty-Four sat across the table from him. He didn't look very powerful dressed in his rumpled orange coveralls, but if Fei said he was an influential man, then she believed her.

His eyes studied her face carefully, but he said nothing for almost a full minute. When he finally spoke, his voice was curious.

"Tell me about your tattoos. What do they represent?"

"These tattoos belong to members of the Andrea Line. The Singularity has twelve lines that form the ruling caste, and the Andrea Line is one of them."

The man glanced over at Grace and Fei, who stood near the bulkhead. "I'm familiar with the ruling caste in general, but now I'm really curious how you managed to get your hands on one of their children."

His gaze returned to One Twenty-Four. "I'm even more curious as to why you would help them. Aren't they your enemies?"

One Twenty-Four considered how much she should tell him. Time was short, and he didn't need to have her complete story to understand the circumstances under which she found herself. She needed to stick to the salient points.

"Children of the ruling caste are raised in crèches. I was separated from mine due to treachery by one of my line sibs. Grace and the marines found me before the guards could execute me and took me with them when they left the transshipment center where the crèche was hidden.

"The moment I was expelled from the crèche, I was no longer a member of the Andrea Line, and they will kill me on sight. I don't want to die, so once I learned more about Grace and Fei, I decided that I had to do everything I could to help them."

She gave the man a steady look, focusing on his eyes. "Did you know that the Empire says that I'm property? That I'm a thing and not a person? One way or the other, I will have to live inside the Empire, but I want to be a person and choose for myself what my life will be."

"I'm familiar with that law, but I can't say that I've thought about it very deeply. It's never been personalized for me before. It's all very ethereal to say that genetically engineered beings aren't human until one is sitting right in front of you. Something about you allowed you to unlock the Singularity computer?"

When One Twenty-Four nodded, he continued. "I understand that you wear that armor for protection, but why do you have weapons? Did you expect to need to fight? Could you fight if you had to?"

"I *have* fought," she declared. "When the armed men aboard this ship tried to stop the squad from going to the bridge, I shot some of them. Perhaps I even killed some, though I'm not sure.

"I don't know how that makes me feel yet, but it had to be done. I wasn't going to let anyone hurt the marines that saved my life.

"I've only known Grace and Fei for a very short time, but I feel as if I've bonded with them more deeply than Keeper or my line sibs. Whatever they need me to be, I will be. Whatever they need me to do, I will do."

"She did kill at least one of the Singularity marines," Fei said quietly. "I've reviewed the helmet cam video, and it was her shot into a plasma gun that caused the charge to prematurely detonate and kill someone in powered armor that was going to decimate the squad.

"Her actions saved a lot of lives. It was quick thinking, and if she were a marine, I'd put her in for a medal."

The man nodded slowly. "Then you're committed far more deeply to your friends than I'd suspected. I'm uncertain how to feel about you fighting. You're a child. You shouldn't have to kill anyone."

"Her life in the crèche was cruel and dystopian," Grace said with sadness in her tone. "She says they started with two hundred children and any that didn't measure up were executed. She knew what awaited her if she failed to meet this Keeper's expectations.

"It astonishes me that she has any emotional stability at all. The fact that she has empathy for *anyone* is a miracle. I don't think anyone in that crèche cared one way or the other about their line sibs. So long as it wasn't them dying, it didn't matter.

"Are you familiar with the traditions that surround raids into the Singularity, Your Grace?"

"Only in the vaguest of terms," he admitted.

"Tradition and the emperor's express command says that we're obligated to personally claim some piece of property to declare as our booty. Something that no one can take from us, no matter its legality or value. Not even the emperor himself."

The man's eyes widened. "Ah, I think I see where this is going. You've declared the girl as your booty, so you can protect her from those that would take her away from you. That's clever.

"However, it's not going to do you much good if you want her to actually have a life. That's where you're hoping that I can help."

He returned his gaze to One Twenty-Four. "Growing up in the crèche as you did, do you even have a concept of what a free life is? I assure you before you answer that you don't. Just as I can't begin to imagine what you went through, the wider universe is going to be a mystery to you for many years."

Having said that, he laughed. "For that matter, it's a mystery to me, too. No one really understands the world around them, they just adapt to the portions of it that they can see and feel. The Singularity stands as an enemy of the Empire, and you're not going to find many people inside the Empire willing to be your friend, even if very few of them would argue in favor of you being property."

"I know what I want from life," One Twenty-Four said seriously. "I want to be an Imperial Marine."

The room was silent after she made the declaration, and she almost said more, trying to justify her position, but decided that sometimes saying nothing was better.

"I know very little about the Imperial Marines," the man said after a minute or so. "You, I'd wager, know even less. Just because you've been in a fight doesn't mean you're suited for that life.

"Yet I suppose it's good to have goals. If one doesn't have things to strive for, they'll do nothing. One thing I know about the Singularity is they have very strong feelings about machines inside their bodies. If you were to become an Imperial Marine, you'd have to set aside that belief.

"And that's even assuming that the Imperial Marines would allow the equipment they require to be installed in the first place. They're pretty picky about that sort of thing."

"About that," Fei said slowly. "After Andrea unlocked the computer, Captain Anders decided to take that complication off the table. He reasoned that if Andrea was going to be fighting, then she needed all the protections that the marines had.

"I concurred with his decision and took her straight to the medical center, where, with her agreement, Doctor DuBois installed Fleet implants and a marine nanogenerator."

"You did what?" Grace said, jerking away from the wall and glaring at Fei. "Without telling me?"

Fei nodded, her face serene. "Captain Anders felt it best if the blame revolving around Andrea was spread around a little. Your lack of knowledge about this means that you can't be punished for it. I'm sorry that I didn't get your approval, but I'm not sorry I took that matter off your plate.

"I understand that you're still pissed, but it's far easier to beg forgiveness—particularly when you have no knowledge that something is being done—than to ask permission."

One Twenty-Four could tell that Grace was furious, but Fei's words made sense to her. The deed was done, and nothing that Grace did at this point could change that. It also meant that whoever was in charge of the Imperial Marines couldn't undo it either.

She'd committed herself to this life, so changing her mind at a later point was no longer an option. Fei's assurance that one could always change their life by taking a step in a new direction became much more difficult when one had proprietary equipment inside their body.

"Do you know who I am?" the man asked.

She shook her head. "No. Someone of importance, or so I'm told."

"I am Reginald Fowler, Duke DeSantis. I command the Parasis Sector militia and rule my namesake world in the name of the emperor. If I choose to become your advocate, it's possible that the law of the Empire might one day change.

"I'd certainly be able to make certain that no one takes you away from Lieutenant Tolliver. It would require you living on DeSantis, but I assure you, it's a wonderful place."

"A... planet? I have no idea what that is."

"Then you're in for quite the experience, and I promise that I'll make it a memorable one once we get there."

He turned to Grace. "As I understand how these raids work, you were released from Imperial service before the raid. To avoid getting orders to do something you don't want to do, I'm afraid that career is done. Can you accept that?"

Grace nodded. "I'd already come to that conclusion myself. If we survive this raid, I'll be able to support Andrea and myself without any difficulty. I'm just going to have to accept that my life as an Imperial Marine is over. That's a price I'm willing to pay to guarantee that Andrea has the life that she deserves."

"My father taught me when I was very young that debts incurred are always paid in full and with generous interest," he said. "You might never anticipate that you'll owe someone for a particular task, and yet when the time comes, you don't turn them away.

"This is not going to be a simple task, but perhaps with my assistance, it's possible. You're going to face resistance at every turn. You're going to find perfectly rational people who will hate you for what you've done and what you're trying to do. Change is hard, particularly when it goes against the grain of what someone believes.

"The fact that the Singularity destroyed my escorts, killed my officers and courtiers, and kidnapped me is going to spark another war. They must've realized this before they acted, hoping that my loss would destabilize the sector I'm in charge of. They'll have been mistaken, but people often fool themselves into thinking that their chances of success are greater than they in fact are."

He once again turned to face One Twenty-Four. "I can't guarantee that I'll manage to change the law so that you're considered a person. I also can't assure you that, even if that happens, the Imperial Marines will accept you.

"What I can do is promise to put the full weight of my support behind you. For what your guardian has done for me, I hereby swear to do so. That means that I'm going to take her under my direct protection, and by extension, you'll be under my wing as well.

"You cannot give me your bond, but on your behalf, I'm going to demand hers. If this is what you *truly* want, you need to know that it will probably bind Grace to my service for the rest of her life. Knowing that, do you still wish to proceed?"

Grace started to say something, but the man held up his hand and silenced her without taking his eyes off One Twenty-Four. "I need to hear what this young woman has to say for herself. Her answer is going to determine how we proceed."

One Twenty-Four swallowed. "I cannot force another into doing something on my behalf that will bind them to another. I'll accept whatever fate the Empire decides to give me on my own."

"Please," Grace said softly. "I'm more than willing to do this for her."

The man smiled. "I know, but the fact that she's unwilling to throw you to the wolves tells me that she's a decent person at heart, even if she is from the Singularity, and that's what I needed to know."

He rose to his feet and turned toward Grace. "The Imperial Marines believed that releasing you from service is a polite fiction to provide cover for their actions to prevent all-out war. However, they're going to discover that they're quite mistaken.

"As you are no longer bound to the Imperial Marines, that frees you up to accept other oaths. Are you prepared to swear yourself to my service?"

Grace nodded. "I am."

"Kneel."

As soon as Grace lowered herself to the floor—which didn't seem to be an easy task in powered armor—the man extended his hands in front of her, palms up. Grace put her gauntleted hands in his and looked up at him.

"Do you, Grace Tolliver, swear to serve me as your personal liege for the remainder of your life or until such time as I choose to release you from my service?"

"I do." Her voice was firm.

"Then I accept your service and, in turn, promise to return that service with protection. As my sworn woman, you shall never want for succor. So long as your sword is held in my service, I shall be your unbreakable shield. On my oath to Emperor Marcus, I so swear."

When Grace made to rise, the man shook his head. "We're not quite done yet. While I'm confident that other accolades will be coming your way, it's probably best to get some of this done before the full scope of your actions becomes clear.

"If you hadn't chosen to be Andrea's champion, it would be far easier for the emperor to reward you as you deserve. As things stand, I suspect that circumstances and the general feelings of the peerage will prevent him from being as generous as he could. That being the case, I'm going to do as your subordinate did and perform the actions that I believe he would approve of so that I will be the one taking the blame.

"The first action is one that I'm certain he'd do in any case. I hereby name you a Knight Commander of the Imperial Order with all prerogatives pertaining thereto."

He smiled at her wryly. "My father was a man of the old school, and I received the colée—a blow to the head—rather than a sword to the shoulder, but we can spare you that, at least. Only the diehard traditionalists insist on something so violent these days."

Grace raised an eyebrow and pointedly eyed her powered armor. "My lord, I'm no wilting flower. I am—I was—an Imperial Marine and a combat officer. You can't possibly rough me up any worse than Sergeant Na did in the advanced hand-to-hand course.

"Don't leave room for anyone to ever say that I was coddled. That kind of insult would be—if you'll forgive the irony—a slap in the face. Do it."

"Then never let it be said that I denied you the full experience." He drew his hand back and slapped her across the face with a loud crack.

One Twenty-Four was shocked, even though she'd known it was coming. Imperials were… strange.

Even though the blow had rocked Grace's head to the side, she returned her gaze to his face and seemed smugly satisfied for reasons that One Twenty-Four couldn't explain. The redness on her face was already fading, probably being fixed by the medical nanites.

"Let that blow be the last one you receive that isn't answered by me, and through me, my liege lord, Emperor Marcus," the man said gently. "Violence offered to you is violence offered to me; offense offered to you is offense offered to me. From this day forward, I and those loyal to me will stand at your side against any foe, no matter their station or power."

He turned his face toward One Twenty-Four. "My father was a hard man, but, in my defense, she did insist."

"If you are the duke—and why is your name different than your title?—then what happened to your father?" One Twenty-Four asked.

"When I said he was a diehard traditionalist, I wasn't kidding. He was killed while hunting, having picked prey that was more than capable of hunting him back. Honestly, I still miss him, but I think that would've changed as I grew older. He could be a hard man, too.

"As for the name, titles remain constant, but family names can and do change over time. The original DeSantis line died out millennia ago due to sickness. The emperor back then appointed a new duke. That new line was extinguished in battle with the Singularity hundreds of years ago, and the Fowlers were raised to the title. And here we are."

Fowler returned his attention to Grace. "My final action is one that the emperor would hesitate to make, so I will risk his wrath by doing it myself. In the name of Emperor Marcus and as his direct vassal, I hereby elevate you to the peerage at the rank of baroness.

"I have more than enough personal land on DeSantis to create the barony. When the emperor created the Duchy of DeSantis, he set aside a healthy chunk of wildland on all the continents for future growth.

"One of those reserves is on our small southern continent. It's a rugged place, full of mountains, imposing hills, and absolutely breathtaking forests. With you as the first holder of this title, I think that I have the perfect name for it: the Barony of Iron Mountain. That suits your personality. Rise, Lady Grace, Baroness Iron Mountain.

"As your co-commander, I'll get around to doing something similar for Captain Anders when time permits. Others like Sergeant Na will get knighted, as well as receive other rewards from the crown through me, but we'll have to sort that out when time permits."

One Twenty-Four didn't understand *any* of what she'd just seen or heard but could tell that Grace was stunned, and not only from the blow to her head. She was going to have to ask for an explanation when they had time.

Even as she was thinking that, a loud klaxon began sounding from overhead. She didn't know what it meant, but Grace was instantly on her feet, and Fei was already pulling One Twenty-Four out of the chair and grabbing her helmet to hand it to her.

Before she could ask what was happening, the overhead speakers came to life, and she heard Captain Anders's voice ringing out authoritatively.

"All hands to battle stations. The enemy destroyers have returned. We're going to have to fight after all."

36

Grace raced to the bridge with Andrea hot on her heels. Na split off and followed Duke DeSantis as he went to get his men ready to help defend the ship. They had plenty of time to get into position. The destroyers were almost certainly still hours away.

The bridge was a hive of activity when she arrived, even if almost all the stations were unmanned. The ship was still in orbit around the gas giant, which might be a good thing, all things considered. If the destroyers didn't think anything was wrong, they might be more susceptible to an ambush.

Not that she was looking forward to a fight like that. While a heavy cruiser could normally handle two destroyers easily, *Gargoyle* was damaged and undermanned. She also lacked the implant systems that would usually allow a Fleet crew to operate the ship at a higher level of effectiveness.

Anders turned at their entrance and acknowledged them with a dip of his head, not slowing as he gave orders to the men and women at the consoles around him. Based on what Grace could hear, it didn't sound as if they were about to get underway anytime soon.

Once he'd finished giving his initial instructions, Anders turned his chair so that he could see her clearly. "The destroyers came through the flip point and are headed our way. They're only moving at cruising speed, so I don't believe they know what's going on at this point. The commercial orbital doesn't seem to be aware that we've seized the ship, so there's no reason anyone else should be either.

"We were still getting all of the primary systems checked out, and we hadn't left orbit yet. Honestly, that might be a lucky break. If we were in motion, that would certainly raise some concerns for them. At least for a little while, we should be able to sit here and lure them closer. If we can lull them into a false sense of security, we might be able to ambush them."

Grace wasn't sure how likely that was, but if their chances in a straight-up battle were poor, they needed to fight dirty. If nothing else, the weapons they had aboard *Bright Passage* should be able to screw up at least one destroyer.

But that would only work if the enemy didn't suspect what was coming.

"How likely are we to fool them?" she asked, stopping by his chair and keeping Andrea in the corner of her vision.

"I wouldn't hold my breath if I were you," he warned. "They were satisfied with a brief acknowledgment that they'd returned to the system and were on their way to meet up with us, but when they get closer, it's an almost certainty that whoever's in charge over there is going to want to speak to the legate.

"When that happens, we'll try to put them off, but as soon as they figure out what's happening, the game is up, and they're going to come in hot and fast."

"So, what do we do? If they're going to come in shooting no matter what tricks we try, how do we make sure that we survive this in good enough shape to get the hell out of the Singularity?"

"We've already moved *Bright Passage* into a different orbit," he said. "No time to recover any of the cargo we liberated, so we'll have to hope the duke honors his promise to pay for them at full value.

"She's going to be a lot closer to them, based on their current course, but since she's still in orbit around the gas giant, they're not going to see her as a direct threat. I'm hoping they'll dismiss her as just part of the scenery and focus on us.

"She's only got the minimum crew required to move and fire her weapons. If she can knock one of the destroyers out of the fight, I'd say our odds are pretty good. We'll almost certainly lose her, but I'm hoping the crew can eject before the destroyers take her out. Basically, this is going to be a situation where they fire the weapons and abandon ship immediately."

Grace didn't like the sound of that.

"Are we going to be able to get enough of our weapon systems online to fight? What about our battle screens?"

He shook his head. "The battle screens are power hogs. Since we only have one fusion plant, and it has stability issues, I'm leery of trying anything that chancy. If we do bring them up, we won't have power for the beam weapons or the engines. We'd be a stationary firing platform.

"The missiles are easier. All we have to do is get enough trained crewmen to operate them, and we'll be able to reload and keep firing. While some of the batteries are still offline due to battle damage, we've got more than they do.

"The problem is that we're a fragile firing platform. Without those battle screens, and without the ability to maneuver, we can be damaged enough to prevent us from escaping once the fight is over. In other words, we'll win the battle and lose the war."

Grace had no experience with space combat, so she'd have to take his word on that. She knew the Fleet officer would use every bit of tactical maneuvering he could to win this fight, but the chances were high that they'd end up being boarded.

"I should probably get the platoon split up between engineering and the bridge," she said with a sigh. "That's where they're going to come if they board us. Since they're almost certainly not going to use the standard docking tubes, we can expect boarding pods similar to the ones we used to get on board. That means we're not going to be able to guess where they'll breach.

"They're also going to be using powered armor. Thankfully, we've got more than enough to equip the entire platoon. Those destroyers do have twice the number of marines we do, though. As the defenders, we'll have a force multiplier, but it could come down to the wire."

"I think you're right," he agreed. "The destroyers are still a couple of hours out, so you need to get everybody armored up and harden all the defenses you can. This is going to give us time to get the missile batteries manned, and we might be able to take out some of the boarding pods before they get to the ship. I'm not going to promise that, but I'm not going to exclude the possibility either."

"I knew the risks when I signed up," she said with a shrug. "I'll take charge of the group guarding the bridge. Sergeant Na will take care of engineering. I'll have to leave some of my people guarding the prisoners because the very last thing we need is for them to get loose in the middle of this fight. If that happens, we're done."

She turned to face Andrea. "I can't detail anyone to guard you, so I'm going to send you to engineering with Fei. You're not trained to use powered armor, and I doubt very seriously that we could get any fitted to you because of your size, so you're going to have to stay concealed and use your weapons more like a sniper.

"And before you decide that you want to argue with me, you need to remember what's at stake. If you take unnecessary risks, one of the marines is probably going to get killed trying to save you. This is not the time to prove how brave you are. This is the time to show how smart you are. Do you understand me?"

Andrea nodded. "I've seen powered armor in operation. I have no desire to be directly in the sights of a weapon like that again. At least not when I'm so ill prepared to defend myself. With your permission, I'll go join Fei in engineering so that she can tell me what she wants me to do.

"If I might make a suggestion, perhaps you should preemptively stun the prisoners before the fight begins. I'm not certain if that violates some rules of behavior for your people, but if they are a threat, you should neutralize them."

Anders pursed his lips and nodded. "Not exactly according to Queensberry's rules, but I think that's an excellent idea. The antiboarding weapons in that section are functional, so when it starts looking like things are going down, I'll trigger them. One less thing to worry about, and your marines can focus on the real threat."

Grace gestured toward the hatch. "Get moving, Andrea. By the time you get to engineering, I'll have already given Fei her orders. Stop by the armory and pick up some of the heavier weaponry. Whatever hiding place you end up in, you're going to want to have weapons that are actually useful against powered armor.

"You're going to have to time your attacks well, because as soon as they realize you're a threat, they'll blast the area where you're hiding.

"I'm certain that Fei will give you the same orders that I am, but I want to stress this right now. Spread those weapons out and make sure that once you fire a shot, you're already moving before they can return fire. That's how snipers stay alive in a close-contact fight like this. Mobility is life."

Andrea nodded. "I'll do that. And remember that you don't have to lead from the front. You should stay inside the bridge and let the rest of your people form the defensive bulwark. If you're out front, you can't be directing them as cleanly as you would be when you're not ducking every incoming plasma shot."

Without waiting for a response, the girl raced out of the bridge.

"You know, if she survives the next few months, I think she might make a decent marine," Anders said thoughtfully.

Grace nodded. "I think you're right."

Then she turned to glare at him. "And just so we're clear, I'm not happy with what you did. I'm her guardian, and you had no right to make a decision like that. I don't want you ever doing anything like that again."

The Fleet officer grinned unrepentantly. "I doubt very seriously that I'll have to. This is more of a once-and-done sort of situation. I'm going to get my ass reamed for doing it, but since that's my only transgression, my career is going to survive. If you'd made that call, they'd lock you up over misuse of Imperial property or some such.

"Sergeant Na is going to get a lecture about following my instructions when she should've said no, but as a noncommissioned officer, she'll probably be shielded from any real consequences, because it's our responsibility. The same thing for the doctor. He was just following orders."

Grace had to admit that Anders was right, but it still galled her.

"Do you think it's going to make any difference?" she asked quietly. "Is the Empire going to change the law to recognize her as a person? Even if they do, will the Imperial Marines accept her as a recruit?"

"I think with the duke putting his weight behind her, there's a decent chance that the emperor will modify the law in some way through the Imperial Senate. There's some political capital in doing that, because it would be just another poke in the Singularity's eye.

"I suspect it would be an exception solely for her. That would get the most outrage from the ruling caste of the Singularity when they find out that she's escaped, which they eventually will.

"As far as getting into the Imperial Marines, that's outside my bailiwick. I'm sure there'll be a lot of resistance, and I'm not certain that even an Imperial noble can get her past it.

"Thankfully, you've got about six years to figure that out. The fact that she already has the hardware is of some benefit. They probably don't want someone with a marine nanogenerator just wandering around.

"Do you think that the duke is going to be able to keep them from taking her away from you?"

Considering what he'd done after Anders had left the compartment, Grace suspected Andrea was safe, so long as they moved to DeSantis. Anders had no idea the bomb that Fowler had dropped on her—and planned to drop on him in turn—and this wasn't the time to tell him, but she was starting to have hope.

Also, she wanted to see the stunned look on his face when it happened. That would pay the smug bastard back for what he'd done without telling her.

"I either have to think that he'll keep her safe, or I'll drown in despair," she said, turning toward the hatch. "Well, I'd best leave you to your work and get my people ready to defend the ship. This is it, Captain. We're in the end game. We either win, or we die."

37

One Twenty-Four raced to find the armory. In spite of hurrying, she didn't get there particularly quickly, since she didn't know where it was located. Luckily, she ran across one of the marines, who then directed her to the room inside what they called marine country.

The selection of armor and weapons inside the room was bewildering, but the marine duo that was guarding the armory directed her to a specific rack of large weapons when she told them that she was supposed to set herself up in engineering to help defend against invaders in powered armor.

The rack held two types of large rifles. One was thicker and was obviously made to be used with powered armor, which would be difficult at best. The other was long but would work with her smaller hands. That made the choice easy.

She wasn't sure precisely what made the longer rifle different than the others, but it was obviously a flechette weapon. Only the flechettes were about four times larger than those used in the weapon she'd been issued, as she discovered when she found the magazines it used.

The weapon looked more than capable of firing them at a

significantly higher velocity as well. If it was designed to penetrate powered armor, it had to be capable of delivering a lot of force.

She found a bag that she could strap across one shoulder that held a number of the large magazines and stuffed it full. Far better to have more than she could possibly need than to run out before the fight was done.

Since Grace had said that she'd be moving from one location to another, One Twenty-Four might as well preposition several weapons so that she could simply run away after she fired each time.

Whatever the case, Fei was going to tell her what she needed to do. The woman had the experience to guide her on how she could contribute to the fighting without needlessly risking her life.

With that thought in mind, she pulled two more of the weapons off the rack and cradled all three of them awkwardly in her arms as she headed for engineering. She was sure that the marines guarding the armory thought she was insane, but she really didn't have time to explain herself.

Thankfully, engineering was much easier to find than the armory. Her new implants were able to translate the signs she passed, and in less than ten minutes, she'd made it to the main hatch for engineering.

There were a significant number of marines stationed outside the room. They were busy setting up heavy defenses and didn't stop her as she made her way past them.

Inside engineering, she found Kayden directing everyone that wasn't a marine and determining what tasks they were supposed to be performing. That kind of surprised her. She hadn't expected an Imperial crew to obey someone from the Singularity.

Of course, the redheaded officer named Kyle was also there, so perhaps his presence was responsible for that.

Fei was standing nearby and saw One Twenty-Four come into the room. She was dressed in powered armor now, just like Grace. Her helmet was held in one arm, and a large flechette rifle like the ones she'd seen in the armory was strapped across her back.

"Three weapons?" Fei asked as she stepped over to One Twenty-Four. "Isn't that a little... ambitious?"

One Twenty-Four shook her head. "Grace said that I had to be ready to abandon any firing position at a moment's notice. I thought it might be best to preposition several of these weapons so that I don't have to try to carry a rifle with me when I run."

Fei pursed her lips and slowly nodded. "That's well thought out. I'm hopeful that you don't have to run that often. I don't expect that the invaders want to completely destroy engineering, so that rules out plasma weapons. They'll be using heavy flechette rifles like the one I'm carrying. They put out more than enough energy to crack the shells on these suits of powered armor.

"Since flechette weapons are silent, and sniper rifles like those more than most, you should be able to fire from a good place of concealment more than once before you relocate.

"By the time the enemy dials in your location, you'll know that it's time to move. Let's go find you a couple of good spots."

The engineering compartment was much larger than One Twenty-Four had anticipated. Fei was able to find several locations behind large pieces of equipment that still had a decent view of the central area where any intruders would force their way in.

After carefully considering the options, they selected three of them, and One Twenty-Four put the rifles in place. With her small size and the low cross-section of the weapons themselves, she wouldn't have to expose herself very much to fire. Thankfully, these weapons wouldn't have that heavy a recoil.

Of course, she'd only fired small rifles, so this larger one probably delivered significantly more force. The weapon had a built-in bipod that allowed her to set it flat so that she could fire while lying down behind it. That meant that the energy of each shot was going to go into her body at an awkward angle along the shoulder.

"This rifle doesn't look like yours," she said to Fei. "What was it that you called it? A sniper rifle?"

"Specifically, it's a heavy sniper rifle. It's designed for long-range fire, but it will work here. Barely. Just make sure you know what's behind each of the targets and that you don't mind destroying it if you miss.

"It fires a heavier flechette than my rifle here and isn't made for general combat. The selector switch only has two positions: safe and fire. Its purpose is to kill at extreme range.

"That gives it the power to breach powered armor at close range —like here in engineering—but the general use is to target someone at a distance of ten kilometers or so without revealing the shooter's position.

"Now, I want you to practice with the interface. Lie down and look through the scope."

One Twenty-Four knew that so long as there wasn't a magazine in the weapon, it was unloaded, thus safe to handle.

"I can use the scope," she objected.

"Of course you can, but now you have implants, and they're going to give you some added functionality that you've never used before and won't even know to check unless I show you how to do it. Now, find someone on the far side of engineering and target them through the scope."

One Twenty-Four did as instructed and quickly had one of the crewmen selected. The man was working at a console, and she lined up the red dot on his torso.

"Ready."

"Connect your implants with the weapon. If you close your eyes for a moment, that might make it easier the first few times. Just try to sense that there's something out there that you can connect with."

She closed her eyes and tried to do as Fei ordered. Strangely, she did feel something and tried to push her awareness into it. That caused a strange connection to form between the weapon and herself, and she was suddenly staring through the sight even though her eyes were closed.

"That's really strange," One Twenty-Four said. "Isn't that kind of redundant? I can just open my eyes and shoot the weapon normally."

Fei laughed. "While that's true, can you anticipate where the next shot is going to need to go? After all, your attention is now focused through the sight, and you can't see anything in the rest of the room. Wouldn't you like to know what everyone else is doing?"

Frowning, One Twenty-Four considered how that might change things and decided to experiment before Fei gave her directions. She willed the weapon to show her the rest of the room, and she could immediately see the entire area in front of her, even though her eyes were closed. The weapon was feeding her information.

"I'm… impressed," she admitted. "This is much more effective at maintaining situational awareness than staring down the sight with my own eyes."

"And it gets better. Instruct your weapon to target multiple people and designate them as such."

One Twenty-Four mentally selected half a dozen people, including Kyle, as temporary enemies, and a sort of reddish outline appeared around each of them in her vision.

"Done."

"Since your weapon is unable to fire, it's safe to pull the trigger. I want you to pretend to shoot the first target and instruct the weapon to move down the target list at its discretion."

One Twenty-Four let her breath out slowly and squeezed the trigger. Nothing happened, of course. However, the weapon seemed to shift on its own to the next target, and she squeezed the trigger a second time, causing it to move on to the next.

She'd been staring down the sight and wondered how the weapon was moving on its own, but as she paid attention to the process, she realized that it wasn't. She was shifting the rifle to a new point of aim after every shot in conjunction with the weapon's targeting.

Somehow, her implants had mated the weapon to her body, and she was now using its targeting information while allowing her implants to control her movements.

"That's excellent, Little One," Fei said. "You're picking this up much faster than I'd have expected. Your implants link up with the computer inside the weapon, and you're using its scanners for target selection.

"You're not seeing it now, but it's capable of determining which enemies coming into your field of view are more of a threat and prioritizing them so that you can eliminate the more dangerous ones first. Its ranking criteria were designed by the Imperial Marines, so trust it more than your own guesses about which targets you should shoot."

She looked up at Fei. "It seems as if your machines can fight better than people. Why don't you just use automated weapon systems?"

"That was tried several times. Machines are indiscriminate, and they can't alter their preprogrammed plans effectively when circumstances change.

"Say there are hostages. How would you make the machine aware that some of the potential targets are off-limits? That's a judgment call that machines just aren't capable of making. They're not sentient.

"Now, let's go around and set up all of your hides. Then you'll practice moving between them. Try to find multiple routes that won't be visible from the main compartment.

"And remember, when you move, there are going to be people shooting at you. If they hit you with a heavy flechette in your unpowered armor, it's going to kill you. Since I've grown rather fond of you, I'd prefer it if you avoided getting shot."

"I'll do my best," One Twenty-Four said dryly.

Over the next half hour, One Twenty-Four continued to refine her plan and was finally satisfied that she'd done the best she could. Fei had returned to the main compartment to continue directing the setting up of barricades to help defend engineering.

One Twenty-Four settled into what she thought was the best initial firing position, loaded her weapon, and tried to relax. Being tense while waiting for the oncoming fight wasn't going to do her any good.

If they were fortunate, Captain Anders would be able to end this fight without the ship being boarded at all. However, she couldn't count on that and knew that she had to plan on fighting here in engineering and perhaps in other portions of the ship.

How times had changed. Just a short while ago, she'd barely won a fistfight with Thirty-One. The girl wouldn't recognize her now. She barely recognized herself.

She'd do whatever it took to protect her friends and survive. Dangling just beyond her reach was a new life. She refused to even contemplate having it snatched away from her now. Better to die first. Or to kill everyone that wanted to stop them.

38

Grace spent the next hour getting the area around the bridge set up for defense. If the Singularity boarded them, the fighting was going to be brutal, but there were some upsides. The bridge was heavily armored to prevent it from being breached, for one.

The second was that boarders wouldn't want to destroy the control systems. That would limit the kinds of weapons they'd be willing to employ.

And that was only if boarders actually managed to get onto *Gargoyle* at all. A heavy cruiser had a lot of firepower, even excluding the beam weapons that made it so potent a fighting platform.

Yes, they'd be more at risk because they couldn't use the battle screens, but once again, the question was going to be whether or not the destroyers would be interested in the outright destruction of the heavy cruiser to begin with.

The enemy was starting out at a significant disadvantage. First, they'd yet to realize that *Gargoyle* had been seized in the first place. Once they'd made that leap, then they had to remotely assess how much of the ship was under the control of the new ownership.

Since it would be unreasonable for the enemy just to assume that the new owners had somehow found a way to override any computer lockouts, they had to be wondering whether or not the ship was just sitting here because she couldn't move. If the lockouts had still been in place, they wouldn't have been able to fire the weapons either.

The smart bet for them would be to assume that the new owners had complete control of the ship, but since they'd acquired that control through unlikely means, it might be a little hard for the destroyer commanders to completely make that leap of faith.

Her basic assessment was that if the enemy even realized the scope of what was going on, they'd try to disable the heavy cruiser while launching their boarding pods. If Anders could get enough of their missile batteries online to overwhelm one or both of the destroyers in that initial exchange, this fight would be over.

The most significant risk was that they'd lose their remaining fusion plant due to damage. If that happened, they'd have to scuttle the heavy cruiser and stuff everyone aboard *Bright Passage*. And if the freighter participated in the ambush and was destroyed as well, they'd be completely and utterly screwed.

She ran her thoughts past Anders as they waited for the destroyers to make their way into the system, and he nodded. "That pretty much mirrors my thinking. It's going to be a toss-up when someone tries to report what they found at Aponte.

"I figure they're going to wait until there's only a slight communications lag before they attempt to do that. No one wants to make their boss sit there waiting for questions to be answered with nothing but blank looks on everyone's faces.

"Most people can accept a couple of seconds, but when you get higher than that, it starts wearing on your nerves fast. They may send a recorded message of what they found before they get here and expect a response. If that's the case, we'll have to start playing around with excuses and see what we can manage."

Grace considered both of those options. Waiting until they were at close range would put the enemy inside their missile envelope. They could then ambush the two destroyers before they even knew what was coming.

So, of course, it made a lot more sense to plan for them to send

Gargoyle a message about what they discovered and demand some kind of feedback.

"What about orbital mechanics?" she asked. "I know the commercial harvesting orbital is moving around the gas giant, so that means that we are too. Are we going to be in their direct line of sight the entire time, or is there a point where we're going to be blocked by the planet or some of its moons?"

"Sadly, no," he said. "They've pretty much got a straight shot in from the flip point, and we're visible all the way in. At least *Bright Passage* is safely on the other side of the orbital, and they'll have no reason to associate her with us. We'll have total surprise if we have to fire her concealed weapons."

Grace really hoped it didn't come to that. She'd much rather have the two destroyers blissfully wander into firing range. A hail of missiles from their flagship would kill them at point-blank range if they didn't even have their antimissile defenses online.

The next hour passed at a snail's pace. The two destroyers made their way toward the gas giant at a leisurely rate and only occasionally focused their scanners toward the planet itself.

According to Anders, both Fleet and the Singularity warships did a lot more active scanning than commercial vessels, just to be sure that the space around them was clear.

But in this case, it didn't seem that they were overly interested in *Gargoyle* or the area around the planet itself. That boded well for their ultimate chances of success if circumstances held.

A noise back at the hatch had her turning her head to see Fowler entering the bridge. He'd changed from his prisoner's coveralls into a deep-blue ship's suit that had no markings of rank. It seemed to be tailored and was probably comfortable.

"Pardon the intrusion," the nobleman said. "Since we're about to risk everything on the toss of the dice, I figured it would be in my best interest to be here. It also doesn't hurt that this section of the ship is the most protected on the ship."

The last bit was said with something of a sly smile.

"She's your ship," Anders said. "You're more than welcome to be wherever you like."

"Until the prize court makes a ruling, that's not true," the duke disagreed. "You've seized this vessel from enemy hands, and until you turn her over inside the Empire, she's yours. I'm absolutely not going to try to put my thumb on the scales to influence what you do, Captain."

"If I can pull this off, it's going to look good on my record," Anders admitted. "If I don't, I probably won't survive to have my ass chewed for making whatever mistakes I make."

"We have an incoming transmission," a man at a console on the far left said. "It looks like it's a report of some kind. Transmission lag is about eight seconds."

"Put it up on the screen."

The image of a man sitting in the center seat of a small bridge appeared. He wore the same kind of uniform as the officers on this ship had, but the insignia were different.

For that matter, so was the layout of the bridge. The details that Grace could see were similar to what she'd seen on destroyers in the past, but this was obviously not an Imperial vessel.

"The news is grave, Legate," the man said. "It appears that there was some kind of sabotage at the transshipment center in the Aponte system. It was destroyed with great loss of life. At this time, the local authorities have not determined who was responsible, and they've requested assistance. What are your orders?"

The man sat there attentively, obviously waiting for a response.

"Well, that limits our options," Anders grumbled. "Send back a response that the legate is currently occupied in engineering. Say that the fusion plant has been fluctuating more significantly in the last several hours and requires his full attention.

"Tell them he's going to want them to report here in person once they arrive in orbit and leave it at that. Hopefully, that'll be enough to satisfy them."

The man sitting at the console did as instructed, obviously using voice only. The man on the screen looked exactly the same as he had before until there was enough time for the transmission to cycle through being sent out and his response coming back in.

The man frowned. "Put Sub-Legate Guarris on, then. I need to pass on a few details immediately."

"Tell him that he's with the legate and that he'll get back to him as soon as he can," Anders said.

Grace had her doubts about whether this was going to work. Then again, now that communications had started, the chances of them actually fooling the enemy were low.

The man on the screen frowned even deeper once the time lag had passed. "Give me video so I can see who I'm speaking with."

"It's not going to work, but tell him that we're having issues with the visual end of the communications gear," Anders said.

Grace knew that wasn't going to work. They were screwed.

The man's expression confirmed her assessment, and it was obvious that he didn't believe a word of what he was hearing. "What's going on? Who has the watch? Who is this?"

"That tears it," Anders said. "No way they're going to buy what we're selling. Don't respond to anything else. Something I read as a kid that applies. 'Say nothing. Let them deduce our lies for themselves.'"

The man waited for a long while, saying nothing. When it became evident that no one was going to answer him, he shook his head.

"I have no idea how you've managed to capture *Ever-Loyal Warrior,* but that's obviously what's happened. I'll give you one chance to surrender before I use force to take her back from you.

"My ships will be in missile range within half an hour, and if you haven't surrendered at that time, I'll use my marines to retake the ship. Or, if I'm being paranoid, you can have Legate Lucius tell me so. Good luck convincing him to lie for you."

The transmission ended, and Anders sighed. "Well, that could have gone better."

He turned to face Fowler and Grace. "I'm not going to fire at them until they're in an ambush position. I could probably open up on them at longer range, and we'd win that missile duel, but the chances of critical damage to this ship are too high.

"The best way to make this work is to lull them into a false sense of security and then hit them between the eyes with a hammer before they suspect what's really going on."

"And how are you going to do that?" Fowler asked. "They're going to be close enough to detect anything we do."

"They're going to disregard *Bright Passage*. She might not be able to kill one of the destroyers, but she can certainly knock it out of the fight. That just leaves one for us to deal with. And, of course, any boarding pods they happen to launch. We'll try to use the antimissile defenses to take them out."

Grace shook her head. "I wouldn't hold my breath if I were you. Boarding pods don't travel at the same speed as missiles, so the targeting is going to be screwy. They're slower, so there's still some chance that you'll hit some, so I'm not going to totally disregard the possibility, but we're going to have boarders."

"We're as prepared as we can be to fight them. You make sure that those ships don't shoot us to pieces, and we'll take care of any boarders that manage to get here in one piece."

"What's your attack plan going to be, Captain?" Fowler asked. "Isn't a missile duel at this kind of range like having a knife fight in your shower?"

"That's quite an evocative turn of phrase you have there, Your Grace," Anders said with a grimace. "It would be ugly, which is why that's not what I'm going to do.

"It's risky—damned risky—but I'm going to use the beam weapons. We're not maneuvering, and we won't have battle screens up, so the power draw should probably be low enough not to trigger instability in the fusion plant."

That did seem risky to Grace, but she wasn't a Fleet officer. If Anders thought that was the best course of action, then she wasn't going to argue. Her job was to fight when the enemy marines reached the ship, so that was what she'd focus on.

Standing there on the bridge and watching the enemy ships come closer was nerve-wracking. They crossed into missile range, and when there was no response from *Gargoyle*, they continued in.

In a show of just how callous the Singularity was about its civilians, they used the commercial orbital to obscure themselves as the range closed. Bad for them, but it meant that the destroyers would come right past *Bright Passage*.

The maneuver certainly upset the civilians, because they immediately started asking what was going on and demanding answers that no one was willing to give them.

"I'm going to stun the prisoners now," Anders said. "Now they'll be out of the fight no matter what happens."

When the action finally started, everything seemed to happen all at once. The destroyers came around the orbital and launched six boarding pods toward *Gargoyle*. *Bright Passage* was perfectly positioned to unload all of her concealed missiles directly into one of the destroyers at point-blank range.

Some of the enemy's automated defenses must've reacted, because the destroyer fired one missile back at the freighter even as *Bright Passage* began jettisoning escape pods. The missile impact didn't cause the freighter to blow up, but Grace doubted the ship they'd been traveling on for so long was going to come out of this in operable condition.

Grace really didn't have an opportunity to guess at how badly damaged the destroyer was before the lights on the bridge dimmed, and *Gargoyle* fired her beam weapons into the undamaged destroyer. That ship didn't have an opportunity to react before it exploded.

Something must've struck the remaining destroyer, because he began tumbling and then abruptly exploded moments later. Neither of the Singularity ships had managed to eject a single escape pod.

That still left the pods racing toward the heavy cruiser. The antimissile defenses did their best but only managed to stop two. The survivors slammed into the aft section of the heavy cruiser, disgorging their marines very close to engineering.

That meant that her forces there would be outnumbered three to one and needed immediate reinforcement. Even with all her marines, this was going to be an ugly fight.

"I think they're all going to go for engineering, but I want you to keep me updated about where every single intruder is," Grace said. "I'll leave you some guards, but I'm taking most of my marines with me. Lock the hatch."

"It looks like they entered the ship right where we were keeping the Singularity prisoners," one of the officers said. "That entire section is open to vacuum."

The overhead lights flickered and then went out. The darkness lasted less than a second before the emergency lights came on, and an alarm started wailing.

"The fusion plant just shut down," the same man said. "It looks like Kayden thought it was about to do something unpleasant."

"Perfect," Anders said. "Get Kyle to give me an update. Kayden is going to be too busy to talk. Tell him that we need to get that fusion plant back online as soon as possible. If another ship comes into this system, we're sitting ducks."

Grace cursed their luck and jammed her helmet over her head, locking it down. She had to lead the majority of her people back to engineering and stop the enemy from permanently crippling the ship, or they were all dead.

39

One Twenty-Four knew that something was about to happen when she felt the ship jolt. The com implant in her head came to life, relating information from the communications gear built into her armor.

"Four enemy boarding pods have breached the ship near engineering," Fei said calmly. "We can expect an attack force twice our size to make an assault on our position shortly. They'll try to disable the ship, and we've got to keep them from doing that.

"The marines outside engineering are dug in and will hold for as long as they can, but we have to count on the fact that they're going to breach us. Our reinforcements from the bridge probably won't get here in time to keep them off of us."

There was a pause, and for a moment, One Twenty-Four thought that the channel had closed, but it was just Fei giving them a moment to think.

"Everyone is counting on us to hold the line. We've got to keep them out of engineering for as long as we can, and even if they get inside, we can't allow them to damage the fusion plant, flip drive, or normal space drives. Keep calm and follow your training. Seal the hatch."

The large hatch at the entrance to engineering slid closed and locked with a loud metallic clang. Moments later, the overhead lights went out, and some kind of alarm began wailing on the other side of the compartment. A second later, dim lights sprang to life, casting everything in the compartment in blue.

"The fusion plant is down," Kayden shouted. "We're not in danger, but it was fluctuating badly enough that I shut it down before it crashed on its own. I'm going to have to do an inspection before I can bring it back online."

One Twenty-Four's helmet adjusted for the low-light conditions, and she was able to see just almost as clearly as she had before the lights had gone out.

She aimed her weapon at the main entrance to engineering and waited. Since the majority of the marines were positioned outside, no one was coming through that hatch until they made more than enough noise for her to realize they were coming.

The fight outside engineering started with a loud explosion, and then dozens of flechette rifles began firing. Even during their attack on the bridge, she'd never heard that level of violence taking place, and it was sobering. Men and women that might have one day been under her control were now coming to kill her and her friends.

She recognized that she should probably be afraid. Unlike the marines, she wasn't trained for this. Her skills were far from the level they'd need to be for her to survive in a melee like what was taking place outside engineering.

If she survived this battle and made it to the Empire, she was going to have a lot of learning to do. She never wanted to feel this helpless ever again. If anyone was going to feel terror during combat, it would be her enemies.

She didn't know enough to even imagine what becoming an Imperial Marine would require of her, but at this moment, she knew it was her destiny. A destiny that those who'd tried to kill her as a child would dearly regret when she became an adult.

The communication net was filled with people reporting on the attack and Fei giving orders, but One Twenty-Four couldn't keep track of everything, and most of the words they used to describe the events in progress just didn't make sense to her. Once again, her lack of experience and training was hobbling her.

Then a series of loud explosions began. One Twenty-Four recognized them at once as the blasts of plasma grenades or perhaps the plasma rifles.

She accessed the marines' statuses in her HUD, and her mouth dried up as she saw that a third of them were dead or injured. The dots that represented them continued to go red and yellow as she watched the violence outside take its toll.

"Breach imminent," the marine One Twenty-Four only knew as Jane said coolly.

The dot indicating her on the HUD went red a heartbeat later as the woman died. Now all of the marines outside of engineering were dead, and the enemy was at the gates.

A few seconds later, an intensely bright explosion caused the hatch to engineering to buckle and come partially loose from the bulkhead. A second blast sent it spinning into engineering with an incredibly loud clang and armored figures very much like the one she'd killed near the bridge rushing through the breach.

The remaining marines, set up in defensive positions inside engineering, opened fire on the intruders, and several of them went down with rips in their armor in places that would be fatal to the person inside.

Two times in a row, One Twenty-Four tried to fire at one of the figures, but they went down before she could squeeze her trigger. The third time, she managed to line up a shot and took an enemy marine in the head. The helmet in One Twenty-Four's sight shattered, and the armored form dropped to the deck.

Even though the enemy marines were dying rapidly, they were apparently just as well trained as the Imperial Marines and taking a toll on the defenders as well. The only plus that One Twenty-Four could see at the moment was that the close combat prevented the enemy from targeting the fusion plant or drives.

Unfortunately, the casualties weren't limited to the combatants. Several of the unarmored crewmen lay scattered on the deck. One of the figures had red hair, and she was certain that it was the Fleet officer, Kyle.

As the Singularity marines found locations where they could seek cover, they began putting pressure on the defenders, and the fight became a free-for-all. One Twenty-Four was able to kill two more enemy marines before someone located her position and sprayed it with high-velocity flechettes.

With only a few moments' warning, she was barely able to roll behind a large piece of equipment. The heavy flechettes searching for her chewed chunks of metal out of the device and shredded the rifle she'd left behind.

Thankfully, One Twenty-Four had practiced for exactly this situation and raced for the second rifle she'd concealed deeper into engineering. It was on top of one of the machines, but she was able to scramble up the handholds that she'd located easily enough. All that climbing rope during physical education was paying off now.

She threw herself down by the weapon, flipped the safety off, and located the person that had been firing at her. The Singularity marine had been searching for her, and his weapon was tracking toward her new location. He must've seen her movement and was trying to line himself up to try and kill her again.

One Twenty-Four fired three shots in rapid succession at her target. One missed, but the other two struck the armor center mass. It looked like the heavy metal shrugged off the first flechette, but the second one must've hit something vital, because the marine fell to the deck and began thrashing around.

She was about to take aim at another of the enemy marines when they scuttled back out through the destroyed hatch, and the remaining troops that were at his side quickly flowed after him.

The sound of flechette guns firing in the hallway told her what was going on. Grace had arrived with the last of the marines, and the enemy was trying to prevent themselves from being trapped in engineering, where they'd be slaughtered.

The quick check of her HUD made her blanch. Most of the marines that had been defending engineering were dead. Many of the rest showed yellow, indicating some form of injury.

She quickly located Fei on the list and almost sobbed when she saw that her mentor was alive but hurt.

One Twenty-Four longed to rush to her side but knew that would be shortsighted. She had to keep her weapon pointed toward the entrance, because the enemy could come running back in at any moment. If they did, it was going to be up to her to help make sure that no more marines died today.

Honestly, she wasn't sure how likely that was. She had no idea how many Singularity marines were still left, but she was convinced that her guardian would make them pay dearly for their intrusion into the ship.

Now all she had to do was wait and see how the fight played out.

* * *

JUST AS THEY were about in position to encounter the enemy, Grace double-checked the command overview in her head and grimaced. Casualties in engineering had been high. Thankfully, both Andrea and Na were still alive, though Na was hurt.

According to Na, the Singularity forces had withdrawn from engineering as soon as her people hit their rear lines. They were in the process of reforming to repel her attack, and she knew she couldn't allow them the time they needed, or there might be none of her people left when this was done.

It was going to be bloody, but they had to break through their defenses fast in order to reduce the number of casualties they were going to suffer. It felt like throwing her friends into the fire—and in a very real sense, it was—but this wasn't the time for delicate probing.

"Charge!" she ordered as she ran forward.

They fired plasma weapons as they ran, vaporizing sections of the corridor in front of them while a few people laid down a withering hail of flechettes. Neither of those things was quite enough to keep the enemy from returning fire, but it certainly reduced the effectiveness of their response.

Things were going about like she'd expected right up until the moment a plasma grenade bounced at her feet. Without thinking, she kicked it back and turned to dive away. It went off in front of the makeshift barricade and hurled her back down the corridor.

Grace landed hard, spinning and flipping. She skidded to a halt, and her HUD announced that her armor was damaged in numerous places. It was still functional—barely—so she levered herself to her feet and turned to assess what had just happened.

It looked as if she'd managed to get the grenade out of the center of their group, but the forward elements had still suffered. The rear echelon was in the process of pouring through the barricades that the Singularity marines had taken over during their assault on engineering, and the fighting was bloody and brutal.

She tried to run to join the fight, but her right leg failed to function. In fact, she couldn't feel it at all. A quick check showed that it was injured but that the armor had sealed it up and applied heavy pain medication to numb the wound.

That was what she got for kicking a plasma grenade.

By the time she'd hobbled to the barricades, the remaining marines inside engineering had put in an appearance and added their fire to her people's, and the fight was over.

The butcher's bill had been extremely high. Her platoon had started out with forty-one people. They'd lost one of their number with Anne Marie Scott's death. Now another twenty-eight had joined her in death.

Of the remaining twelve marines, eight of them—including herself—were injured, some of them gravely.

"Uninjured marines, form a perimeter," Na ordered as she staggered out of engineering. "The rest of you, help me get our injured out of their armor so that the medics can get them to the medical center at once."

The NCO turned to Grace. "Are we going to have more intruders?"

Grace shook her head and found a comfortable wall to lean against before her leg collapsed. "No. That should be the last of them unless another ship drops in for a visit. My HUD says that Andrea came through uninjured. How bad are you?"

"My back is chewed up pretty good, and at least one flechette got through. The armor slowed it down enough that I'm not dying, but I'm going to have to have my turn getting it pulled out.

"Kyle is dead. He got caught in the crossfire. Kayden is working on the fusion plant now. He had to shut it down, but he thinks he'll be able to get it back up after he checks it.

"If so, then I suppose we're going to get away, at least from this system. Then we have to hope that we don't run into anyone else before we get out of the Singularity."

That would be about their luck—survive the fight here and then get caught by somebody else before they could get away.

"Let's hope that he gets the power back online, because *Bright Passage* isn't going to be taking us anywhere," Grace said as she struggled to get her helmet off. "She took a missile, and I'm pretty sure she's not going to be usable at this point.

"I'd imagine Kayden is glad that the Empire bought it off him, because trying to get insurance to pay for this would be a screaming bitch."

Andrea came out of engineering at a run. She looked torn about whether to go to Grace or look at Na. After a moment's indecision, she raced to Grace's side.

"Where are you hurt? How bad is it?"

"My leg, and I have no idea how bad. I'm leaving the armor on until I get to the medical center because it's going to keep me from bleeding out."

The girl looked worried but nodded. "This was the last of them? The fighting is over?"

"For now, at least." She looked into Andrea's eyes and smiled. "You really pulled your weight. I'm so proud of you. You're going to make one hell of a marine when this is all over."

Personally, Grace was done with the Singularity. It was time to go home.

40

Thankfully, it hadn't taken Kayden long to restore power to the ship, and six days later, One Twenty-Four stood on the bridge as *Gargoyle* entered the border system they'd chosen. They'd picked this one because of some of the classified data that she'd helped Corporal Gomez pull out of the computer.

The marine had been severely injured in the fighting but was still able to do his part to get them safely out of the Singularity. Grace and Fei had also been hurt, but to her relief, both had recovered completely.

With her overrides, she'd been able to unlock many—though not all—of the files that Gomez had wanted to see. That had given them a treasure trove of data about the Singularity incursion into Imperial space that had led to the capture of this ship and the destruction of several militia vessels.

More importantly, it had details about which systems inside the Singularity were reinforced and where those reinforcements had come from. That information had led them to this system.

It had also allowed them to strike at all three of the secondary targets that Grace and Captain Anders had mapped out with Kayden Harmon. They had up-to-date records of where ships were going to be that gave them confidence that they could hit those targets and get away cleanly.

In each case, they gave the people in the orbital time to evacuate and blew it up with missiles without even slowing down all that much. It wasn't as if the targets were going to resist an Imperial heavy cruiser, after all.

This final system was uninhabited and, according to their scanners, unoccupied. If that proved true, they'd make one more flip and be into unaligned space. From there, they'd circle around the fighting that was likely still going on and find another place to cross into the Empire.

One Twenty-Four was worried about Grace, Fei, and the marines. There had been twelve survivors after the boarding action. Four of those injured marines had since died. Of the eight remaining, one still might die.

Grace's injury had easily been taken care of by some time in the regenerator. The same had been true of Fei's back injury. Corporal Gomez's hurts would take longer to mend, but the doctor said that he would eventually make a full recovery.

Injuries and deaths among the crew in engineering had been less onerous, but that didn't mean that they'd escaped unscathed. Commander Kyle had been hiding behind what he'd likely thought was sufficient cover only to have a heavy flechette punch all the way through it and him.

All of that loss had proven emotionally draining for everyone, including her. She'd taken part in the marine ceremony to remember the fallen, which had been combined with the remembrance for the Fleet personnel that had died and the militia crew as well.

It was a somber affair that had brought her to tears. So many people that she'd known hadn't survived, and she was still trying to figure out how to deal with that.

Thankfully, today would be the day that they slipped away from her former home. Once they'd done so, the Singularity wouldn't be able to track them down. Not easily and not in time to intercept them.

By now, she was certain that the Singularity was marshaling what forces it could to hunt for *Gargoyle*. The commercial orbital near where the battle had taken place had undoubtedly passed along every bit of information they could, but it would've taken time to assemble a force capable of taking on the rogue heavy cruiser.

Bright Passage had proven too damaged to salvage, so they'd dropped it into the gas giant, putting it forever beyond the reach of any human. That also saddened her.

Those thoughts consumed her until they reached the final flip point and the heavy cruiser left the Singularity. She'd forever left her home behind but only after it had rejected her. She was now the enemy of her former people but not yet the friend she wanted to be to the Empire.

Perhaps in time, she'd gain access to the things that her friends took for granted, but she knew that there would be more fighting ahead for her. She'd have to battle to receive recognition as a human being. If she wanted to become an Imperial Marine—which she did —it was going to require intense effort and perseverance.

As soon as the flip was complete and they'd left the Singularity, Fei put a hand on her shoulder and edged her toward the main hatch. "Come, Little One. Let's leave the rest to their tasks while we look forward to what we need to do next."

"When will you leave?" One Twenty-Four asked. "I know that you have your career to return to when we get to the Empire. Do we have a month left? Less?"

The woman smiled down at her. "We have much more time than that. I've been talking with Grace, and after considering my options, I've decided that I'll be sticking around to help train you."

One Twenty-Four brightened at the news. "Truly? I'd like that."

Fei laughed. "You say that now, but by the time I'm finished with you, you'll be cursing my name."

"But what about being an Imperial Marine? Are you sure you want to leave something like that behind?"

Fei led her out into the corridor, and they started the walk back to marine country. "I'll miss some portions of the work, yes, but I think this is a fight worth fighting and that you're worth fighting for.

"Together, Grace and I are going to make sure that you're

afforded every opportunity that any normal person would have and that you have a chance to become an Imperial Marine.

"You're going to have a difficult time doing so, but if you're willing to fight and accept the fact that you'll be discriminated against every step of the way, you *can* succeed.

"Things that everyone else takes for granted will be denied to you. Successes that should be earned will turn into failures, because some people will go to great lengths to see that you fail.

"How could I not fight for someone like that? And who knows, perhaps once you're accepted into the marines, I'll rejoin. I'm a young woman, after all."

The thought of that brightened One Twenty-Four's thoughts. "Then let's get about it. I'm told that I have a lot of training to catch up on."

* * *

GRACE RAPPED on the hatch and waited. When the hatch slid open, she stepped into the duke's office.

Much like the briefing room, it was well appointed. The desk was made of the same wood as the conference room table, and the sealed hutches along the walls also matched what was present in that compartment. It was just down the corridor from the briefing room, though they hadn't known that at the time.

He rose from behind his desk and gestured for her to join him at a pair of chairs at a small table nearby. As soon as she'd sat, he secured a pair of glasses and a bottle of dark-amber liquid from one of the hutches.

"I hope you like single malt, because I think that we both could use a good drink after everything we've been through. This is the best I have, which also makes it what we should use to toast your fallen comrades."

"While I'm not much of a beer person, I won't turn down a good whiskey."

And that was true enough. She usually didn't get into hard liquor, preferring wine, but whiskey would work.

He poured them both two fingers of the amber liquid and took the seat next to her, setting the bottle between them. Without saying a word, he raised his glass in a toast.

Grace tapped the edge of her glass gently against his. "To absent friends."

They drank, and she marveled at how smooth the alcohol was. Whenever she'd allowed herself to sample one of the various flavors of whiskey, it was never such a pleasant experience. Maybe she was going to have to reevaluate her assessment based on the quality of the booze.

Once they'd settled back into their seats, he gave her a searching look. "How are you doing? After a fight like that and losing so many people, I'm worried about you."

"It hurts," she admitted. "To come so far and then be slaughtered at the end guts me. The doctor tells me that we're almost certainly going to lose Young, so that means we only have seven survivors out of forty-one marines. I lost eighty percent of my people, and there wasn't a damned thing that I could do about it."

Fowler nodded. "Even though I command the militia, I'm not a military man. I won't even pretend to understand how much that hurts. I will say that I can't imagine how you could have done anything differently, though. Frankly, it's a miracle that any of you survived. I have difficulty believing that we got away at all."

Grace sighed and looked away from him. "It's hard for me to imagine, too. The smart thing for me to do once we get back to the Empire is to talk to a counselor. I'm no longer going to have access to anyone inside the Corps, so I'll have to find someone on the civilian side who has a clue what I've been through."

"I disagree," he said firmly. "No matter how they want to play this, you took this injury in service to the Empire, and they'll damned well let you see someone that has the background to understand who you are and what you've been through.

"If they give you any grief at all on this matter, I'll make it a point to visit the commanding officer on the marine base at DeSantis. I believe I can make him see reason. If not, I can make his life a living hell."

He sighed and shook his head. "I've already spoken with Captain Anders, and he's set course back for the Empire in a long loop it's going to take us probably two months to travel. We want to take the most obscure paths that he can find to get there, because your man isn't going to be able to do anything with either fusion plant.

"With God's grace, the one we have left will get us where we need to go, but we're not going to push it. We can't afford to take that kind of risk. If we run into an enemy warship, they're going to stomp us."

"I don't mind taking it easy for the next couple of months," she said. "I'll be happier once we reach the Empire. Now that they've had a chance to bring all of the missile batteries online, we should be able to deal with any smaller vessels that consider giving us grief.

"We'll just hope that we don't run into anything our size or bigger. Or a swarm of smaller ships. And before you get worried about it, Anders says the chances of us actually encountering a force like that are slim."

Talking about Anders made her smirk a little. He'd been floored when the duke had knighted him—also as a Knight Commander of the Imperial Order—and then ennobled him as a baron on DeSantis as well. It wasn't going to keep the man from returning to Fleet to serve, but being Commander Lord Jay Anders, Baron Greenfield would open a hell of a lot of doors.

Once they finished the drink, Fowler offered to pour another, and she accepted. Normally one was her limit, but she felt so tired, and the warmth inside of her weakened her resolve.

"Have you considered what our best option is for protecting Andrea until we have the situation settled, at least initially?" she asked.

"The course we've picked is going to take us into the Empire inside the area my militia controls, and we'll make directly for DeSantis," he said. "DeSantis is the seat of governmental control for the entire sector, and so my authority extends all the way to the border. No one is going to stop us once we make the crossing.

"Your life is going to be filled with turmoil as we get you set up. It'll take me at least a week to get the lands transferred and make your title an official act. What I did is certainly valid and grants you all of the protections of the peerage, but I'll be happier once all the T's are crossed and I's are dotted."

She nodded. "And I'd imagine things are going to get worse once I make my official declaration that Andrea is my booty. That's going to cause a firestorm."

"It's something that we can handle. You're a woman that's experienced in battle, and this is no different, even if the war is fought with words and political maneuvering. Just understand that your enemies are going to be as skilled with those weapons as you are with powered armor and a flechette rifle. Worse, their attacks will be just as dangerous.

"I've got some few skills in those areas myself, and I'll be able to bring some allies on board to help fight at your side, but this isn't going to be easy, and it isn't going to be quick.

"Andrea is twelve now, and it may take until she's of age to finally win all of the protections and access that we both want for her. Be strong, and remember this is going to be a series of skirmishes. Some we'll win, and some we'll lose. As long as we win the war, it'll all be worth it."

Grace knew that to be true. She had no idea what the battlefield was going to look like and how she was going to fight on it, but it was going to be unlike anything she'd ever done before. Yet she'd give it the same tenacity that she'd give any other fight. Andrea deserved no less.

"If that's how long it takes, that's how long it takes. Na told me that she doesn't intend to reenlist. She's going to stay and help train Andrea for what's coming. Our goal is to teach her everything that we can about the Imperial Marines by the time she's accepted as a recruit.

"They're going to be looking for any reason whatsoever to deny her entry or to kick her out if she makes it in, I'm sure of that. Far be it for me to say that the Corps is hidebound, but it is. She's going to need to already be one of the most skilled people there on day one if she's going to have a chance."

"The two of you are well suited to doing that," Fowler said with a nod. "Sergeant Na spoke with me about that yesterday, and you're in luck.

"For reasons both inscrutable and obscure, the Singularity packed one of the marine pinnaces absolutely full of equipment, weapons, and other bric-a-brac of a military nature. Not just Imperial gear but Singularity as well. Up to and including enough powered armor for all of you, also in both Imperial and Singularity versions.

"Since she's allowed to claim one object and all its contents as her booty, she's taking it *all* with her when we arrive at DeSantis. I'd imagine that will cause a lot of wailing and gnashing of teeth, but it's the law."

He said that last with just a touch of smug satisfaction.

Grace felt her eyes narrowing. "Really? The armory seemed pretty full when I was in there the day that we took the ship. I wonder where all that gear came from and how it got into the pinnace."

"It's a mystery," he declared. "One that I'm not going to worry about. Frankly, I'm more distraught at Captain Anders's choice of booty. He's taking my desk. Luckily for me, he's at least allowing me to retrieve my belongings first.

"If anyone gets too overwrought, I'll just remind them that she could've claimed *Gargoyle* and everything in her. I'm sure they'll give in to the inevitable once they compare the cost of the pinnace and everything aboard her against an entire heavy cruiser. They'll scream and moan, but they'll capitulate. Eventually.

"Besides, the cost for that pinnace filled with military equipment pales beside how much the rare elements and flip drives that were destroyed were worth. Believe me when I say that there will be a plethora of things for them to take umbrage at."

Fowler swirled the whiskey in his glass. "While that seems to takes care of everything necessary to training Andrea to be an Imperial Marine, how are we going to get her the general education and socialization that she needs to become an Imperial citizen?

"Honestly, even after having spoken with her, I still don't really understand the world she comes from. It's hard to form a bridge when I can't clearly see the other side of the river."

"Kayden is going to help with that," Grace said. "Since he no longer has a ship to take care of, he's decided that Andrea is his new pet project. He'll stay on DeSantis with us and help her transition from the Singularity to the Empire.

"He admits that he doesn't really understand the environment that she was raised in either, but he's in a much better position to help us than anyone else. And besides, I kind of like having him around. Between the four of us, we should be able to protect and educate Andrea until she's an adult."

They sat in silence for a while. When the drink was done, Fowler poured one final measure of whiskey into their glasses and rose to his feet.

"Then let us toast our future endeavors," he said somberly. "To Andrea and shepherding her through the fight to come. May she never waver."

Grace raised her glass and thought of everything that Andrea might one day achieve. It would be worth the price of admission.

"To Andrea."

* * *

WANT to get updates from Terry about new books and other general nonsense going on in his life? He promises there will be cats. Go to TerryMixon.com/Mailing-List and sign up.

DID YOU ENJOY THIS BOOK? Please leave a review on Amazon. It only takes a minute to dash off a few words and that kind of thing helps Terry make a living as a writer and gets you new books faster.

WANT the next book in this series? Grab *Imperial Recruit* today or buy any of Terry's other books, which are listed on the next page.

VISIT TERRY's Patreon page to find out how to get cool rewards and an early look at what he's working on at Patreon.com/TerryMixon.

ALSO BY TERRY MIXON

You can always find the most up to date listing of Terry's titles on his Amazon Author Page.

Note: the links below (ebook only, obviously) redirect you to my website where you can click a button to go to Amazon. This allows me to participate in Amazon's associates program and earn a little more. Sorry for any inconvenience.

The Last Hunter

The Last Hunter

Bonds of Blood

Alpha Strike

The Enemy Revealed

Command Authority

The Grand Conspiracy

Shield of Humanity

Fog of War

Ships of the Line

Operation Liberty

The Empire of Bones Saga

Empire of Bones

Veil of Shadows

Command Decisions

Ghosts of Empire

Paying the Price

Recon in Force

Box Sets

The Empire of Bones Saga Volume 1

The Empire of Bones Saga Volume 2

The Empire of Bones Saga Volume 3

The Empire of Bones Saga Volume 4

Humanity Unlimited Publisher's Pack 1

Humanity Unlimited Publisher's Pack 2

ABOUT TERRY

#1 Bestselling Military Science Fiction author Terry Mixon served as a non-commissioned officer in the United States Army 101st Airborne Division. He later worked alongside the flight controllers in the Mission Control Center at the NASA Johnson Space Center supporting the Space Shuttle, the International Space Station, and other human spaceflight projects.

He now writes full time while living in Texas with his lovely wife and a pounce of cats.

TerryMixon.com

[a] amazon.com/author/terrymixon

[f] facebook.com/TerryLMixon

[p] patreon.com/TerryMixon

[BB] bookbub.com/authors/terry-mixon

[g] goodreads.com/TerryMixon

www.ingramcontent.com/pod-product-compliance
Lightning Source LLC
Chambersburg PA
CBHW072314020726
47501CB00002B/501